THE NAUGHTY GIRLS
BOOK CLUB

Sophie Hart lives in London with her boyfriend and her collection of naughty books. She likes to spend her time going on nice holidays, making half-hearted attempts to exercise, and lusting after Daniel Craig.

SOPHIE HART

The Naughty Girls
Book Club

AVON

AVON

A division of HarperCollins*Publishers*
77–85 Fulham Palace Road,
London W6 8JB

www.harpercollins.co.uk

A Paperback Original 2013

1

Copyright © Sophie Hart 2013

Sophie Hart asserts the moral right to
be identified as the author of this work

A catalogue record for this book is
available from the British Library

ISBN-13: 978-0-00-751494-6

Set in Sabon LT Std by Palimpsest Book Production Limited,
Falkirk, Stirlingshire

Printed and bound in Great Britain by
Clays Ltd, St Ives plc

MIX
Paper from
responsible sources
FSC **C007454**

FSC™ is a non-profit international organisation established to promote the responsible management of the world's forests. Products carrying the FSC label are independently certified to assure consumers that they come from forests that are managed to meet the social, economic and ecological needs of present and future generations, and other controlled sources.

Find out more about HarperCollins and the environment at
www.harpercollins.co.uk/green

1

'You've been a bad girl, Christina . . . A very naughty girl . . .'

Christina gazed up at Alexander, her eyes dark with longing, her face flushed. 'I'm sorry,' she panted helplessly. 'I won't do it again.'

'I need to make sure of that,' Alexander said, as he stalked across the room. He'd removed his shirt, and his torso was taut and muscular. 'I need to teach you a lesson.'

His gaze turned to the candle that blazed on the bedside table, the flame dancing and twisting.

As Christina stared, the wax spilled over from the slim, white candle down to the antique silver holder. She watched as it cooled and hardened.

'I think you know exactly what I have in mind,' Alexander murmured, his voice low and husky.

Christina could only nod, mute with longing.

'But first – the sweetness,' Alexander promised, as he moved towards her, bending down to kiss her lips, her neck, her collarbone.

Christina moaned in delight as his mouth moved lower . . . past her navel . . . over the soft, white mound of her stomach . . . and then lower still, before finally, exquisitely, she felt his hot lips on the delicate, pink flesh of her—

Estelle Humphreys glanced up in panic and slammed the book shut, hastily shoving it beneath a pile of papers. Her heart was pounding wildly, while her ears strained to listen.

The noise came again – *thump, thump, thump* – and Estelle realised with relief that it was just her fourteen-year-old son, Joe, in the flat upstairs. The racket meant that he'd finished his homework and turned on his music – Kasabian, by the sound of things.

She stood motionless for a moment, feeling her heart rate return to normal and her cheeks turn from flaming red to their more usual milky shade.

Guiltily, she removed the copy of *Ten Sweet Lessons* from underneath the distinctly less exciting pile of HMRC forms, and stared at it. The cover was deceptively innocent – a dark grey background, with a single red ribbon looped across it – but *Ten Sweet Lessons* was an erotica novel that was currently causing a sensation up and down the country. Selling thousands of copies every day, it had topped the bestseller lists for weeks. And it was the closest Estelle had come to a shirtless man with hot lips and an unbridled desire for a very long time . . .

With a sigh of longing, she stashed the book in her handbag, tied her mousey-brown-with-a-hint-of-grey hair back in the scruffy ponytail it was trying to escape from, and turned to the worksheets that were spread across the counter in front of her.

Back to reality.

The accounts for her little cafe made grim reading, as she calculated the day's receipts and entered them on a spreadsheet. The takings had plummeted in recent weeks, and it didn't seem as though anything Estelle did could reverse that trend. She knew that this time of year was always tough – after the Christmas rush, everyone cut back on their little treats, and no one wanted to venture out in the chilly February weather. But if business didn't pick up soon . . . well, it didn't bear thinking about.

Forty-two-year-old Estelle had opened Cafe Crumb five years ago when she and her husband, Ted, had got divorced. Married life had left her feeling as though her own identity was slowly being swallowed up by the demands of being a wife and a mother, so after she and Ted had split (realising they made much better friends than spouses) Estelle had resolved to do something for herself.

And she had, she thought proudly, surveying the little

cafe with its red and white checked tablecloths, a single red gerbera in a white vase on each table. As it was now the end of the day, everything was wiped down and perfectly clean, the window cleared of its usual delicious-looking selection of cakes and pastries.

It might not be much, but it was *hers,* Estelle thought with satisfaction.

But for how much longer? she wondered with a shudder, as she looked down again at the depressing figures. They seemed to swim in front of her tired eyes.

Of course, she had her regular customers – the businessmen who rushed in for their morning latte with a buttery croissant for their daily commute into Bristol city centre; the yummy-mummies who dropped by for gossip, green tea and a low-fat muffin after dropping the kids at school; the lunchtime rush who chomped their way through piles of toasted sandwiches; and the afternoon pensioner crowd who loved their traditional cream teas – but there just didn't seem to be enough of them anymore.

And if she lost the business, Estelle realised, hardly even daring to consider the possibility, she lost their home too – the flat above the shop where she and Joe lived. Poor Joe. He was a good kid, but he seemed to be at that stage where every time she turned around he'd grown another six inches, none of his clothes fitting him for more than a month at a time. He tried not to ask for too much, but Estelle knew what it was like at that age – to fit in, you had to have the right trainers, the newest phone, the latest games console. It was all just so expensive.

Anxiously, Estelle reached for a slice of lemon drizzle cake, breaking off a corner and popping it into her mouth. *Mmm*, she sighed in satisfaction. It was moist, tangy and delicious, just as it should be. At least there wasn't a problem with her baking. She just needed to get more people through the doors to try it out . . .

A movement from across the road caught her eye, and she looked out through the cafe windows which were dotted with droplets of condensation. It was dark outside, but in the amber light of the streetlamp she could see two people coming out of Bainbridge Books, the local independent bookshop.

Estelle's heart lurched as she realised it was the owners, Mary and Alan Bainbridge, and that the couple were locking the door for the very last time. A few boxes of books stood forlornly on the pavement outside – the ones they'd been unable to get rid of in the closing down sale – and even from here Estelle could see that Mary was close to tears as Alan fished the key out of his pocket.

Instinctively, Estelle grabbed one of the stiff, white cake boxes from the shelf behind her – usually reserved for her big-spending customers – and began filling it with an assortment of goodies. Two slices of pecan pie, a large slab of ginger cake, a couple of glazed doughnuts topped with hundreds and thousands. Oh, and some of her special double-chocolate brownies. She knew how much Alan loved those.

Hurriedly, Estelle snatched up the cakes and dashed outside, the bell clanging behind her.

'I brought you these,' Estelle blurted out as she crossed the street, proffering the box, which Mary took gratefully.

'Thank you, Estelle,' she said, her voice wobbling dangerously. 'It's very kind of you.'

'It certainly is,' echoed Alan, as he took the box from his wife and peeped inside.

'I'm just so sorry to see you go,' Estelle told them helplessly, wishing there was something more she could do. Mary and Alan had run Bainbridge Books for over thirty years, but they simply couldn't afford to keep it open any longer. They were moving down to Devon to be closer to their grandchildren, and though Estelle knew they'd been planning their retirement for a while, they certainly hadn't wanted to leave like this – unable to sell their business, and forced to close due to lack of custom. It was a chilling reminder of what could happen to her if things didn't pick up.

'Well, we all have to move on,' Alan replied stoically. 'Times change.'

'I'll miss you,' Estelle swallowed, feeling overcome with emotion. She'd loved the atmosphere in the cosy little bookshop, and had whiled away many a happy hour with the friendly owners, chatting about books over a cup of tea and a generous slice of battenberg.

Mary was shaking her head sadly. 'Oh, we've had some wonderful times in there,' she sniffed, staring through the window at the now-abandoned shop, with its bare walls and rows of empty bookshelves. 'You know what I'll miss the most?' she confided, her eyes glistening with tears behind her oversized glasses. 'Talking to all of our customers every day. Everyone thinks that reading is such a solitary occupation, but it doesn't have to be,' she insisted.

Estelle nodded in agreement as Mary continued speaking, warming to her theme. 'All the best books should be shared and discussed and debated. It's a centuries' old tradition. People have always loved stories. Oh, I'll miss this place so much!' she sobbed, dabbing at her eyes with a soggy tissue.

Estelle reached out towards her, enfolding Mary in a comforting hug. It was so true what Mary had said, she thought, remembering all the chats they'd shared, from debating their favourite Jane Austen novel to discussing the merits of Mr Rochester versus Heathcliff as a romantic hero. Not that she'd have admitted to Mary about reading *Ten Sweet Lessons,* Estelle thought guiltily, remembering the creased paperback hidden at the bottom of her bag.

Suddenly, she pulled away from Mary as though she'd just had an electric shock. 'That's it!' Estelle exclaimed. Her eyes were sparkling, her face shining with enthusiasm.

'That's what, dear?' Mary asked, looking at her

husband in confusion. Peter simply shrugged, staring nervously at Estelle as though she'd gone mad.

'The solution to my problems,' Estelle squealed. '*You*, Mary Bainbridge,' she declared, throwing her arms around her once again, 'are a genius!

2

'Bruce Willis would definitely be in my top five favourite action movie heroes of all time. Don't you think?'

'Mmm-hmm,' Rebecca answered her husband distantly. It was Friday night and they were walking home from the cinema, arm-in-arm against the cold night air. There was a light frost on the pavement, and overhead the stars dazzled in the inky black sky.

'Bruce, definitely,' Andy confirmed, nodding thoughtfully. 'Then Arnie, of course. And Sly Stallone. Who else?'

'Hmm?'

'Who else would you have in your top five favourite action movie heroes of all time, darling?'

'Umm . . . I'm not sure,' Rebecca replied uncertainly.

Andy glanced across at his wife. 'Are you okay, sweetheart? You seem a little preoccupied tonight.'

'No, I'm fine,' Rebecca insisted. She pulled her knitted

beanie hat further down over her choppy brunette bob, and hoped Andy would change the subject.

'All that marking to do this weekend, eh?' he commented. 'What was it again – Year Ten coursework on the Tudors?'

'That's the one.'

'Never mind. I'll stay out of your way. I wanted to make a start on stripping the wallpaper in the spare room anyway.'

'Right.'

'And then next week,' Andy broke into a beaming smile as he turned to Rebecca, 'there's a big treat in store.'

'Is there?' she asked hopefully.

'Oh yes. The new *Spiderman* movie is being released,' he grinned, not noticing the way his wife's face fell. 'Whaddya think? Me, you, a medium-sized bucket of popcorn . . .'

'It's a date,' Rebecca replied weakly.

'Are you *sure* you're okay?' Andy pressed after a few moments. 'You just don't seem as excited as I thought you would be.'

Immediately, Rebecca felt bad. 'I'm fine,' she repeated, forcing a smile. 'I'm just feeling a little bit out of sorts. It's been a long week, I suppose, and work's been really busy . . .'

'Righto.' Andy seemed satisfied with the explanation. 'At least you've got me to cheer you up, eh?' he grinned, giving her a friendly nudge.

They carried on walking in silence, as Rebecca tried

to work out just what exactly was wrong with her. She'd been like this for weeks now, and couldn't shake the general feeling of . . . what? Restlessness? Boredom?

Rebecca and Andy had been married for over a year now and everything was . . . *fine*. Not amazing, not incredible, just . . . *fine*. They'd quickly adapted to their little routine of quiet nights in during the week, a Friday night trip to the cinema, and weekends spent doing DIY. There was nothing wrong per se; it was just that it never changed, with every week becoming a carbon copy of the one before.

Everything had seemed so exciting after Andy proposed, Rebecca remembered with a pang. She'd revelled in her role as the bride-to-be, throwing herself into scoping out venues, trying on dresses, choosing the exact flowers for her bouquet. She'd been rushed off her feet, juggling her job as a history teacher with planning her dream wedding, but she'd loved every minute of it.

The wedding day itself had been perfect, the honeymoon in Sorrento utter bliss, and then . . . reality hit. Was it so unfair to admit that she was finding her life now a little dull?

It wasn't Andy's fault, of course. He was easy-going (perhaps a little *too* easy going at times) and nice looking too, even if his sandy hair was starting to thin, and that cute little belly she'd teased him about at first was becoming a permanent fixture. All of their friends said they made a great couple, and Rebecca knew she should be grateful for her settled, untroubled life.

But there was part of her that couldn't help but wonder if this was all there was from now on. She was only thirty-three, but she was starting to feel old before her time, and recently she'd had the horrible suspicion that she was turning into her mother.

It was abundantly clear to Rebecca that she and Andy needed to put the *oomph* back into their relationship – and soon. There was no way she wanted to turn into one of those couples you sometimes saw in restaurants, the ones who sat together in silence because they'd run out of things to say to each other some time back in 2005 . . .

'Hey, why don't we go to the pub?' Rebecca burst out suddenly.

Andy looked at her doubtfully. 'The pub?'

'Yeah!' Rebecca tried to inject some enthusiasm into her voice. 'It's not too late – we could still make last orders. It might be fun . . . something different . . .'

She trailed off, as Andy broke into a huge yawn.

'The thing is, I've had such a long week and I was really looking forward to my bed tonight. Maybe next week, eh?'

'Uh-huh. Maybe next week,' Rebecca echoed, forcing a smile. Inside, she felt herself deflate like a punctured tyre. What had happened to the pair of them? They hadn't been like this when they were dating. She desperately wanted to do something spontaneous, but Andy's idea of going wild seemed to be ordering an extra-large popcorn on their weekly cinema trip. Not to mention his

DIY obsession – recently, stripping the wallpaper was about as exciting as it got in the bedroom too . . .

Yes, Rebecca was realistic, and knew that the initial throes of passion would fade over time, but she hadn't expected her sex life to dry up quite so completely. Since they'd got married, sex was a rarity. They hadn't even consummated their marriage on their wedding night; Andy had got roaring drunk with his old university friends and passed out, fully clothed, on their four-poster bed before Rebecca had time to unlace her corset. Perhaps she should have taken that as a sign, she realised with a sigh.

Even when they did find the time and energy to make love, it had become somewhat . . . routine. Rebecca could predict the two or three positions they'd work through, before cuddling briefly, turning off the light and falling asleep. She was too embarrassed to talk to any of her friends about the situation, and too scared to bring up the subject with Andy. What if it meant that she was abnormal? Or that Andy didn't fancy her anymore? But the truth was, Rebecca was becoming increasingly frustrated – in more ways than one.

'Bex, come and look at this!'

She heard Andy shout and realised that she'd walked on without him. He was browsing in one of the shop windows, reading a poster that had been tacked up.

'What is it?' she called.

'Come and see!' He waved her over, grinning excitedly.

13

Reluctantly, Rebecca retraced her steps. Knowing Andy, it was probably a plant sale at the local church, or an announcement that the Phoenix Cinema was running a back-to-back showing of the *Star Wars* movies.

'What is it then?' she asked wearily, as she came up alongside him.

Triumphantly, Andy pointed to the poster in the cafe window:

Hungry for books?

Join the Cafe Crumb book club!

We'll be meeting every other Thursday to talk books, life, everything . . .

Email Estelle@cafecrumb.co.uk for details

The coffee and cake at our first meeting will be free ☺

'You want to join a book club?' Rebecca asked in confusion. Andy was more of a newspaper guy, occasionally reading the biography of some sporting hero. She'd never known him to willingly pick up a novel.

'Not me!' he burst out. '*You!*'

Rebecca rolled her eyes at him. 'Why would I be interested in that?' she snapped, feeling another wave of disappointment at just how hopeless her husband could be sometimes. 'It'll be a load of old fogies rambling on about *War and Peace*,' she complained, as she stomped off down the street.

Andy looked hurt as he ran to catch up with her, and they fell into step outside the butcher's. 'Oh. I thought you might enjoy it. It'd be a chance to get out of the house, meet some new people. And you like reading, don't you?'

'True,' Rebecca admitted. Not that she had much time for it these days. Pretty much the only things she read now were badly written history essays from her Year Tens.

'Never mind. It was just a thought,' Andy said cheerily, recovering his usual easy-going demeanour. Sometimes it was this that annoyed Rebecca the most. She wished he'd show some passion occasionally.

She remembered when they'd first started dating, how Andy hadn't been able to get enough of her. She recalled them falling out of a bar or a nightclub, the way he would pull her into an alleyway for a passionate kiss and perhaps a cheeky fumble . . . It was all so thrilling, so illicit – the feeling of his hands on her body, and the knowledge that they could be discovered at any moment. Even the memory got her juices flowing, Rebecca thought excitedly, looking longingly at the shop doorways as they passed. She wished Andy would grab her masterfully, press his body against hers and have his wicked way . . . But those days seemed to be long gone, and the fantasy was all she had left now.

Rebecca stopped and turned around, looking back at

the cafe. There was a young woman standing outside wearing a bold black and white houndstooth-print swing jacket with a red scarf and red kitten heels. Her legs were encased in black fishnet tights, and her dyed black hair was backcombed into a funky beehive, rockabilly style.

She looked cool, feisty and, best of all, she was studying the poster intently.

As Rebecca watched, the woman pulled an iPhone from her handbag (which was red patent and shaped like a pair of lips) and began tapping in the details on the poster.

Rebecca smiled to herself. Maybe the book club wouldn't be full of old fogies after all.

3

It was 6.57 p.m. on the Thursday of the first ever Cafe Crumb book club meeting, and Estelle was standing to attention behind the counter, looking around anxiously. No one had arrived yet, and there was an unpleasant churning sensation in her stomach. What if this whole thing was a disaster?

She knew that holding a book group wasn't going to be the answer to all her financial woes, but it was a start, and Estelle was willing to work as hard as it took to see her little cafe succeed. Even if she could get a handful of new customers through the door, it was better than nothing, and if they brought their friends, who then brought their friends . . . From little acorns, mighty oak trees grow – wasn't that how the saying went? But for that to happen, she needed people to turn up tonight.

Perhaps she looked too formal, Estelle thought

suddenly, like a soldier at the ready, beside her teapot. Perhaps she should go and sit down instead.

Earlier that evening, she'd pushed the other tables back against the walls and set two together in the middle of the cafe, surrounded by half a dozen chairs. Estelle sat down on one of them, flicking casually through her copy of *Tess of the D'Urbervilles*, the text she'd chosen for their first session.

No, this wasn't right, she chastised herself. Now she looked *too* laid-back, or like she hadn't read the book and was frantically cribbing at the last minute. It was much better to be doing something.

She jumped up again, checked her watch (7.02 p.m.) and put a pot of coffee on to brew. There, that was better, she thought with satisfaction, glancing around once again to check that everything was in order. The counter was lined with a selection of cakes – squares of carrot cake, chocolate brownies, shortbread biscuits liberally dusted with sugar. Estelle hoped to goodness that someone turned up or else she'd look like a loony, stuck with an enormous pile of cakes going stale, like Miss Havisham in a pinny instead of a wedding dress.

Where on earth was *everyone?* she wondered in exasperation. The replies to her email address had been positive enough – a few definites and a handful of maybes, not to mention an awful lot of spam.

Estelle glanced up at the clock once again – 7.06 p.m. The silence in the little shop was deafening, and for once there was no thudding rock music coming from the flat upstairs. Joe had gone straight to his Dad's after school tonight, and wouldn't be back until later. Ted now lived with his new wife, Leila, in the Bedminster area of Bristol, a couple of bus rides from Estelle's cafe in Clifton.

Funny how men could move on so quickly after a divorce, Estelle reflected sadly. It always seemed much harder for women – at least, it was for her. She was so busy running the cafe and looking after Joe that there never seemed to be any time for love . . .

The bell clanged and Estelle spun round, startled. A very tall, lean, young man was standing awkwardly in the doorway. He wore wire-rimmed glasses with brown corduroy trousers and an old-fashioned overcoat. Despite looking like he was in his late twenties, he dressed like he was in his late sixties.

'Oh! You're here!' Estelle exclaimed, a little too enthusiastically.

'Am I in the right place?' he asked hesitantly, running a hand nervously through his messy brown hair. 'For the book club?'

'Yes!' Estelle squeaked, wishing her voice would drop a couple of octaves. 'This is here . . . I mean, this is the place. The book club that is. You're the first! Yes. Welcome!'

The man nodded, looking warily at Estelle. Then he glanced around, noting the empty cafe, and Estelle suddenly panicked that he might decide to leave.

'Can I take your coat?' she asked, practically

manhandling him out of it. 'And do help yourself to cake. Do you prefer tea or coffee?'

'Tea, please,' he replied, sitting down self-consciously and taking a copy of *Tess* out of his battered old satchel. 'Milk, two sugars.'

'Oh, I'm terribly sorry, I didn't introduce myself,' Estelle apologised, looking extremely flustered as she dashed over with his tea, a piece of shortbread balanced precariously on the saucer. 'I'm Estelle,' she said, wiping her hands on her skirt then holding one out to him.

'Reggie,' he replied, as they shook hands.

'Oh, *you're* Reggie,' said Estelle, bustling round the table to cross a name off her list. 'You know, I expected you to be older.'

Reggie forced a smile. 'That happens a lot,' he said tightly. 'It's the name.'

'Yes, well . . .' Estelle instinctively felt that she'd said something wrong. 'It's lovely to have you here, Reggie,' she clumsily tried to change the subject. 'Very lovely to have a man here tonight. Oh!' Estelle clapped a hand over her mouth and blushed scarlet. 'I didn't mean . . . Well, I meant . . . Book clubs are usually full of wom— Oh!'

Fortunately for Estelle, the bell clanged again, and a woman entered. She looked to be in her sixties, her silver-grey hair cut into a short, sleek crop. She was dressed elegantly, in a smart camel-coloured coat and expensive-looking scarf.

'Good evening, and welcome to the Cafe Crumb book

club.' Estelle moved towards her, recovering herself. She was determined to behave more professionally this time. 'My name's Estelle, and this is Reggie,' she said, indicating Reggie sitting at the table.

'Very pleased to meet you Estelle, I'm Sue. And Reggie,' she nodded at him. 'That was my grandfather's name,' she added with a smile.

Reggie didn't smile back, simply raised an eyebrow. He looked distinctly unimpressed.

'May I take your coat, Sue?' Estelle leapt in, trying to defuse the situation. 'And what would you like to drink?'

'Coffee would be lovely, thank you,' Sue smiled graciously, as she slipped off her coat to reveal a cream silk blouse and smart navy trousers.

'Do help yourself to cake,' Estelle told her, barely having the chance to hang up Sue's coat before the door swung open once again.

'Hello everyone, I'm Gracie,' announced the newcomer, smiling round at everyone. Her jet-black hair was styled in Victory rolls at the front, but tumbled in loose curls down her back, and her lips were painted with bright-red lipstick.

'Ooh, it's lovely and warm in here, isn't it?' she continued, as she took off her jacket to reveal a fifties-style polka-dot dress. There was a small rose tattoo by her collarbone, and a much larger one of a Betty Grable-type pin-up girl on her upper arm.

'Gracie, it's lovely to meet you. I'm Estelle,' said Estelle, rushing forward to introduce her to everyone. They all waved their hellos, as Estelle hurried off to get her a drink.

'So what did everyone think of the book?' demanded Gracie, pulling out her copy and slamming it down on the table.

'Are we starting already?' asked Sue.

'Well . . . perhaps we could wait a few more minutes,' Estelle suggested, glancing at the clock to discover it was now 7.15 p.m. 'There was one more person who said she would be coming . . .' she broke off as she checked her list. 'Gracie – you're here. And Sue . . . Yes, a lady called Rebecca said she would definitely be here. Perhaps we could wait for her?'

Everyone murmured their agreement, then went back to what they were doing. Sue sipped her coffee awkwardly; Gracie was skimming through her book, underlining certain phrases with a purple glitter pen; and Reggie was tapping his foot irritably. The silence was fast becoming unbearable.

'Anyone for more brownies?' Estelle called out desperately, thrusting the plate under Reggie's nose.

She span round as the door opened once more and Rebecca burst through.

'I'm so sorry,' she panted, pulling off her woollen beanie and cosy parka. 'I stayed late at work, but then the bus got stuck in traffic. Have I missed anything? Have you started yet?' she asked, barely pausing for breath.

'You're fine,' Estelle reassured her, as she brought over

a pot of tea and a jug of coffee so everyone could help themselves to top-ups. 'Rebecca, is it?'

Rebecca nodded breathlessly as she slid into a seat, quickly pulling out her copy of *Tess*.

'We decided to wait for you,' Estelle smiled kindly. 'This is Sue, by the way. And Reggie. And Gracie,' she finished.

'Oh!' Rebecca exclaimed, as she noticed the woman she'd sat down next to. 'I saw you outside here the other week, looking at the poster. I'm so glad you came,' she beamed. 'I love your dress, by the way.'

'Thanks,' Gracie grinned. 'It's from Lola's Vintage, on Park Street. Do you know it?'

Rebecca shook her head, as she helped herself to a square of carrot cake.

'You should check it out. It's really cool.'

'Thanks, I will,' Rebecca smiled back.

'Are we expecting anyone else, or should we get started?' Reggie asked, and Estelle detected a touch of impatience in his tone.

'No more definites,' she told him.

'And it *is* twenty past seven,' Sue added. 'If anyone else turns up, I'm sure they could just join in.'

'Yes, good point,' Estelle agreed, feeling a little apprehensive now that they were actually about to start. She'd never been to a book club meeting before, let alone chaired one, and the fact that she desperately wanted tonight to be a success made her far more nervous than she would otherwise be. From a financial perspective, Estelle couldn't help wishing that a few more people had turned up, but the small, cosy group was intimate and unthreatening – perfect for making her debut as a book club host.

'Right, let's get going,' Estelle began, clapping her hands together authoritatively. 'Who'd like to start?'

She looked expectantly around the table, but everyone stayed silent. 'Anyone?' Estelle pleaded, trying to keep the note of desperation from her voice.

Reggie scratched his nose, and the sudden movement caught Estelle's attention.

'Reggie? Perhaps you'd like to give us your thoughts on *Tess*.'

'Um . . .' Reggie shifted awkwardly in his seat. 'Well, if you don't mind, I'm actually just here to observe.'

The four women looked back at him in confusion.

'*Observe?*' Estelle repeated.

'Yes.' Reggie's face was flushed, and he looked embarrassed. 'I'm doing my PhD, you see,' he explained, pushing his glasses up his nose. 'At the university. My thesis is on how literature brings communities together, and I thought this would be a good place to observe first-hand . . . so to speak . . .' he tailed off.

'I see,' Estelle replied, feeling a stab of disappointment. She'd hoped for a lovely group of people, all having a pleasant discussion about books, but now it seemed as though Reggie saw them as nothing more than lab rats.

She looked around the table, trying to gauge the reactions of the others. 'Does anyone have a problem with that?'

Gracie narrowed her eyes. 'I'm not a monkey in a zoo, you know,' she said petulantly.

'Would you rather Reggie didn't attend the meetings?' Estelle asked nervously.

Gracie stared at him, with a long, assessing gaze. 'No,' she announced finally. 'He can stay.'

Estelle breathed a sigh of relief, grateful that she didn't have to break up an argument before the first session had properly got underway. 'And have you read the book, Reggie?'

'Yes, I have,' he confirmed.

'Well, if you would like to interject at any point and give us your opinions, please do,' Estelle encouraged him. 'I'm sure the group would be the richer for it. Now, Sue, how did you find *Tess*?'

Sue cleared her throat. 'Overall, I enjoyed the novel,' she began. 'I thought it was moving, and thought-provoking, and I felt very sorry for Tess. I'm glad I read it, but it's not something I'd read again – parts of it were very long-winded and dull.'

'Thank you, Sue,' Estelle said uncertainly. It wasn't quite the ringing endorsement she'd hoped for, but she supposed that having a variety of opinions was the point of a discussion group. 'Would anyone like to add anything to that? Gracie?'

'I think Tess had a hellish life,' Gracie dived in. 'She went through one horrible experience after another, and I don't see how anyone could enjoy reading about a poor young woman being thrown from one miserable scenario to the next. In fact, it made me wonder about Thomas Hardy – I bet he was a real misogynist to make her go through all that. I mean, what kind of a man was he, dreaming up all those vile situations? Quite frankly, I think the way Tess was treated was utterly disgusting, and the double standard for women in those days was appalling.'

'Okay . . .' Estelle began slowly, somewhat thrown by the strength of Gracie's opinions. 'So, was Tess a victim of fate, or should she be held responsible for her own mistakes?' Estelle asked, consulting the list of questions she'd hastily put together before the meeting.

'How could any of what happened to Tess be her fault?' Gracie shot back. 'It was all because of that bast—' Here Gracie broke off and looked around apologetically. 'Sorry, *Alec's* fault. And then Angel should never have treated her the way he did either, especially when he'd already had an affair with some trollop.'

'Excellent, thank you for your contribution, Gracie,' Estelle cut in quickly, conscious of Sue's look of disapproval at Gracie's choice of language. 'And what role does the landscape itself play in *Tess*?' Estelle asked, hoping she'd chosen a less controversial topic.

There was silence around the table, the only sound coming from Reggie furiously scribbling on his notepad.

'Rebecca?' Estelle asked, noticing that Rebecca hadn't yet spoken. 'How do you think the landscape affected the action?'

Rebecca giggled nervously. 'I'm not really sure . . . I feel like I'm back at school, to be honest,' she admitted. 'Stuck in English class.'

Sue was nodding in agreement. 'I know what you

mean. It reminds me of the essays we had to write at grammar school.'

'You know, *Tess* is still on the syllabus,' Rebecca told her. 'At the school where I teach. It's like being a pupil coming here tonight – I guess now I know how they feel,' she laughed.

'Well I think it's all misogynistic drivel,' Gracie declared, tossing the book down dismissively. 'Why can't we read Caitlin Moran instead?'

'Something more modern *would* be good,' Rebecca chimed in.

'Yes, what *is* going to be our next read, Estelle?' Sue asked politely.

Estelle looked up to find everyone watching her expectantly. Even Reggie had stopped taking notes and was staring at her.

'Umm . . .' she hesitated, stalling for time. She glanced at the notebook in front of her, where she'd written:

Next week: *Crime and Punishment* – Fyodor Dostoyevsky

Oh dear, Estelle panicked. If they thought *Tess of the D'Urbervilles* was dull and old-fashioned, what were they going to make of *Crime and Punishment*? She'd thought she couldn't go wrong with classic, literary texts, but obviously she'd been mistaken.

Estelle badly wanted this venture to do well – she knew it was ridiculous, but to her it was almost symbolic of Cafe Crumb's fate. If she could make a success of the book club, then perhaps the cafe might have a future.

Right now, though, she was standing on the brink of failure. Estelle could see the way everyone was looking at her, doubt and scepticism in their eyes, and she knew she had to do something drastic.

Quickly, she grabbed her handbag and began to rummage through. She'd written down some other ideas before she finally settled on *Crime and Punishment* – perhaps one of those might provide the magical answer she was looking for.

Damn, thought Estelle, ploughing through old tissues and emergency tampons and Joe's letters from school. Where was the list she'd made? She finally spotted it, crumpled at the bottom, and hastily tugged it out, bringing most of the contents of the bag with it. Suddenly, the floor beside her was littered with faded receipts, loose change, packets of chewing gum – *and*, she realised, a feeling of shame creeping over her, a very battered copy of *Ten Sweet Lessons*.

'What's that?' asked Sue, craning her neck to look around Reggie.

'*Ten Sweet Lessons*!' burst out Gracie, looking shocked. 'Wait a minute, isn't that . . .?'

'Is that what you're reading, Estelle?' demanded Rebecca.

Estelle looked up, her face glowing like a beacon, to see them all staring at her accusingly. Oh, this was so humiliating! Here she was trying to run a serious book group, and now she'd blown her cover, revealing that all along, she preferred mass-market, low-brow erotica.

'Sort of . . .' Estelle began slowly, trying to brazen it out. But her brain no longer seemed to be connected to the words that were coming out of her mouth, and she heard herself say, 'I was actually testing it out in advance of the next meeting. It's going to be our next read.'

Trying to regain her dignity, Estelle bent over and picked the book up off the floor, placing it squarely on the table in front of her. 'Yes, that's right,' she continued more confidently, ignoring their shocked expressions. '*Ten Sweet Lessons* by CJ Jones. I hope there are no objections?'

There were gasps from around the table as they stared at her in disbelief, shock written across their faces.

'B . . . But that's . . . *porn*,' Sue burst out, whispering the word under her breath.

'Erotica, I'd say,' Estelle replied thoughtfully. 'Although it's a very fine distinction – something we could discuss at the next meeting, perhaps?'

'Well I've heard that it's deeply misogynistic,' Gracie began furiously. 'And that it sets feminism back fifty years.'

'You could always read it and make up your own mind,' Estelle couldn't resist saying, her eyes sparkling mischievously. 'I'd love to hear your opinions next time.'

'I wouldn't mind seeing what all the fuss is about, actually,' Rebecca admitted shyly.

Estelle smiled at her, grateful for her support. 'Thank you, Rebecca. Reggie?'

Reggie said nothing, his cheeks crimson as he stared at the ground like he wanted it to swallow him up.

'Good, then that's settled,' Estelle said firmly, feeling a remarkable sense of calm now that she'd taken control and made her decision. 'The next read for the Cafe Crumb book club will be *Ten Sweet Lessons* by CJ Jones. The meeting will be held two weeks today, and I look forward to seeing you all back here to find out exactly what you thought of it.'

4

Reggie carefully placed his spaghetti bolognese in the microwave, setting the timer impatiently.

The kitchen was a bombsite as usual, he realised, glancing around. He lived with five other students that he'd met through a house-share advert in the local paper, and they occupied one of the large Victorian houses on Pembroke Road in Clifton. Although he made an effort to keep his own room relatively clean, the communal areas were out of control. The sink was filled to the brim with used crockery floating in grimy, grey water, and old takeaway cartons were piled precariously on top of the overflowing bin that no one could be bothered to empty. The cleaning rota that he'd stuck to the fridge with a novelty magnet was torn, stained and ignored by everyone.

As the plastic tray circled endlessly in the microwave, it struck Reggie that there were more exciting ways to spend a Friday night. Perhaps he'd go crazy and open a bottle of wine – there was that nice Shiraz he'd picked up, the one that had been on special offer at the local Co-op, and—

Reggie jumped as he heard the front door bang. A few moments later, a young woman burst into the kitchen, wrapped up tightly against the cold. She had shaggy blonde hair with long dark roots, and wore skinny jeans with chunky boots, a cropped leather jacket and an enormous ethnic scarf wound several times around her neck.

'Hi Reggie! How are you?' It was his housemate, Selena, an MA student reading Sociology.

'I'm fine. Just . . . um . . . cooking,' he said bashfully, indicating the microwave.

'Ah. Tesco's Finest?' Selena guessed.

Reggie shook his head. 'Marks and Spencer.'

'Well, it *is* Friday night. Why not treat yourself?' Selena joked, dropping her bag on the floor and unwrapping the gigantic scarf, before shrugging off her jacket to reveal a skimpy, low-cut vest top.

Reggie blushed and quickly averted his eyes. Selena was undoubtedly a very attractive woman, and Reggie wasn't quite sure how to deal with one of those.

'Hey, I just had a text from Alex,' Selena told him, as she checked her phone. 'He's in the pub with Matt and Josh. I'm heading out to join them if you want to come.'

'Thanks, but I've got the . . . er . . .' he trailed off, gesturing at the microwave once more.

'No rush. I'm going to grab a shower first, so you've got time to eat.'

'Um . . .' Reggie stalled. 'I've got a few things that I really should be . . . you know . . . getting on with.'

'Sure, no problem,' Selena shrugged. 'We'll be in the Rose and Crown if you change your mind.'

Reggie felt bad for refusing. He hardly ever joined his housemates on their regular nights out, but pubs and clubs weren't his natural territory. He always felt uncomfortable sitting in a large group, especially one dominated by blokey-blokes all talking loudly about football and rugby, or trying to outdo each other with dirty jokes and laddish banter. Reggie usually ended up sitting silently in the corner, nursing a pint, wishing he'd never come out in the first place.

No, tonight he would just stay in and a watch a film in his room. Maybe type up the notes from that awkward book club meeting he'd attended last week. Which reminded him . . .

'Selena?' he called after her.

'Yeah?' She turned in the doorway to look at him. 'Changed your mind already?'

'No, sorry,' he apologised. 'I was just wondering . . .' He broke off, unsure how to ask the question. 'This probably sounds ridiculous but . . . I mean, I'm *sure* you haven't, but I was just wondering . . .' Reggie pushed his glasses up his nose self-consciously, as the heat rose in his cheeks. Selena was staring at him curiously, and his words tumbled out in a rush. 'Have you read *Ten Sweet Lessons*?'

Selena took one look at his terrified face and burst out laughing. 'Oh God, yeah. Of course I have!'

'Really?'

'Absolutely. Pretty much everyone I know has read it. All the girls definitely have, and quite a few guys too. Even my mum's read it!'

'Oh.' Reggie couldn't hide his surprise. 'So . . . um . . . what's it like?'

'Filthy,' Selena replied with a grin. 'Really graphic, and dirty – and great fun, of course. Totally addictive.'

Reggie stared at the floor, suddenly finding that he couldn't meet Selena's eyes.

'But . . . But it's very badly written isn't it?' he stammered. 'That's what I've heard.'

'Well, it's not great literature, but it isn't pretending to be. You don't read low-brow erotica thinking it's going to be Tolstoy. You read it for . . . other reasons. And it does exactly what it says on the tin,' she smirked, her eyes twinkling. 'Why? Are you thinking of letting it entertain you?'

'No, no. Oh gosh, no, it's not my sort of thing,' Reggie bumbled. 'Not my sort of thing at all. Just something I'd heard . . . for research . . . my thesis . . .'

The microwave pinged and Reggie span round, grateful for the distraction.

'Well I'd offer to lend you my copy, but my friend Sarah's got it at the moment,' Selena explained. 'And then Gemma wants to borrow it after that, so . . .'

'Oh, no, it's fine,' Reggie insisted, as he tipped his

bolognese into a cereal bowl, hastily washing a fork as there were no clean ones left in the drawer. 'I wasn't asking to . . . It's fine.'

'Okay. Well, I'd better head to the shower. You're sure you don't want to come to the pub?'

'No, thank you. But you guys have a good night.'

'Will do,' Selena smiled, then turned and walked out into the hallway. 'Oh, I nearly forgot,' Reggie heard her shout. 'Something arrived for you from Amazon today.'

She came back through to the kitchen, holding out the distinctive brown package. 'What is it? *Ten Sweet Lessons*?' she teased.

'No, of course not,' Reggie panicked, almost snatching it out of her hand. 'It's . . . something very serious and academic.'

Selena pulled a face. 'Rather you than me. See you later,' she called over her shoulder.

Tucking the parcel under one arm, and grabbing his dinner firmly with the other hand, Reggie sprinted upstairs to his own room, locking the door behind him.

He sat down on the single bed and placed the package on the far corner of the duvet, eyeing it warily as though it was a bomb that might explode at any moment. Then he switched on his laptop, loaded up an episode of *Game of Thrones*, and slowly ate his meal.

Fifteen minutes later, Selena called out, 'Bye Reggie,' and the front door slammed.

Reggie paused his laptop and sat for a moment, listening intently, but the house was silent. Cautiously, he eased himself towards the parcel. The bed springs squeaked and Reggie froze, guilt surging through him, before he told himself not to be so ridiculous. Recovering himself, he leaned over, grabbed the cardboard package, and swiftly tore it open.

There it was. The oh-so-familiar book cover he'd seen everywhere recently – in the window displays of Waterstones, in the number one slot at WHSmiths, even on the shelves of his local supermarket. It had been discussed endlessly on TV talk shows, the subject of innumerable newspaper features and magazine articles.

It was dark grey, with a single red ribbon snaking across the front: *Ten Sweet Lessons* by CJ Jones.

Reggie realised he was holding his breath as he stared at it, unable to shake the feeling that he was doing something very naughty. Then he reached forward and picked it up, flipping it over to read the blurb on the back.

When innocent university graduate, Christina Cox, lands a job as PA to reclusive millionaire Alexander Black, she imagines a boring role looking after an elderly invalid all day. She doesn't expect Alexander to be a handsome and charming bachelor barely older than she is, or the intense sexual attraction that develops.

It soon becomes clear that Alexander has a much darker, more dangerous side than Christina could ever have imagined, as she finds herself drawn into a world of desire and depravity that's impossible to resist . . .

As Christina pushes her female sexuality to the limit, has she fallen too deep into seduction and does she have the power to surrender?

'Jane Eyre *re-imagined by the Marquis de Sade*' **– The Independent**

'*Erotic literature has come of age . . .* The Story of O, *brought skilfully and scandalously into the twenty-first century by CJ Jones*' **– New York Times**

Casually, Reggie flicked though the book. Words seemed to jump out at him: *tongue, licking, wetness, hot.*

Heart pounding, Reggie snapped it shut. This was *far* too embarrassing. There was no way he could do this. To put himself through the mental torture of reading such . . . *trash*, and then to go back to the book group and discuss it with those gossipy women . . . No. That was simply not going to happen.

Reggie hadn't even made up his mind about whether or not he would return to the Cafe Crumb book club. The previous meeting had been excruciating enough, without adding a sex-fuelled novel into the mix.

He jumped up off the bed, opening his wardrobe and taking out the bottle of wine he'd stashed there (Reggie had learnt the hard way not to leave any alcohol in the communal areas of a shared student house). He poured himself a large glass and took a calming sip of the rich, fruity Shiraz, closing his eyes as he savoured the flavour.

When he opened them again, *Ten Sweet Lessons* was sitting right where he'd left it, like a piece of evidence from a crime scene.

Stop being so ridiculous, Reggie told himself sharply. It was just a novel, like any other. Okay, so it was erotica, but so were works by Chaucer, DH Lawrence and Anaïs Nin, all of which he'd come across during his undergraduate degree in English Literature. There was nothing at all to be ashamed of.

Whether or not he decided to attend the next meeting, he might as well read the book now that he'd bought it. Just for research purposes of course. He would think of himself as an impartial investigator, detaching himself from the content and examining the novel from a purely academic point of view.

Yes. That's what he would do.

Reggie opened *Ten Sweet Lessons* and began to read.

5

'Come on, Joe! That's it – run! Come on, come on . . . hit it . . . Yeah! Goal!'

Estelle jumped up and down on the freezing touchline, whooping loudly as she threw her arms in the air. She was barely recognisable, buried beneath layers of clothes to combat the crisp, early morning air, as she watched her son tear around the football pitch. His teammates jumped on him triumphantly, wrestling him to the ground, and as Joe eventually climbed out from underneath the pile of bodies, his long, skinny legs coated with mud, his mop of dark hair mussed untidily, he smiled shyly, and Estelle could tell he was thrilled.

'Yay, go Joe!' she shouted again, cupping her hands around her mouth like a megaphone.

Turning to her side, she high-fived her ex-husband, Ted. She was proud to say that the two of them had remained friends after their marriage had broken up, and often turned out together to support Joe. They liked to present a united front for the sake of their only child, and knew how important his football was to him.

Joe played with a local team every Sunday morning and, without fail, Estelle would go and watch him. Cafe Crumb was closed on Sundays and, whether it was just a regular practice or a home match against another team from the youth league, Estelle would trek along to the local park. The weather this morning was particularly bitter, as the first days of March brought a final blast of winter. The bare trees were stark against the slate-grey sky, and the ground was frozen in parts, muddy where the grass had been rubbed away.

The referee blew his whistle, and the teams ran back to their places.

'Isn't he great?' Estelle said proudly.

Ted nodded, putting his hands back in his pockets to keep warm. 'Ah, he's grand. One good thing we did together, eh?'

Estelle nodded, surreptitiously looking over at her ex. They'd known each other for almost twenty years, and time had taken its toll on him – as it had done on her. Ted's hair was thinner, and almost fully grey now. His face was lined, with deep creases that formed when he smiled, and his jowls had started to sag. But he was still a handsome man, and the roguish charm she'd originally fallen for was very much in evidence. Ted possessed a natural Irish charisma, twinkling blue eyes, and a melodious accent that brought to mind the green hills of Connemara where he'd been raised. His new wife, Leila, was fifteen years younger than he was, but Estelle could understand why she found this craggy, older man attractive.

'So how's everything with you?' Ted asked, as the match kicked off again.

'Alright, I suppose,' Estelle shrugged. 'Nothing new to report.'

'And how's it going with the cafe?'

'Not so well,' she admitted ruefully. 'Things are a little quiet at the moment, but they'll pick up. You know how it is at this time of year.' Her sense of pride kicked in, and she found herself reluctant to tell him the extent of her troubles.

'Y'know, I was really proud of you when you set up that little business. Never thought you'd do it.'

'Thanks . . .' Estelle replied uncertainly, wondering how to take Ted's comment. 'Oh, that reminds me – are you still alright to have Joe this Thursday?'

'I'll check with Leila, but I don't see why not.'

'Great. I'll remind him to go straight to yours after school. Just give him his tea and send him back later.'

'Sure. Why, what are you up to? Off on a date or something, are you?' Ted asked slyly.

'Don't be daft,' Estelle chided, waving her hand dismissively. 'I've started a book group actually, at the cafe. Didn't Joe tell you?'

Ted shook his head. 'You know what teenagers are

like. Not interested in anything unless it's about them. So, a book group, you say? Tell me more.'

'There's not much to tell really. Just something to bring a bit more custom into the cafe. You know Bainbridge's across the road finally closed down? It was terribly sad. I felt so sorry for them.'

'A real shame,' Ted agreed.

'And I thought it might be a nice idea to start a reading group. Give me a chance to meet some new people, and have a good old natter about books.'

'Ah, you always did love to have your head in a book,' Ted reminisced. 'So what sort of things will you be reading at this club?'

'Well . . .' Estelle cleared her throat, playing for time. 'At the last meeting, we discussed *Tess of the D'Urbervilles*.'

'Did you now?' Ted's eyebrows shot up. 'Very impressive. You must have got more high-brow in your reading choices since we were together. I remember how you used to love all those trashy thrillers, and the cheesy romance novels too.'

'Mmm-hmm,' Estelle replied vaguely, keeping her eyes firmly fixed on where Joe was sprinting up and down the pitch.

'So what are you reading next?' Ted pressed. 'It'll be your Charles Dickens, or your William Shakespeare or something, I bet.'

'Not quite,' Estelle confessed. 'Have you heard of *Ten Sweet Lessons*?'

Ted threw back his head and roared with laughter.

'Have I heard of it? You'd have to have been living under a rock not to have heard of that book, so you would. And there was me thinking you were running a serious book club.'

'It *is* serious,' Estelle protested indignantly. 'We don't confine ourselves to merely the classics,' she retorted haughtily. 'As *Ten Sweet Lessons* is so popular, it's the perfect novel to discuss, and I'm sure it will provoke a wide range of opinions.'

Ted nodded knowingly, his blue eyes dancing. 'And the fact that it's a wicked dirty read has nothing to do with it.'

Estelle started laughing, breaking down under Ted's teasing. 'Oh, stop it you,' she giggled, whacking him in the chest with her handbag. 'It's the perfect book for *you* – older man leading a younger woman astray. Don't let Leila read it or else she'll start getting ideas.'

'Oh, she's already read it.'

Estelle raised her eyebrows. 'Has she?'

Ted nodded. 'Leila's not much of a reader, but all her friends were talking about it, and she'd seen it in the magazines so she decided to give it a whirl. She barely spoke to me for three days straight.'

'Oh, bad luck,' Estelle shouted, as the opposing team scored, and a dejected Joe slunk back to the centre line. She was grateful for the distraction – it felt odd to be discussing *Ten Sweet Lessons* with Ted, knowing that it had given his new wife so much pleasure. Estelle knew it was ridiculous, but she had thought of it as *her* secret,

43

her little discovery. The idea of Leila fantasising about Alexander Black too was somehow disconcerting – as was the image of Leila and Ted trying out some of the raunchier scenes in the book . . .

'Actually, I've been meaning to talk to you about Leila,' Ted began.

'Have you?' Estelle replied warily, wondering what Ted could possibly want to tell her. She certainly didn't want all the grisly details of how *Ten Sweet Lessons* had spiced up their sex life.

'Yes, well, both of us actually. We've got a bit of news, and I wanted to ask your advice about how to tell Joe.'

'Mmm?' Estelle said distractedly, as an opposing player tackled Joe and he fell to the ground with a heavy thump. She stepped forwards instinctively, but Joe bounced right back up and kept on running.

'Leila's pregnant,' Ted announced. 'We're going to have a baby.'

'Oh!' Estelle cried out, her hands flying to her face. 'I mean, that's wonderful news, Ted. Congratulations,' she finished sincerely, turning to him with a smile, and trying to suppress the flurry of emotions racing through her. Of course she was pleased for the pair of them, but there was another part of her that felt as though she'd just been punched in the stomach. All of Estelle's worries about loneliness and growing old were brought into sharp focus; it was impossible not to question the way her own life was going when confronted so starkly with someone else's happiness.

'Thanks, Estelle. That means a lot to me, and I know it will to Leila.'

'*Ten Sweet Lessons* must have really done the trick.' The words popped out of her mouth before Estelle even realised what she was saying.

'Yes, well, we've certainly been a lot more experimental since she read it. I didn't even know half of the things that were out there – floggers and gags and all kinds of paraphernalia, if you know where to look. It's certainly very different to when you and I—'

Ted stopped talking suddenly, aware that his comments weren't entirely appropriate. A red flush stole over his face, and Estelle had the unusual experience of seeing Ted lost for words. There was very little that embarrassed her ex-husband.

'So when's she due?' Estelle asked finally, breaking the awkward silence that had sprung up between them.

'Mid-September. She's about ten weeks gone at the moment, and once she's had her twelve-week scan we'll officially start telling people, but I wanted you to know before that. You – and Joe,' he explained.

Estelle nodded, wondering what was coming next.

'I did wonder if it might be better coming from yourself first. Just to forewarn him, so to speak. Obviously, we'll talk to him about it afterwards, but it's a sensitive subject, and he can be a wee bit quiet when Leila's around. I thought if you paved the way first . . .' Ted looked at her pleadingly.

'Okay, I'll talk to him,' Estelle capitulated, as the final

whistle blew and she began cheering once again, while Ted whooped and fist-pumped the air. Joe's team had won four-two, with Joe scoring the final goal for his team.

'We're probably embarrassing him no end,' Estelle laughed, glad that the conversation was on safer territory.

'What are parents for?' Ted smiled back at her.

Joe came striding across the pitch towards them, receiving hearty claps on the back from his teammates.

'Nice one, Joe! Well played, mate,' they called, as they ran past him.

'You star!' Estelle exclaimed as he reached her, pulling him into a hug. 'Now put a jumper on before you freeze.'

'Mum . . .' Joe rolled his eyes, as he reached into his kit bag and dutifully grabbed a sweater. Then he bent down and unlaced his boots, swapping them for a pair of battered old trainers.

'Well done, son,' Ted grinned, ruffling his hair. 'Are you ready to go?'

Joe nodded, and the three of them set off walking towards the car park. They were loading Joe's bag into the boot of Estelle's Ford Fiesta, when Tony, Joe's coach, jogged over towards them. A dark-haired man in his mid-forties, he had a well-built, athletic body and dark brown eyes.

'Great match today, Joe,' he grinned.

'Thanks, Tony.'

Tony nodded in acknowledgement at Estelle and Ted.

'You've got a good kid here. Proper little David Beckham, this one.'

'I hope so,' Ted chuckled. 'I wouldn't mind his salary.'

'And you're definitely alright for the upcoming away match?' Tony asked, addressing Joe. 'You're not on holiday or anything?'

'I don't think so. We're not going away anywhere, are we Mum?' Joe asked.

'No, I'm afraid not. No luxury vacation for us anytime soon,' she smiled.

'We've got an away match in a couple of weeks, against Bath Under-fifteens,' Tony explained. 'It's during the Easter holidays, so we're holding it on a Tuesday afternoon. Is that okay? The bus will pick up from the car park here, and we'll be back by early evening.'

'I don't see a problem,' Estelle agreed. 'I'll be working though, so Joe, you'll have to make your own way down here. Will that be okay? Unless – Ted, will you be around?'

'Afraid not. I'll be at work too, nose to the grindstone as usual.'

'Where do you live?' Tony asked, turning to Estelle.

'I own Cafe Crumb, so we live above there. Do you know it?'

'I most certainly do! I didn't realise that was your place. You do the best Chelsea buns in all of Bristol!'

'That sounds like us,' Estelle beamed. 'And all home-made too. Do you come in very often? I don't recall seeing you,' she admitted.

'Well, my colleagues usually do the pastry run,' Tony confessed, as Estelle smiled.

'Ah, that explains it. I'm usually very good at remembering my regulars, and I'm sure I'd have remembered you.'

Ted was listening to their conversation, a frown on his face. 'So what's happening with Joe?' he cut in gruffly.

'I can pick him up and drop him back too, if you'd like,' Tony offered. 'I live just off Hotwell Road, so it's on my way. Chris, my son over there, is Joe's age, and he'll be playing as well.'

'Well that sounds perfect, thank you, Tony. Is that good for you, Joe?'

'Yeah, sure,' Joe agreed easily.

'That's settled then,' Tony nodded, looking pleased. 'I'll let Joe fill you in on all the details.'

'Great. Have a good week.'

'You too.' Tony smiled at them all and strode off.

'Well, I'll see you on Thursday, son,' Ted said, as he reached over to give Joe a goodbye hug. 'Your mother says you're coming to mine, while she hosts her little book group. Is that alright?'

'No problem. See you then, Dad.'

'Come on, Joe. Let's get you back,' Estelle told him, bristling at Ted's rather patronising dismissal of the book club.

She suddenly felt very tired, not relishing the long day of baking and nagging Joe to finish his homework that loomed ahead of her. The news of Ted and Leila's baby had hit her harder than she expected, and it seemed to bring home the fact that she'd never really moved on after her divorce; the responsibility of running the cafe and caring for Joe hadn't allowed for much else. It wasn't fashionable to admit it, but sometimes she wished she had someone to take care of her, to talk through her problems with . . . and to take her to bed at night, she thought, feeling her cheeks grow warm.

Her sex life had been non-existent since she'd separated from Ted, and she hadn't relished hearing about him and Leila swinging from the chandeliers. For Estelle, it had been so long since she'd been with a man that she wasn't even sure she could still remember how! They said it was like riding a bike, but that was something else she hadn't done for years. Her old pushbike was sitting in the back yard, covered in rust and in need of a good oiling – much like herself.

'Mum?' Joe asked, looking at her curiously.

Estelle glanced up, flustered, her face burning. She realised she was sitting in the driver's seat, staring into space, a host of inappropriate thoughts running through her mind.

'Sorry, love, I was miles away,' she apologised hastily, turning the key in the ignition and reversing out of her parking space at speed. There was no point daydreaming about meeting her own Alexander Black, she told herself sharply. Joe and Cafe Crumb were the priorities in her life now, and as long as she had those, nothing else mattered.

6

Sue moved her hands over the rails of clothing, luxuriating in the feel of the different fabrics beneath her fingertips. There were silk blouses in bold jewel colours; crisply pressed cotton shirts in formal whites and baby blues; and cashmere sweaters in pale pastel shades.

In spite of the fact that spring had not yet fully sprung, the shops were already stocking their summer collections, ready for when the days lengthened and the temperature rose. Sue glanced covetously at the rows of beautiful dresses: delicate floral prints in sheerest chiffon, long maxi-dresses with jewelled necklines. She watched as a woman picked one up and held it against herself, checking out her reflection in a nearby mirror.

How lovely to be young and pretty and choosing your new wardrobe, Sue thought with a stab of envy. She picked out a blouse and held it up to the light, admiring the pattern of tiny black swallows against the cream-coloured fabric.

But what was the point anymore? Sue wondered sadly, putting it back and walking hastily away.

She caught the escalator back down to the ground floor, weaving her way through the perfume hall where a sales assistant wearing too much make-up tried to spray her with the latest celebrity fragrance. Sue politely declined, drifting over to the Chanel counter and wondering if she should splash out on a bottle of perfume. Perhaps Chanel No. 19 – she'd always loved that one. It had been her favourite when she was younger, when she and her husband, George, were first courting. But how could she justify it now? George would say she was being frivolous, frittering away their pension money on luxuries she didn't need.

Before she could be tempted by anything else, Sue walked briskly towards the exit signs, leaving the department store and heading out onto the street. For a moment, she was shocked by how quiet it was, but then she realised it was Tuesday morning – hardly prime shopping time. Most people were in work right now, she reminded herself. Not everyone was retired, like she was.

She checked her watch to find it was almost 11.30 a.m. The afternoon seemed to stretch out in front of her, yawning and empty without anything to fill it. What on earth was she going to do with the rest of the day?

Since Sue had retired three months ago, she'd encountered this problem on a regular basis. At first, she'd been looking forward to it, eagerly planning all the things she would do with her new-found freedom – travel, read, try out new recipes, perhaps take up yoga or learn a new language. After all, there were evening classes in practically everything at the local college, and she would be spoilt for choice. But somehow, it hadn't quite worked out that way.

The long, lazy lie-ins that Sue had envisaged had never happened. Her body clock still woke her at seven a.m. each day, and while George slept on beside her, she would rise quietly to make a start on cleaning the house – she couldn't help herself. Without fail, she would blow-dry her hair and apply a little make-up, worrying that if she let her standards slide now, she might never get them back. It would be the start of a long slow descent into slobbing out and not caring about how she looked, like one of those people on *The Jeremy Kyle Show*.

This morning, Sue had decided to treat herself to a shopping trip. She'd come into Bristol city centre with the aim of spending a leisurely, indulgent few hours browsing the new season fashions. It was something she used to love doing, and something she never quite had the time for when she was working. This morning's trip, however, had only depressed her even more. Why bother buying nice clothes if you never had occasion to wear them? She could hardly sport a fitted pencil skirt to do the vacuuming, or a smart tailored suit to do the washing up.

Maybe she should go food shopping instead. Yes, that might solve the problem. She could plan an elaborate menu for this evening's meal and spend a good chunk of the afternoon preparing it, then she could—

'Sue?' a voice called. 'I thought it was you!'

'Sandra!' Sue exclaimed. 'How are you?'

'Good, thanks! I'm just taking an early lunch break as I'm on my way to the dentist's. How about you? You must be spending the day shopping like the lady of leisure you are now – lucky thing!'

Sue smiled weakly. She and Sandra had worked together at the Windlesham Group, a large insurance firm based in the city. Sue had joined the company over twenty years ago, after her two children had started school and she'd gone back to work part-time. She'd seen the firm go through huge changes over the years, expanding from a start-up business with a handful of staff, to a thriving corporation that employed almost two hundred people. Sue's own role had grown in line with Windlesham's development, and by the time she retired, she was head of Human Resources, overseeing the entire department.

'So how is everyone?' Sue changed the subject. 'Tell me all the gossip.'

'Oh, there's nothing to tell really.' Sandra waved her hand dismissively. 'Same old, same old. Although Richard Maynard got promoted to head of UK Operations – can you believe it? None of us saw that coming! And Tessa Stevenson is pregnant again. She's due in June, so we're still deciding what to do about that. We might get a temp in, or it's possible we can split her workload between Dan and Aisha . . .'

As Sandra chattered on, Sue realised just how out of the loop she felt. They might have been uneventful, everyday happenings as far as Sandra was concerned, but they felt like a lifeline for Sue.

'And how's Beverley getting on?' she asked, referring to her replacement. Beverley was in her early forties, two decades younger than sixty-two-year-old Sue, and had made a big step up by taking on Sue's position.

'Oh, she's fine. Taken to it like a duck to water, as they say. Not that we're not missing you, of course,' Sandra added hastily. 'We've had to take on some new people as the company's expanding again. Windlesham's have won a big new contract with Bristol council, and there's talk of moving to new offices – perhaps that fancy new business park out near Filton.'

Sue swallowed, forcing herself to smile brightly. Everyone was managing just fine without her – better, in fact. She knew it was irrational, but it made her feel utterly useless.

'So what have you been up to?' Sandra asked eagerly. 'I remember you had all these plans when you were leaving. It must be wonderful having so much free time to do exactly what you want.'

'Oh, I haven't been doing much really . . .' Sue replied vaguely. 'We're thinking of going on holiday soon, but we're still deciding where.'

'Ooh, that sounds lovely. You're so lucky, not having to work anymore. I guess I'll just keep playing the lottery and crossing my fingers!'

Sue laughed politely.

'Anyway, I must dash,' Sandra continued. 'You remember how lunch breaks always fly by – we can't all be ladies of leisure!'

'Send my love to everyone,' Sue told her, as Sandra waved a hasty goodbye and dashed off down the street.

For a moment, Sue remained motionless, frozen to the spot in the middle of the pavement. Out of the corner of her eye she caught a glimpse of herself in a shop window and almost didn't recognise herself. Who was that old woman, with the grey hair and the lined face? Inside, she felt as though she was in her twenties, a young woman with her whole life ahead of her. But the reflection told a very different story.

Suddenly overcome by an overwhelming desire to escape, Sue turned on her heel and hurried towards the car park. This whole shopping expedition had been a disaster, and she didn't want to stay here any longer. She wanted to be back at home, in the safety of her own house – not some stupid old woman out roaming the streets, vainly searching for a purpose.

George was snoozing in the armchair, a copy of the *Daily Mail* crumpled in his lap and Radio 4 playing in the background, when Sue walked in. The slam of the door jolted him awake, and he bolted upright, blinking rapidly to clear the sleep from his eyes. His reading glasses had slid down his nose, and he pushed them hastily back up before straightening out his paper.

'George?' Sue called out, as she opened the living room door.

'I didn't expect you to be back so early,' he confessed, trying not to look guilty. He knew Sue didn't like him lazing around the house, especially when it was only a couple of hours since he'd got out of bed. In George's mind, he didn't see what the problem was. Neither of them had anywhere they needed to be, so what did it matter if he chose to have a little mid-morning nap? Fortunately for George, Sue seemed distracted, and failed to notice her husband's sleep-lined face and bedraggled appearance.

'I wasn't really in the mood for shopping,' she shrugged disconsolately.

'Oh.'

They sat in silence for a few moments, George wondering if it was acceptable to go back to reading his paper.

'Guess who I saw today?' Sue began.

'Um . . . I don't know. Who?'

'Sandra Farley. From Windlesham's,' she prompted, as George continued to look clueless.

'Oh,' he said again, hoping he'd chosen the right tone of voice. In recent years, he'd largely stopped paying attention when Sue talked about her work. Did his wife even like this Sandra woman? 'How was she?' he tried.

'She seemed very well. Apparently they've got a big new contract, so they're looking to expand – perhaps to that new business park in Filton.'

'Good job you're not still there, eh?' George remarked. 'You wouldn't want to be bothered with travelling out there every day.'

'It's supposed to be really nice,' Sue continued. 'Plush new offices set in landscaped gardens, with a Starbucks on site. There's even a gym for everyone who works there.'

'Well there you are then – what would you be interested in a gym for?'

'I might!' Sue retorted indignantly. 'Plenty of women my age go to the gym.'

'What are you planning to do? Bulk up like one of those bodybuilders?' George sniggered. 'Or maybe you're thinking of running a marathon? I'm afraid those days are long behind you,' he added, still chuckling to himself.

Sue pursed her lips like she'd just sucked on a lemon. 'I'm going to make a drink. Would you like one?' she asked shortly.

'Ooh, I'd love a cup of tea,' George replied, oblivious to the fact that anything was wrong. 'Thanks, love.'

As his wife disappeared into the kitchen, George heard her call out, 'Apparently the HR department are managing very well without me.'

'Well of course they are.' George raised his voice to reply. 'You didn't expect the company to collapse after you left, did you? If there's one thing I've learnt about business, it's that no one is irreplaceable, no matter how important you think you are.'

He thought Sue might have muttered something in

reply but it was hard to hear as the kettle rose noisily to boiling point.

'What was that, love?' George shouted. But Sue didn't answer.

She came back through a few moments later, carrying two mugs of tea.

'So, what shall we do today?' she asked brightly, her bad mood seemingly forgotten.

George felt his heart sink. Every day it was the same, as Sue attempted to drag him out to garden centres and furniture shops, craft fairs and exhibitions. She'd even started talking about exotic holidays to far-flung destinations, weekend breaks to European cities. Didn't she understand that he'd retired?

Until recently, George had worked as an engineer, and seemed to spend his whole life rushing around and striving to meet tight deadlines. Especially when the children were still at home, he'd often felt as though he never had a minute to himself.

Retirement, in comparison, was a veritable paradise! He had no commitments, no responsibilities, and that was just how he liked it. He could take all the time in the world to read the paper or do the crossword, enjoy a leisurely lunch and potter in the garden, or watch a film if the weather was bad. That took him nicely up to his evening meal, expertly cooked by his wife at the same time every day, and then there was always something good on TV these days – all those channels! Perhaps he'd pick a gentle detective drama, or a documentary. Sue never minded too much what he watched – she always had her nose in a book, or would be on the Internet researching things to do.

If it had been a particularly taxing day, George reflected, he might fall asleep in front of the television, but without fail he'd be in bed by midnight.

'I hadn't really planned anything, to be honest,' he admitted, taking a sip of his tea. 'I've got a few jobs to do round the house,' he continued vaguely, although that wasn't strictly true, 'so I thought we could just stay in and I'd get on with those . . .'

He saw the tiniest flicker of irritation cross his wife's face.

'We could drive up to the Cotswolds,' she suggested, as though he hadn't spoken. 'Like we used to when the kids were little. Then we could find somewhere nice to have our dinner – a country pub, or a little restaurant. We could even stay overnight,' she continued, her voice rising with excitement. 'After all, we're not in any hurry to get back, are we?'

George glanced out of the window. It had started raining lightly, and the trees were swaying violently in the wind. It was a day for staying indoors with the central heating turned up, not a day for traipsing around the countryside.

'Maybe another time, eh? Let's organise something for next week. Besides, haven't you got that book club thing tomorrow night?'

'Yes, that's true,' Sue agreed, instantly perking up as

she remembered *Ten Sweet Lessons*. If only her husband could be more like Alexander Black – passionate and impulsive, instead of dull and grumpy.

If truth be told, she was finding *Ten Sweet Lessons* absolutely fascinating. Of course, the writing was hardly comparable with Oscar Wilde or Virginia Woolf, but Sue was utterly hooked, and could understand why countless other women were too. It was pure fantasy, offering an erotically charged glimpse into a world which she'd never experienced.

For Sue, sex had always been largely functional, with little or no focus on her pleasure. George was the only man she'd ever slept with, and Sue had gone through life thinking of sex as something of a chore – an act which, for the most part, was to be endured, rather than celebrated. But the experiences Christina described in *Ten Sweet Lessons* had left Sue feeling unexpectedly envious. Even if she was in her early sixties, was it too much to demand a satisfactory sex life before it was too late? Her ageing limbs might not be able to contort themselves into a dozen different positions, but if George was willing to be a little open-minded, she might be able to reach the heady, climactic heights described in the novel.

Right now though, Sue couldn't see any way of opening up to her husband. The gulf that had sprung up between them was just too wide, and the idea of telling him how she felt was unthinkable.

'There you are then,' George pronounced with satisfaction, bringing Sue rudely out of her reverie. 'Let's leave going out for another day. It's nice that you've joined that little book group though,' he added thoughtfully. 'Something to keep you occupied.'

Sue opened her mouth, intending to snap back with an angry retort, but then closed it again, an expression of defeat crossing her face. She slumped down in her chair, taking a sip of tea.

'Yes,' she agreed tonelessly. 'I suppose you're right.'

'Well, there you are then,' George repeated, shaking out his newspaper and turning to the sports pages. As far as he was concerned, the conversation was over.

Neither of them spoke and the air lay heavy between them, just the ticking of the grandfather clock in the hallway to break the silence.

7

The second meeting of the Cafe Crumb book club began very differently to the first. Although Estelle still worried about whether or not anyone would turn up, her concerns proved unfounded, as Sue, Rebecca and Gracie all arrived before the seven p.m. start time.

They queued up at the counter for their drinks and cakes (for this time, refreshments and snacks weren't free) and sat down quickly, three distinctive copies of *Ten Sweet Lessons* on the table in front of them.

The atmosphere was completely different to the last meeting. There was no air of boredom, tapping of feet or heavy sighs. Everyone sat bolt upright and eager to begin. There was a buzz in the air, and it was as though everyone couldn't wait to start.

There was, however, no sign of Reggie.

'Have you heard from him, Estelle?' asked Sue.

'No, I haven't,' she replied, coming over to sit with them and placing her own copy of *Ten Sweet Lessons* on the table.

'I wonder if he's going to show up.'

'Do you think we scared him off?' Gracie grinned wickedly.

'Well, it's got to be fairly unnerving for the poor boy,' replied Sue. 'A nice young man like that, and then he has all us women to contend with. Not to mention the subject matter for this week,' she finished, tapping the book lightly.

'He probably didn't read it,' Rebecca sniffed dismissively.

'Or maybe he did and feels intimidated,' Gracie chimed in. 'Maybe he didn't feel he could measure up to the famous Alexander Black.'

'Mmm, Alexander Black,' drawled Rebecca, pretending to swoon.

Gracie rolled her eyes. 'What? That disturbed sicko, with his pathological need to control everything and take advantage of a younger woman?'

'Yep, that's the one,' replied Rebecca with a giggle. 'He can take advantage of me any time.'

'Should we just get started?' wondered Estelle, looking anxiously at the door.

'Yes, let's,' said Gracie. 'Besides, even if Reggie does turn up, it's not like he's going to say anything. He'll just sit in the corner and makes notes about us.'

'True,' Estelle agreed uncomfortably. 'Although I would

like to encourage him to join in if at all possible. It seems a waste otherwise.'

'And it could be good to get a man's perspective on these things,' added Sue. 'See if *Ten Sweet Lessons* is as much of a turn-on for men as it is for—' She broke off suddenly, flushing as she realised that she'd just revealed more information than she intended to.

'Well, it sounds as though *you* enjoyed the book,' Estelle smiled, unable to help herself. 'What did everyone else think?'

There was a burst of noise, as everyone began speaking at once, and Estelle laughed, holding up her hand for silence. 'This is a little different to the last session!'

'This was *so* much more exciting than *Tess of the D'Urbervilles*,' Rebecca grinned.

'It was certainly wilder, but I don't know if you can compare it to a classic like that,' objected Sue.

'They both feature women being oppressed – whether by societal norms in *Tess*, or physical subjugation in *Ten Sweet Lessons*. Why can't anybody write a book about strong women?' Gracie complained.

'Great everyone, that's really interesting,' cut in Estelle, feeling like a referee. Everyone was so eager to speak; she instinctively felt she'd done the right thing by choosing such a controversial book. 'So given everything that's just been said, why do you think *Ten Sweet Lessons* has proved to be so popular? Rebecca?'

'Sex,' she blurted out.

'Absolutely. Sex sells,' agreed Gracie. 'Whether the

book is of any quality or not doesn't matter. It sells on notoriety alone.'

'Oh, come on Gracie, you must have enjoyed it a little bit,' Rebecca pressed. 'You'd have to be dead from the waist down not to read about all that spanking and sexy stuff without feeling some urges of your own. I don't know about anyone else, but I wanted to jump on my husband every time he walked through the door.'

'I have to admit, it made me thoroughly envious,' Sue admitted. 'I didn't know that most of that sort of thing went on, let alone have the opportunity to try it.'

'It's great, isn't it?' Estelle enthused. 'It's as though *Ten Sweet Lessons* has suddenly made it okay to read this sort of novel. It makes you feel very naughty for doing it, but that's part of the appeal.'

'I know! I read it on the bus,' Rebecca agreed. 'More than once I found myself sitting looking at everyone else, hoping they couldn't tell what I was thinking. It's like having a sexy secret.'

'I also found it quite frustrating,' confessed Sue. 'It made me realise what I'd been missing out on all these years, and wondering if that's what everyone else was getting up to while I'd been – if I may speak frankly – lying back and thinking of England.'

'Well my ex and I never did anything like that,' Estelle admitted, marvelling at how openly the women were speaking in front of each other. 'Although maybe we'd still be married if we had! You know, spiced things up a little,' she finished ruefully, thinking of what Ted had said about him and Leila.

'It's given *me* a few ideas,' Rebecca giggled.

'I just don't get what the big deal is,' Gracie protested. 'It's not like we've never read about sex before, so why is this book so popular?'

'I think it's the novelty factor,' Rebecca said thoughtfully. 'I mean, I've never read anything like this before, and it wouldn't have occurred to me to pick it up unless everyone else was raving about it. But it's made it acceptable – mainstream even – to read erotica.'

'How about you, Sue?' asked Estelle. 'What did you make of it?'

'Well, like Rebecca said, I've never read anything quite like this before,' Sue replied, fiddling self-consciously with her necklace. 'I mean, obviously it's very graphic in parts. And this whole idea of pleasure and pain – that's something I've never really considered. Some of the content really was extreme and shocking. But ultimately, I think the book's appeal comes from the fact that, at its heart, it's a simple love story. A romance almost.'

'Ahh, I love a good romantic spank on the bottom,' sighed Rebecca, making everyone laugh.

'But it *is* an interesting point, Sue,' Estelle continued. 'Is it *actually* erotica? Is it just a romance novel with added sex scenes? Or is it nothing more than porn?'

At that moment, the door opened. Reggie walked through, just as Estelle was finishing her sentence. As he heard the word 'porn', a slow blush spread across his face, burning from his neck all the way up to his forehead. 'Um . . . I . . .' he began, looking like he could happily have turned around and run as fast as he could away from Cafe Crumb.

'Reggie!' Estelle called out, as the other women immediately fell quiet, their previous openness deserting them. Somehow, discussing their urges and fantasies in front of Reggie wasn't quite the same. 'You're here! How lovely that you came back. We're all very pleased to see you. Now sit down,' Estelle told him, standing up and pulling out a chair. 'What can I get you to eat? I'm afraid you'll have to pay for it this week.'

'I'll just have a tea . . .' he began. 'And a piece of whatever cake you've got left.'

'Two sugars in your tea, is that right?'

'Yes, that's right,' Reggie agreed, still looking terrified as he set his bag down on the floor and pulled out his own well-thumbed copy of *Ten Sweet Lessons*.

'You read it!' Rebecca exclaimed in shock.

'Yes,' Reggie mumbled. 'Just for research – for the book club, I mean,' he explained quickly, as Gracie sniggered. 'Not for any other kind of research.'

'We didn't think you'd come back,' Gracie challenged him, as Estelle shot her a sharp look.

'I almost didn't,' Reggie admitted. 'But . . . you know . . . for the sake of my thesis . . .'

'Right,' Gracie nodded, a teasing glint in her eye. 'You're very dedicated.'

'We were just talking about how to categorise *Ten*

Sweet Lessons,' Estelle explained. 'About whether it's romance, or erotica . . .'

'Or porn,' put in Gracie helpfully.

'Yes, thank you, Gracie,' smiled Estelle. 'What do you think Reggie? Or do you have any thoughts on the book in general?'

'Um . . .' He looked horrified to be put on the spot. 'I didn't know women liked this sort of thing. I mean, it's so popular. Is this really what everyone out there's reading?'

'*I'm* not!' Grace burst out. 'I thought it was offensive, misogynistic, badly-written tripe.'

'Don't hold back Gracie,' Estelle couldn't resist teasing her.

'The whole premise of the book is just horrible!' Gracie burst out. 'You've got this young woman – Christina Cox – who's willing to do anything Alexander Black says. To debase herself in any way, and go through the "ten sweet lessons" to ultimate submission. It's simply not a good message to be putting out there – that violence towards women is acceptable.'

'But it's *her* choice,' Rebecca protested. 'If anything, she's the one in control. Any power that Alexander Black has over her comes from what she gives him. I think it's a really sexy idea.'

'I disagree,' Gracie shot back. 'It's not her choice at all. She only goes along with the spanking and shackles to please him; because she loves him, and hopes she can change him. The relationship is entirely on his terms.'

'Well I liked it,' Rebecca said firmly. 'And I think you're reading far too much into it. It's just a fun bit of escapism.'

'Well, if BDSM is your idea of fun . . .' Gracie smirked.

'I didn't mean it like that!' Rebecca blushed.

'And it's totally unrealistic,' Gracie continued. 'Nobody has that many . . . I mean, not like . . . not that many *times* . . . it's just not possible . . .' she finished, as everyone began giggling once more.

'Now come on, everyone,' Estelle managed, through her own laughter. 'We're all grown-ups here.'

'But isn't that the point, Gracie?' Rebecca continued. 'It's escapism. It's bigger than real life – if you'll pardon the pun. Everyone knows that whereas men get turned on visually, women need something more . . .'

'So it *is* porn,' Gracie declared triumphantly.

'I think it's more like a fairytale,' cut in Sue. 'You have the handsome, rich, older man living alone in his mansion like some storybook prince, and he rescues the young, pretty woman and whisks her off to an amazing life that's far removed from her everyday drudgery. It's a classic fairytale.'

'It's certainly not what *I* dreamed of when I was growing up,' Gracie quipped. 'Being handcuffed to the bed and whipped until my bottom bled . . . hardly the stuff little girls dream of.'

'Yes, but who knew it could produce such earth-shattering orgasms?' Rebecca deadpanned.

Reggie stood up so quickly he almost knocked his

chair over. 'Estelle, could you tell me where the toilets are, please?'

'Certainly. They're just in that back corner, over there,' she indicated, as Reggie practically sprinted across the cafe to escape.

'Oops, do you think I scared him off?' Rebecca whispered guiltily.

'He'll be climbing out of the toilet window as we speak,' Sue added wickedly.

'Maybe now would be a good time to have a little break,' Estelle suggested. 'Anyone for a top-up?'

The others murmured their assent, getting up from the table and ordering a fresh round of coffee and cakes. Estelle was delighted as the money dropped with a chink into the till, and the conversation didn't stop while the women were queuing.

'All I'm saying,' Gracie was explaining earnestly to Rebecca, 'is that the heroine – Christina – was like a wet dish cloth. She was so annoying. At times I just wanted to give her a good slap.'

'I think she might have enjoyed that,' Rebecca grinned. 'Honestly Gracie, I think you're getting far too worked up about it. Have some more cake,' she suggested, taking a large bite out of hers.

'What about Alexander Black?' asked Estelle, as she sat down again. 'What do we all think of him?'

'Mmm, I think I'd give everything I own for one night with Alexander Black,' Rebecca raved. 'He's *such* a sexy character. So manly and masterful.'

Gracie looked disgusted. 'I think he has major issues, and shouldn't be allowed near women, personally.'

'But imagine having a man who adored you that much,' Rebecca began dreamily. 'Someone who worships the very ground you walk on, all his energy and passion and desire focused on you, as the sole object of his lust . . .'

Gracie snorted derisively. 'I'd rather not be treated like an object, thank you very much.'

'I have to say, I agree more with Rebecca,' Sue admitted. 'Alexander is a rich, powerful man with a commanding presence, and I think that most of us ladies find that attractive. Especially these days, when more and more women are building successful careers and forging ahead in so many areas, sometimes – and it's not fashionable to admit it – you want to be with a man who can take charge and really be in control.'

'Very interesting, Sue,' Estelle nodded. 'I hadn't thought of that.' She turned, as Reggie crept sheepishly back across the room and slunk back into his seat.

'Don't worry, Reggie,' Estelle smiled. 'You didn't miss very much. Although Sue did make a very interesting point about career women wanting a man who can dominate them. What do you think to that? Has that been your experience?' she asked, hoping to draw him into the discussion.

Reggie's eyes seemed to widen behind his glasses, as he looked anxiously at each woman in turn. He swallowed nervously, but his throat felt constricted, and he took a soothing sip of tea before he spoke.

'I mean, it can certainly be very intimidating for a man
. . . if *that's* what women want,' he began, nodding
towards the book. 'Someone who's very confident and
. . . so on. We can't all be like Alexander Black, I'm
afraid,' he finished, his tone apologetic. In spite of his
large frame, he seemed to physically shrink as he spoke,
disappearing under the penetrating gaze of the women.

'We don't *all* want an Alexander Black, you know,'
Gracie retorted. 'And what's wrong with having normal
sex? Why do fantasies always seem to involve all this
weird, fetish stuff?'

'I'll make you a badge for next week – "Vanilla and
Proud".' Rebecca teased, making quote marks in the air
with her fingers.

Gracie stuck her tongue out in retaliation.

'Thank you, ladies,' Estelle said firmly, bringing their
exchange to an end. 'And thank *you*, Reggie,' she
continued in a softer tone, thrilled that he'd actually
made a contribution. 'Well I think that just about wraps
us up here. Does anyone have any final thoughts?'

There was a moment's pause then Sue began to
speak. 'Being a little bit older than most of you – well,
all of you,' she smiled, looking round, 'I think I would
make the point that it's all been done before. Every
generation thinks they're the one to discover sex, and
they all reinvent it in a slightly different way. In the
eighties, it was all about the big, glossy airport novels
– you know, the Jackie Collins-type bonkbuster. And
then in the nineties, the craze was for true life

72

confessions – whether French housewives or high-class call girls.

'When I was very young, there was all that hoo-hah about *Lady Chatterley's Lover*, as it was finally allowed to be published after having been banned for obscenity. But if you read it now, it's so tame as to be laughable, almost. It's certainly nothing like *Ten Sweet Lessons*.'

'I've never read *Lady Chatterley's Lover*,' Rebecca admitted.

'Me neither,' said Estelle.

'I always imagined it would be absolutely filthy, but is that not the case?' Rebecca questioned Sue.

'Well, it does have its moments,' she conceded. 'I think the language was one of the most shocking things in it, back then.'

'Why don't we make that our next book club read?' Estelle burst out, with a flash of inspiration. 'Then we could compare it to *Ten Sweet Lessons*, and see how the language and the styles vary. Plus it'd be a great excuse to read one of the classics.'

'I think it's a fantastic idea, Estelle,' Rebecca backed her up.

'Thank you, Rebecca. What do you think, Gracie?'

Gracie pursed her lips, looking mutinous. 'As long as it's not another soppy woman being subjugated by a man with issues.'

A smile twitched at the corners of Estelle's mouth. 'I'm sure there'll be more to it than that, if we look deeply enough. Reggie, does *Lady Chatterley* suit you?'

'That's fine . . . whatever you want. As I say, I'm largely here in an observational capacity, so . . .' he trailed off.

'Well I'm glad we're all in agreement,' beamed Estelle. 'So the next meeting will be in two weeks' time, and the book we'll be discussing is *Lady Chatterley's Lover*. Make sure you come armed with plenty of thoughts and opinions, and I'll see you all in a fortnight.'

As everyone filed out of the door and Estelle locked up behind them, she couldn't keep the smile from her face, a warm glow of satisfaction stealing over her. Tonight had been a success! There had been discussion and debate, whilst the meeting itself had been lively and friendly. *And* she'd made a small profit.

She could hardly wait to get stuck into *Lady Chatterley's Lover*. Estelle had enjoyed *Ten Sweet Lessons* immensely, half-thrilled and half-terrified by the sensations it had stirred within her – sensations she'd thought were long gone, and had doubted she might never experience again. And now the group was moving on to one of the most famous pieces of erotic literature ever written, one renowned for its explicit love scenes and scandalous use of language. She couldn't wait to see what the next meeting would bring!

8

'Keyes . . . Marian Keyes . . .' Gracie murmured under her breath as she paced round the library, trying to locate the right home for the copy of *Rachel's Holiday* she was carrying.

Found it! She thought triumphantly, checking the reference number on the spine and slotting it in between Cathy Kelly and Sophie Kinsella.

She returned to the trolley she was pushing and picked out *The Take* by Martina Cole.

'How are you getting on with those returns, Gracie?' asked Simon, her manager.

'Almost done,' she told him cheerily, as she whizzed past him to the *Crime and Thriller* section, where she found one of the library's regular patrons browsing the shelves. 'Hello, Mr Harris.'

'Hello, Gracie,' replied the elderly gentleman. 'Lovely day, isn't it?'

'It is indeed,' she said happily. The sun was shining, the warm yellow light streaming in through the wide library windows. It was one of those glorious spring days when it felt like winter might finally be in retreat, and you started to believe that summer was on its way back.

'Tell me, do you have the new Harlan Coben?' Mr Harris enquired.

Gracie frowned. 'That's only just been released, so it might be another few days until we get it in. Would you like me to reserve it for you when it arrives?'

'If you could, I'd very much appreciate it.'

'No problem,' Gracie beamed, making a mental note to do just that when she returned to the front desk. 'In the meantime, have you read *Long Dark Road* by Alex Hayter? He's a new author, very similar to Harlan Coben. I think you might enjoy it.'

Mr Harris took the novel from her and examined it, turning it over to read the back cover. 'Thank you, Gracie. I like the look of this. Yes, I'll definitely give it a whirl.'

'We aim to please,' Gracie grinned, as she set off once again.

Gracie had worked in Clifton library for almost five years now, and although she'd initially seen it as a stop-gap after university – something to tide her over until she got a 'real' job – she enjoyed it so much that she'd long since abandoned any ideas of moving on. Gracie loved the calm, steady pace of the library, the regular customers that she'd got to know, and the sense of being at the heart of the community, of organising speaker meetings and book readings with local authors. Unlike many of her friends who'd left Bristol to go to university and never returned, seduced by the bright lights of London or Manchester or Edinburgh, Gracie was content with her lot in life. Born and raised in Bristol, and now living in Clifton with her mother, as long as she had enough money to go out with her friends on a Saturday night, and treat herself to some new clothes now and again, she was quite satisfied.

At twenty-seven years old, she thought it might be nice to have a regular boyfriend, but a series of unsuccessful dates and a love of feminist literature had left her feeling that it wasn't a necessity. Women didn't even need men nowadays, after all – babies could be created in a test tube! Her own father had left when she was a toddler and was in and out of her life sporadically, occasionally remembering her birthday, or sending a card at Christmas. By and large, he was a waste of space. Gracie had grown up believing that men couldn't be relied upon, and her mother, Maggie, had reinforced that view. Maggie had never remarried, and had impressed upon her only daughter the importance of self-reliance and financial independence from men. As such, Gracie had developed strong opinions that she wasn't afraid to share, and had extremely high standards when it came to finding a boyfriend.

'Ooh, that's a lovely outfit, Gracie,' she heard a voice say, as she passed through *Contemporary Fiction*.

'Thank you, Mrs Jaworski,' Gracie replied, as she turned and saw the small, Polish-born pensioner looking her up and down.

Gracie was wearing a fitted black pencil skirt, with a tight white blouse and oversized red belt, teamed with red patent kitten heels and seamed stockings. Her dark hair was loose, with a red silk handkerchief looped underneath and knotted on top.

'You always look so nicely turned out,' Mrs Jaworski was saying. 'So many young people today just don't make an effort, and the girls these days are always wearing jeans or trousers. It's nice to see someone dressing like a lady for once.'

Gracie smiled to herself, wondering whether to engage Mrs Jaworski in a debate about a woman's right to choose what she wanted to wear, and how it was only in the last century that it had become acceptable for women to even *wear* trousers in this patriarchal society. On reflection, she decided not to. 'What are you reading today?' she asked instead.

'I'm looking for something different,' Mrs Jaworski replied, her tone serious. 'Tell me, have you read this *Ten Sweet Lessons* that everybody's talking about?'

'Yes, I have,' Gracie nodded.

'And what did you think?'

Gracie pulled a face. 'I didn't really like it, and I'm not sure it would be your kind of thing either. Maybe you should just stick with a nice Josephine Cox.'

'I might be old, but there's life in me yet,' Mrs Jaworski

chuckled. 'I'd like to see what all the talk is about. It's supposed to be very naughty, isn't it?'

'*Very*,' Gracie emphasised. 'It's all handcuffs and candle wax. It doesn't leave much to the imagination, let me tell you!'

Mrs Jaworkski's eyebrows lifted so high they almost disappeared into her wiry grey hair.

'Fascinating. Do you have it in stock?'

Gracie laughed, as she skimmed the shelves and found the last remaining copy. 'Now don't say I didn't warn you,' she teased, as she handed it over. 'Is there anything else I can help you with today?'

'Not now, thank you. I'll carry on looking, and come to the desk when I've chosen everything.'

'No problem. Just let me know.'

Gracie returned the last couple of books to their homes and made her way over to the counter. She tapped into the computer, making a note to reserve the new Harlan Coben for Mr Harris.

'Are you busy, Gracie?' asked Simon, who was officiously stamping a pile of books.

'Almost finished,' Gracie replied, as she hit the enter key and the 'reserved' notice popped up.

'Great. When you're done, could you go and help that gentleman over there? He's looking a little lost.'

'Which gentleman?' Gracie asked in confusion.

'The one with his back to us, wearing a grey coat.'

Gracie stared across the library and frowned. There was something very familiar about the man's lean frame and messy brown hair, not to mention the battered satchel he was carrying. Gracie approached him slowly, an odd feeling in her stomach.

'Excuse me,' she began.

The man turned around, and his mouth dropped open in shock.

'Reggie!' Gracie exclaimed. 'It *is* you.'

Reggie looked startled. 'Hello, Grace,' he began nervously.

'It's Grac-*ie*,' she retorted, pursing her lips into a fine line. 'What are you doing here? Making notes on us outside of the book club too?'

'No, of course not,' he replied, angry spots of colour appearing on his cheeks. 'Besides, you're the one who came over to say hello to me. I didn't even see you.'

'I *work* here,' Gracie shot back. 'My manager sent me over because he thought you looked like you needed some help.'

'Oh, I see,' Reggie replied, caught off-guard. 'Well, I could do with some help actually. I . . . um . . . I can't seem to find a copy of *Lady Chatterley's Lover*.'

Gracie raised her eyebrows. 'So you *are* planning to come to the next meeting?'

'Yes, most probably. After all, it's very important for my—'

'For your thesis. Yes, you mentioned that,' Gracie finished sarcastically, and Reggie blushed even deeper. 'I'm afraid *Lady Chatterley's Lover* isn't in stock.'

'How do you know without checking?' Reggie shot

back suspiciously, worrying that she was trying to fob him off.

Gracie tried hard to keep a straight face, but couldn't hide her triumphant smile. 'Because I've already borrowed it. Librarian's privileges, you see. It means I get first dibs.'

Unable to help himself, Reggie began to laugh. 'Well, I can't compete with that, can I? I suppose I'll have to buy it instead. Isn't there a little bookshop around here? Bainbridge Books, or something like that?'

'It closed down,' Gracie told him glumly.

'Right. Well, I'll have to go to the big Waterstones in town. Or maybe I could look in the university library next time I'm in.'

'I can check the system if you like,' Gracie offered, taking pity on him. 'See if it's in stock in any other libraries nearby.'

'Would you?' Reggie asked gratefully. 'That would be very useful.'

'Of course.'

'I used to have a copy,' Reggie explained, as he followed her over to the main desk. 'But I don't know where it is now. It's probably in a box somewhere at my parents' house, with all the other books from my undergraduate degree.'

'Did you study English?' Gracie asked.

Reggie nodded.

'Me too! I specialised in feminist writing. My thesis was on *First Wave to Second Wave: Feminist Writing from Mary Wollstonecraft to Simone de Beauvoir.*'

Reggie looked amused. 'Now why doesn't that surprise me?' The words slipped out of his mouth almost before he realised what he was saying, and Gracie turned on him angrily.

'There's nothing wrong with having a little self-respect. Not all women are as pathetic and submissive as books like *Ten Sweet Lessons* imply.'

'Ah, you weren't a fan of that, were you?' Reggie grinned, his eyes twinkling as he teased her.

'Look, you can't deny that books like *Ten Sweet Lessons* are a totally unrealistic representation of a male-female relationship,' Gracie began hotly. 'They offer an unhelpful stereotype that women – and men – simply can't live up to.'

'In what sense?' Reggie challenged her.

'In every sense!' Gracie was becoming increasingly frustrated. 'They imply that everything – in the bedroom – is going to be amazing, and sometimes it's just not. I mean, you can't just – *you know* – so easily and so frequently. Not *every* time,' Gracie faltered, tying herself up in verbal knots and wishing she'd never started this rant.

'It's supposed to be a fantasy,' Reggie continued, aware that he was infuriating Gracie, and enjoying watching her become increasingly animated. 'Anyway, maybe some people can – *you know* – so easily and so frequently.'

'Well I haven't ever . . . like that,' Gracie retorted, eager to win the argument, but revealing more about herself than she intended.

'It's all a question of chemistry. Maybe with the right person you *could* . . . It's about buttons. Pushing them, I mean . . .' Reggie finished awkwardly, jabbing at the air in a clumsy mime.

'Great technique, Reggie,' Gracie broke down in helpless giggles.

'It's not . . . I mean . . . That's not what *I* do . . .'

'Really?' Gracie shot back, relishing the fact that the tables had turned, and Reggie was now the one squirming with embarrassment. 'What *do* you do? Maybe you could outline your technique for us at the next book club meeting.'

Their voices were growing louder, and Gracie's manager looked across sharply.

'Gracie,' he hissed. 'It's not very often that I have to tell the *staff* to be quiet, but you and your friend are disturbing people.'

'Sorry Simon, I—'

'And I'm not sure your conversation is entirely appropriate for the workplace either,' he added pointedly.

Gracie caught Reggie's eye and saw that he was trying not to laugh. It was impossible to keep a straight face, and soon they were both grinning naughtily at each other, like schoolchildren being told off by the headmaster. Gracie found herself wondering how on earth they'd ended up on this subject. The last person she'd have expected to be discussing sexual chemistry with was *Reggie*.

'So do any other libraries have it?' Reggie whispered,

his eyes dancing as he leaned over, resting his elbows on the counter.

'Have what?'

'*Lady Chatterley's Lover.*'

'Oh, yeah, I'd forgotten about that!' Gracie quickly typed in the title and squinted at the screen. 'There are three copies in the central library. We can order one for you, and it'll be here tomorrow after three, or I can reserve a copy and you can pop in yourself to collect it.'

'Um . . .' Reggie pondered the issue for a moment. 'I'll call in. I'll be over that way this afternoon.'

'Okay,' Gracie nodded, feeling unexpectedly disappointed. 'I'll put it on hold and it'll be there waiting for you.'

'Great. Thanks, Gracie.'

'No problem.'

'Well . . . I guess I'll see you at the next meeting.'

'I guess you will. If you turn up, that is.'

'Oh, I'll turn up,' Reggie insisted. 'You lot aren't so bad after all, you know.'

'Oi!' Gracie exclaimed, narrowing her eyes. 'And don't worry – I won't tell everyone at Cafe Crumb about your appalling seduction technique,' she smirked.

'You'd better not, or else I'll tell everyone I witnessed you being inappropriate in a library,' Reggie returned, causing Gracie to giggle, and Simon to glare fiercely at them once more.

'I'd better get back to work,' Gracie whispered apologetically.

'Okay. Oh, I might be a little late for the next meeting – I have a seminar that afternoon which is likely to overrun. Could you tell Estelle for me?'

'Of course.'

'Thank you.'

'My pleasure.'

'See you there then.'

'Bye, Reggie.'

'Bye, Gracie.'

Gracie watched him walk out of the door into the dazzling spring sunshine, and realised she was smiling.

Outside the library, as Reggie strolled down the path and back out onto the street, he found himself mentally replaying what had just happened.

His mind had been full of the research notes he needed to make today, and seminars that he thought it might be useful to attend, so his only thought when entering Clifton library had been to pick up a copy of *Lady Chatterley's Lover* as quickly and as painlessly as possible.

Then he'd bumped into Gracie, and what had started out as a somewhat hostile encounter had quickly turned into something . . . what, exactly? *Fun*, Reggie supposed, the realisation taking him by surprise. 'Fun' and 'Reggie' were not words which usually went together.

But he'd enjoyed chatting with Gracie; he found her intelligent, sparky and challenging, and she'd made *him* feel the same. The way she'd teased him when they'd somehow ended up talking about the most outrageous of subjects . . . it was a long time since he'd laughed like that.

Reggie made his way towards the city centre, a spring in his step as he marched along. It was almost as though he'd made some kind of a breakthrough back there, managing to be self-assured and humorous – flirty, even. The sensation was all too rare, but he liked the person he became when he was relaxed and confident.

To Reggie's surprise, he found himself fervently hoping that Gracie liked it too.

9

The delicious smell of baking filled the flat; an intoxicating
blend of warm scones, freshly mixed chocolate brownies
and rich coffee cake. The windows had steamed up from
the heat of the oven, the atmosphere cosy as Estelle moved
busily around the kitchen, humming away to Radio Bristol
which was playing quietly in the background. She peered
through the door of the oven to check on her cupcakes
which were rising nicely, then moved back to the cluttered
work surface, pouring a large bowl of cookie dough into
the food mixer and turning it on.

The living space above Cafe Crumb was small and
comprised of two bedrooms – one each for Estelle
and Joe – and a bathroom, with the front door opening
directly into the tiny living-cum-dining room. But by far
the largest room was the kitchen; Estelle had had it
specially extended, she needed the extra space for all the

baking she did for the cafe. It was undeniably hard work – every night after the shop closed Estelle would whip up fresh batches of a dozen different cakes and sweets, ready to sell the next day. On Sundays, after watching Joe play football, the rest of Estelle's day would be taken up with making industrial-sized quantities of pastry to freeze and use later in the week, as well as preparing stock for the next day and putting the last week's accounts in order. Sometimes it seemed never-ending.

But Estelle enjoyed her hectic routine. There was something calming and deeply satisfying about weighing all the ingredients, mixing the dough and rolling it out, then loading everything into the oven and seeing the alchemy which took place as buns rose like magic, and pastry turned flaky and golden.

This Tuesday evening, with Joe away at the U15 match in Bath, Estelle was on her own. Tony had picked him up in the early afternoon and would be dropping him back soon, Estelle realised, as she checked the clock on the wall.

She sprinkled the counter top with flour and had just begun rolling out the cookie dough when she heard Joe's key in the lock.

Estelle came out of the kitchen to greet him, brushing her hands on her flour-covered apron.

'How'd it go, love?' she asked, as he sauntered in, leaving the front door open.

'Fine. We won,' he replied with a grin, as Estelle shrieked in delight.

'You little star!' she exclaimed, running over to give him a hug. Joe endured his mother's squeezes for a few seconds, before wriggling free.

'Oh, I nearly forgot, Tony's here,' he added casually, grabbing a muffin from the rack that was cooling on the side before disappearing into his bedroom.

'What? Joe—' Estelle began in confusion. She stepped forwards and saw Tony standing outside the front door, waiting at the top of the metal stairway that led directly up to the flat from street level. He was wearing dark jogging bottoms with a grey hooded fleece, and the sporty look emphasised his fit, strong body. Much to Estelle's shame, she realised that since reading *Ten Sweet Lessons* she'd begun paying far more attention to the male physique, and her eyes scanned over him appreciatively.

'I'm so sorry about that, do come in,' Estelle told him, suddenly very aware that her face was flushed from the heat of the oven and she was wearing her scruffiest old clothes.

'That's alright,' Tony waved away her apology.

'I can't believe Joe left you outside like that! I'll have a word with him later,' she promised, as she smoothed back her hair, conscious of what a state she must look.

'Oh, it's no problem,' he repeated. 'I know what teenagers can be like.'

'Well, thanks so much for dropping him back,' Estelle said gratefully. 'What was the score? He didn't even tell me.'

'Six-four,' Tony beamed. 'It was a great match, and Joe scored a hat-trick.'

'Did he?' Estelle exclaimed, thrilled. 'Oh, I wish I'd been there.'

'You'd have been very proud. He's a great little player.'

'I'm just pleased that he's found something he's so passionate about. I wish he got that excited about doing his homework,' Estelle laughed. 'Can I get you anything to drink?' she offered, realising that they were standing awkwardly just inside the door. 'A cup of tea or coffee? Something stronger?'

'I'd better not,' Tony declined. 'I've got Chris waiting outside in the car, so I can't stay long. I just wanted to come up with Joe and make sure he got in okay.'

'Oh, of course,' Estelle nodded. 'But at least let me give you some cakes to say thank you. I've just made a fresh batch of Chelsea buns,' she told him, moving through to the kitchen. 'You said they were your favourites – is that right?'

'Well remembered,' Tony beamed, as he followed her, his eyes lighting up at the rows of cakes arranged on wire cooling trays. 'I suppose it would be impolite to refuse.'

'Absolutely,' Estelle agreed, as she picked up two enormous Chelsea buns, bursting with fruit and coated in icing. 'Now I've only just finished glazing these, so they'll still be a bit sticky. I'll give you a couple – one for Christopher too,' she explained, as she slotted them in a paper bag and expertly twisted the corners so that the paper sat safely above them.

'Mmm, they smell wonderful. It's a real operation you've got going here,' Tony observed, staring round appreciatively at the piles of meringues, fairy cakes and flapjacks. 'Like I said, I didn't realise you owned Cafe Crumb. I'll definitely start popping in more often.'

'Oh you must,' Estelle insisted. 'And Lord knows I could do with the extra business.'

'Things a little quiet, are they?' Tony asked gently.

'Oh, it's nothing to worry about,' Estelle replied quickly, wondering why on earth she'd opened her mouth in the first place. 'This time of year is always quiet. It'll pick up when the weather gets warmer,' she said brightly.

There was a beat of silence, and Estelle thrust the bag of buns towards him. 'Here you go.'

'Thank you,' he replied warmly. 'I'll certainly look forward to these.'

'You're very welcome.'

'Is your husband not around today?' Tony asked, as he headed towards the door.

'My husband?' Estelle replied, looking confused.

'Yes – the man who was at the match the other Sunday.' Now it was Tony's turn to look discomfited. 'Oh, I'm sorry. Have I said something I shouldn't? You're usually together at training, and I thought he was Joe's dad, but are you two not . . .?'

'Oh,' Estelle laughed, trying to ease the tension. 'We're divorced,' she explained. 'We're very lucky to be on such good terms, to be honest. We get on much better now we're not married.'

'I see,' Tony nodded. 'I'm sorry – I just assumed.'

'Nothing to be sorry about,' Estelle brushed off his concern. 'Ted remarried a couple of years ago. In fact, his new wife, Leila, is expecting a baby. I spoke to Joe about it the other day – Ted thought it might be better coming from me – and he's been a bit quiet since. I hope he's alright. It must be a bit strange for him.'

'And you too, I'd have thought,' Tony said softly. 'I wouldn't worry too much about Joe,' he continued. 'Chris is just the same – holed up in his bedroom most of the time, and pretty uncommunicative when he *is* around. I'm sure it's just a regular teenage thing.'

'Thanks, Tony,' Estelle smiled, looking relieved. 'I'm sure you're right. After all . . .' She broke off, and began sniffing the air. 'Can you smell–'

Her words were interrupted by a deafening beeping noise, causing Estelle to let out a loud squeal and clamp her hands over her ears. She dashed into the kitchen, to see black smoke billowing from the oven.

'Oh no!' she exclaimed, as she grabbed her oven gloves and wrenched open the door, pulling out a tray of what looked like lumps of coal – the charred remains of the cupcakes she'd placed in there earlier.

Quickly, she flung the windows open, pushing them as wide as they would go and fanning the smoke outside. Tony followed her lead, then yelled over the noise, 'Where's your smoke alarm?'

'Out here,' Estelle shouted back, as she ran into the

living room and pointed at the ceiling, dragging a chair over from the dining table.

'It's fine, I can reach it,' Tony assured her, as he stretched up to press the button. In spite of the unfolding crisis, Estelle couldn't help but notice the sharply defined muscles of his stomach as his jumper rode up, or the smattering of dark hair leading down from his navel and disappearing beneath the waistband of his jogging bottoms . . .

'Estelle?' came a shout from outside. 'Estelle, are you okay?'

The front door burst open and Ted stood there, looking around anxiously as he took in the clouds of smoke and screaming alarm. At that moment, Tony hit the off button and the loud wailing stopped, their ears taking a second to adjust to the silence.

'Is everything okay?' Ted demanded, his breath coming fast from his short sprint up the stairs. His hair was a mess, and he looked older than Estelle remembered.

'All sorted now,' Tony assured him.

'I don't know what's the matter with me today,' Estelle began, feeling unusually flustered – whether from the narrowly averted fire, Ted's unexpected arrival, or the sight of Tony's muscular body, she couldn't say. 'I always set the timer on the oven, just in case, but I must have forgotten.'

'Something must have distracted you,' Ted said, looking suspiciously at Tony.

Estelle sensed the uneasy atmosphere, although she

had no idea why Ted was behaving that way. 'Tony just dropped Joe off,' she explained. 'You remember last week at the football he said he'd bring him back after the match. They won – six, four.'

'Well, that's great.' The faintest hint of a smile appeared, Ted's face softening somewhat at the news.

'How are you doing?' Tony asked pleasantly, as he strode across to shake Ted's hand.

'Very well, thank you,' Ted replied, all three of them standing there awkwardly once more.

'Did you want something?' Estelle addressed Ted, utterly at a loss as to why he'd just appeared in her house.

'Oh . . . Well I was just passing,' Ted began, seeming somewhat taken aback by the question. 'I thought I'd bring these Nike trainers for Joe. He mentioned he wanted a pair when he was at mine the other week.'

'Oh Ted, I wish you'd discuss these things with me,' Estelle wailed. 'I told him he couldn't have them – he's got more than enough pairs and he never wears half of them. It undermines what I say if you get him things regardless.'

Ted's tone was defensive. 'I just wanted to treat my own son, Estelle. It's hardly a big deal.'

Estelle raised an eyebrow, biting back half a dozen responses. To her, it looked suspiciously like a guilt present – something to temper the news of Leila being pregnant – but she didn't want to have it out with him while Tony was here. If anything, she was embarrassed that Tony had had to witness the scene between her and her ex, especially after she'd been telling him how well they got on now.

'I think I'll be making tracks,' Tony said, sensing the atmosphere. 'If you're sure you'll be okay?' he added, his gaze trained on Estelle.

'I'll be fine,' she smiled, her stomach feeling strangely fluttery inside at the way he was looking at her.

Ted was watching their exchange with a growing sense of annoyance. 'Of course she'll be fine – we used to be married.'

'I know.' Tony looked amused. 'I just meant after the fire – I didn't mean with you.'

'Oh . . . well . . .' Ted made a series of harrumphing noises, but had the good grace to look embarrassed as Estelle shot him a sharp look.

'And don't forget these,' Estelle added, pressing the Chelsea buns into Tony's hands. Their fingers brushed, and she jumped back in alarm, her cheeks flaming. 'Thanks so much for all your help,' she managed breathlessly.

'All part of the service,' he grinned, his eyes crinkling at the corners. 'I'll see you both at football practice no doubt – unless I pop past the cafe first,' he added to Estelle.

'Make sure you do,' she trilled, closing the door as he headed down the stairs.

'What are you smiling about?' Ted asked, narrowing his eyes.

'Nothing. What are you talking about?' she shot back defensively. 'And why are you being so strange today? You've had a weird attitude since the moment you walked in.'

Ted simply shook his head, as though refusing to answer her question. 'He seems very friendly,' he continued, nodding towards the door where Tony had just departed.

'Yes, he does. He seems like a nice man,' Estelle replied, attempting to hold eye contact with Ted, and hoping her blushes wouldn't give her away. Because the truth was, she was beginning to think that Tony was a very nice man indeed.

10

'Honey, I'm home!' Andy Smith called out in a faux-American accent, chuckling to himself. It had become something of a ritual, using the same joke whenever he walked through the door of the semi-detached house he shared with Rebecca, and he never seemed to tire of it.

Putting his suitcase down carefully in the hallway, he wandered through to the kitchen where Rebecca was making dinner. The schools had broken up for the Easter holidays and Rebecca was on holiday for two weeks, so in true 1950s housewife style she'd been cooking the evening meal, ensuring it was ready when Andy returned from work.

Andy let his arms snake around her waist and leaned in for a kiss. 'Mmm, you smell nice, darling,' he told her, as he nuzzled her neck. Then he took a step back, holding

Rebecca at arm's length and eyeing her suspiciously. 'Have you had a haircut?'

'Andy, I've gone blonde!' Rebecca giggled.

'I thought there was something different!'

'Do you like it?' Rebecca asked flirtatiously, stroking her hair and pirouetting in front of him. 'Of course, it's not *blonde* blonde,' she gabbled. 'I'm hardly Marilyn Monroe platinum. But Karen in the hairdresser's suggested trying some highlights, and I just thought – why not?'

'You look beautiful,' Andy told her genuinely. 'But of course, you always do to me.'

'Aww, thank you, Andy,' Rebecca smiled, pulling him in close and taking him by surprise with a long, deep kiss. 'Do you really like it though?' she couldn't resist asking, looking up at him from beneath freshly mascara-ed lashes.

'I really do. It's very different actually. It kind of feels like I'm cheating with another woman – quick, get out before my wife comes home,' he quipped, as Rebecca laughed.

'Dinner's nearly ready, by the way,' she told him. 'It'll be about ten minutes.'

'Righto. What are we having?'

'I've got some gorgeous fresh salmon, so I'm grilling that, with new potatoes and veggies. And I've got you a lovely cream cake for dessert, which you're not to let me anywhere near.'

'Righto,' Andy said again. Rebecca was obviously on

one of the health kicks that she embarked on from time to time. When they'd got married, just over a year ago now, she'd slimmed down to a size ten, but her weight had been creeping up ever since. Andy knew that she blamed the comfort of married life for her expanding waistline – they'd swapped going out on dates and dancing the night away for evenings in eating takeaways and watching reality TV. Rebecca was now a curvy twelve-to-fourteen, and although Andy loved her whatever her size, he knew that Rebecca was always trying to lose a few pounds.

He kissed her once more, then went upstairs to the bedroom where he swapped his corporate suit for a more comfortable pair of old jeans and long sleeved t-shirt. He noticed a crush of shopping bags piled up against the wardrobe, overflowing with new clothes and goodies wrapped in tissue paper. Andy smiled to himself. Rebecca was obviously making the most of her time off.

Jogging downstairs, he discovered the lights in the dining room had been dimmed, and that Rebecca had lit long white candles in silver holders. The table was beautifully dressed, with a fresh white cloth and the linen napkins they only used on special occasions, and Rebecca was pouring from a chilled bottle of white wine into two wine glasses.

'What's all this?' Andy asked in surprise.

'I just thought it might be nice to make an effort,' Rebecca replied, trying to sound casual. 'Show my husband how much I appreciate him.'

'I could definitely get used to this,' Andy smiled, looking round approvingly. 'Do you need a hand with anything?'

'No, sit down. I've got it all under control.' Rebecca squeezed his shoulders as Andy lowered himself onto the dining chair, then she walked coquettishly back to the kitchen, her bottom wiggling as she tottered on her heels.

'Dinner is served,' Rebecca announced, as she returned with the plates and set them down. 'So, how was your day?' she asked, as she slid into the seat opposite her husband.

'Oh, you know,' Andy sighed, taking a sip of his wine. 'That issue I told you about with Graham's commission still needs to be resolved. Honestly, Mark Ravens is such an idiot. All he needs to do is make a decision, but he won't. He doesn't know what he's doing, he really doesn't – I've no idea how he ended up getting promoted in the first place . . .'

As Andy rambled on, Rebecca sighed inwardly. She'd really tried to make an effort tonight, still worried that everything was getting a little stale in their relationship. *Ten Sweet Lessons* had opened her eyes to the possibilities that were out there, and she was eager to experiment, to try and put some sparkle back in their sex life. But when Andy went on like this . . .

He must have noticed the way his wife's eyes had glazed over, because he stopped himself abruptly. 'I'm so sorry, darling,' he apologised, suddenly coming to his senses. 'I should really try and leave work at work. It's not very interesting for you, is it?'

Rebecca looked at him with an expression that said it all.

'Right,' Andy said brightly, changing the subject. 'Tell me about your day. Did you buy some lovely new things at the shops?'

'I bought this dress,' Rebecca told him, perking up immediately as she stood up and twirled around. The dress was a deep blue colour, nipped in at the waist and flaring out over her thighs. It was closely fitted and cut low at the front, showing off an impressive cleavage.

'Very nice,' Andy nodded approvingly. 'Is it for work?'

'I thought it might be a little too revealing for that,' Rebecca laughed, looking down at her bulging breasts encased in the soft fabric.

Andy followed her eye line. 'Quite right,' he coughed, feeling his throat grow thick. 'You'll be distracting all those boys. As a matter of fact, you're distracting me right now.'

Rebecca smiled triumphantly, bending down low to top up his wine glass. Finally, some interest from her husband! The new dress and romantic meal hadn't been in vain after all.

'Are you trying to get me drunk, Mrs Smith?' Andy asked, his eyes dancing.

'And what if I am, Mr Smith?' she replied, her voice all husky.

'I think that new haircut *has* turned you into a new person,' Andy joked

Rebecca didn't reply, unexpectedly hurt by his comment.

Didn't he realise that this wasn't just some passing fad? That she'd been unhappy and frustrated for months now? She topped up her own glass, sat back in her chair, then speared a forkful of salad and chewed thoughtfully. After she'd swallowed, she asked quietly, 'Are you happy, Andy?'

Andy looked startled. 'That's a big question. Um . . . yes, I suppose I am. Yes, I'm happy enough with my little lot,' he confirmed.

'I mean . . . are you happy with *us*?'

'Yes, of course I am. I love you very much and I'm very happy with everything. What's this about, Rebecca?'

Rebecca ignored the question. 'And are you happy with everything . . . in the bedroom?'

Andy frowned. 'Well, it's not exactly as I would like it, of course.'

'Really?' Rebecca's tone was sharp.

'It's all a bit stale and worn out, isn't it?'

Rebecca's eyebrows lifted even further.

'But once we get rid of that saggy old mattress it'll be much better. Then I still need to get the new wallpaper up, give the skirting boards a fresh lick of paint . . . Oh!' Andy exclaimed, as the penny dropped and he suddenly realised what Rebecca meant. He looked mortified. 'I mean . . . I misunderstood. Yes, yes, of course, I'm happy. Of course I am. Everything's fine . . . Right?'

'I suppose,' Rebecca shrugged.

'I mean, we don't . . . *you know* . . . as often as we used to, but that's normal, isn't it?' Andy protested, taking a large slug of his wine to hide his embarrassment. 'We're not teenagers anymore. We're grown-ups, with lives and responsibilities and occasional headaches . . .'

'But would you like it to be more exciting?' Rebecca pressed.

Andy thought about it. He thought about all the things that got in the way of their love life, like work and tiredness and worrying about paying the mortgage. Then he looked at Rebecca's thrusting cleavage and felt that delicious stirring in his groin, realising that underneath the accountant exterior, he was still very much a red-blooded male.

'Well . . . I wouldn't say no . . .'

Rebecca's lips broke into a curving smile. 'It's just that I was reading this book recently – have you heard of *Ten Sweet Lesssons*?'

Andy almost choked on his potatoes. 'I didn't know you'd read that!'

'Oh yes,' Rebecca informed him. 'I read it on the bus, on the way to work and back.'

'You can't read something like that on a bus!' Andy's eyes were bulging. 'What will people think?'

'Oh, don't be such an old stick-in-the-mud! It's totally acceptable – nobody cares these days.'

'Well,' Andy harrumphed, looking perturbed. 'Was it . . . a good read?' he asked curiously.

Rebecca nodded, looking up at him seductively. 'It's given me one or two ideas . . .'

Andy hastily drained his glass of wine and poured

himself another, finishing off the bottle as he anxiously wondered what was coming next.

'I was thinking . . . It might be fun to try out some new things in the bedroom. And I don't mean a new lampshade,' she added quickly, before Andy got the wrong idea. 'There were all sorts of things in the book,' she continued, trying not to lose her nerve. 'Spanking, bondage . . .' Rebecca stretched out her foot underneath the table, running it along Andy's leg all the way up to his crotch. Using her toes, she began gently stroking him through his trousers. 'Do you fancy trying anything like that?'

Rebecca's eyes were sparkling. Andy sat bolt upright, his food completely forgotten.

'What have you done with my wife?' he joked weakly. 'Bring back the brunette one.'

'Fine,' Rebecca snapped, withdrawing her foot sharply. She grabbed her empty plate and stood up, an expression of hurt on her face. She'd gone out on a limb to try and spice things up between them, really making an effort to get their relationship back on track, but her husband seemed more interested in making stupid jokes than ravishing her across the dining room table.

Andy realised he'd said the wrong thing, yet again. 'No, no, I didn't mean . . .' he scrambled to reassure her. He reached out to take her arm, stopping her in her tracks. 'Please, sit down again, darling,' he implored.

Rebecca hesitated, then did as Andy had asked.

The room had grown darker as the light outside

faded. Shadows danced across the contours of Rebecca's face, the candlelight bathing her features in a soft, warm glow. Andy caught his breath at how beautiful she looked.

'Rebecca, I love you very, very much,' he began, taking her hand across the table. 'I'm sorry for always doing the wrong thing or saying something stupid, but I never, ever want to hurt you. You're a beautiful, sexual, sensual woman, and I am putty in your hands. Use me as you will,' he added with a smile, and to his delight, Rebecca burst into giggles – a sure sign that he was forgiven.

Rebecca looked at him for a moment, tilting her head to one side as though considering him. 'Do you want to know a secret?' she asked finally, her tone playful.

Andy nodded eagerly.

Rebecca stood up and walked slowly round the table towards her husband, never breaking eye contact until she bent down to whisper in his ear. Suddenly she felt powerful, able to seduce her husband like a character from a novel. If she played this right, she could soon be living out her own *Ten Sweet Lessons* fantasy. 'I'm not wearing any underwear right now,' she murmured, her breath hot against the skin on his neck.

Andy's heart began to pound, his eyes widening in delight. Involuntarily, he looked over at Rebecca's new dress, reaching out and running his hands over the smooth curve of her bottom where, as promised, there were no tell-tale panty lines.

Then he stood up manfully, throwing down his napkin with wanton abandon. 'Suddenly I'm not hungry anymore,' he growled, grabbing Rebecca's hand and striding masterfully upstairs towards the bedroom, a delighted Rebecca following behind.

11

The next meeting of the Cafe Crumb book club was so popular that Estelle had people beating down the doors. Well, almost.

After closing the cafe at six, and heading upstairs to quickly shower, change, and grab a bite to eat, Estelle came back down at ten to seven to hear a knock on the front door. Looking through the glass, she saw Sue and Rebecca huddled in the doorway, trying to keep out of the rain.

'You're early!' Estelle exclaimed, as she swiftly unlocked the door to let them in.

'We just couldn't wait,' Rebecca giggled.

'We're eager beavers,' Sue smiled, as she removed her rain-soaked jacket.

'What a nice outfit, Sue,' Estelle complimented her. She was wearing a long-sleeved, wraparound dress in dark green, with smart brown boots.

'Do you think so? I've had this dress for years. It's so old,' Sue confessed.

'You've got a lovely figure,' Estelle told her sincerely. 'And you've got such a wonderful sense of style.'

'Thank you,' Sue replied, looking surprised. 'I wish my husband was as complimentary as you. Honestly, I swear, I could turn up wearing the bedroom curtains and he wouldn't bat an eyelid.'

'Well I think you look great,' Estelle smiled at her. 'And Rebecca!' she cried, as Rebecca pulled off her beanie hat. 'You've changed your hair!'

Rebecca self-consciously smoothed down her blonde bob. 'Do you like it?' she asked hesitantly. 'I've just had a few highlights put through it. I thought it might be nice now that the weather's getting warmer. Plus it's a chance to test whether blondes really do have more fun!'

'It looks gorgeous, doesn't it Estelle?' Sue assured her, as Estelle nodded and began pouring out the teas and coffees. 'I just hope your husband's more appreciative than mine.'

'I'm not sure about that,' Rebecca laughed. 'Although he did actually notice, so that's something at least. He said he feels like he's having an affair with another woman.'

'Ooh, I imagine you could have all sorts of fun with that.' Sue raised an eyebrow. 'If only I was thirty years younger. Could I have a slice of coffee cake please, Estelle?'

'You're not that old,' Rebecca said dismissively. 'And you can still have fun at any age, can't you?'

'So they tell me,' Sue sighed. 'I imagine it helps if your other half has the enthusiasm to do something other than sit in front of the television and watch war films every evening.'

'Well you'll just have to make him an offer he can't refuse,' Rebecca advised, as she pointed at the meringues. 'One of those please, Estelle. They look delicious. Buy yourself some lovely new underwear and stand slap-bang in front of the TV yelling "Take me now",' she continued, turning back to Sue. 'Or if all else fails, give him a naked lap dance. He'll definitely notice you then. Won't he, Estelle?'

'Oh, I don't think I'm the best one to be giving out marriage advice,' she said wryly. 'My husband and I split up five years ago. He's all settled with his younger woman, and I spend my days looking after our son and baking cakes. *Ten Sweet Lessons* and *Lady Chatterley's Lover* are about as passionate as it gets for me right now. Although, I must admit, I'd be open to a little excitement.'

'But there are plenty of ways a woman can have fun on her own,' Rebecca raised her eyebrows suggestively. 'Perhaps not as easily as a man, I grant you, but there're all sorts of things out there these days.'

Estelle burst into laughter. 'Oh, I don't think I'll be bothering with any of that. Especially not with a teenage son in the house.'

'Doesn't he stay over with his friends sometimes?' pressed Rebecca. 'You shouldn't neglect that side of your life,' she advised sternly.

'Is there no man on the horizon?' Sue asked. 'No gentleman caller?'

'Chance would be a fine thing!' Estelle joked, feeling somewhat embarrassed to have the focus of the discussion on her and her love life. She was just wondering how to change the subject when the door clanged and Gracie walked in.

'Gracie!' Estelle called out, relieved.

'Hello everyone,' she smiled. She looked round to see the others sitting there with their empty plates and half-drunk cups of tea, copies of *Lady Chatterley* out on the table. 'Am I late?' she asked, puzzled, as she checked her watch.

'No, we were both early,' Rebecca explained. 'How are you, my lovely?'

'Great, thanks. Ooh, you've changed your hair! I love it.'

'Gracie, can I get you anything?' asked Estelle, jumping to her feet and heading back behind the counter.

'Do you sell mint tea?' Gracie enquired. 'I'll have one of those please. And . . .' she scanned the display of mouth-watering cakes. 'A chocolate brownie please. The biggest one you have,' she grinned cheekily.

'We're just waiting for Reggie, and then we can get started,' Estelle explained, as she passed Gracie an enormous brownie, bursting with generous chunks of chocolate.

'Oh, I just remembered! Reggie asked me to tell you that he'd be here a little later tonight. He has a seminar to attend, or something.'

'But he's definitely coming?' Estelle confirmed, as Gracie nodded.

'I'm surprised that poor boy keeps coming back,' said Sue. 'Especially as he's not even here for the books *per se.*'

'I think he quite enjoys it,' Gracie mused. 'Now he's getting used to us all, I mean.'

'Hang on a minute,' cut in Rebecca, her brow creased in thought. 'Since when have you and Reggie been best friends? How do you know all this?'

'Oh,' Gracie laughed, trying to sound casual. 'He came into work. I work in Clifton library you see, and he popped in to borrow a copy of *Lady Chatterley's Lover.* He didn't know I work there, *obviously,*' she added, feeling her cheeks start to redden, much to her annoyance. 'But then he couldn't borrow it because I'd already checked out the last one,' she gabbled, pulling her copy out of her black furry bag and placing it on the table. 'See?'

'Riiiight,' Rebecca nodded, trying not to smile.

For once, Gracie seemed lost for words, sipping her tea delicately and avoiding eye contact with the others.

'So should we just get started, and Reggie can join in when he arrives?' suggested Estelle.

'Sounds good to me,' Sue agreed.

'Right. So what did everyone think of *Lady Chatterley*?' Estelle began. 'Opinions, ideas, first impressions?'

111

There was a thoughtful silence, and then Rebecca spoke up. 'I see what you meant, Sue, when you said it's not very shocking these days – it seems laughable that it was banned for obscenity when there are far worse things out there now.'

'It just shows you how far we've come in fifty years, doesn't it?' Sue added. 'When you think that this was banned for its content, but now you can pick up *Ten Sweet Lessons* in any supermarket, along with your weekly shop.'

'Some of the language was still very explicit though,' Rebecca added, 'and not what I expected.' She flicked quickly through the book, hoping no one would notice that it automatically fell open on the dirty pages. 'Oh, I can't find the exact quote, but Mellors says something to Connie like, "Tha's a good bit of cunt",' Rebecca giggled, as she hammed it up in a bad Yorkshire accent. 'Could you imagine if someone said that to you?' she demanded, as the women sniggered.

'I think the sex scenes are distracting, in some ways,' Sue spoke up. '*Lady Chatterley* is a very well written book, and it's trying to make serious points about the class system. But all of that is overshadowed by the debate about the morality of the novel – the language and the content.'

'Oh, but DH Lawrence knew what he was doing,' Rebecca protested. 'You don't *accidentally* write scenes like that. They may have been integral to the novel, but I'm sure he knew they wouldn't pass without comment.'

'*Are* those scenes integral?' Estelle wondered. 'Or is it merely titillation?'

'I think they are integral,' Rebecca nodded. 'The whole point is to show the difference between the uptight upper classes – and Connie's husband's physical *and* emotional impotence – contrasted with the earthy physicality of the gamekeeper, Mellors. He's rough and uncouth, but highly sexual. Grrrr,' Rebecca growled at the end, as everyone burst out laughing once more.

'Gracie, you've been very quiet so far,' Estelle noticed. 'What are your thoughts on *Lady Chatterley*? How does it fit in with your feminist values?'

'Surely Constance has more balls than the other heroines we've been reading about?' Rebecca cut in. 'She's eager to break out of the life that she's living, and quite happy to ignore social conventions.'

'I just don't like this idea that women are so ruled by their sexuality,' Gracie protested. 'We see it time and time again – that women will drop all their values and beliefs for what is basically a good shag!'

'Guilty!' Rebecca quipped, raising her hand, which caused more raucous laughter.

'Oh Rebecca,' Estelle chuckled. 'You're so funny.'

'I have to admit,' Rebecca began, her eyes sparkling naughtily, 'that whilst I *did* read the book – I promise I did, by the way – I also bought the DVD adaptation, the one starring Sean Bean.'

'Now *that's* dedication,' Sue joked.

'Oh, that man is just *perfect* in it,' Rebecca gushed.

113

'There's one scene where he's shirtless, chopping wood . . .' she closed her eyes, smiling at the memory.

'I think I remember that being on television,' Estelle pondered. 'Is that the one with Joely Richardson as Lady Chatterley?'

'That's the one,' Rebecca exclaimed. 'Isn't it good? I just loved the scenes between the two of them.'

'Do you think I might be able to borrow it?' asked Sue.

'Of course! Just be warned that your husband might not be able to measure up to the delectable Sean Bean,' Rebecca drooled.

'So,' Estelle cut in, as she consulted her list of questions, keen to get them back on track once again. 'Do you think Mellors is a good romantic hero?'

'Oh yes!' Rebecca answered immediately.

'Yes, I think so too,' Sue agreed. 'He obviously has that rugged, earthy appeal that we've already mentioned. And because he works outdoors doing physical labour, it's a given that he'll have a strong, muscular body.'

'Fit,' cut in Rebecca, nodding vigorously. 'Fit as f—'

'—*And*, I was going to say,' Sue quickly interrupted, 'that he's clearly very good in bed. He takes her to new sexual heights, and she experiences things she's never experienced before.'

'Simultaneous orgasms,' cut in Rebecca helpfully.

'Yes, thank you,' smiled Sue. 'That's what I was alluding to.'

'I can see why that kind of man appeals,' Gracie added

thoughtfully. 'You know – the strong, silent type, with all that brooding passion just below the surface . . .'

She broke off, as the door opened and Reggie came in. He was dressed in drainpipe jeans and a navy-blue anorak, carrying a large rucksack crammed with books.

'Hello Reggie,' Estelle smiled. 'Come and sit down, and I'll get you a drink.'

Reggie took a seat beside Rebecca, and she turned to him and smiled. 'So, to bring you up to speed, Reggie, Gracie here was just telling us how she goes for the strong, silent type in a man.'

'I was talking about Mellors!' Gracie burst out, looking horrified in case Reggie thought she was somehow referring to *him*. Everything that she'd said when she was alone with the other women seemed to take on a whole new meaning with Reggie in the room, the subtle change of atmosphere meaning she suddenly became far more aware of what she was saying. 'We were discussing *Lady Chatterley's Lover*,' Gracie explained hastily, 'and I was saying how some women can find men like Oliver Mellors appealing – though not me personally, and—'

'Which cake would you like, Reggie?' Estelle shouted over, to spare Gracie's blushes.

Reggie instantly jumped up, eager to be away. 'What's the biggest?' he pondered, before pointing at a large slice of Victoria sponge. 'I'll have that please. I didn't have time for any lunch today, so I'm starving.'

'I can make you a sandwich if you like,' Estelle offered. 'It's no trouble.'

'Well . . .' Reggie looked extremely tempted. 'If you're sure, that would be marvellous. Whatever's easiest.'

'Ham?' Estelle suggested. 'Cheese? Ham and cheese?'

'Ham and cheese, please,' Reggie grinned.

'Coming right up! The rest of you, don't stop talking, just because I'm busy,' Estelle instructed, as she moved around behind the counter, pulling Tupperware containers out of the industrial-sized fridge. 'You go sit down and join in,' she smiled at Reggie.

He slid back into the seat beside Rebecca, but this time it was Sue who turned to him. 'What did you think of *Lady Chatterley's Lover*, Reggie? I imagine it was probably more up your street than *Ten Sweet Lessons*.'

'Yes. Yes it was,' Reggie nodded gratefully, pushing his glasses up his nose. 'I think this had far more literary merit than *Ten Sweet Lessons*.'

'Well that goes without saying,' Gracie cut in sarcastically, back to her usual bolshie self.

Reggie hesitated, before carrying on, 'And I found the historical element quite fascinating too – set against the background of the coal mines and industrial unrest – and the rigid social structures . . . in the post-war era . . .' He swallowed nervously, aware that the women were looking at him. 'That's all.'

'Yes, we've touched on some of those elements already,' Sue said kindly. 'Before you arrived, we were talking about the impact of class, and the social pressures on Constance.'

'Right,' Reggie nodded, but he'd clearly made his

contribution for the session and was unwilling to say anymore. Instead, he pulled out his notebook and began scribbling.

Gracie looked at him and rolled her eyes.

'I must say, I found the central relationship much more believable than in *Ten Sweet Lessons*,' Sue cut in quickly, before Gracie could make a withering comment which might upset Reggie.

'I agree,' Estelle called across the cafe, as she spread mayonnaise on a baguette and began slicing some cucumber.

'As I said before,' Sue continued, 'Alexander and Christina's relationship in *Ten Sweet Lessons* is almost like a fairy story. It's a fantasy – not real. But you believed in these characters – in Connie and Mellors – and believed that a relationship like that might take place.'

'Don't you think that it relies heavily on stereotypes?' wondered Gracie. 'You know – the working class gardener just wants . . . well, a shag, basically, whilst all the intellectuals are too busy talking about passion to fully experience it?'

'Good point, Gracie,' nodded Reggie, almost before he knew what he was saying. Everyone stared at him for a moment, as Gracie smiled shyly, and Reggie lowered his head once more.

'But you could say that stereotypes exist for a reason,' Rebecca fired back.

'I must say, this book – and *Ten Sweet Lessons* – seem to provide so much rich material for discussion,' Estelle mused, as she came back over with Reggie's sandwich. 'I was just wondering, do you think we should perhaps make it the theme of the Cafe Crumb book club? I mean, we don't have to stick with it forever, but we could look at different variations on the erotic novel theme – everything from the bonkbuster, to historical erotica, and the famous books that have made their mark. You know – how every generation found satisfaction in the bedroom,' she giggled. 'What does everyone think?'

'I think it's a fantastic idea,' Rebecca enthused.

'Me too,' agreed Sue. 'It's been quite an education already, and I think I'd prefer erotica to plodding through some dull-as-dishwater novel that's "worthy" and critically acclaimed.'

'Hear hear,' chimed in Rebecca.

'Gracie?' asked Estelle. 'What do you think?'

'I suppose I'm happy to give it a whirl,' she agreed grudgingly. 'But they'd better not all be about pathetic women being dominated by sadistic men. I'd prefer to read something which portrays the heroine in a more positive light.'

'Well, we could all choose a novel,' Estelle suggested. 'Each session, everyone could take a turn at suggesting something for next time. How does that sound?'

There were nods and mutterings, as everyone murmured their assent.

'Reggie, are you happy with this idea?' Estelle turned to him.

'I . . . Well, it's your book group,' Reggie said

nervously, through a mouthful of food. 'You can make the decisions. I'm only here to observe.'

'Oh, stop all that, Reggie,' Rebecca couldn't resist teasing him. 'You're as much a part of this club as any of us.'

'Yes, you're a very valued member of the group, Reggie,' Estelle backed her up.

Reggie turned pink with pleasure, unused to such praise and feeling strangely warm and fuzzy. It was rare that he experienced such feelings of acceptance.

'Thank you. Yes. That would be . . . quite an eye-opener,' he finished.

'So who'd like to make the first pick?' asked Estelle. 'Does anyone have any ideas?'

There was silence around the table.

'I don't want this to be like school, but if no one volunteers, I'll have to choose someone. Sue, how about you?'

'Oh!' Sue exclaimed, looking uncomfortable as everyone turned to her. 'I don't know if I know any . . . I mean, my knowledge of erotica is non-existent I'm afraid. I'd need to look into it a little more . . .'

'It doesn't have to be anything highbrow or obscure,' Estelle reassured her. 'It could even be something you've already read, that you'd like to re read and think the rest of us would enjoy too.'

'Well . . .' Sue frowned thoughtfully. 'I don't know if it counts as erotica, as such, but I enjoyed it very much and it's a really fun read. It's something that everyone should read once, if they haven't already – in my opinion, anyway . . .' she paused, realising that everyone was waiting expectantly. '*Riders* by Jilly Cooper,' she announced finally. 'Does that count?'

'Ooh, what a perfect choice,' Estelle exclaimed. 'I read it years ago, so it'd be great to read it again. It's a classic of that genre.'

'I've never read it,' said Gracie.

'Me neither,' chipped in Rebecca. 'Although I'd love to. And it'd be nice to have something a bit lighter and more modern after *Lady Chatterley's Lover*.'

'That's settled then,' Estelle said happily. 'The next read is *Riders* by Jilly Cooper, and the next meeting will be two weeks today. That's the 11th of April, I think.'

'Oh no!' Gracie exclaimed. 'I completely forgot – I won't be able to come.'

Estelle's face fell. 'Oh dear, that's a shame.'

'There's a Fifties Night on at the community centre, and I've said I'll go.' Gracie dropped her gaze and looked embarrassed. 'I'm performing, actually.'

'Performing?' repeated Estelle.

'Yes. I'm singing,' Gracie explained, her cheeks flushing even deeper.

'I didn't know you were a singer,' Estelle cried. 'How wonderful!'

'Oh, I'm not really,' Gracie shook her head modestly. 'Not at all. I've actually never performed in public before, and I'm pretty terrified, to tell you the truth. But it's something I've always wanted to do, so I'm taking the plunge. You have to try these things, don't you?'

'I'm so impressed,' Rebecca said, sounding awestruck. 'I wish I could sing. You're so brave.'

'I don't know about that,' Gracie demurred.

'I'm sure you'll be fantastic,' said Sue.

'Me too,' Reggie spoke up. 'I bet you've got a great voice.'

'Hey, I've just had a brilliant idea!' Rebecca exclaimed. 'Why don't we all go to support you?'

'Yes!' echoed Estelle. 'Can we do that? I mean, it's not a private event or anything is it?'

'No, not at all. It's at the community centre on Church Street – anyone can go. There's going to be a band and dancing. Oh, but you have to dress up in fifties style. You're all welcome – that's if you're sure . . . Although I'll be terrified,' Gracie admitted, burying her face in her hands.

'I love the fifties style,' enthused Rebecca. 'Your outfits every week are always so gorgeous.'

'Yes, I think it would be fun to dress up,' added Estelle.

'I bet you do,' Rebecca winked, causing Estelle to blush furiously.

'What will you be singing?' enquired Sue.

'*Summertime* – the Ella Fitzgerald version.'

There were squeaks of approval from the others, and cries of, 'I love that song!'

'That settles it then,' Estelle said decisively. 'We'll all go. We can just put our meeting here back by a week, and hold it in three weeks' time instead – does that suit everyone? Perfect! Gracie, if you want to email me the details as you've got my address, then I'll forward them on to everyone,' Estelle suggested. 'See you all at the Fifties Night!'

12

'Hello you,' Rebecca grinned, as Gracie came hurrying towards her.

'Hi! Hope you haven't been waiting long,' Gracie said, as the two women hugged.

'No, not at all. I came past Lola's Vintage on my way here – it looks amazing!'

'It is,' Gracie assured her. 'Let's go!'

They made their way down the street, chatting animatedly as they walked the short distance to the vintage shop. It was the first time they had been out together without the rest of the book group, and Gracie hoped there wouldn't be any awkwardness, but so far they were nattering away as though they'd known each other for years.

'Thanks so much for your email,' Rebecca told her. 'It's such a shame the others couldn't make it.'

'I know,' Gracie agreed. She'd sent round a group email a few days ago, asking if anyone fancied a shopping trip to find outfits for the Fifties Night, but Rebecca was the only one who'd agreed to come. Estelle was working, while Sue had made plans to visit her daughter. Reggie, unsurprisingly, had also declined.

'You didn't really expect Reggie to say yes, did you?' Rebecca chuckled. 'I very much doubt it's his sort of thing. He's a funny one, isn't he?'

'I thought he *might* say yes,' Gracie leapt to his defence. 'And he's not that odd. I think he's quite sweet actually.'

'Oh really?' Rebecca replied, raising an eyebrow as she sneaked a sidelong glance at Gracie. But before she could question her any further, they arrived at Lola's Vintage.

'I can't believe I've never been in here before,' Rebecca marvelled, staring through the window at the clothes on display. There were 1940s tea dresses in feminine floral prints and dazzling 1960s kaftans in neon brights.

'I'm a regular,' Gracie smiled, as she pushed open the door and they went in. 'Hi Yasmin,' she called to the girl behind the counter.

'Hi Gracie!' Yasmin greeted her, as she turned and saw them. Yasmin was dressed in classic Swinging Sixties style, with a black-and-white geometric-print mini dress, knee-high boots and a black peaked cap. 'How are you today?'

'Great thanks. This is my friend, Rebecca,' she

introduced her. 'We're going to a Fifties Night next week, so we're looking for outfits.'

'Ooh, that sounds fun,' Yasmin exclaimed. 'Well, you know where everything is. Do you want a hand, or shall I leave you to it?'

'We'll just browse for the minute, thanks Yas.'

Beside her, Rebecca was staring round in awe. 'I want everything!' she laughed, running her hands lightly over a full-length silk gown from the 1920s, which was hanging next to a row of beaded flapper dresses. 'Wow, look at that!' she squealed, spotting a silver jumpsuit that looked as though it was made entirely from tinfoil.

'It's like a giant dressing-up box,' Gracie beamed happily, thrilled that Rebecca was enjoying herself so much.

'I *need* these in my life,' Rebecca declared, as she grabbed a pair of heart-shaped sunglasses with thick white rims. 'Here, try these,' she added, passing Gracie a pair of round, John Lennon-style glasses.

The two women posed together in the mirror, pulling faces and bursting into giggles.

'Gorgeous, darling,' Rebecca intoned, in an over-the-top cut-glass accent.

'Now put those back,' Gracie admonished, trying to be serious. 'We need to stay focused.'

'Okay,' Rebecca reluctantly agreed, replacing the sunglasses and resisting the temptation to try on an outrageous coral-coloured hat with full veil and flamingo feathers.

The clothes were grouped according to decade, and Gracie led the way to the 1950s rail, rifling through and pulling out anything she thought might be suitable.

'These would be a great choice, and I think they'll really suit your body shape,' she said, holding up a pair of polka-dot swing dresses, one in red and one in blue.

'Do you think so?' Rebecca asked, running her hands over her hips self-consciously. 'I'm not quite the slim size ten I once was.'

But Gracie waved away her concerns. 'The brilliant thing about 1950s clothing is that it's *so* flattering for a woman's figure. If you've got boobs and a bum and a waist, this style will make you look incredible,' she continued, holding the dress up against Rebecca.

'Would you like me to put those in the changing room for you?' asked Yasmin.

'If you could, that would be fantastic. I think there'll be quite a few though!' Gracie warned her.

'No problem,' Yasmin said, taking the two dresses and heading to the curtained-off area in the corner of the shop.

'What are *you* planning to wear?' Rebecca asked Gracie, as she continued to select outfits and hand them over to Yasmin. There was a nautical shift dress in navy and white, and a pink pouffy prom dress, which Rebecca immediately vetoed.

'I've ordered something from the Internet,' Gracie explained. 'It's gorgeous, but I'm worried I might look a bit overdressed.'

'Oh, just go for it,' Rebecca insisted. 'Everyone's going to be dressed up, and as you're singing you want to be the star of the show.'

'I think I might prefer to fade into the background,' Gracie admitted, looking worried. Whenever she thought about performing in public, a wave of nausea swept through her body, nerves clutching at her stomach.

'I don't believe you! Look at what you're wearing today,' she continued, indicating the skin-tight Capri pants and gingham bustier Gracie was sporting. 'You dress so gorgeously every day that you'll really have to pull out all the stops on Thursday.'

'Thanks Bex,' Gracie smiled gratefully. 'Right, I think I'm done. Is there anything else you fancy trying?'

'Not from this rail,' Rebecca replied, looking longingly at a beautiful silk-chiffon ball gown, hanging in the 1930s section.

'Then let the transformation begin,' Gracie smiled, as Yasmin pulled back the changing room curtain, and Gracie bundled Rebecca inside.

It was over an hour later that Rebecca finally made her decision. Piles of discarded clothes lay on the changing room floor, and her head was spinning. In the end, she plumped for the classic, halter-neck, polka-dot dress in blue with the addition of a white net underskirt which gave it shape and peeped out tantalisingly from beneath the hem. Gracie had insisted she looked gorgeous in it, and Rebecca trusted her opinion.

The style – sexy and flirty – was hugely different to what Rebecca would usually go for and it felt like a brave choice. Rebecca felt proud of how confident she was becoming, the new decisions she was making.

'Thank you so much for all your help, Yasmin,' Rebecca told the long-suffering sales assistant, who'd been running back and forth fetching different sizes, helping with tricky zips and making expert suggestions.

'I almost forgot!' Gracie exclaimed, as they made their way to the till. 'You need shoes, too!'

They headed over to the shoe rack, where Gracie instantly pounced on a pair of sparkly Buffalo trainers with six-inch wedge heels. 'I used to have a pair of these when I was a kid! They were so fashionable in the nineties,' she remembered fondly. 'All the Spice Girls wore them.'

'Put the trainers down, Gracie,' Rebecca warned sternly, as she slipped her feet into a pair of red patent Mary-Janes with a bow decoration at the front.

'They're perfect!' Gracie exclaimed. 'Imagine if you wore them with little white ankle socks – you'd look so cute!'

'I'd look like an overgrown schoolgirl,' Rebecca disagreed.

'Andy might like that!' Gracie replied suggestively.

'Very true . . .' Rebecca agreed thoughtfully, wondering if Andy might like her to dress up for him. The erotica reads had sparked off all sorts of new ideas. 'And speaking of Andy – I really need to get him something too. Do you sell menswear?' she asked Yasmin.

Yasmin frowned. 'We don't have very much, I'm afraid. There's just not the same demand as there is for women's clothing. But we have a few pieces – how about this?' she suggested, pulling out a Frank Sinatra-style fedora hanging on a hook above their heads.

'Ooh, that could work,' Rebecca exclaimed, taking it from Yasmin and holding it up admiringly. 'He's already got a nice suit, so maybe he could rock that whole "Rat Pack" look.'

Gracie found herself unable to resist a jive-skirt with a bold cherry pattern, and the two women paid for their purchases, leaving with bulging shopping bags.

'Thanks Yasmin, see you soon,' Gracie called, as they headed back out onto the street.

'Whew, I'm exhausted,' Rebecca sighed. 'I never knew shopping could be so tiring.'

'It is when you're doing it right,' Gracie grinned.

'Like so many things in life,' Rebecca giggled. 'Thanks for all your help today, by the way. I'm thrilled with my outfit.'

'You looked gorgeous in it – very sexy,' Gracie affirmed. 'I think Thursday's going to be a really good night.'

'Definitely,' Rebecca agreed. 'It's so nice that everyone from the book club's going to be there.'

'So what do you want to do now?' Gracie asked, as they meandered along. The sun had come out, and the afternoon was growing warm. She rolled up the sleeves on her cropped cardigan, enjoying the heat on her bare skin. 'We could get some lunch, or look round some more shops.'

'Hmm. I was actually just wondering whether I should get a waistcoat for Andy as it might make his suit look more authentic. Do you know anywhere that sells them? I don't really want to buy a brand new one as he'll probably never wear it again.'

'We could try the charity shops if you like,' Gracie suggested, happy that their shopping trip wasn't over yet. She was enjoying Rebecca's company, and it was rare for Gracie to have a really girly day like this. 'The other vintage shop I know doesn't have menswear, and we've still got plenty of time left if you fancy a browse.'

'Sounds like a plan,' Rebecca replied cheerfully. They strolled along in the sunshine, browsing in shop windows and chatting happily about clothes, books and 1950s hair and make-up. The more they talked, the more they found that they had in common, giggling over the book club reads as the conversation took a racier turn.

'Ooh, look at that,' Rebecca cooed, stopping in her tracks as she stared at a sexy-looking bra and knickers set in a shop window. 'Isn't that gorgeous?' It was more outrageous than she would usually go for but she was feeling brave, buoyed up by the decisions she'd already been making.

'I love it, but that's even better,' Gracie replied, pointing at a naughty black lace set, with matching suspender belt.

'That *is* gorgeous. Although I didn't think it would be your kind of thing,' Rebecca admitted.

'Just because I'm a feminist doesn't mean I don't like

nice underwear. I'm all for wearing sexy bras, not burning them,' Gracie grinned.

'Maybe I should get some new underwear to go with my new dress. What do you think?' Rebecca suggested.

'Sounds like a good excuse to me. Shall we have a look?'

'Yes, let's,' Rebecca said eagerly, like a child at Christmas as she stepped inside.

'Ooh, suspenders,' Rebecca murmured, as she fingered a garter belt, thinking how much Andy would enjoy seeing her kitted out in the full set.

'Ooh, yes I love real suspenders,' Gracie admitted. 'They're great with the 1950s wardrobe, and always make me feel very feminine.'

'Blimey, look at all this stuff!' Rebecca exclaimed, as they moved further into the shop. Past the underwear display was a more risqué section, with nurse's uniforms and French maid's outfits.

'Those look a little chilly,' Gracie giggled, as she pointed out a pair of crotchless panties.

'Tell me, would you *ever* wear that?' Rebecca demanded, holding up a fishnet, all-in-one body-stocking.

'I don't think I'd fit in it. It looks like one of those net bags you get your oranges in! Oh, but that *is* nice, though,' Gracie went on, as she moved over to look at a boned black corset with purple ribbons.

'It's beautiful,' Rebecca agreed. 'I honestly think that reading *Ten Sweet Lessons* has opened up a whole new world for me. Andy and I had sort of stopped making an effort since we got married, but the book club reads have really inspired me. There's all sorts of things out there that I've never tried, and it's fun to dress up and feel sexy.'

'I know what you mean,' Gracie agreed. 'I'd always been really dismissive of stuff like this,' she said, nodding at a particularly risqué set of red and black underwear. 'But recently I've been wondering if I'm missing out. It's certainly got me curious . . .'

'Do you need any help there, ladies?'

Rebecca and Gracie turned round guiltily as a shop assistant approached them. She was dressed smartly, all in black, but her hair was dyed magenta and she had a piercing through her bottom lip.

'We're fine thanks,' Rebecca assured her. 'Just browsing.'

'Well let me know if you need any help. That really is beautifully made,' she said, indicating the corset Gracie was holding. 'And then we have sex toys over here too,' she finished, indicating the back of the shop.

'I didn't see those!' Rebecca squealed, looking slightly alarmed.

'Me neither,' Gracie added hastily.

'Oh yes, we have a good selection,' the sales assistant informed them, stepping towards the display. 'I don't know if you're looking for anything in particular, but *this one* is really good,' she continued, pointing out an alarming-looking purple device in the shape of a wishbone.

Intrigued, Rebecca and Gracie slowly moved towards her.

'This really provides coverage in all areas,' the assistant explained, not at all phased by discussing vibrators with two complete strangers. 'Firstly internal – where this button hits your g-spot – then clitoral and anal too.'

'Have you tried it?' Rebecca couldn't resist asking.

'Yes, we get to try a lot of them out. We like to be able to give our customers an honest opinion,' she smiled. 'Or if you're looking for something discreet, this one's great,' she continued, picking up a gadget that was shaped like a lipstick. 'You can just pop it in your handbag and no one knows. It's great for if you're on the move.'

Unable to help herself, Gracie burst into giggles. 'I think someone might notice if I was using that on the bus.'

'Oh my God, look at that one!' Rebecca squealed, pointing at an enormous implement made of black rubber. 'It's huge!'

'Yes, that one's slightly more . . . specialist, shall we say,' the woman smiled knowingly. 'Well, I'll leave you to have a look. Let me know if you have any questions – I'd be happy to help. Oh, and they all come with a free pack of batteries when you get to the till.'

'Thank you,' Rebecca told her, in a dignified manner. As soon the assistant was out of earshot, she collapsed into giggles. 'I never expected this when we came shopping today,' she sniggered. 'You take me to all the best places, Gracie.'

'Hey, you were the one who wanted to come in here!'

'Look how much that one costs,' Rebecca marvelled.

'All that money, just for a vibrator. And it looks like a shoehorn.'

'Put it down, you don't know where it's been,' Gracie joked.

'Well, that woman did say she tries them all out,' Rebecca dead panned.

'Yuck,' Gracie pulled a face. 'Hey, do you think they have a second-hand section?' she quipped, and the two women collapsed into giggles once more.

'You know, maybe we should get something for Estelle,' Rebecca said thoughtfully, once her laughter had subsided.

'What?' Gracie asked, sounding shocked. 'Why?'

'At the meeting last week – just before you arrived – we touched on this area, and she was saying – well she *implied* – that she doesn't really do anything about that side of her life. All of her time is taken up with running the cafe and looking after her son, and there's no man on the horizon. It seems such a shame. She's only about ten years older than me, and I wouldn't like to think everything would just completely stop in that department.'

'I know what you mean,' Gracie sympathised. 'But we can't buy her a . . . *vibrator*,' she continued, lowering her voice as she said the word. 'We don't even know her that well. Imagine we turned up at the next book club, waving it around and shouting "Hey Estelle, we bought you this, thought you might like it. And *do* tell us how you get on with it, we'd love to know . . ."'

Rebecca thought about it for a moment. 'Okay, so you

might have a point,' she conceded, giggling at the image Gracie had painted. 'Maybe I'll get something though . . .' she began, her eyes scanning the shelves. 'Oh my, look at all these whips, and spanking paddles. It's just like *Ten Sweet Lessons*. Alexander Black probably comes here to get his supplies,' she joked. 'God, could you imagine if we bumped into him? I'd just die!'

Gracie rolled her eyes. 'He's *fictional*, Rebecca.'

'But there've got to be some single, drop-dead gorgeous, deeply kinky multi-millionaires prowling the sex shops of Bristol, haven't there?' Rebecca asked hopefully, as Gracie laughed.

'Do you know, I read that sales of all this stuff have gone up by two hundred per cent, or something ridiculous, since that book came out.'

'I can see why,' Rebecca replied, thoughtfully stroking a pair of fluffy handcuffs. 'This looks fun,' she said casually, holding up a 'Bondage Starter Kit' containing handcuffs, an eye mask and a feather tickler.

'Not you as well, Bex,' Gracie sighed, looking disappointed. 'Don't tell me you're subscribing to all this female submissive rubbish.'

'It's just a bit of fun,' Rebecca retorted. 'And anyway, who says I'm the submissive?' she added cheekily, as Gracie pulled a face indicating she'd really rather not know. 'It's alright for you – you're younger than me,' Rebecca continued. 'But when you've been together for a while, you have to make the effort to spice things up a little. How about you – do you have a boyfriend?'

'No,' Gracie replied, shaking her head. It wasn't a subject she usually talked about, but she felt comfortable confiding in Rebecca. 'I've had a few relationships, but nothing longer than about a year. It's been ages since my last boyfriend. I guess I'm taking a break for a while – although it's not entirely my choice.'

'Maybe you should get one of those then,' Rebecca teased, pointing at a Rampant Rabbit.

Gracie flushed crimson. 'I've already got one,' she confessed, in hushed tones. 'I live with my mum, so I have to keep it well hidden. I'd just *die* if she found it.'

'Good girl,' Rebecca grinned, looking at Gracie in a whole new light. 'You know what? I *am* going to get this,' she said, picking up the starter kit. 'Purely for research purposes, of course.'

'Of course,' Gracie nodded. 'Just don't tell me how you get on – I really don't want to know.'

'Fair enough,' Rebecca agreed. 'Now let's pay for these and find a nice pub to have some lunch. I need a drink after everything we've been through this morning.'

'Make mine a stiff one,' Gracie couldn't resist quipping, as the two women burst into hysterical laughter once more.

13

Sue and George were on their way to visit their daughter, Helen. She lived near Oxford, in the small town of Abingdon, along with her husband, Peter, and their three-year-old daughter, Bella.

George was driving, and they were pottering along the motorway in their smart BMW at a steady sixty-five m.p.h. He was listening to *Saturday Live* on Radio Four, chuckling to himself occasionally at something the presenter said. Neither of them spoke.

Sue longed to start a conversation – but about what? They had nothing new to say to each other these days. She and George lived in each other's pockets, together almost twenty-four hours a day, every day. Neither of them had done anything that the other didn't know about, or held an opinion that their other half wasn't already aware of. Sue knew exactly what George thought about reality television and the price of petrol and England's cricket prospects, while George was well-versed in Sue's views on everything from the European Union to the height of next door's garden fence.

Of course, the one thing he *didn't* know about was her new-found love of erotic literature, but Sue doubted he'd be interested anyway. He'd probably crash the car in alarm if she attempted to talk about *Riders* with him, initiating light conversation about sex in the stables or suggesting he might like to try being spanked with a riding crop.

Eventually, Sue cleared her throat. 'It'll be lovely to see Bella again,' she said, opting for a thoroughly innocuous topic.

George nodded in agreement, never taking his eyes off the road.

'I bet she's got big now. I mean, I know Helen's sent photos, but you never quite realise until you actually see her in the flesh, do you?'

George was still nodding away, giving no actual response. Sue suspected he was more interested in the radio than in what she had to say. She glanced out of the window to see the other cars speeding past them. When an ancient Fiat Panda driven by a woman who looked about ninety zoomed by, Sue couldn't keep quiet any longer.

'Put your foot down, George.' She tried to joke, but her tone was sharp. 'It'd be good to get there before dark.'

'There's no rush, Sue,' George replied evenly. 'Let's just take our time and not have an accident.'

'Just because we're both retired doesn't mean we have to do everything at snail's pace,' she sniped.

'I've been driving for over forty years now and have never had so much as a point on my licence. I don't want to start now,' George responded tautly.

Sue pursed her lips and turned her head away from him, staring out of the window as the familiar sights of the M4 flashed by.

A few miles further on, she began to feel a little calmer. 'We still haven't booked anything for our summer holiday,' she tried again, fighting to keep her tone light. 'It'll be creeping up on us before we know it. Have you had any thoughts about where we should go?'

'Ah, there's plenty of time,' George replied. 'No point in rushing into these things.'

'I was thinking of Tuscany,' Sue suggested. 'It's supposed to be beautiful. We could hire a villa – perhaps one with a swimming pool.'

'What would we do out in the middle of Italy by ourselves all day?' asked George, not relishing the thought of a week without his usual routine of *Murder She Wrote* in the afternoon, followed by *Pointless* at teatime.

'Well, we could drive out into the local area – there're some lovely little towns nearby – and we could do wine tastings or even a cookery course. I was researching it last night on the Internet. If you don't want to stay in one place, we could drive around – move from one town to the next and stay in a *pensione* – that's their equivalent of a B&B.'

George said nothing for a moment, and the silence hung heavily in the air. Finally, he spoke, 'I don't like the sound of all that driving.'

Sue let out a frustrated sigh that she didn't bother to hide. She couldn't help it. However she looked at it, she was assailed by the nagging sensation that life was passing her by. Now that she and George were both retired, they had so much spare time on their hands, but were completely failing to make the most of it. Sue was starting to get ridiculously excited about attending the Cafe Crumb book club; it was a rare opportunity for her to get out of the house, to interact with other people, and share their lives and opinions. More than that, it had got her thinking about the new experiences she wanted out of life – intellectual, cultural *and* sexual . . .

'I've been meaning to mention,' she began, becoming animated once more. 'You know the book club I've been going to? One of the girls from there – Gracie – has invited us all to a Fifties Night in the community centre. She's going to be singing, and there'll be a band . . . Everyone has to dress up.'

'Very nice,' George commented distractedly.

'Yes, it should be. I think everyone from the group is going. One of the women – Rebecca – mentioned that she was taking her husband, so I thought it might be nice if you and I . . .' Sue trailed off, wondering if George was even listening to her.

'What's that, love?' he asked, after a moment.

Sue gritted her teeth and tried to stay calm. 'I was just saying, it might be nice if you and I went to this Fifties Night together. You know, had a night out for a change.'

'Me?' George burst out. 'Oh no, I don't think so.'

'But why not?' Sue sounded exasperated.

'Well . . . I don't know these people, do I?'

'And you'll never get to know them unless you meet them,' Sue pointed out logically. 'I didn't know them until a few weeks ago, but they're a perfectly nice group of people.'

'And how old is she? This young girl who's singing?' demanded George.

'Gracie? I'm not sure. In her late twenties, I think. Yes, late twenties.'

George frowned. 'Don't take this the wrong way, love, but do you not think you're being a little ridiculous, running around with a group of twenty-year-olds? I know you're obviously going through some kind of . . .' George paused, wondering how to best phrase his words, '*phase at the moment, and that things have been a little difficult* for you since you retired, but honestly, they probably just asked you to be polite. You don't want to go making yourself look silly now, do you?'

Sue's mouth flapped open and closed like a dying goldfish. She was livid, unable to speak for a moment. She had half a mind to tell George to stop the car then she could get out and walk the rest of the way to

Oxfordshire. Better still, throw *him* out of the car, while she drove off without looking back.

'How *dare* you!' Sue finally exploded. 'Those people are my friends. *Of course* they want me to join them.'

'Sue, you barely know them—'

'And yet I've had more fun with them over the past few weeks than I've had with you for the last forty-odd years,' she retorted furiously, intent on hurting him.

George rolled his eyes, muttering under his breath, 'Oh, here we go . . .'

'Well it's true,' Sue insisted, her eyes blazing with anger. 'You never want to do anything, or go anywhere. It's bloody boring, quite frankly,' she snapped, months of frustration pouring out. 'If *you* want to sit at home and stagnate, you're quite welcome to do so, but don't drag me down with you. I want more out of life.'

'Would you listen to yourself?' George was incredulous. 'You're sixty-two years old, woman! You're supposed to be winding down. Now is not the time to be running around nightclubs like some bloody teenager.'

'I don't want to go to nightclubs! I just want to do normal things that people of our age do – go on holiday, take up golf, eat at nice restaurants. There's a whole world out there, George, and you'll never see any of it if you don't get out of your damn armchair.'

Sue didn't think she'd ever been as angry as she was right now. Her face was puce with rage, and she could cheerfully have throttled her husband right there and then.

George was shaking his head. 'Women . . .' he tutted to himself. 'I thought the menopause thing was bad enough, without having to live through whatever phase you're in now.'

Sue sat bolt upright, eyes narrowed, lips white with anger. It took a lot for her to swear, but she was ready to let him have it with both barrels.

'You know what, George? You can just sod off. Sod. Right. Off,' she finished furiously.

George didn't answer, simply indicating left and taking the Swindon exit off the M4. There was still an hour left to go until they arrived at their daughter's house. Neither of them said a word to each other for the rest of the journey.

Sue's temper hadn't subsided by the time they pulled up outside the modern, detached house in Abingdon.

Having been married for almost four decades, Sue and George were well practised in the art of continuing their day normally, without having to actually speak to one another. As they stepped out of the car, stretching their limbs after the long journey, their granddaughter, Bella, came barrelling out of the house towards them.

'Look at you!' Sue exclaimed, as she scooped her up in her arms and covered her in kisses. 'Look how much you've grown!'

'Hi Mum,' grinned Helen, as she followed Bella out onto the driveway and her husband, Peter, shook hands with George. 'How are you? How was the journey?'

'Oh, not bad,' Sue said casually, placing Bella back on the ground. 'There was a bit of traffic getting out of Bristol, but nothing major.'

'Grandma, come and see my new wendy house,' Bella insisted, grabbing her hand and pulling her inside.

'Bella, give Granny and Granddad a chance to catch their breaths,' Helen told her, as she ushered them inside and closed the door behind them all. 'Can I get you both a drink?'

'A cup of tea would be lovely, thank you,' Sue replied, avoiding eye contact with George.

Helen disappeared into the kitchen, while Bella ran back and forth to show off various items from her toy box, pirouetting in front of them, and singing songs she'd learnt at nursery.

'She's so full of life, isn't she?' Sue commented archly to Peter. 'It's so nice to see. It must be lovely to find so much joy in the world, instead of looking on each day as a chore,' she finished, with a pointed look at her husband.

'Yes . . . She's always on the go,' Peter agreed uncertainly, finding Sue's comment a little odd.

As Sue smiled innocently, Helen stuck her head out of the kitchen. 'Pete, we're almost out of milk. Do you mind nipping out to the shop?'

'No problem,' Peter replied, standing up and reaching for his coat.

'I think I might come too,' George interjected, as he got to his feet. 'I wouldn't mind a stroll after sitting in the car for all that time.'

'It wouldn't have been quite so long if you'd put your foot down a bit,' Sue muttered under her breath.

'What was that, dear?' George asked sweetly.

'Nothing, darling,' Sue replied, with a tight smile. 'Enjoy your walk.'

Helen and Peter looked at each other in confusion, Peter shrugging his shoulders slightly as Helen flashed him a questioning look.

The two men departed, and as the front door slammed shut, Helen sat down beside her mother. 'Is everything okay with you and Dad?' she asked, her eyes full of concern.

'That man is driving me bloody insane,' Sue hissed furiously.

'Mum! Not in front of Bella.' Helen nodded towards her daughter, who was sat on the floor playing happily with her crayons.

'Sorry,' Sue apologised, lowering her voice. 'But honestly, Helen, I feel like I'm about to crack up. Being cooped up with him, day in, day out, in that house is becoming utterly unbearable, it really is. I'm thinking about divorce.'

'You can't say that!' Helen gasped. 'You don't mean it.'

'Don't I?' Sue raised an eyebrow. She looked straight at her daughter with an unwavering gaze, realising with a pang how much Helen looked like her father. Where Sue's face was much finer and sharper, Helen and George shared the same rounded cheeks and snub noses.

'But I don't understand . . .' Helen faltered. 'What's the problem?'

'It's just . . . We don't seem to have anything in common any more,' Sue explained desperately. 'Since I retired, I've been eager to do and see things – you know, go travelling, have some long weekends away, that sort of thing. But your father never wants to do *anything*. He'd be quite happy to spend every day between now and when he dies sitting in his armchair watching re-runs of *Bargain Hunt*.'

'I'm sure it'll come right in the end,' Helen assured her. 'It must take a bit of readjusting, when you're both used to being so busy, to suddenly have to deal with what's basically a huge lifestyle change.'

'Well it had better adjust quickly,' Sue retorted. 'I can't take much more of this.'

'Maybe . . . Maybe you need to compromise a little more, Mum,' Helen suggested gently. 'If Dad wants to relax a little – and let's face it, he's earned it after working flat out for forty years – then perhaps you should let him. He didn't even have a break to have babies. I mean, they didn't *have* paternity leave back then, did they? So maybe you can't do something *every* day. Let him have his rest during the week, and then maybe you can have a couple of days away at the weekend or something. You've got to be reasonable.'

'I *am* being reasonable,' Sue hissed under her breath, attempting to keep her voice down so as not to disturb Bella. 'He literally doesn't want to do *anything*. I can't get him to commit to a trip to the supermarket, let alone a holiday to Italy.'

Helen looked uneasy. 'Perhaps you don't always have to do things together. You could join some groups on your own – even take a weekend away by yourself. It might be good for the two of you.'

'Then what's the point of being together?' Sue asked sadly. 'Tell me, if we're going to live solo lives and spend our time bickering when we *are* together, then where's the fun in that?'

Helen didn't seem to have an answer, and Sue sighed despondently. 'I *have* tried, Helen. I know you think it's all my fault, but—' she held up a hand as Helen went to interrupt her. 'I joined a book group, at the local cafe. I thought it would get me out of the house, and I'd get to meet some new people. And I have. It's been great fun.' Here, Sue lowered her voice once more. 'We've actually been reading erotica novels,' she confessed with a giggle, as Helen's eyes widened. 'We started off with *Ten Sweet Lessons,* and it's gone from there really.'

'Mum!' Helen exclaimed. 'I don't want to know about you reading that! No, there are some things that a daughter never wants to hear.'

'Have you read it?' Sue demanded, as Helen reluctantly nodded. 'Isn't it wonderful? I mean, obviously it's badly written, etc. etc., but it's such an escapist, romantic read. We're doing Jilly Cooper at the moment, and all I'm doing is reading about people leading these hectic, thrilling lives, while I'm stuck at home, vegetating. I'm just so jealous of those characters! Does that make sense?'

'I suppose . . . But life can't be like fiction, Mum. People read books like that for escapism – it doesn't mean that they're all going to run round having affairs and so on. Oh God – you're not having an affair, are you?'

'Chance would be a fine thing,' Sue shot back. 'I'd leave your father in an instant if Alexander Black came knocking at my door.'

'Mother!' Helen exclaimed once again, wondering if Sue had taken leave of her senses.

'Have *you* ever tried these things?' Sue pressed on regardless. 'You're obviously younger than me – is *Ten Sweet Lessons* what passes for normal nowadays? Your father and I never did anything like that, and to be honest, I wouldn't mind giving it a go. Who knows, I might enjoy being tied up.'

A horrified Helen had her hands clamped firmly over her ears. 'LA LA LA LA LA,' she sang loudly. 'I can't hear you!'

'Okay,' nodded Sue, accepting that she'd perhaps gone a little too far. 'But take this morning for example. Everyone from the book group is going to a Fifties Night. There's a real mix of us – all different ages – and one of the girls is singing. There'll be fifties music, and we all have to dress up . . . You know the kind of thing? I asked your father if he wanted to go, and he refused point blank. *"I don't know these people. They're too young for you*",' Sue mimicked him. 'He had the cheek to tell me that I was making a fool of myself by going out with them. I tell you, I'm starting to think the real fool is me, for sticking with him for so long.'

Both women jumped as they heard the front door open, and Pete and George walked back through, Pete blissfully unaware of the strained atmosphere.

'The milkman's here,' he called brightly, chuckling as he handed the carton over to Helen.

'Thanks, Pete,' she said, hastily getting up and kissing him on the cheek. 'I guess I'll go make the tea, then.' She seemed almost relieved to get away.

Helen dashed through to the kitchen, as Sue's shoulders slumped dejectedly. She felt like a stroppy teenager, misunderstood by the world, and with everyone else advising what was best for her own life.

She glanced over at George, who was settling down on the sofa beside her and reaching for the remote control. Feeling an uncontrollable surge of irritation, she jumped to her feet.

'I think I'll go give Helen a hand,' Sue declared, thinking what a sad state of affairs it was when she could no longer bear to be in the same room as her own husband.

14

Rebecca closed the front door behind her, groaning in relief as she dropped her bag in the hallway and kicked off her heels. It had been a tough day at work, and all she wanted was a nice hot bath before she got ready for the Fifties Night.

'Andy?' she called out.

There was no reply and for a moment she simply stood luxuriating in the silence before heading upstairs to their bathroom. They'd had it redecorated a few months ago, with Rebecca aiming for a slinky, boudoir feel – all black and white floor tiles, a claw-foot bath and a large, silver-framed mirror above the sparkling white sink.

She turned on the taps and poured in the new bath oil she'd bought, watching as it foamed up in the water, the sweet smell of vanilla and honey scenting the air.

Then she padded across the hallway to their bedroom, slipping out of her work clothes and pulling on the white silk nightgown that she loved, the one that made her feel like a glamorous film star.

She was hugely looking forward to the Fifties Night, relishing the thought of an evening out with her husband where he could meet all her new friends from the book club. In all honesty, Rebecca was just excited to be doing something with Andy that didn't involve the garden centre or a DIY superstore. Tonight, they could have a few drinks and dance the night away, recapture the youth that felt so lost to her now.

Rebecca opened her wardrobe, rifling through and stopping at the dress she'd chosen during her shopping trip with Gracie. It was draped tantalisingly on a padded coat-hanger – the ones she saved for her best items of clothing – with the stiff, net skirt hooked underneath. Rebecca laid it on the bed reverently. She knew she looked good in it. The style totally flattered her figure, making the most of her small waist and large breasts, while the halter-neck emphasised the curve of her shoulder and her shapely upper arms.

With her dress now ready to go, Rebecca opened her underwear drawer to pick out suitable lingerie. As she gently rummaged through, letting her fingers trail over brightly coloured thongs, silky boy shorts, and white cotton panties, she came across the bondage starter kit she'd bought, hidden at the back. Her gaze lingered on it, her hand hovering over the box. She really had to bring up the topic with Andy. She felt sure he'd be as enthusiastic as she was – once he'd got over the initial shock of course.

Covering it up once again, she quickly pulled out a polka-dot bra, which she knew pushed her cleavage up to eye-popping levels, and a pair of matching bikini briefs in the same design as her dress, before hurrying back through to the bathroom.

The bath was almost full, great white waves of foam floating on the surface. Rebecca turned off the taps then took out a dozen tea-lights from the mirrored wall cabinet, scattering them around the bathroom – on the windowsill, the sink, on top of the cistern. The effect was beautiful; atmospheric and romantic.

Then she slipped off her robe, hanging it on the back of the bathroom door and standing naked for a moment in front of the mirror as she inspected her body with a critical eye. Yes, she could do with losing a few pounds, perhaps toning up a little, but Rebecca knew she had a woman's body and overall she was happy with her shape. She ran her hands lightly over her body, noticing the way her nipples stiffened instantly beneath her fingertips, then cupped the whole of one breast in her hand, feeling the weight. She let it fall gently back into place, her gaze running down further as she took in the rounded hips, the swell of her tummy, the dark fuzz between her legs. She might not be a supermodel, but she felt like a sexual, sensual woman. Besides, Andy had never had any complaints.

Rebecca stepped into the tub, lowering her body beneath the bubbles and letting her head come to rest against the cool porcelain. She closed her eyes and breathed deeply, allowing her muscles to relax.

Her brain, however, wouldn't stop running at a mile a minute, planning all the things she had to do. There was her Year Ten coursework to grade, lesson plans to write up for her Year Nines. She also needed to ring her mother, and remember to buy a card for her cousin's birthday, plus they were running low on essentials in the kitchen, so she needed to grab some bread, milk and orange juice from the corner shop. And when she found five minutes, she could finally settle down properly with *Riders*. It was a huge slab of a book, almost the same shape and weight as a brick. Rebecca was only a couple of hundred pages into it, but she loved it already. It was fun and sexy and made her feel naughty. Come to think of it, she'd been feeling naughty on a regular basis since the book club had started on those erotic reads . . .

Rebecca jumped as she heard the front door bang, and a few seconds later Andy called out, 'Honey, I'm home.' Rebecca smiled at his predictability.

'I'm upstairs,' she shouted, as she listened to him go through his usual routine of putting down his bag and heading through to the kitchen to grab himself a drink. After that, he made his way to the living room, where Rebecca knew he'd be checking the post that she always left out on the coffee table.

She stuck her leg up in the air, watching the water and

bubbles trickle down her smooth skin, as she flexed her foot and admired the shape of her calf. Sometimes, she thought with a sigh, she wished Andy would just come bounding up the stairs and have his wicked way with her.

Eventually, she heard his heavy tread on the stairs, the top step creaking as he reached the upstairs landing.

'I'm in the bath,' she called out, in what she hoped was a sultry, seductive tone.

Moments later, Andy opened the door, his eyebrows shooting up in surprise as he took in the low lights and the flickering candles. 'Well, this is all very nice,' he smiled.

He'd loosened his tie and undone the top button of his shirt, something Rebecca found inexplicably sexy. He looked like a hotshot City worker, or a powerful New York businessman. It was the kind of gesture Alexander Black might make, right before he ravished Christina Cox.

Andy leaned over the bath to give his wife a lingering kiss. As he went to stand up, she playfully tugged on his tie, pulling him down to meet her lips once again before releasing him. Rebecca could see the questioning look in his eyes as he moved away.

'How was your day, darling?' she asked solicitously.

Andy sighed, sitting down on the toilet lid. 'Not bad, I suppose. Long, but fairly productive. How about you?'

Rebecca rolled her eyes. 'My Year Nines were running wild for some reason. They were completely giddy all afternoon – and they're raging bags of hormones at that age, which doesn't help. Honestly, sometimes it feels more

154

like crowd control than teaching. But let's not talk about that now,' she continued, changing the subject. 'Let's talk about something fun.'

'Well we've got the Fifties Night tonight,' Andy reminded her. 'Are you excited about it?'

'Definitely,' she nodded. 'It'll be like a date night with my handsome husband. And I'm looking forward to a bit of dressing up,' she added flirtatiously.

'What time does it start?' Andy asked, appearing not to pick up on Rebecca's double meaning.

'Seven thirty.'

Andy checked his watch. 'Right, I guess I'd better start getting ready soon. Will you be in the bath for long? I'd like to grab a quick shower before we go.'

'I'll be out soon,' Rebecca assured him. Her pulse rate quickened as an idea flitted through her mind, and she wondered if she dared to voice the suggestion. Fixing her husband with her most come-hither stare, she murmured, 'Or you can share my bath if you like?'

Andy hesitated for a moment, his body frozen in indecision, then a smile spread slowly across his face. 'You mean . . .? Okay,' he agreed, his eyes twinkling as Rebecca giggled and slid further under the bubbles.

He bent down and swiftly pulled off his socks – something Rebecca was grateful for, as she found it terribly unsexy when he left his socks on until the last minute. Barefoot, Andy slowly undid his tie, sliding it off and cracking it like a whip, which made Rebecca giggle even more.

'You'd better behave tonight, Mrs Smith,' he warned, raising an eyebrow. 'Or else I'll have to teach you a lesson.'

'I think I might enjoy that,' Rebecca returned, biting her lip in anticipation.

She watched, feeling like a voyeur, as Andy unbuttoned his shirt, letting it drop to the floor in a careless heap. Then he unfastened his trousers, coming to stand beside the bath in just his boxer shorts.

'And the rest,' Rebecca teased, unable to take her eyes from the growing bulge in his pants. 'Keep going with the striptease.'

Without missing a beat, Andy pulled off his boxers and strode into the bath, causing the water to slosh violently, foam landing on the floor tiles as the two of them wriggled around, trying to find a way that the small bath could accommodate them both comfortably.

'This always looks a lot sexier in the films,' Rebecca laughed.

Andy pretended to be affronted. 'Are you saying I'm not sexy?'

'Oh, come here my sexy husband,' Rebecca pouted, as she leaned in for a kiss. They were sitting facing each other and Andy pulled her in towards him. 'Ooh, what's that?' Rebecca squealed, feeling his hardness press into her stomach. 'I don't know what it is, but it's enormous!'

'Just shut up and kiss me,' Andy growled masterfully, as their bodies pressed together once again, their skin slippery and wet and covered in soapy bubbles. They kissed deeply, and Rebecca was beginning to feel wildly turned on, the tell-tale butterflies low in her belly.

Finally they broke away, keeping their faces so close that their noses were touching. Rebecca could see every detail of Andy's skin; the tiny pores, the rough stubble on his jaw, the drop of bath water trembling on the end of an eyelash.

'I love you,' Andy said suddenly, his words so simple and honest that Rebecca felt them clutch at her heart. 'And I'm sorry I can't always be the wild, exciting husband that you want—'

Rebecca put a finger to his lips, cutting him off. 'Sssh,' she whispered. 'I love you too. And you're exactly what I want.'

She saw the desire flame in his eyes and they kissed again, until Rebecca pulled away, a wicked smile on her face. Not breaking eye contact, she picked up the bottle of shower gel from the side of the bath and squeezed a generous amount into her hands. Then she began to smooth it over Andy's chest, her hands moving in smooth circles as she worked it into a lather, covering his shoulders, his arms, his torso and moving down until her hands disappeared under the water and Andy's eyes widened in delight.

Following Rebecca's lead, Andy did the same, squeezing the slippery gel onto his palms and starting on her collarbone before moving down to her breasts. They were full and heavy in his hands, his thumbs circling her taut, caramel-coloured nipples, before he too moved towards the water, his hands gliding over the rounded tummy beneath her belly button and continuing to explore.

Rebecca's breathing had sped up, her eyes locked on Andy's as they continued to pleasure each other. Right now, she wouldn't have traded him for anyone in the world. Not Alexander Black or Oliver Mellors or even George Clooney. He was doing exactly what she wanted and her body was responding eagerly.

By the time his hands slipped below the water, sliding smoothly between her legs and into the secret place where she was longing for him to touch her, Rebecca was lost. She arched her back, pressing herself into his hands with wanton abandon. She was completely unselfconscious, not caring what she looked like as she gave in to the pleasure of the moment.

Andy could only marvel as he watched her, leaping beneath his touch. It made him feel proud, and like a man, that he could have this effect on her. He wasn't stupid or blind – he knew Rebecca had been unhappy recently, racing through those book club erotica reads as though they were the only thing that gave her any satisfaction. They hadn't even celebrated their second anniversary yet, and Andy was as anxious as Rebecca that their relationship shouldn't go stale. He'd been crazy about her when they first got together, but then . . . life seemed to get in the way.

Well, he would start making more of an effort, he vowed. Rebecca seemed keen to spice up their sex life, so why should he argue?

He stopped what he was doing for a moment, and Rebecca slowly opened her eyes, gazing at him languidly. There was a dreamy, faraway expression on her face, and her irises were enormous as she looked at him. Her cheeks were flushed, her lips wet and parted.

Gently, Andy slid his hands under her bottom, lifting her up and lowering her down onto him.

'You know, we're going to be late,' he whispered, as he began to nuzzle her ear.

'I don't care,' Rebecca responded, as their bodies connected and all other thoughts just melted away.

15

Reggie pulled his bedroom curtains closed and headed over to his laptop, loading up Spotify and browsing the playlists.

Perfect, he thought to himself, as he found one entitled 'Classic 1950s Hits'. He clicked on it, and moments later Jerry Lee Lewis singing *Great Balls of Fire* was blasting out over his speakers.

Conscious of his housemates, Reggie turned it down a little, then stared at himself in the cheap, three-quarter length mirror that hung on the wall, assessing his reflection critically. In his sandy-coloured trousers, brown-checked shirt and buttoned-up cardigan, he looked as lean and gawky as a teenage boy who'd just been through a growth spurt and hadn't yet filled out. Reggie's problem was that, at twenty-nine years old, he should really have filled out by now. His Adam's apple seemed to protrude like an arrow from his neck, his chin always covered in a fine layer of fluff that never quite developed into a fully-grown beard. His face was angular, with prominent cheekbones, his blue eyes hidden behind wire-rimmed glasses, and atop his whole face was an unfashionable, untameable mop of messy brown hair.

'Let the transformation begin,' he whispered to his reflection.

Slowly unbuttoning his cardigan, he peeled it off, then stripped down until he was almost naked, standing in nothing but a pair of white cotton boxer shorts. He sprayed himself liberally with Hugo Boss aftershave, hoping that tonight would be the night he finally emerged, butterfly-like, as a new, improved version of himself. Reggie 2.0 would be cooler, more confident, well respected – and, of course, he would always get the girl.

He couldn't help but think of *Ten Sweet Lessons*, and the question he'd asked at one of the early book club meetings – was Alexander Black really what women wanted? Apparently so, given the way that the entire female population seemed to be going crazy for the book. They longed for a man who was powerful, charming, handsome and more than a little dangerous. Reggie sighed. He was so far from being that man that it wasn't even funny. But, for one night at least, he could try.

Replacing the aftershave bottle neatly back on top of his second-hand chest of drawers, Reggie padded over to his wardrobe, rifling through until he found his smart, black suit – the one he wore for interviews and funerals.

Then he pulled out a crisp, white shirt that his mother had ironed for him the last time he went home, and the skinny black tie he'd bought for a pound at the local Oxfam shop. Adding black loafers and a slim black belt, he checked out his reflection once again.

Not bad, he thought, twisting from side to side to view himself from all angles.

Next up was face and hair. Inspired by pictures he'd seen on the Internet, Reggie had decided to experiment with Brylcreem, and had bought a pot of the stuff in Boots especially for tonight. He scooped out a generous dollop, rubbing it between his hands before running it through his hair – hesitantly at first, but becoming braver once he felt he had the situation under control. He rinsed his hands in the small basin in his room, then picked up his comb and began the styling process, dividing it into a side parting then pulling it up to make a small quiff on the left hand side, while slicking it down on the right.

Not bad at all.

Now it was time for the pièce de résistance. Rummaging around in the top drawer of his desk, Reggie located an old pair of glasses with thick, black frames. He took off his usual wire-rimmed ones, swapped them over, and the look was complete.

Checking himself out in the mirror, Reggie smiled. He could have walked straight off the set of a 1950s movie.

He was admiring his reflection when the music segued into *Hound Dog* by Elvis Presley. Tentatively, Reggie tried out an Elvis lip curl, raising the corner of his mouth in what he hoped was a sexy sneer. His look was more Buddy Holly than Elvis Presley, but Reggie wasn't about to be limited by such distinctions. He began to wiggle his hips, shaking his legs and bouncing on his toes, like Elvis in his *Jailhouse Rock* era.

Reggie was getting carried away as he watched himself in the mirror, miming along to the music on his laptop as he imagined himself looking out over an imaginary crowd, scores of screaming girls yelling out his name in the front row . . .

'Reggie?'

There was a sharp knock at the door, and Reggie jumped in panic. Heart thumping, he whirled round. He saw the door handle turn, but fortunately he'd remembered to lock it, so whoever was calling his name was denied entry.

'Who is it?' he yelled, as he quickly turned off the music.

'Reggie?' The voice shouted again. 'You in there, buddy?'

It was his housemate, Josh. Reggie sighed inwardly. If he was being honest, Josh was an idiot – certainly not someone Reggie would have *chosen* to live with. But the problem with house-shares was that you got very little say in who you ended up with.

'Yeah, hi Josh. I'm just . . . um . . . getting changed.'

'Sure, sure. Are you decent, mate? Open the door.' Josh was studying medicine, and was one of those rugby-playing, party guys who was good looking and popular with everyone. He wore trendy jeans with polo shirts that showed off his well-developed pecs, and he was always tanned, even in winter. He and Reggie had little in common and it didn't help that he had the knack of making Reggie feel vastly inferior.

'Just a minute,' Reggie stalled. 'What do you want?'

'We're all going out tonight, and Selena said we should ask you. We're gonna start out at the Rose and Crown, then grab a taxi into town and see where the night takes us. Probably end up somewhere shit like Reflex. You fancy it?'

'Sorry, I'm busy,' Reggie yelled back.

'Come on, Reggie, staying in and working on your thesis doesn't count as being busy. Come out and have a few drinks, pull some birds, yeah?'

'I can't,' Reggie insisted. 'I really *am* going out.'

'Bollocks,' Josh shouted back. 'You never go out you sad bastard.'

'Well I am tonight,' Reggie replied, trying not to take offence. 'I've got . . . other plans.'

'Reggie, mate, open the door,' Josh repeated. 'I can't hear you properly.'

Reggie hesitated, wondering what to do. He had hoped to sneak out of the house without seeing any of his flatmates, but Josh was so insistent . . .

'Come on, mate. What's going on in there? You doing something shady, are you?'

'No, of course not!' Reggie retorted indignantly. He could feel his cheeks growing hot, his pulse racing. Unable to see any other option, Reggie took a deep breath and unlocked the door.

'Motherfucker!' Josh exclaimed crudely, as he took in Reggie's appearance. 'What the hell are you wearing?'

'I'm going to a Fifties Night,' Reggie explained, attempting to say the words with a dignity he didn't feel.

'What, you're actually going outside the house dressed like that? Like, in public?' A slow smile crept across Josh's face, then he let out a long, loud wolf-whistle. 'Oh man, you've gotta come downstairs and show everyone.'

'I don't think so . . .'

'Yeah, man,' Josh insisted. 'Hey everyone,' he yelled downstairs. 'Reggie's off to a Fifties Night. He looks like a total knob!'

'What?' came a shout from downstairs, and Reggie heard the scrape of chairs as people stood up, moving towards the staircase.

'Come down and show everyone,' Josh repeated, an inane grin on his face.

Reggie felt trapped in a nightmarish scenario. There was no way he wanted to show the others – who would undoubtedly take the mick even more than Josh had – but he knew there was no way of escaping. He had to go through with it, however great the humiliation.

Reluctantly, Reggie acknowledged defeat, his head slumped as he followed Josh downstairs into the kitchen, where his other housemates and their friends were sitting round the big table, drinking bottles of beer. Once again, he was clearly the outsider.

As soon as they clapped eyes on him, they broke out into rowdy cheers and raucous laughter. There was about half a dozen people in total, but it felt like more, as Matt jumped up from his chair, bent double in hysterics, and Pankesh took a photo with his mobile, the flash momentarily blinding Reggie.

'I'll tag you under "Loser",' Pankesh guffawed. Like Josh, Pankesh was a medical student and everyone knew that they were notorious for their partying. Reggie wouldn't have trusted either of them to do the washing up properly, let alone diagnose an illness.

Selena was there too, staring at him sympathetically. 'You look great, Reggie,' she told him. 'Really . . . smart. It suits you,' she smiled. She was dressed for clubbing, wearing some tiny dress that showed off her bulging cleavage and long, slim legs. Reggie didn't know where to look.

'Thanks,' he said awkwardly, wishing the ground would open up and swallow him. He didn't know whether to be pleased that Selena had leapt to his defence, or humiliated that she'd had to do so.

'Spin round, give everyone the full effect,' Matt was shouting, as Reggie tried to pretend he hadn't heard.

'So is this party going to be full of old people?' yelled Josh, as Pankesh quickly took up the theme.

'Aw, don't tell me you're trying to shag a granny? What, you can't get someone your own age so you're chasing after someone's nan?'

Reggie simply stood there, a strained smile on his face

to try and imply that he was thoroughly enjoying being the butt of all their jokes.

'Hey, maybe we should crash it boys, what do you reckon?' Josh jeered. 'Sounds like fun.'

'Don't,' Reggie said too quickly, his face betraying his panic at the idea.

'Alright mate, it's only a joke. I've got better stuff going on anyway.'

'Great, well, have a good night and I'll be off,' Reggie said, trying to keep his tone casual but backing towards the door with every step. His inner Alexander had well and truly abandoned him at this point, and his only thought was to get out of there as quickly as possible.

'Whatever, mate. Enjoy your freak show.'

'What a dickhead,' Reggie heard one of them say as he closed the kitchen door, quickly followed by Selena interjecting, 'Leave him alone.'

But Reggie didn't want to hear anymore. He made his escape through the front door, slamming it behind him and bolting down the path without looking back.

16

'Ta-dah! Well, what do you think?'

Estelle emerged from her bedroom in a cloud of perfume, and pirouetted into the living room.

Joe looked up from where he was playing *Football Manager* on his Xbox, and sniggered. 'You look like a numpty.'

'Great. Thanks, Joe,' Estelle retorted huffily, but she knew her fourteen-year-old son wasn't the best person to pass judgement.

Estelle thought she looked pretty good, all things considered. She'd been so busy with the cafe that she hadn't had time to organise a proper costume, and had been forced to scrape one together from whatever she could find in the depths of her wardrobe. There was a pair of denim pedal-pushers that she hadn't worn for years; a fitted, yellow V-neck jersey; and some pale pink court shoes that she'd bought for a wedding and worn only once. Estelle had accessorised with a matching pink scarf, which she'd knotted round her neck. She'd planned to do something with her hair – perhaps put it in curlers then wear it in soft waves – but in the end she hadn't had time, quickly scooping it up into a high ponytail instead. The style suited her – she looked petite and youthful, like a cast member from *Happy Days*.

'Now are you sure you'll be alright tonight?' Estelle asked Joe, her forehead creasing in concern. 'Call my mobile if you need *anything*. I'm not far away – just on Church Street – so I can be back in less than ten minutes. Oh, and don't open the door to anyone. And don't use the oven. And don't eat too many cakes.'

'I won't,' Joe agreed distractedly.

'And you're sure – absolutely *positive* – that you'll be alright?' Estelle pressed.

'Yup, I'll be fine.'

'I really don't like leaving you on your own. It's such a shame you couldn't go round to your father's tonight, but he and Leila—'

'Have gone away for a few days, yeah, yeah, I get it. I suppose I'd better get used to it.'

'What does that mean?' Estelle questioned.

'Well, when the new baby comes, Dad won't want me there at all, will he?'

'Oh Joe . . .' Estelle came over and sat down on the sofa, next to where he was sprawled on the floor. She stroked his hair softly like she used to when he was a baby, but he shook his head irritably, brushing off her hand. 'You know that's not true. Your dad loves you, and he'll still love you when the baby comes. Of course he will.'

Joe snorted disbelievingly. 'Leila'll try and stop me coming over. I hate her. And Dad's missing my football game this weekend 'cos he's away with *her*.'

'Oh Joe, don't say things like that,' Estelle pleaded. 'Of course Leila won't stop you going to their house. She knows that, whatever else happens, Ted will always be your dad, and there's no way she'd try to come between you. She probably feels a bit awkward around you, but you really shouldn't hate her. She *is* your dad's wife, and he'd want you to try and get on. After all, you'll have a new brother or sister soon.'

'*Half* brother or sister,' Joe shot back. 'It's not the same thing.'

Estelle looked at the clock and bit her lip anxiously. 'Joe, sweetheart, I've really got to go or else I'm going to be late. We can talk about this tomorrow, yeah? And I'll have a word with your dad too, if you want.'

Joe shrugged. 'Whatever.'

'Now are you sure you'll be okay on your own?' Estelle asked once again, as she pulled on her coat and picked up her handbag.

'Yes, Mum, I've said I'll be fine.'

'I won't be back late. Love you.'

Joe muttered something incomprehensible, and went back to his game.

* * *

Estelle could hear the music before she even entered the building. The band were playing *Tutti Frutti* by Little Richard, and she could hear the crash of the drums, the chatter and laughter of people having fun. Quickly checking her appearance in her compact mirror, Estelle pushed open the door and went inside.

Very little had been done to the decor – it was still the same old community centre, with its scuffed wooden floor and ancient noticeboards advertising events that had long since been and gone. But the atmosphere was lively, with people dressed in all manner of 1950s styles, from the ones who had gone all out and hired Elvis Presley costumes, to those like herself, whose outfits were distinctly more home-made. The six-piece band, comprising a drummer, lead and bass guitarists, saxophonist, trumpet player and a man on the keyboard, were set on a dais at the far end of the hall, and behind them a banner proclaimed 'Welcome to the 1950s!'

Glancing around her, the first person Estelle spotted was Rebecca, resplendent in her polka-dot dress. Her hair was styled in soft, blonde curls and she wore bright red lipstick that co-ordinated perfectly with her outfit. She looked like an old-fashioned movie star.

'Rebecca, you look gorgeous,' Estelle told her, as she made her way over and kissed her on the cheek.

'So do you,' Rebecca replied. 'Look at you! I don't know how you stay so slim when you own a cake shop. I'd be the size of a house! Oh, this is my husband, Andy,' she added hastily. 'Andy, this is Estelle who runs the book club.'

171

'Ah, so you're the one who's responsible for my wife reading all those naughty books,' Andy chuckled. 'Can I just take this opportunity to say thank you very much,' he joked, slipping an arm around Rebecca's waist and giving her a little squeeze.

'Oh, stop it you,' she giggled, blushing, but looking thrilled all the same.

'Well, it's certainly been an eye-opener,' Estelle smiled. 'Have you seen any of the others yet?'

'Gracie's here – just over there, by the bar,' Rebecca pointed her out. 'She's very nervous. Let's go over and say hello, then we can get you a drink.

The three of them made their way over to the bar area, which was really just a long trestle table serving cocktails in plastic tumblers.

'They can't have glass because of health and safety, apparently,' Rebecca explained. 'But the cocktails are yummy! What can I get you? Tom Collins? Martini? I've just had a Manhattan, and it was delicious.'

'Ooh, I'll have a Tom Collins, please. Gracie!' Estelle squealed, as she caught sight of her. 'You look incredible!'

'Do you think so?' Gracie asked nervously, pulling at the hem of her skirt. 'I was worried it might be a bit much.'

'Oh no,' Estelle shook her head. 'If you've got it, flaunt it!'

Gracie was wearing a replica of the famous white Marilyn dress from *The Seven Year Itch*, except that her version was a dazzling red. She had painted her nails to match, and her hair was rolled at the front, pinned up at the back, with a large red flower clipped to the side.

'I just hope . . .' she began, then trailed off, looking over Estelle's shoulder towards the entrance at someone who'd just arrived. Estelle turned to see who it was.

'Reggie!' she exclaimed, as he began making his way over towards them.

'Hello, Estelle,' he said, as he kissed her awkwardly on the cheek. 'You look lovely.'

'Thank you. And so do you. Very suave,' she grinned, as she took in Reggie's outfit.

'And Gracie . . .' Reggie turned to her. 'You look . . .' For a moment he simply stared at her, his jaw practically on the floor. 'Incredible,' he finished finally.

'Doesn't she?' Estelle echoed.

'Your outfit's great,' Gracie complimented him. 'Very geek-chic.'

'Thanks.' He took off his glasses and rubbed them on his tie, aware that they were steaming up.

'I'm so pleased that you made it,' Gracie continued, beaming at him. 'I know it's not really your sort of thing, but I'm sure you'll have a great time.'

'I hope so,' Reggie replied, replacing his spectacles. Trying his best to sound confident, he attempted to summon his inner Alexander and asked, 'So what time are you on? I can't wait to hear you sing.'

'About half past eight, I think. Maybe closer to nine if they're running behind,' Gracie told him, suddenly looking utterly terrified as she remembered her upcoming performance. 'That's if I haven't run away by then. I might just lock myself in the broom cupboard where nobody can find me.'

'I'll go with you if you want,' Reggie blurted out, almost before he was aware of what he was saying. A look of acute embarrassment swept over his face, as he tried to take back what he'd said. 'I didn't mean . . . I just meant that . . . um . . . Whilst it would be lovely to be in a cupboard with you, I didn't . . .'

'Oh look, there's Sue,' Estelle broke in, grateful for the distraction. She'd been starting to feel like a spare part in their conversation. 'I'll go over and say hello.'

She made her way over to the entrance, where Sue and a gentleman she didn't recognise were hovering. Estelle waved at her above the crowd, and noticed that Rebecca and Andy were also heading that way.

'Sorry we're late,' Sue apologised as they reached her. '*Someone* was having trouble with his costume,' she added, rolling her eyes. 'This is my husband, George, by the way.'

'Hello, George. Well, it looks as though all the trouble was worth it,' Estelle said sweetly. George was wearing black trousers and a white shirt, with a bright blue Teddy Boy jacket and a bootlace neck tie, which he was tugging at uncomfortably.

'Does this look right?' he asked Estelle, as Sue let out a frustrated sigh that she didn't bother to hide. 'I thought it made me look like a cowboy, but it came with the outfit. I couldn't decide.'

'You definitely don't look like a cowboy,' Estelle assured him, as Rebecca chimed in.

'Nice to meet you, George. We've heard lots about you,' she said innocently, stopping in her tracks as Sue shot her a warning look. 'Oh! Not *too* much, obviously. Nothing bad or anything . . . This is my husband, Andy, by the way,' she finished awkwardly, as the two men shook hands.

Estelle felt someone tap her on the shoulder, and heard a male voice say, 'I thought it was you!'

She span round to see Tony stood behind her, dressed like Danny Zuko from *Grease*. He was wearing tight black jeans, an even tighter white t-shirt that showed off his powerful chest, and a black leather jacket, while his dark hair was styled in an enormous quiff.

'Tony! What are you doing here?'

'Well, I thought it sounded like a fun evening,' he grinned.

'Oh yes, I didn't mean . . . That sounded awfully rude of me,' Estelle apologised. She turned to the group, who were watching them with interest. 'Everyone, this is Tony, my son's football coach. Tony, this is Rebecca and her husband Andy, and Sue and her husband George.'

They all made small talk for a few minutes, until Rebecca said tactfully, 'Sue, we'll show you where the drinks are,' and left them to it.

'It's lovely to see you,' Estelle told him, trying to recover herself. 'I just didn't expect you to be here. Who did you come with?'

'I'm here on my own,' Tony explained.

Estelle looked surprised. 'Is your wife staying at home with Christopher?'

'No . . .' Tony looked uncomfortable. 'Chris's on his own tonight. I'm . . . My wife passed away,' he explained not meeting Estelle's gaze. 'It was a few years ago now.'

'Oh, I'm so sorry,' Estelle apologised, feeling terrible. 'I didn't know.'

'It's fine,' Tony assured her. 'Chris was quite young and . . . So it's just me and him now,' he finished, trying to sound upbeat. 'I don't usually come to things like this, but now Chris is older it's easier to leave him by himself, and I need to start making more of an effort to get out and meet new people. One of the guys at work had a leaflet for tonight, so it seemed like a good place to start,' Tony explained. 'What about Joe? Is he staying at Ted's?'

'No, I've left him home alone too,' Estelle told him guiltily. 'He's got the mobile phone on standby, and a list of dos and don'ts as long as my arm, but I'm still worried. It's not something I do very often.'

'You can't help but be anxious,' Tony agreed. 'Even when they're grown up, with families of their own, we'll still be worrying about them.'

'You're right there,' Estelle chuckled.

'You look lovely tonight, by the way,' Tony told her. 'That style really suits you.'

'This?' Estelle flushed, waving away his compliment.

'It's literally something I pulled out of the back of the wardrobe. I was in such a rush finishing work that I barely had time to do anything. There were these two old dears in the cafe, chatting away, and they weren't in any hurry to leave, no matter how many hints I dropped. Their tea had gone cold and they'd finished their cakes, but still they wouldn't go.'

'Well, I think you look great,' Tony insisted. 'So how do you know those other people?' he asked. 'The ones you introduced me to.'

'Oh, they're members of my book group. Did I tell you about that?' Estelle asked, seeing Tony's puzzled expression. 'To be honest, it's something I started to try and bring a little more business into the cafe. We meet every couple of weeks – we're actually supposed to be meeting tonight, but we decided to come here instead. Gracie – one of the members – is singing tonight. There she is, over there – the girl in the red dress, with the dark hair.'

'Oh yes, I see her.' Tony had to raise his voice to be heard over the noise of the band and the chatter of people. The hall was starting to get busy, and he moved in closer to Estelle.

'And the tall man next to her – that's Reggie. He's a member too.'

'You seem like a very varied group,' Tony smiled. 'I'm not much of a reader myself, but it sounds like a great idea. I might join in. What kind of books do you read?'

Estelle hesitated, thinking how awkward it could be

discussing graphic sex scenes with Tony sitting beside her. It would be completely impossible for her to concentrate. 'Erotica, mainly,' she said finally, deciding to brazen it out. 'We tried the classics, but it didn't really work out for us, so we've become quite a niche group.'

'Really?' Tony raised his eyebrows, unable to work out whether or not she was joking. 'You know, every time I talk to you, I find out something surprising about you.'

'Oh, I'm really not that interesting,' Estelle protested, trying to avoid his penetrating gaze, and finding herself staring at his well-developed pectoral muscles instead.

'I disagree. Can I get you another drink?' Tony asked, noticing that Estelle's Tom Collins was almost empty.

'Thank you,' she smiled, finally looking up at him and meeting those dark eyes. 'I'd like that very much.'

17

'Ladies and gentleman . . .'

Brian, the band leader, took to the microphone and surveyed the crowd, his view hindered by a huge black wig with enormous quiff and fake sideburns.

The crowd had stopped dancing as the music died down, and they turned to listen to what Brian was saying.

'We're going to have a little change of pace now,' he began, in a faux-American accent, clearly enjoying being the centre of attention. 'Slow things down for all you lovers out there . . .'

He raised an eyebrow meaningfully, and the crowd let out a series of cheers and whoops.

'Singing Ella Fitzgerald's version of *Summertime*, please welcome our very own . . . Gracie Bird!'

There was loud clapping and shouts of approval as Gracie climbed up to the stage, her head bowed bashfully.

She looked absolutely ravishing, her dark hair shining under the stage lights, while the red dress fitted her perfectly, clinging to every curve.

'Thank you, everyone,' she said nervously, taking hold of the old-fashioned silver microphone. 'I hope you enjoy it.'

She turned her head and gave the briefest of nods to the band, who immediately struck up the intro. Then Gracie took a deep breath and began to sing.

Her voice was beautiful: warm and rich and utterly captivating. She closed her eyes as she sang, swaying sensuously to the music.

'Fish are jumpin'. . .'

Everyone in the shabby community centre was transfixed. No one spoke; plastic cups of cocktails were left hovering in mid-air, as all eyes were fixed on Gracie. She'd managed to bring the bustling, buzzy room of people to a complete standstill.

Reggie was hovering at the back of the crowd, his height meaning he had a clear view over everyone's heads. He was watching Gracie sing, open-mouthed with amazement, unable to take his eyes off her.

Rebecca glanced across at him and saw the expression on his face. She nudged Sue gently and nodded in his direction. Sue followed her gaze, smiling knowingly as she saw the way he was staring at Gracie.

As the song progressed, Gracie began to grow in confidence, her powerful voice building in strength and depth. She opened her eyes, gazing dreamily out over the crowd.

It was a powerful sensation, being able to hold an audience in the palm of your hand, but Gracie was still nervous. It was like walking a tightrope, and Gracie knew that she could fall at any moment, breaking the spell that she'd woven.

It was the first time she'd ever sung in public – the first time she'd sung outside of her bedroom, in fact. Ever since she was little, Gracie had always loved dancing around her room, using her hairbrush as a pretend microphone, so when she'd heard they were looking for acts for the Fifties Night, she'd signed up in a moment of madness. She'd barely slept in the week leading up to tonight, a nagging feeling of anxiety plaguing her every waking hour, but now she was up on stage she was invincible.

The feeling was orgasmic. In fact, Gracie could say with confidence that standing centre stage in the Clifton community centre was better than any sex she'd ever had – although that perhaps said more about the shortcomings of her previous lovers than anything else.

The last note faded, and for a moment there was only silence. It was as though everyone in the audience was mesmerised, reluctant to break the spell that had descended upon them. Then, slowly, the clapping started, and then the cheering, and suddenly the hall was a riot of excited noise, all of it directed at Gracie.

'Thank you,' she murmured shyly into the microphone, although she could barely be heard above the stamping and the whistling. Cheeks flaming, she broke into a huge grin as she took in the reaction of the audience, weeks of tension being released as the adrenaline raced through her body.

Then Brian was onstage beside her, leading the applause and taking over the microphone.

'What about that, ladies and gentleman? Wasn't she fabulous? Give it up for Graciiiiiie Bird!'

At the back of the hall, Reggie longed to rush forward and congratulate her too, but by now she was surrounded by a tight circle of admirers, and he was too embarrassed to push his way through and speak to her in front of everyone. He would leave it for a while, he decided, until the attention had died down and he could perhaps talk to her alone later in the evening.

He couldn't help but compare himself to the men in the novels they'd been reading – the rich and powerful Alexander Black in *Ten Sweet Lessons*, or the rugged, manly Oliver Mellors in *Lady Chatterley's Lover*. Both of them had a confidence and a masculinity that Reggie would never have. Men like that had women falling at their feet, but Reggie felt certain that if he ever asked a girl out, she would laugh in his face.

He'd had a couple of abortive relationships whilst at university, but these tended to be the result of awkward drunken fumbles that neither of them knew how to get out of afterwards. The prospect of asking someone he actually *liked* out on a date – someone like Gracie for example – seemed nigh-on impossible.

Reggie sighed in frustration, wishing for the thousandth

time in his life that he could be someone else. He'd really made an effort tonight, and thought he looked good in his sleek suit, sipping on a Martini. But in reality, he felt ridiculous, his old insecurities always ready to resurface and undo any progress he might have made. For the moment he would simply stay here, by himself, and later – perhaps – he would go over and speak to Gracie.

Estelle and Tony were applauding loudly, as they watched Gracie step down from the stage and meet her adoring public.

'She was brilliant,' Tony commented, thoroughly impressed with her performance.

'Wasn't she?' Estelle gushed, looking thrilled. 'I had no idea she was so good.'

The band struck up *Rock Around the Clock*, and the dance floor quickly filled up once again. There were some couples jiving professionally, while others were just letting loose and enjoying themselves.

Tony watched them for a moment before turning to Estelle. 'Would you like to dance?' he asked, standing up and holding out his hand.

Unable to help herself, Estelle broke into a wide smile.

'Why not?' she replied, taking hold of Tony's hand and following him onto the crowded dance floor.

Rebecca and Sue were gossiping at the edge of the dance floor, as Andy and George made slightly awkward conversation over by the drinks table.

'You managed to convince George to come after all, then,' Rebecca noted.

Sue rolled her eyes. 'Yes, eventually. Not without a blazing argument or three. I'm telling you, Rebecca, never retire.'

'Oh, surely it's not that bad!'

'Well, perhaps you and Andy will make a better job of it than George and I have. But honestly, it's as though we've been so busy all these years that it's stopped us from realising we no longer have anything in common.'

'I'm sure you do! I think you need to reconnect somehow,' Rebecca advised. 'Rediscover what it was that made you fall in love in the first place. Have you thought about spicing up your love life?' she enquired. 'All these books we've been reading have given Andy and me some new ideas.'

'Oh, we're too old for all of that,' Sue waved away her suggestion, too embarrassed to admit that the same thoughts had crossed her mind.

'Of course you're not,' Rebecca insisted, somewhat tipsily. She'd been sampling all the cocktails and her inhibitions were lowered. 'What about massage?' she continued, ignoring the look of doubt on Sue's face. 'Andy and I bought this special oil that smells like strawberries. You can get it on the Internet if you don't want to buy it in a shop, or just use moisturiser. And the massage doesn't have to lead onto anything else – it's just a really nice experience, and it's good for your health too. You can get to know each other's bodies again.'

'Perhaps . . .' Sue replied doubtfully. 'Gosh, look at

Estelle!' she exclaimed, changing the subject. 'She seems to be enjoying herself.'

Rebecca looked over to where Tony was whirling Estelle around the dance floor. They made a good looking couple, and Estelle couldn't seem to stop smiling, laughing helplessly every time Tony struck an Elvis-style pose.

'Interesting . . .' Rebecca raised one eyebrow slyly. 'Who did she say he was again?'

'Her son's football coach, I think.'

'You can tell. He's got a great body,' Rebecca said matter-of-factly.

'He's certainly a very handsome chap,' Sue commented. 'Lucky Estelle.'

'Do you think it's serious?' Rebecca mused.

'Who knows? We'll have to pin her down and interrogate her next week.'

'Exactly. We'll shine a bright light in her eyes and make her tell us everything!'

Sue chuckled as she looked around the room, her gaze landing on Reggie. 'Bless, look at Reggie over there. I feel a bit sorry for him.'

'Where is he? Oh yes, I see him,' Rebecca nodded, spotting Reggie stood by himself at the back of the hall. He was staring longingly at Gracie, who was still surrounded by a gaggle of admirers.

'Reggie!' Rebecca yelled, trying to get his attention above the music. 'Hey, Reggie!'

It took a moment for him to realise that someone was

calling his name. Startled, Reggie looked at Rebecca, who began frantically waving him over.

'Reggie! Come here!'

He made his way through the crowd, leaving his empty glass on the drinks table as he passed. 'Hello,' he said awkwardly, as he reached them.

'Hi, Reggie. Wasn't Gracie good?' Rebecca got straight to the point, looking meaningfully at Sue.

'Yes, she was. She was wonderful,' Reggie said dreamily, staring over at her.

'Go and ask her to dance,' Rebecca encouraged him.

'What? Oh no,' Reggie looked horrified. 'No, I can't do that. Besides, I can't dance.'

'*Everybody* can dance,' Rebecca contradicted him. 'It's not hard. Go on – just ask her.'

'But—'

'What have you got to lose?' Sue added.

Reggie swallowed, looking nervously between the two women, and once again trying desperately to conjure up his inner Alexander. He didn't know which was the more terrifying prospect – asking Gracie to dance, or Rebecca's reaction if he didn't.

'Do it, Reggie,' Rebecca repeated fiercely, balling her fist like a sports coach giving a pep talk.

Reggie's breathing was coming fast, as he exhaled heavily through his nostrils like a boxer preparing to enter the ring. 'Okay,' he blurted out finally. 'I will!'

He marched off determinedly, parting the crowd and making a beeline directly for Gracie.

Rebecca and Sue watched him proudly.

'Did someone mention dancing?' Andy asked, coming up behind Rebecca and slipping his arms round her waist.

'Ooh, is that an offer?' Rebecca giggled.

'It certainly is.'

'Well if you're asking, I'm dancing,' Rebecca quipped, as they made their way onto the dance floor.

George looked over at Sue. 'What do you say? How about it?'

'You want to dance?' Sue couldn't hide her surprise.

George shrugged amiably. 'Why not. Let's go show these young ones how it's done,' he replied, whisking a delighted Sue into the centre of the action.

Reggie pushed his way rather rudely through the circle of people surrounding Gracie.

'Reggie!' she breathed, delighted to see him.

Reggie was struck dumb. Confronted by the sight of Gracie right in front of him, he suddenly couldn't remember anything he wanted to say.

'I . . . um . . . That was amazing,' he managed finally. '*You* were amazing.'

'Did you like it?' Gracie asked shyly.

'You were incredible. I had no idea you could sing like that.'

'Neither did I,' Gracie admitted. 'But it seems to have gone down well. Everyone's been so nice about it.'

'I was just wondering if . . . um . . .' Reggie coughed, clearing his throat, as Gracie stared at him curiously.

'Would you like . . . I mean, you probably won't . . . I mean, I can't even . . . Would you like to dance?' he blurted out finally.

Gracie broke into a wide grin that made her eyes sparkle. 'I'm actually gasping for a drink,' she told him honestly. 'I haven't had anything since I came off stage, and I've been sticking to water all day, so . . .'

'Oh, of course,' Reggie looked mortified. 'How stupid of me – I should have thought . . . Yes, why on earth would you want to dance with me? You go get a drink and I'll see you later. In fact, I think I'll go home right now . . .'

'Reggie,' Gracie cut in, placing a hand on his arm and interrupting him mid-ramble. 'If you'd like to get me a drink, that would be wonderful. And then afterwards, I'd love to dance with you. I'll have a Martini, if you're asking,' she prompted him, as Reggie simply stared at her, seemingly unable to comprehend what she was saying.

'Oh! Right . . . right . . .' he managed finally, a slow smile spreading across his face. 'Yes, of course I can do that. Don't go anywhere. One Martini, coming right up!'

He strode off masterfully across the dance floor, unable to stop grinning and feeling exceptionally proud of himself. If he carried on at this rate, he thought, a jaunty swing to his step, he might very well be able to give Alexander Black a run for his money.

It was getting late, but the night showed no signs of slowing down. The band was still pumping out the hits to a packed dance floor, drinks were being pressed into people's hands, and everyone seemed happy and relaxed, the atmosphere buzzy and good-natured.

'I think I might need to take a breather for this one,' Estelle confessed to Tony, as the band struck up *Johnny B. Goode*. The pair of them had danced and flirted the night away and Estelle was on cloud nine. She couldn't remember the last time she'd felt this good – managing to put aside her worries about Joe and Cafe Crumb, in favour of sheer, unadulterated fun with a gorgeous man who made her feel incredible.

'Of course. No problem. I'll go get us some drinks,' Tony said, as Estelle found a pair of empty seats, and Tony returned shortly afterwards carrying two Tom Collins.

'This will have to be my last one, I'm afraid,' Estelle said with genuine regret. She didn't want this night to end. 'I have to get up early tomorrow and open the cafe. No rest for the wicked.'

'I need to be heading off soon, too,' Tony replied. 'I don't want to leave Chris for too long, plus I'm on the early shift tomorrow.'

'What do you do?' Estelle asked, taking a sip of her cocktail. 'I forget that you're not a full-time football coach.'

'Actually, I'm a fireman,' Tony confessed with a smirk.

'You're not!' Estelle exclaimed in disbelief, clapping a hand over her mouth as she remembered the incident the other week where she'd nearly burnt down her own flat. 'Tell me you're joking.'

189

'Scout's honour,' Tony grinned, holding up his fingers. 'And I was very glad to see that your smoke alarm's in full working order. Good of you to test it while I was there.'

Estelle blushed, feeling as though she'd somehow been caught out. Her blushes grew even deeper as an image popped into her head of Tony in his full fireman's regalia. Talk about an erotic fantasy – that vision could fuel her dreams for weeks! And his profession explained his superb physique, Estelle realised, idly wondering what he'd look like wearing just his helmet . . .

'So I was thinking,' Tony began, interrupting Estelle's thoughts. She was glad it was dark so he couldn't see how red her cheeks were. 'You mentioned you were trying to think of ways to drum up more business. Does Cafe Crumb have a website at all?'

'No, it doesn't,' Estelle confessed. 'It's something I keep meaning to do, but I never seem to get the time to look into it. And it's so expensive.'

'It doesn't have to be,' Tony shrugged. 'I set one up for the football team – did Joe tell you about it? Now why doesn't that surprise me,' he smiled, as Estelle shook her head. 'Teenage boys aren't the most communicative people, are they? But seriously, you should take a look. It has all the dates for practices and matches, plus a section where the players can confirm who's available. I'd like to soup it up a little – maybe put on player profiles, and add a message board where they can all discuss how the games went and so on, but I haven't got round to it yet.'

'It sounds great,' Estelle said enthusiastically. 'I'll get Joe to give me the details.'

'If you like, I could help you do one for Cafe Crumb,' Tony offered. 'It won't be anything amazing I'm afraid – I'm not really a technical person – but I can do the basics. You could have your opening hours on there, and the menu. Maybe details of any events you've got coming up, like the book club, plus customer reviews or special offers. Whatever you want.'

'Would you really do that?' Estelle asked in disbelief.

'Of course,' Tony agreed easily. 'Just let me know when you're free. You'd have to buy a domain name, of course, but I can always help you with that if you're not sure how.'

'That would be amazing!' Estelle enthused, her eyes dancing. She wanted to throw her arms around him and kiss him, but she wasn't sure if that would be appropriate, and she was fairly sure the cocktails had impaired her judgement. It was at moments like this that she longed to be candid and forthright, like the characters they'd been reading about. She wished that she had the confidence to whisper in his ear exactly what she wanted him to do to her, to let him take her to bed and show her what she'd been missing out on.

'I'd be happy to,' Tony said, looking pretty pleased with himself.

Estelle raised her glass to take a celebratory sip, but realised it was empty. With a deep sigh of disappointment, she checked her phone and saw that the time was shortly after eleven. Fortunately, there were no missed calls from Joe – just an earlier text saying that everything was fine and he was heading to bed.

'I really have to go,' Estelle said, her voice full of regret. 'I planned to be back by now. But thank you so much for offering – it's a brilliant idea. I have your number, so I'll be in touch about it soon,' she finished, getting to her feet.

Tony stood up too. 'I can walk you back if you like,' he offered. 'It's not far, and you shouldn't be walking around by yourself at this time,' he added gallantly.

'Well, if you're sure . . .' Estelle replied, feeling giddy with excitement.

'Anyone who bakes Chelsea buns as perfectly as you do deserves to be looked after,' Tony laughed.

'Well . . . thank you,' Estelle replied, turning pink with delight. The man seemed to get closer to perfection every time he opened his mouth. 'I'll just go say goodbye to my friends, and then I'll be back.'

She flashed him a smile, her pulse rate accelerating wildly as he smiled back at her, then looked around the room to locate the others.

The first people she saw were Gracie and Reggie, tearing up the dance floor. Reggie was trying some comedy jitterbug-type dance, waving his arms and kicking his long legs, as Gracie laughed hysterically and threw in a few moves of her own. Sue and George were also dancing together, although somewhat less outrageously than their younger counterparts.

Estelle spotted Rebecca and Andy taking a breather by the drinks table, and made her way over.

'Hasn't it been a fantastic night?' Rebecca cried tipsily. 'And wasn't Gracie fabulous?'

'It has, and she was,' laughed Estelle, amused by how happy Rebecca seemed. She and Andy were stood with their arms around each other, their bodies resting comfortably side by side. 'I'm afraid I've got to head off now. I've left Joe on his own, and I've got to be up early tomorrow.'

'Oh, that's a shame,' Rebecca frowned. 'I've barely seen you tonight – you've spent all your time with that hunky man over there.'

'Oi!' Andy interrupted good-naturedly.

'Not as hunky as this one, of course,' Rebecca corrected herself, stroking his chest.

'He's waiting to walk me home, actually,' Estelle confessed.

'Estelle!' Rebecca squealed so loudly that Estelle worried Tony might hear her. 'That's brilliant! Don't do anything I wouldn't do,' she added, with a less-than-subtle wink.

'Don't worry, I won't,' Estelle said, hoping she wasn't blushing too noticeably. 'I don't want to interrupt the others while they're dancing, so would you say goodbye to everyone for me? And I'll see you next week for our usual meeting.'

'I'll be there. And I want *all* the gory details,' Rebecca insisted with a grin.

'It was lovely to meet you, Andy,' Estelle continued, tactfully ignoring Rebecca's comment as she kissed them both on the cheek and hurried towards the exit where Tony was waiting for her.

18

It was almost midnight, and the band had played their final song. The last remaining revellers had slow-danced to *Love Me Tender*, and now the community centre was emptying out, as Sue and George said their goodbyes and headed out into the darkness.

Sue shivered – she was wearing a classic trench coat over her outfit, but the material was thin and the night air was chilly.

'Are you cold?' asked George. He didn't have anything on over his Teddy Boy jacket, but a warming nip of Scotch before he left had fortified him nicely.

'A little,' Sue admitted.

'Come here, love, I'll keep you warm,' George said cheerily, pulling her towards him a little too forcefully.

'Be careful, George,' Sue scolded him, as she almost tripped in her heels. But whether George didn't hear her, or chose to ignore her, she wasn't sure – he simply wrapped his arm tightly around her, and the pair walked on.

'I had a good time tonight,' Sue reflected, sounding satisfied.

'Yes, me too,' George admitted.

'See!' Sue pounced on his words. 'I knew you'd enjoy it once you got there.'

'Yes, well . . .' George muttered grudgingly.

'We should do this kind of thing more often,' Sue pushed on. 'You know – have a night out, go dancing . . . Gracie was telling me that they hold jive classes in one of the bars in town – I've forgotten the name of it now – but maybe we could—'

'Let's not talk about this tonight, Sue,' George cut in, a slight edge to his voice.

'It was only a suggestion,' she replied defensively. 'Seeing as you enjoyed tonight, I thought you might be more amenable to trying out some other things.'

They walked along in silence for a few moments, before George finally spoke. Trying to keep his tone light, he commented, 'Like I said, we've had a good time tonight. Let's not spoil it, eh?'

'Alright,' Sue agreed, deciding to hold her tongue for once.

The moon was full and bright as they walked along, lit by the amber light of the streetlamps. A group of young people, barely old enough to be drinking, staggered past them. They had clearly just left a nearby pub, and they were all laughing and joking around.

'Seems like a lifetime ago, doesn't it?' George reflected wistfully.

'What?'

'Being that age.'

'It *is* a lifetime ago,' Sue smiled.

'I reckon we could still give them a run for their money,' George grinned. 'We showed those young 'uns how it's done tonight. You and me, tearing up the dance floor!'

'So you don't think my friends are too young for me, then?' Sue couldn't resist asking.

'Well we *were* practically the oldest there, but I think we held our own. And your lot all seemed very nice. Andy seemed like a good chap – even if he does support Chelsea. And that Gracie's got a cracking pair of lungs on her.'

'Oh, she was wonderful, wasn't she?' Sue gushed. 'I didn't know she had it in her – she certainly kept that quiet.'

'And your friend who owns the cafe – Elsie, is it?'

'Estelle,' Sue corrected him.

'Yes, that's the one. What about her and that bloke she went home with?'

'I don't think she went *home* home with him,' Sue remarked. 'She has a teenage son, and I don't think she's that kind of woman. But I think she'd like to get married again one day – you know, find someone to make her happy.'

George snorted. 'Marriage? Happiness? Now there are two concepts that don't always go together.'

'And don't I know it,' Sue shot back, hitting him playfully on the arm. The subject was somewhat close to the bone, given all the arguing they'd been doing recently, but tonight they were getting on better than they had done for weeks.

As they approached their driveway, Sue broke out of George's embrace in order to find her door key. With its white-washed walls and low roof, their detached house resembled a country cottage; it was set back from the road down a short path, and the outside light came on automatically as they drew near.

Sue realised she was still a little tipsy – or 'tight', as Jilly Cooper would say, she thought with a smile – as it took her three fumbling attempts to get the key in the lock. Oh, but those Manhattans had been deliciously moreish!

Eventually, she managed to open the door and George followed her inside.

'Mmm, it's good to be home,' he sighed, heading through to the lounge and sinking into his favourite armchair.

'Oh no you don't,' Sue scolded him. 'I'm not having you falling asleep fully clothed down here. Up you get – we'll go straight to bed if you're tired.'

For once, George didn't complain. 'I like it when you're forceful,' he winked.

In spite of herself, Sue smiled at his comment. 'Do you want a cup of tea or anything first?'

'No thanks, love. I don't want to be up all night,'

George replied, heaving himself out of the chair. 'Oh, my whole body's going to feel sore tomorrow. Perhaps I overdid it a bit with all that dancing.'

'Finding it difficult to keep up with the youngsters after all?' Sue teased. 'Well, you are a granddad now.'

'Speak for yourself, Grandma.'

'Hey, I'm a glamorous granny,' Sue protested.

George laughed, then winced as he rolled his shoulders. 'My poor old bones. My back's stiffening up already.'

Sue hesitated for a moment, looking at George as though she was trying to decide whether or not to say something. Finally the Manhattans kicked in and, remembering Rebecca's pep talk, she said coyly, 'I could give you a massage if you like.'

'Eh? What's that?' George asked, thinking he'd misheard.

'A massage,' Sue repeated, trying to sound casual. 'It's supposed to be good for bad backs – it'll ease your muscles and make you feel relaxed.'

George narrowed his eyes, looking at her suspiciously. 'How come you know so much about it all of a sudden?'

'Oh, I just read about it somewhere,' Sue replied airily, not wanting to admit exactly *where* she'd read about it – in the kind of novels where a sensual massage is merely the forerunner to something much more filthy. It had been a long time since anything like that had taken place under Sue's roof, but you never know what might happen, she thought hopefully, realising that the erotic reads had affected her more than she'd expected. Her eyes had been

199

opened to a world of romance and passion and sensuous pleasure, and she longed to experience it for herself.

'So, what do you say?' she challenged him, raising an eyebrow suggestively.

'Alright then,' George called her bluff. 'You're on.'

'Come on then,' Sue murmured. 'Get into the bedroom and take your shirt off.'

'It's been a while since I've had an offer like that,' George chuckled. 'Can we turn the heating up first?'

Sue rolled her eyes, following him upstairs to the chintz-patterned bedroom, where George began stripping down to his underwear.

'And your vest too. Come on Georgie boy, I want to see some flesh,' she giggled, running her gaze over her husband's exposed body. If she squinted, she could almost imagine it was the toned, chiselled body of David Beckham stood in front of her, rather than George in his baggy Y-fronts.

'What about you?' George insisted. 'I'm not lying here in the altogether if you're not.'

'Well I don't know what kind of massage parlours you've been frequenting, but it's my understanding that the masseuse stays fully clothed,' Sue teased.

'I'm sure you'd be much happier out of those silly fifties clothes,' George persisted.

'Okay, I'll slip into something more comfortable,' Sue played along, sliding out of her dress and folding it neatly over the wing-back chair in the corner. She took her summer dressing gown out of the wardrobe and wrapped it around her – a light, silky garment which allowed her to move easily.

'Lie down on your front,' Sue told George.

With a grunt, he did as he was told.

'Now close your eyes and enjoy,' Sue said softly, as she knelt on the bed beside him. 'Where does it hurt?'

'Everywhere,' George mumbled, his face squashed into the duvet.

Sue began to sweep her fingers over his skin, rubbing the muscles gently to warm them, before starting work on the knots beneath his shoulder blades.

'Ohhhh, that feels good,' George groaned.

'Hang on a mo, I've just remembered something,' Sue exclaimed, jumping off the bed and dashing downstairs to the kitchen.

'Don't stop now!' George complained, prostrate and frustrated, until Sue returned carrying a bottle of olive oil. 'What on earth are you going to do with that?' he asked, looking alarmed.

'It's easier to use some sort of oil. It acts as a . . . lubricant,' she explained, her cheeks reddening as she said the word.

'But you can't use olive oil!' George protested. 'I'm not a salad!'

'It's fine, George. Don't fuss,' Sue scolded him. 'It's one hundred per cent natural and completely safe to use.'

'I suppose you read that somewhere too, did you?' George huffed, as he lay back down, burying his face in the pillow.

'I did, as a matter of fact,' Sue said, glad George couldn't see the way she was blushing. In actual fact, her choice had been inspired by a particular scene in *Ten Sweet Lessons*, where Alexander and Christina had used all manner of foodstuffs on each other's bodies. The things they'd done with olive oil and a large courgette had made Sue's eyes bulge – they certainly hadn't used them to whip up a tasty Mediterranean snack.

But George didn't need to know that, Sue thought, as she poured out a capful and warmed it between her hands. She drizzled it gently onto George's skin, smoothly rubbing her hands over his shoulders once again. This time they slid with ease, the sensuous feeling of skin on skin.

'How's that?' Sue murmured.

'I feel like a turkey being basted for the oven,' George muttered, but as Sue worked her magic, his complaints quickly gave way to a series of contented sighs.

While Sue kneaded away, she found herself wondering what people would think if they could see her now – a sixty-two year old woman straddling her sixty-five year old husband, trying to put the spark back into their relationship with the aid of some kitchen condiments.

In spite of everything she'd said to her daughter last week, Sue did want to get her marriage back on track. It was simply a case of both of them making compromises, both of them making more of an effort with each other. And since George had come out with her tonight, she was giving him a little reward in return.

Sue's hands moved in long, lazy sweeps down her husband's back, and she observed him as he lay there, his body relaxed. Of course, he was quite different, physically, to the man she'd married all those years ago. His hair was grey now, thinning at the sides and bald on top. Where once his torso had been firm and tight, the skin was now slack, moving loosely under her hands. The muscles were soft and untoned, with flabby love-handles around his waist and wiry grey hairs scattered across his back and thighs.

But he was hers, and she loved him.

Sue knew that she, too, was no longer the same person she'd been in her twenties. Gravity had taken its toll on her face, her breasts, her stomach and she was helpless to fight back. Her skin was lined, her hair silver-grey. But, as husband and wife, they had to look after each other. *For better or for worse* – wasn't that what they'd pledged?

Sue's hands moved down to George's lower back, her thumbs circling the hollow at the base of his spine, increasing the pressure.

'Does that feel good?' she asked softly.

'Mmmmm,' George replied distantly. He sounded deeply relaxed.

'That's good.'

Sue poured out more oil and continued to work, using her palms to smooth out his muscles, and letting her fingertips knead away the gristly little knots.

Her hands moved lower, sliding beneath the waistband

of George's underpants. Unbidden, a naughty thought flitted across Sue's mind. It had been some time since she'd last investigated what lay beneath George's Y-fronts, but if he was anything like he used to be, he certainly wouldn't complain if she initiated something.

And why shouldn't she make the first move? Sue thought indignantly. The characters in the books she was reading didn't hesitate to go for what they wanted, so why shouldn't she?

Tantalisingly, Sue let her hands slide around her husband's waist, gradually moving them beneath his underpants. Her fingers travelled lower, an inch at a time, her oily fingertips sliding smoothly over his skin.

She inhaled sharply, a long-forgotten tingle of excitement fizzing through her veins as she realised she finally felt brave enough to tell her husband exactly what she wanted, what she'd been fantasising about since reading those erotic books. Her breathing grew shallow, her body craving the satisfaction that had largely eluded her throughout her married life.

Closing her eyes, Sue allowed herself to remember the feel of George's hands on her body, his fingertips caressing her bare skin, how it felt to have him inside of her, moving together . . .

'George . . .' she whispered seductively.

There was no reply.

She moved lower still, her hands locking onto their target so there could be no mistaking her intentions as she began stroking softly.

'George . . .? George!' she demanded, more sharply this time.

But the only response she got was a gentle snore, as George's eyelids drooped and his mouth dropped open. Sue sat back on her heels in disgust as she realised that, to her intense disappointment, George had fallen fast asleep.

19

'What happened?'

It was the first thing Rebecca said when she bounded through the door of Cafe Crumb for the book club meeting. She was even earlier than for the previous session, but this time Estelle was prepared and had re-opened the cafe at 6.45 p.m.

'*Nothing* happened,' Estelle insisted, knowing exactly what Rebecca was referring to.

'What, no kiss? Nothing?'

'He was the perfect gentleman,' Estelle said primly.

Rebecca pulled a face. 'How boring,' she declared, looking hugely disappointed. 'If only you were characters in a Jilly Cooper novel,' she sighed wistfully, pulling her copy of *Riders* out of her bag. 'He'd have thrown you across his saddle and had his wicked way with you in the hayloft by now.'

'Rebecca!' Estelle exclaimed, feeling the telltale heat rise in her cheeks. If she was being honest, that was exactly what *she* wanted too.

'Sorry,' Rebecca apologised, her eyes twinkling. 'I'm getting carried away. And sorry if I said anything embarrassing the other night – I enjoyed those cocktails rather too much.'

'I'm sure it was all fine,' Estelle reassured her. 'Did you have a good night?'

'I had a great time, and so did Andy. I wonder if there'll be another one soon?'

'Ooh, there's a thought. We'll have to ask Gracie.'

They both turned as Sue hurried in, taking off her coat and hastily hanging it up. 'So, what's all the gossip? Have you asked her, Rebecca?'

'Yes, and she's not spilling.'

'Ah, well a lady never tells,' Sue winked at Estelle.

'There's nothing *to* tell!'

'What's that saying?' Rebecca smirked. 'Methinks the lady doth protest too much.'

'You did make a lovely couple,' added Sue. 'He's a very handsome chap, and you looked good together.'

'Thank you, but Tony happens to be a lovely gentleman who just walked me home, that's all. Our sons play football together, and we have a lot in common.'

'Oh, it's all so perfect!' Rebecca squealed, refusing to be put off by Estelle's denials.

'Is he divorced, then?' wondered Sue.

'No. It's terribly sad, actually. His wife died a few years ago.'

'How horrible!' Sue burst out. 'So he's raising his son on his own?'

Estelle nodded. 'Chris seems like a really nice kid. He and Joe get on well.'

'It's so romantic,' Rebecca breathed. 'And terrible and awful *obviously*,' she added hurriedly, as Estelle and Sue stared at her, horrified. 'He's like a character from a romantic novel – the tragic (yet extremely handsome) widower, looking for love . . .'

'I think you've been reading too much,' Estelle teased. 'We might have to stop you coming to the meetings.'

'Oh, don't do that!' Rebecca cried. 'I'd miss your custard slices far too much. Speaking of which . . .'

'Oh yes, of course,' Estelle apologised, scurrying behind the counter. 'That's what happens when you distract me.'

'Her mind's on other things,' Sue said to Rebecca in a stage-whisper, causing the three of them to burst into giggles.

'Did I mention he's a fireman?' Estelle couldn't resist adding, as she poured out their drinks.

Rebecca's mouth dropped open. 'Shut up! Tell me you're joking.'

'Every word is true.'

'That explains the hot body,' Rebecca said knowledgeably.

'Has he shown you his helmet yet?' asked the normally reserved Sue, as she and Rebecca guffawed once more.

Estelle rolled her eyes. 'Alright, let's get all of the jokes out of the way now, then we can proceed in an orderly fashion.'

'Has he asked you to hold his hose?' Rebecca was laughing so much she could barely speak.

Fortunately for Estelle, Gracie walked in at that moment, causing them all to burst into spontaneous applause.

'There she is, Little Miss Songbird,' Rebecca called out gleefully, as Gracie bent down into a low curtsey, holding her skirt out to the side. She was wearing the one with the cherry design that she'd bought when shopping with Rebecca, and she'd teamed it with a tight, white V-neck.

'You were wonderful – like a young Ella Fitzgerald,' Sue gushed.

'I didn't like it . . . I *loved* it,' droned Estelle, doing her best impression of Simon Cowell.

'Thank you, everybody,' Gracie smiled, clearly thrilled with their reaction. 'And thanks so much for coming. I'm really pleased with how it all went. Everyone's been so nice about my performance.'

'Well you deserve it,' Rebecca insisted, giving her a hug.

'We were just talking about what a good time we'd had, actually,' Estelle told her. 'Will there be another Fifties Night anytime soon?'

'Yes, I think so,' Gracie nodded. 'They hold them fairly regularly – usually once a month – so I'll check and get back to you.'

'Super. Even George enjoyed it!' Sue laughed.

'How is everything with him?' Rebecca asked gently.

'Oh, you know . . . *Plus ça change* . . .'

But she didn't get chance to say anything further as Reggie walked through the door and everyone turned to look at him.

'Hello,' he smiled, seeming more confident than usual. He was clearly getting used to being around the women. He nodded at them all, then his gaze fell on Gracie. 'Hi,' he said shyly.

'Hi,' she replied, unaware that the others were watching them intently.

'So, can I get you two anything to eat or drink?' Estelle cut in. 'Then we can get stuck into some Jilly Cooper.'

Gracie and Reggie placed their orders (Victoria sponge with tea, and walnut cake with coffee, respectively), then everyone went to sit down at the main table, their copies of *Riders* in front of them.

'It's such an iconic front cover, isn't it?' Rebecca marvelled, staring at the famous picture. It showed a woman's very pert bottom in tight, white jodhpurs, being cupped by a man's hand. On the left hand side, a riding crop discreetly entered the shot.

'It's excellent,' agreed Sue. 'Naughty and suggestive all at once, but without being too offensive, or gratuitous.'

'Just like Jilly's writing,' quipped Estelle. 'So, what did we all think?'

'I adored it!' Rebecca exclaimed. 'I can't believe I'd never read it before. It's exactly the sort of thing I like, and it has such a great, gossipy tone. It's a really naughty romp!'

'Ah, yes,' Estelle agreed. 'The naughtiness! There's certainly a lot of that.'

'But Jilly does it so well,' Sue affirmed. 'There's an awful lot of sex, but it's not explicit – not like *Ten Sweet Lessons*.'

'I wouldn't even call it erotica,' Rebecca added. 'But there are so many allusions to sex, and the whole book is just so . . . sexy!'

'I know what you mean,' nodded Estelle. 'It seems as though everyone's at it constantly, swapping partners, jumping in and out of bed with each other. Everyone's so highly sexed.'

'Lucky them,' said Sue, archly.

'Doesn't it make you want to live in Rutshire?' sighed Rebecca.

'Even the name is hilarious,' giggled Gracie. 'And what is it that's so sexy about horses?'

'Horses?' spluttered Reggie.

'No, I didn't mean *that*,' Gracie quickly corrected herself, as the others laughed. 'Is the horsey world really at it all the time?'

'It's a naturally sexy sport,' Rebecca said knowledgeably. 'All those riding crops and leather straps. Plus, those tight breeches show *everything* – you can't hide the size of your bulge in a pair of those,' she chuckled.

'And everyone's always outdoors and sporty, so they're all fit and healthy,' added Sue, secretly wishing George was up for a little *al fresco* action – although there was little chance of that when she could barely drag him away from the television.

'Do you know you can actually buy horse harnesses and fake tails and everything, if that's what you're into? Isn't that weird?' Gracie informed them.

'Well it certainly left me wanting to be ridden,' Rebecca declared, without a trace of embarrassment. 'Although maybe the tails and everything is a little extreme. But honestly, Rupert Campbell-Black could tie me up in the tack room and teach me a lesson with his riding crop whenever he chose.'

'Rebecca!' Gracie exclaimed, sounding disappointed. 'What is your obsession with men who behave like total shits? Every book club, it's the same thing.'

'It's not just me!' Rebecca replied defensively. 'I'm sure loads of other women fall madly in love with him when they read it. Yes, he's an arrogant bastard, but he is so damn sexual and dangerous and charming. Mmm!' she finished, her eyes sparkling wickedly.

'I think it's because Andy's such a nice guy,' Estelle suggested. 'So your fantasies revolve around being used and abused by a bit of rough.'

'Isn't that what everyone wants?' Rebecca insisted. 'A nice guy – but not too nice. He needs to have a bit of edge to him too.'

'Rupert Campbell-Black has too much edge,' Gracie disagreed, suddenly very aware of Reggie sitting across from her. The more she described the kind of man she wanted, the more she realised that Reggie came very close to fitting the bill.

'Reggie,' Estelle said loudly, and Gracie jumped in panic, worrying for a second that Estelle could read her mind. 'What did *you* think of *Riders*?'

'Long!' he shot back instantly, which made everyone laugh. 'What was it, nine hundred pages or so? And I felt like this was the trashiest book we've read so far.'

'Trashier than *Ten Sweet Lessons*?' Estelle asked in surprise, as Reggie nodded.

'This was more like a soap opera. As you said, everyone just seemed to be swapping partners, sleeping with whoever they wanted. I suppose the backdrop of the showjumping world was interesting – although a little too detailed at times. Overall, I think it's definitely a book for women.'

'Sexist,' Gracie piped up.

Reggie shrugged, his cheeks flushing as he turned to her. 'Like Rebecca said, most women fall in love with at least one of the heroes. There are some really strong male characters, and I definitely think it's a female fantasy.'

'So a roll in the hay wouldn't be your fantasy then?' Rebecca interrogated him.

Reggie stared at her, his mouth flapping open and closed as he wondered how best to respond. In truth, he had found many of the scenarios very sexy – anyone reading about all that romping was going to get turned on – but there was no way he would dare admit that to this group of women. 'I'm certainly no Rupert Campbell-Black,' he finished diplomatically.

'Good,' Gracie leapt to his defence. 'You don't need to be.'

Everyone turned to look at the pair of them, as Gracie stared back defiantly. A smile twitched at the corners of Estelle's mouth, while Sue and Rebecca exchanged meaningful looks, much as they had done while watching them at the Fifties Night.

Reggie avoided eye contact with everyone, his heart beginning to beat faster. Was it possible that Gracie *did* actually like him? Of course, she'd agreed to dance with him last week, but he'd been emboldened by alcohol, while she was on a high after her performance. He'd walked her home at the end of the night, but had been too shy to make a move, leaving her at her door with a polite goodnight. For all Reggie knew, she'd woken up the following morning and regretted being so friendly towards him. But remarks like that gave him cause to hope . . .

'Well, perhaps we should let you choose the book for the next session, Reggie,' Estelle suggested kindly. 'That way, we can hear about a man's fantasy for a change.'

'Good idea!' Rebecca spoke up. 'I like the sound of that.'

'My turn?' Reggie asked, playing for time and wondering what on earth he was going to suggest. Of course, there were obvious choices like Jackie Collins, but that wasn't really Reggie's cup of tea. He could go for something educational, like Chaucer, he mused, wondering what the women would make of that! Then of course, there was more literary erotica such as Anaïs Nin, he remembered, scouring his brain for authors he'd come across during his undergraduate degree. But none of them seemed quite right. He wanted something historical, but something that would *really* provide a subject for debate. A text that would show them he wasn't as square and prudish as they all thought he was.

'Reggie?' Estelle asked gently. 'Someone else can always choose if you can't think of anything.'

'The Marquis de Sade,' he declared triumphantly.

'What?' asked Rebecca, looking confused. 'I've never heard of it.'

'That's the author,' Reggie explained quickly. 'An eighteenth-century French writer.'

'Sounds fascinating,' Rebecca groaned, stifling a yawn, and wishing he'd picked something more fun.

'He wanted to explore how shocking and depraved you could make a novel,' Reggie explained, as Rebecca began to look more interested. 'Believe me, you won't be falling in love with any of the characters in this. Has anyone read the Marquis de Sade before?' he asked.

Everyone shook their heads, as Sue said, 'Didn't he write *120 Days of Sodom*? That's supposed to be horribly shocking.'

'It's not an easy read,' Reggie agreed. 'But I think if we're exploring this kind of work, we should cover all bases. How about *Justine*?' he suggested. 'It's a novelette, so it'll be quicker, but still just as outrageous.'

'Honestly Reggie, how bad can it be?' Rebecca scoffed, thinking that Reggie was probably exaggerating. She imagined he'd led a fairly sheltered life, so anything involving slightly abnormal sexual practices would undoubtedly scandalise him.

Reggie smiled, knowing exactly what Rebecca was thinking. 'Well, just read it and find out for yourself.'

For a moment no one spoke, a strange atmosphere falling over the cafe as everyone contemplated their next read and wondered exactly how depraved *Justine* could possibly be. Little pockets of conversation started up again, but the meeting was clearly winding down, and before long Sue was draining her teacup and saying goodbye. Estelle began tidying away the used crockery, while Rebecca and Gracie gossiped away, apparently in no rush to leave.

It was all Reggie could do not to pack up his things and hurry out of the door himself – usually he escaped at the first opportunity – but tonight he'd hoped to grab a word with Gracie. The longer she spent talking to Rebecca however, the more he began to lose his nerve. Maybe he could leave it for another week, he told himself, fastening his briefcase and carrying his empty plate over to Estelle.

'I really should be making a move,' he heard Rebecca say. 'Andy will be wondering where I've got to. Goodnight, Estelle,' she called. 'Thanks for another great meeting, and I'll see you soon.'

Estelle came over and everyone said their goodbyes,

then Reggie followed Rebecca and Gracie outside as Estelle locked up behind them. He took out his mobile phone and began fiddling with it, trying to kill time as the two women resumed their conversation.

'Are you okay, Reggie?' Rebecca asked curiously, noticing the way he was hovering beside them on the pavement. They were discussing the best way to style your hair for a lasting curl, and she didn't think he'd have any interest in that conversation.

'Yes, fine,' he said brightly, on the verge of giving up and going straight home. Then he stopped himself, turning back around and addressing the women once again. 'Um . . . no, actually. Rebecca, do you mind if I have a word with Gracie? I mean . . . Gracie, can I speak to you?'

'Yeah, of course,' Gracie agreed.

'I'll see you both in a fortnight then.' Rebecca raised her eyebrows, looking meaningfully at Gracie. 'Have a good night – call me if you want to chat before then.'

'Bye, Rebecca,' Reggie said politely. He watched her walk off, nerves jangling in the pit of his stomach. He'd been feeling so brave earlier, contributing to the discussion and suggesting the Marquis de Sade, but now, all alone with Gracie, his courage had deserted him once more.

She smiled up at him, and Reggie couldn't help but notice the startling green colour of her eyes. Her lashes were long and dark, the lids lined with thick black liner. He shook his head sharply, realising he was staring.

'So what did you want to talk to me about?' Gracie asked, smiling encouragingly.

'Um . . .' Reggie cleared his throat anxiously then smoothed down his jacket. He hoped he looked okay – he'd made an effort tonight, wearing a new pair of jeans with a smart shirt, and he'd attempted to mould his hair into some kind of style, rather than leaving it fluffy and untamed.

'I really enjoyed the Fifties Night,' he began. 'Your singing was unbelievable. And you looked . . . unbelievable,' he repeated, suddenly unable to think of any other adjectives.

'Thank you,' Gracie said shyly.

'What I was wondering . . .' Reggie stopped for a moment, taking a deep breath. 'I was wondering whether . . . whether you might like to go out somewhere together . . . you and me . . . without the rest of the book club. We could go for a drink, or for something to eat, or to the cinema . . .?'

'You mean, on a date?' Gracie interrupted, before Reggie could list all the venues he could think of.

'Yes, exactly like that,' Reggie confirmed. Then he panicked, and added hastily, 'Or not, if you don't want it to be. You don't even have to say yes. We can just forget that this whole conversation took place and never tell anyone about it and—'

'Reggie,' Gracie cut in once more. But she was laughing this time. 'Yes, Reggie, I would like to go for a drink or a meal or to the cinema or any other location with you. That would be really nice,' she smiled, her long, dark hair falling prettily around her face as she gazed up at him.

'Really?' Reggie exhaled slowly, the relief visible on his face. 'Right. Well,' he bumbled, breaking into a wide smile as he realised what had just happened. He'd asked Gracie out and she'd said yes! He felt like some all-conquering hero, a ladykiller who could give Rupert Campbell-Black a run for his money. Except that Gracie didn't want Rupert Campbell-Black. She wanted *him*!

'That's excellent,' he grinned, unable to keep the smile off his face. 'Absolutely . . . excellent.'

20

Estelle was standing nervously outside Tony's house. She patted her freshly styled hair to ensure it hadn't gone frizzy, then smoothed down her jacket. She'd spent ages trying to find the perfect outfit, and had finally settled on a loose jersey top, cut lower than she would usually wear, and a pair of tight-fitting jeans with some quilted ballet pumps. She wanted to look good, but not as though she was trying too hard. Her hair was cut in a long, sleek bob, and was shining with health now that she'd finally had those ratty split ends cut off. She'd even put a colour through it – a warm chestnut shade to cover the grey hairs that had been peeking through.

Estelle had added light make-up, and she had to admit that she was feeling good. And why shouldn't she take care of herself? she thought defiantly. Inspired by all those erotic novels she'd been reading, Estelle had become far more aware of her own sexuality, and she wanted to rediscover that side of herself. She was afraid that she'd begun to turn into a dowdy, middle-aged, workaholic, and that was certainly not the way she wanted her life to go.

She glanced across at Joe who was standing beside her, looking at her curiously.

'Why are you being weird, Mum?'

'I'm not being weird!' Estelle shot back defensively. 'How am I being weird?'

'You're just . . . I dunno . . . acting weird. Like you're nervous or something.'

Estelle laughed a little too loudly. 'Why would I be nervous? Honestly Joe, you have the strangest ideas sometimes . . .'

The door opened, and Estelle stopped talking.

Tony stood there, smiling broadly, and it was all Estelle could do not to melt into a puddle on the doormat. Instead, she grinned goofily back at him. He was wearing a polo shirt, with smart jeans, and his feet were bare – something Estelle found inexplicably sexy. She suddenly felt ridiculous for making such an effort with her appearance, worried that Tony would think she was wildly overdressed.

'Hi Estelle, hi Joe, come in. You look great, Estelle,' he told her, as he kissed her on the cheek.

Estelle caught the scent of soap and aftershave and that deliciously indefinable masculine smell. Memories came flooding back of dancing with him at the Fifties

Night, their bodies pressed close as they moved together, and she felt a rush of excitement in parts of her body that hadn't been excited for a very long time . . .

'Have you done your hair differently?' Tony asked, his hand still resting on her shoulder.

Estelle could feel the light pressure of his fingers through the thin fabric of her top, and tried her very best to behave normally. 'Yes, I have,' she replied brightly. 'Just a haircut – nothing special.'

'Are you okay?' asked Tony, his eyes narrowing as he looked at her closely. 'You seem a little . . .'

'Weird,' Joe cut in. 'Doesn't she? That's what *I've* been saying. You're being weird, Mum.'

'Well, I don't know if that's the word I'd have used,' Tony said diplomatically. 'Anyway, how're things with you, Joe?'

'Yeah, all good,' Joe said brightly. 'I'm playing upfront for the school first team now, even though you don't normally get to do that until at least Year Ten. Mr Hughes says that the way I take free kicks reminds him of Ronaldo.'

'Hey, that's fantastic.' Tony looked impressed.

'I knew you'd understand,' Joe grinned. 'Mum never knows what I'm talking about. Is Chris around?'

'Yeah, he's in his room. Just head up – you know where it is.'

'Cool. See you later,' Joe added, as he fist-bumped Tony and headed out of the room. Moments later, they heard the pounding of his feet as he stomped up the stairs.

'He's brought a couple of computer games with him,'

Estelle explained to Tony, wishing she could think of something clever and witty to say instead. 'That should keep them occupied for a few hours.'

'While we get on with some business of our own,' Tony commented, raising his eyebrows.

Was it Estelle's imagination, or were those dark eyes of his sparkling mischievously? Oh, how she longed for him to sweep her up in those strong fireman's arms, carry her off into the sunset and do all manner of unspeakable things to her!

'Did you bring your laptop?' Tony asked, startling her out of her daydreams.

Estelle patted the bulky bag that hung off her shoulder and stared helplessly into those warm, chocolate eyes as she tried her hardest to focus on the reason why she was there. After speaking with him at the Fifties Night, Estelle had taken Tony up on his offer to help her put together a website for Cafe Crumb. She'd made a start on her laptop by writing up the text she wanted to be included, and she'd even done some rough sketches of how she imagined the site would look, but tonight Tony was going to help her put it all together.

Estelle was excited to see it all take shape, and she hoped that a website would give sales a welcome boost. The cafe's takings had been increasing steadily in recent weeks, but that was to be expected as the weather warmed up. Perhaps, with an extra push, she could get the business back on an even keel, with a little spare money left over to treat her and Joe occasionally.

'Great,' Tony smiled. 'We'll get started soon – I'll just fire up the computer.' He headed over to the desk in the corner of the living room, and bent over to flick a switch. Estelle couldn't help but stare as she watched the way his body moved, those powerful muscles flexing as he stretched.

'Would you like a drink?' Tony asked, as he straightened up.

'Tea would be lovely, thank you.'

'Are you sure I can't tempt you with anything stronger? You must get sick of the sight of tea and coffee. I've got a couple of bottles of wine in the kitchen . . .?'

Estelle smiled. 'Are you trying to get me drunk?' she teased, and was gratified to see that Tony looked the tiniest bit guilty at her comment. 'Go on then, I'll have a glass of wine. Just the one though, as I'm driving.'

'Great. Red or white?'

'Red, please.'

'Coming right up. Make yourself comfortable – I'll be back in two minutes.'

As he left the room, Estelle let out a long, shaky breath, trying to slow her racing pulse. She plopped down on the oversized sofa, and looked appraisingly around the room. Everything was neat and tidy, and the house was decorated in a modern style, with lots of sleek, dark furniture and an enormous flat screen TV – perfect for Tony and Chris to crash out and watch football, Estelle thought fondly. But the room was clearly lacking a woman's touch. There were no tastefully selected ornaments, no contrasting cushions on the sofa, no framed family photos on the mantelpiece.

Estelle turned as Tony came back through, carrying two glasses of wine. He passed one to her, and she hastily gulped down half the contents before reminding herself to take it easy. The room was warm and the alcohol hit her system immediately. She felt herself begin to relax, as Tony sat down in front of the computer. His legs were spread, his thighs strong and muscular, and Estelle found herself wondering what it would be like to have them wrapped around her, to be crushed beneath that powerful body. She couldn't help it. All her spare minutes were spent reading the erotica novels for the book group, and it seemed to be affecting her whole way of thinking.

It didn't help that it was such a long time since she'd met a man she was interested in, and now it was almost as though she'd forgotten how to behave. Her mind kept taking off on wild flights of fancy, and she felt sure Tony must be able to tell exactly what she was thinking.

He pulled up a chair beside him and patted the seat. 'Come and sit here,' he suggested.

Estelle rose unsteadily to her feet and walked towards him. Once again, she felt overwhelmed by being so close to him physically, taking in the sheer size of his body, the smell of his skin. She felt she might swoon, like a character in a Victorian novel.

'So how's everything with you?' Tony asked, swirling the red wine before taking a long swallow.

'Great, thanks. Really good,' Estelle squeaked, nodding furiously.

'I'm glad. Did you enjoy the Fifties Night?'

'Oh yes,' Estelle insisted, seemingly unable to stop nodding. 'I had a wonderful time.'

'Me too,' Tony agreed, as he looked at her intently. 'Dancing, drinking, and great company.'

Estelle didn't respond, feeling herself flush under his gaze. Was he talking about her? she wondered excitedly. Did he mean that *she* was great company?

The computer made a beeping sound, and Tony turned away from her. 'Right, we're all ready to go.'

'Thanks so much for helping me with all of this,' Estelle told him. 'I really appreciate it. And I'm so excited to have a website for Cafe Crumb. I feel like we're finally embracing the modern era!'

'Don't get your hopes up too much,' Tony warned. 'Like I said, I'm something of an amateur at these things. But I'm happy to help if I can. You deserve to be successful,' he finished softly.

'Thank you,' Estelle murmured, realising that she even found the sound of his voice attractive.

Don't be silly, she told herself sharply. *He's probably not the slightest bit interested in you. He's probably got women falling at his feet.*

'I brought some sketches,' she said, swiftly changing the subject, and scrabbling around in her bag as she tried to compose herself. She pulled out a handful of A4 sheets on which she'd made rough drawings and notes for how

226

she wanted the website to look. It was a very traditional design, with the home page looking like a smart shop front.

'And I thought we could use this cupcake motif throughout,' she continued, reminding herself to remain businesslike, as Tony leaned in to look at the designs. She could feel the warmth of his body against hers, and took another fortifying sip of wine.

'These look fantastic,' enthused Tony, sounding genuinely impressed.

'I'd like to keep the colours quite simple,' Estelle rushed on. 'Perhaps black, white and . . . pink? Or do you think that's too feminine? Black, white and yellow might be better. Or red. Reddy-orange,' she carried on, aware that she was gabbling but seemingly unable to stop herself.

'I'll leave that sort of thing to you,' Tony told her easily. 'You're probably much better at picking colours and the – what do they call it? – the *aesthetic* side of things than I am. We can start off with a basic template, like this,' he continued, clicking the mouse a couple of times. 'And build around it.'

Estelle watched him as he got stuck in and, little by little, her website began to take shape. She could see the concentration on his face, finding something incredibly sexy about the intensity with which he worked. She observed his body too, his strong torso hunched over the keyboard, the way his sheer size seemed to dominate the room. He was so masculine, Estelle thought with a dreamy sigh. And he was so very different to her ex-husband.

Whereas Ted relied more on his charm, Tony's strengths lay in his physicality. Estelle couldn't help but wonder how that dominant, physical side would come out in the bedroom . . .

Absorbed in his work, Tony unconsciously ran a hand over the rough stubble on his chin. Estelle found herself wishing that she could do the same; she longed to stroke the smooth skin of his forehead, to brush away the eyelash that had fallen onto his cheek, not to mention what she wanted to do to those soft, plump lips of his . . .

'I'm sorry, what?' Estelle was jolted back to reality, as she realised Tony was speaking to her.

'Are you sure you're okay?' he asked his voice full of concern. 'It seemed like you were staring at me.'

'Oh, yes, I um . . . just spotted an eyelash. On your cheek,' Estelle rambled. 'I guess I'm easily distracted,' she laughed, trying to make light of the situation.

'Gone?' Tony asked, wiping his hands roughly over his face.

'No – the right cheek,' she instructed. 'Not quite, it's still there . . . um . . .' Before Estelle had chance to think about what she was doing, she was reaching out to touch him, brushing the eyelash gently away with the tips of her fingers.

For a moment, neither of them moved. They were so close, and Estelle's heart was pounding. Their eyes were locked on each other, and Estelle could see the way his pupils had dilated, so that the irises seemed even darker than usual. He moved towards her, and for a crazy second

Estelle thought he was about to kiss her. It was as though they were the only people that existed, just the two of them, all alone, and—

They heard the noise at exactly the same time and quickly sprang apart. Chris thundered down the stairs, his feet pounding on the carpet. Then the door burst open and the moment was lost.

'Just getting drinks,' he called out, as he tore through the living room on his way to the kitchen. 'Hi, Mrs Humphreys,' he added, as an afterthought.

Neither Estelle nor Tony looked at each other, and the diversion gave Estelle chance to catch her breath. She began to worry that she'd imagined it all, or that Tony thought she was a stupid, desperate woman who'd been about to throw herself at him. She hoped she hadn't made a fool of herself.

Chris sped back through, carrying two glasses of orange squash. 'I'm whupping Joe's ass on FIFA,' he shouted gleefully. 'Wayne Rooney just did a sick bicycle kick!'

'Chris, language!' Tony called sharply, as Chris rushed out of the door. 'Sorry about that,' he apologised to Estelle.

'That's quite alright,' she said primly, folding her hands in her lap and focusing on them instead of looking at Tony. 'What were you saying before?'

'Before? Oh, yes, I was asking if you'd got the text with you,' he replied, equally business-like. 'You said you'd written up the website content on your laptop.'

'Oh, yes, I've got the sex here. I mean the text!' Estelle quickly corrected herself, her hand flying to her mouth at the Freudian slip. 'The text. Yes, it's on here,' she finished, burying her head as she pulled her laptop out of its bag and letting her hair fall across her face so Tony couldn't see how much she was blushing.

She busied herself with opening the laptop and turning it on, and when she finally turned to Tony, he was grinning at her. 'Have you found the er . . . text?'

'Yes, it's just here.'

'Great. Do you mind if I take a look?'

Tony took the laptop from her and quickly skimmed over what she'd written. 'Perfect,' he declared. 'I'll email it across to myself, then I can put it straight into the text boxes.'

He tapped on the Internet icon, clicked on a couple of menus, then a webpage flashed up and both of them froze.

The screen was suddenly filled with lingerie, sex toys and bondage wear.

Neither of them spoke. Neither of them knew what *to* say.

'I'm so embarrassed,' Estelle managed finally. Her cheeks were flaming, and all she wanted to do was run straight out of the front door and never see Tony again.

'Don't be,' Tony insisted. 'It's all my fault – I must have hit the wrong thing and brought up your history . . .'

'It was for research,' Estelle cut in quickly. 'For the book group. I told you we'd been discussing erotic novels,' she reminded him desperately. 'Lots of them refer to . . . this sort of thing,' she continued, her gaze landing on a pair of jiggle balls. 'So I was just finding out what it was all about. Broadening my education, I suppose you could say,' she finished, trying to laugh off the mortifying experience.

'Right.' Tony was nodding slowly, his face inscrutable. Estelle wished she knew what he was thinking. Did he see her as some sad, sex-crazed lunatic going through a midlife crisis? Was he offended by the website?

'So,' he began, his lips twitching in the beginnings of a smile. 'Did you buy anything? For research purposes, of course.'

'No!' Estelle insisted hotly, although that wasn't strictly the truth.

'So you're not wearing a pair of nipple tassels under there then?' he teased, nodding at her top.

Estelle shook her head, noticing the way his eyes lingered on her body. She felt her stomach start to squirm, excitement and adrenaline surging through her veins. It had been so long since a man had made her feel like this! She wished that she was braver, that she could make the first move and finally experience all of those things she'd been reading about.

Estelle gazed up at Tony, her breath coming fast, and saw that look in his eyes once again. No, she wasn't imagining it this time. It was really going to happen. He leaned in towards her and . . .

The living room door crashed open and Chris burst

through once again. Tony hastily slammed the laptop shut, as Chris sailed by, oblivious.

'We need snacks,' he informed them, returning from the kitchen with two bags of crisps and half a packet of biscuits.

Estelle bit her lip, unsure whether to be amused or frustrated that Chris was so successfully blocking her love life. Perhaps it was a sign, she thought to herself. Perhaps someone was trying to tell her that falling for Tony wasn't such a good idea. After all, he was her son's football coach, the father of one of Joe's good friends. Getting involved with him could be far too complicated.

No, better to keep things simple and professional, Estelle decided reluctantly, as she took the laptop back from Tony, avoiding his questioning gaze.

'Right, where were we?' she asked brightly, as she calmly closed down the offending page and retrieved the document she'd been working on, ignoring the way her heart was pounding. From now on, it was back to business.

21

'Oh darling, you look gorgeous!'

'Do I?' Gracie asked disbelievingly. She was wearing a leopard-print dress with a sweetheart neckline, and matching peep-toe heels. Her hair was styled half-up and half-down, pulled back with an oversized black bow. Nervously, she tugged at the hem of her dress, staring uncertainly at her mother.

'Of course you do. You'll blow his socks off,' Maggie assured her. A large, glamorous woman swathed in a multi-coloured kaftan, she was curled up on the sofa reading *Theodora* by Stella Duffy, but she put the book down when she saw the expression on Gracie's face. 'Are you okay, darling? Feeling a bit nervous?'

'I'm fine,' Gracie insisted. 'Besides, it's not really a date, as such. More of a meeting between friends.'

'Riiiight,' Maggie nodded sceptically. 'So where's he taking you, this . . . Reggie, is it?'

'Yes, Reggie. I'm not sure. He said it was going to be a surprise.'

'Let's hope it's a good one,' Maggie said wryly, taking a sip of the gin and tonic that sat on the low Moroccan table beside her. 'So is he the one from this book club of yours?'

'That's right,' Gracie confirmed, applying a final slick of fuchsia lipstick in the mirror above the fireplace, then dabbing her wrists with eau de cologne.

Maggie looked puzzled. 'I thought you didn't like him? I thought you said he was rude and pompous and didn't have a sexual bone in his body?'

Gracie flushed, as she remembered her words. 'Well, perhaps I judged him a little harshly at first.'

'That doesn't sound like you,' Maggie teased, thinking that forming instant, sweeping opinions sounded exactly like her daughter. Although, Maggie had to admit, that was largely her fault. She'd always encouraged Gracie to take a strong stance and hold firm to her beliefs.

'Well I hope for your sake he's better than some of those oddballs you've dated in the past.'

'Oh, here we go . . .' Gracie muttered under her breath.

'That last one – what was his name? Jackson?'

'Jason.'

'Yes, him. You found him wearing your underwear, didn't you?'

234

'Apparently he was going through an experimental phase . . .' Gracie reminded her, through pursed lips.

'And the one before that? I've forgotten his name now, there've been so many—'

'Not *that* many, Mum!'

'Well who was the one who was secretly married to that South American girl?'

'That was Christian, and it was only for the visa. Anyway, it was months ago.'

'How time flies,' Maggie sighed.

'Look, I'd really appreciate it if we could change the subject,' Gracie pleaded. She knew her relationship history wasn't the best, but moments before she set off on her date with Reggie didn't seem like the best time to trawl through it.

'And you think this one seems normal, do you?'

'Well, I don't know if I'd say normal . . .' Gracie confessed, thinking of Reggie's many idiosyncrasies. 'But he seems very sweet. Very . . . different.'

'So will you be wanting to bring him back here afterwards?' Maggie asked, her eyes twinkling. 'Should I make myself scarce?'

'Mother!' Gracie exclaimed.

'Well I don't know, do I?' Maggie retorted. 'Especially not with everything you've been reading recently. It might be giving you ideas. What are you on at the moment?'

Gracie hesitated, before admitting, '*Justine* by the Marquis de Sade.'

'Bloody hell! That's a bit extreme,' Maggie exclaimed. 'Don't go scaring the poor boy off.'

'Actually, it was his suggestion.'

'Really? Now you've completely changed my opinion of him. He'll be shackling you to the walls of his dungeon and wrecking your maidenhead if you're not careful.'

Gracie let out a sigh of exasperation. 'You see, this is exactly why I told Reggie I'd meet him there.'

'What on earth do you mean?' Maggie's face was a picture of innocence.

'You'll just embarrass me if he comes here!'

'That's what mothers are *for*, darling,' Maggie protested, as she stood up to give Gracie a kiss on the cheek. 'Have a fabulous time. And remember – if he does anything you don't want him to, apply a swift knee to the bollocks and run as fast as you can.'

'Thanks, Mum. Great advice as ever,' Gracie replied sarcastically. Then she checked her appearance for the final time, swung her black patent handbag over her shoulder, and walked out of the door.

Reggie was already waiting outside the pub when she arrived. He was wearing a smart jacket over a navy blue shirt, with skinny, dark grey cords. Gracie could tell that he'd made an effort, and she had to admit that he was looking pretty good. He could rock the geek-chic look very well when he chose to, she thought with a smile.

'I wasn't sure if you'd come,' Reggie admitted, looking relieved when he spotted her.

'Of course. Why wouldn't I?'

They eyed each other awkwardly, unsure whether to kiss or hug, before settling for a formal handshake. Then they both burst out laughing at their own ridiculousness, and Reggie leaned in to kiss her politely on the cheek.

'You look . . . amazing,' Reggie said genuinely, his eyes raking over her.

'Thank you,' Gracie said shyly, wondering why she was so nervous – it was only Reggie, for heaven's sake! 'You look good too.'

'Thanks,' Reggie replied. 'I thought I'd treat myself to a new pair of socks.'

'Oh,' Gracie frowned. 'Is that a joke?'

'Yes,' Reggie nodded seriously. 'Yes, it is.'

'Right, well, you might want to warn me if you're going to try that again – then I know when to laugh.'

'Fair enough,' Reggie agreed cheerfully.

'So should we head inside?' Gracie asked, motioning towards the pub.

'No,' Reggie replied firmly, shaking his head.

'No? Why not?'

'Because we're not going to the pub.'

'We're not?' Gracie questioned, wondering what on earth was going on.

'No. The pub was just a decoy.'

'So where *are* we going then?'

Reggie grinned, looking pretty pleased with himself. 'Follow me.'

He strode off quickly, and Gracie had to run to catch

up with him. 'You're not an axe murderer are you?' she asked, thinking that her mother's advice might come in handy after all.

'Not the last time I checked. That's a joke, by the way.'

'Thanks for letting me know – ha, ha, ha.'

She followed Reggie across the road, where he came to a sudden halt. 'Here we are,' he announced triumphantly.

'The cinema?' Gracie frowned, as she stared up at The Phoenix. 'Why all the secrecy? We could have just met here instead.'

Reggie took a step to the side, revealing the poster he'd been standing in front of. 'I thought we could go and see this.'

'Oh!' Gracie exclaimed, inhaling sharply. Her whole face lit up, her eyes sparkling as she looked up at Reggie and then back at the poster for *Some Like It Hot*. It showed Marilyn Monroe sandwiched between Jack Lemmon and Tony Curtis, giving a playful wink. 'How did you know?' she asked in delight.

'You mentioned that you liked it,' Reggie reminded her. 'When we were dancing at the Fifties Night. It turned out that the Phoenix were doing a special showing of it, so I thought—'

'Oh Reggie, it's perfect!' Gracie exclaimed happily, throwing her arms around him. 'It's probably my favourite film of all time, but I've never seen it on the big screen before.'

'Well now's your chance,' Reggie smiled, his cheeks

turning pink at Gracie's reaction. He could feel her body pressed against his, the softness of her breasts against his chest and her silky hair brushing his neck. 'Well . . . um . . . shall we?' he suggested, as Gracie untangled herself and they made their way into the cinema.

'I'll get this,' Gracie offered, as Reggie ordered a large tub of popcorn.

'No, it's fine,' he insisted.

Gracie narrowed her eyes. 'I don't want you coming over all male chauvinist on me, Reginald White,' she threatened. 'I'm perfectly capable of paying for my own popcorn.'

'I know you are,' Reggie replied mildly. 'But I'd like to get this. My treat. Don't worry,' he added, as he saw Gracie open her mouth to protest. 'You can pay next time.'

He walked off towards the screening room before she had time to register what he'd just said. Then the penny dropped and Gracie broke into a wide smile, shyly taking his hand as they sat together in the darkness.

'Oh, that was just brilliant,' Gracie sighed happily, as they emerged two hours later, from the wackiness of 1920s Chicago to the reality of the twenty-first-century Bristol suburbs. 'Wasn't she just beautiful, and funny, and . . . well, perfect?'

Like you, Reggie longed to reply, but he stopped himself from saying anything too cheesy and simply nodded in agreement. He looked over at Gracie's glowing face and thought how rare it was to see her so unguarded. She was showing the same vulnerability he'd seen on stage when she was singing, and it was such a change from her usual feisty, bolshie attitude. Not that Reggie minded when she was like that – he enjoyed the challenge, the way she knew how to push his buttons – but it was nice to see her relaxed, and not immediately shooting down everything he said.

'So, what shall we do now?' Gracie asked dreamily, as she linked her arm through Reggie's and thought how sweet he was. He'd made such an effort, planning a wonderful surprise like that; there were few guys who would be so thoughtful. She remembered what her mother had said earlier, reminding Gracie of how she'd accused him of being pompous and arrogant, and felt increasingly guilty. But it was true what she'd said about him being a nice guy, and the more Gracie got to know him, the more she liked him. And she was starting to like him a lot.

'We could head to the pub, if you like?' Reggie suggested. 'Back to where we started.'

'Do you like pubs?' Gracie asked curiously, as people spilled out of the cinema and onto the pavement around them. She crushed the empty popcorn container she was carrying and put it in the bin.

'Um . . .' Reggie stalled. 'Sometimes. I'm not really into those packed chain bars like you get in town, the ones full of noisy undergrads downing cheap shots.'

'So you prefer old men's pubs?' Gracie giggled.

'I suppose you could say that,' Reggie agreed, good-naturedly. 'I think I'm an old soul at heart.'

'I know what you mean. I sometimes think I was born in the wrong decade. I love everything about the Fifties – the music, the films, the style of dress . . .'

'But not the Women's rights, I expect,' Reggie couldn't resist adding. 'I can't see you being a stay-at-home housewife.'

'Oh, I wouldn't have been! I'd have been out there, blazing a trail . . . Well, I hope I would anyway,' Gracie admitted. 'So, where should we go?'

'I don't mind. As long as it's not somewhere trendy and mass-market. That's not really my scene.'

'Don't worry,' grinned Gracie. 'I know somewhere much cooler.'

'What *is* this place?' Reggie asked incredulously, as he stepped inside. 'I've never even noticed it before.'

'See? You're not the only one who can do surprises,' Gracie beamed. 'Hi Betty,' she called to the woman behind the counter. 'Two large strawberry milkshakes please,' she requested, before leading Reggie over to a red faux-leather seated booth.

They were in a mock 1950s American diner, complete with an old-fashioned jukebox playing in the corner and dazzling neon signs above the long, stainless steel counter. The floor was tiled in black and white check, and the walls were decorated with iconic images of all-American heroes: James Dean astride his motorcycle; Elvis Presley

241

in his rhinestone-encrusted jumpsuit; Marilyn Monroe on the set of *The Seven Year Itch*, her famous white dress billowing around her.

'I'm paying for these,' Gracie insisted, as Betty brought over their enormous milkshakes served in giant metal shakers.

'I wouldn't dream of disagreeing.'

'Good. Especially as you're just a poor student, and I'm a working woman.'

'Well, I can't argue with that,' Reggie smiled, as he leaned forward to take a sip of milkshake through the oversized straw. 'Mmm, this is good!'

'I told you! I meant to suggest to Estelle that she should start doing milkshakes. I think they'd go down a storm.'

'Speaking of Estelle, how are you getting on with the book club read?'

Gracie looked straight at Reggie and raised an eyebrow. 'Reginald White, you're a dark horse, aren't you?'

'What do you mean?'

'Pretending to be all quiet and innocent then casually suggesting that we read the Marquis de Sade. It's absolutely filthy – by far the most outrageous thing we've read.'

'It's a classic piece of literature,' Reggie said in a serious tone, pretending to be offended.

'Oh, that's your excuse is it? So *Justine*'s acceptable, but *Ten Sweet Lessons* is just some mass-market piece of fluff for bored housewives?'

Reggie smiled. 'I never thought I'd see the day when you were defending *Ten Sweet Lessons*.'

'I'm not!' Gracie retorted. 'Just playing devil's advocate. But since you asked, I'm finding *Justine* . . .' She took a long slurp of milkshake as she thought about the right description. 'Disturbing. But absorbing. And educational.'

'*Educational*?'

'You know what I mean!' Gracie blushed, almost wishing they'd gone to the pub so at least she could cover up her nerves with alcohol. Everyone always thought she was so confident, but she was actually quite shy – she covered it up with strong opinions and bluster. 'So is all of this helpful for your thesis?' she changed the subject. 'How are you getting on with it?'

Reggie pulled a face. 'Okay, I suppose.'

'What, are the ladies of the Cafe Crumb book group not giving you what you want?'

Reggie smirked. 'You might want to rephrase that, Miss Bird.'

Gracie blushed, as she realised what he was implying, surprised at Reggie making a joke like that. Perhaps he was becoming more confident than she'd realised. 'I just meant—'

'I know what you meant,' Reggie smiled. 'The book club's been great, actually. I've enjoyed it much more than I expected to. In fact, the notes I have from there are by far the most interesting part of my thesis. The rest of it seems a little dry, to be honest.'

'What's it about, again?'

'*The Cohesive Power of Literature in Communities*

243

throughout the Bristol and Avon area from the Middle Ages to the Present Day.'

'Right . . .' Gracie said thoughtfully. 'And you're wondering why it's a bit dry?'

'Perhaps I was being somewhat pretentious when I chose the title,' he admitted, as they both began to laugh.

'I must admit, I was amazed that you kept coming back to the book group,' Gracie confessed. 'I was talking to the others not long after we all started, and we didn't think you'd stick it out.'

'I surprised myself, really,' Reggie acknowledged, looking straight at Gracie. 'Perhaps there was something that kept bringing me back.'

His eyes were soft, and Gracie couldn't help but smile at the comment. 'And what might that be?'

Reggie shrugged. 'Estelle's cakes. They're amazing,' he deadpanned, as Gracie threw her straw at him. 'Hey, watch the jacket! It's new.'

'New? Don't tell me you bought it 'specially for tonight?'

'I might have,' Reggie admitted. 'You always look so good that I thought I'd better make an effort.'

'Do you think so?' Gracie asked in surprise.

'Yeah, you always look great,' Reggie insisted. 'It's a very cool style.'

'Thank you,' Gracie replied. 'Not everyone *gets* it.'

'I know what you mean. Not everyone *gets* me either.'

'Never mind. We'll never be fashionable, and there's no point in trying.'

'Geeks forever,' Reggie grinned. Purely instinctively, he reached across the table and put his hand over hers.

Gracie looked at it for a moment, unsure how to react. Her eyes widened, and she realised she was holding her breath. 'Geeks forever,' she whispered back shyly, smiling at him. She moved her hand out from underneath Reggie's, then laced her fingers through his, enjoying the feel of his skin against hers.

'Now that's much more equal,' Reggie commented, as he squeezed her fingers gently. 'I forgot you don't like to be dominated.'

'I don't know if I'd say that,' Gracie said flirtatiously. 'There are quite a few things I've read about recently that I might be interested in trying . . .'

She let the comment hang, waiting for the full force of it to impact on Reggie. He coughed loudly, almost choking on his milkshake.

'Why don't you tell me all about them,' he murmured once he'd recovered, 'and I'll see what I can do . . .'

22

'George,' Sue hissed, digging her husband in the ribs.

It was a Tuesday morning and they were lying in bed. The sun was streaming in through the curtains, lighting up the room, but George simply mumbled something incoherent and rolled over so that his back was to his wife.

Sue could feel her blood pressure rising already. She glanced over to look at the radio alarm on the bedside table and saw that it was already 9.12 a.m. This was ridiculous! It would be almost lunchtime before they made it out of the house.

'George!' Sue demanded, shaking him roughly.

Blearily, George looked round at her, squinting as he opened his eyes. 'Whassamatter?' he muttered drowsily. His face was lined with sleep, and tufts of grey hair were sticking out of his head at all angles.

Sue, however, didn't find this sweet or endearing as she once might have done. In fact, this morning it annoyed her more than ever.

'We have to get up *now*, George,' she insisted. 'Otherwise we won't get to Stourhead before midday.'

George contemplated this for a moment, before finally proclaiming, 'Let's go tomorrow, shall we? I feel like a lie-in this morning . . .' And with that, he rolled over once again and began to snore gently.

Sue stared at him for a moment, her mouth hanging open in disbelief. Then she threw back the duvet and leapt out of bed, stomping through to the bathroom. Driven by a fury, she raced through her morning routine in record time, and was ready to leave the house half an hour later. She was moving on autopilot, unaware of what she was doing; all Sue knew was that she couldn't bear to be in that house with that man for another second.

Snatching up her handbag, Sue slammed the front door with a huge sense of satisfaction and set off walking. She had no idea where she was going – she simply wanted to get as far away from George as she could, and blow off a little steam with some strenuous physical exertion.

She'd so been looking forward to her day out. They'd planned to go to Stourhead in Wiltshire, a stately home set in world-famous landscaped grounds. The weather looked set to be beautiful, and they could have strolled through the gardens, had lunch in the cafe, perhaps taken a boat trip on the lake . . .

Sue had researched it all on the Internet and planned their trip meticulously – even right down to the outfit she was going to wear. George had agreed to it all last week, and now he couldn't even be bothered to get out of bed, she thought, as she marched along furiously, her feet pounding the pavement.

Almost before she realised where she was going, Sue found herself outside Cafe Crumb. She stopped walking, staring forlornly through the window at the delicious-looking cakes on display. Her stomach rumbled hungrily. In her haste to leave, she hadn't eaten breakfast. And why shouldn't she treat herself now that her day had been spoilt? Besides, she could really use a friendly face right now.

Sue pushed open the door and heard the familiar jangle of the bell, lining up at the counter where Estelle was busy serving. It felt odd to be in Cafe Crumb when there were other people there, Sue reflected. She had got used to it belonging to just the book group, and now it felt as though everyone else was intruding on *her* cafe.

'Sue!' Estelle exclaimed, looking surprised and pleased all at the same time. 'What are you doing here?'

'I was just in the neighbourhood and thought I'd pop in,' Sue said casually, not quite ready to reveal the details of her argument with George just yet.

'What a wonderful surprise!' Estelle beamed. She looked more closely at Sue, sensing that something was wrong; her friend looked angry and drawn, a far cry from her usual immaculately presented self. 'Is everything okay?' Estelle asked in concern.

Sue let out a heavy sigh. 'Oh, it's nothing really. Just that George and I are arguing again, and I really couldn't stand to be around him any longer. Could I order something to eat? I left the house in rather a hurry . . .'

'Of course,' Estelle nodded in understanding. 'What can I get you?'

'I'll have a toasted teacake and a large coffee, please.'

'Coming right up. Take a seat and I'll bring it over.'

Estelle was as good as her word, heading across a few minutes later with a steaming mug of coffee and a thickly buttered teacake, bursting with juicy pieces of fruit. 'Now tell me all about it,' she insisted, sitting down opposite Sue.

'Oh, I don't want to bother you if you're busy . . .'

'Nonsense,' Estelle insisted, glancing round at the largely empty cafe. There was an old man by the window nursing a cup of tea, and a young girl who looked like a student tucking into a hearty breakfast while typing on her laptop. 'It won't pick up until lunchtime.'

'Well, if you're sure,' Sue said hesitantly.

'Of course! A problem shared is a problem halved, and all that.'

'I only wish it were that simple,' Sue began sadly, as she sipped her coffee.

With a little prompting from Estelle, she soon spilled the details of everything that was troubling her. The way that George never wanted to do anything; her fears that they no longer had anything in common; her growing unhappiness with her marriage; and her grown-up children's insistence that she was going through some kind of later-life crisis.

'I just don't know what to do,' she concluded unhappily. 'What do you think?'

'It's hard to say,' Estelle replied diplomatically. 'You need to consider what's best for you, of course. But if you think there's a chance to work it out with George, you should try. You can't throw away forty years of marriage like that.'

'I *am* trying,' Sue insisted. 'It's almost like he doesn't want to, as though he can't actually see that there's a problem.' She looked anxiously round the little cafe, and lowered her voice. 'I hope you don't mind me telling you this, but I'm getting increasingly frustrated with our sex life – or lack thereof. I blame *you* for that,' she joked.

'Me?'

'Yes. Since I've been coming here and reading all these books, I've looked at sex in a completely different light. I don't know what it was like with you and your ex-husband – you're younger than me, so perhaps you had more idea – but for me, sex was almost entirely . . . functional,' she finished, finally finding the right word. 'You know – we did it so we could have children, and to keep George happy of course, but I never really felt I was getting much out of it. And now I know there are all these amazing experiences I could have had . . .' Sue trailed off. 'Do you know, I envy you, Estelle.'

'Me?' Estelle repeated, astonished. 'Why?'

'Look at you – you're a single woman in the prime of life. You've got all these possibilities open to you. You can go on as many dates as you please, and meet handsome, charming, interesting men . . .'

'Believe me, there aren't many Alexander Blacks out there,' Estelle insisted.

But Sue wouldn't be put off. 'You're an independent woman, running your own business. Every day you're busy, you have somewhere to go, things to do . . . Your life has a purpose.'

'It's really not like that,' Estelle protested, shocked that anyone would be jealous of her life. 'It's hard work, and I'm on the go non-stop. I constantly feel guilty that I don't spend enough time with Joe, but I feel like I have to work all the hours I can to relieve the financial pressure. I'm just a middle-aged divorcee, struggling to keep my business going – I really don't see anything to envy there!'

'Sorry,' Sue apologised. 'I didn't mean to trivialise things – I know that everyone has their own problems. I suppose it's a case of the grass always looking greener . . .'

'I think you need to speak to George about how you're feeling,' Estelle advised. '*Properly* speak to him. You seemed to be getting on okay at the Fifties Night.'

'Yes, that was a good night,' Sue admitted, 'but it's gone downhill from there. The other night,' she began, lowering her voice conspiratorially, 'I started looking at holidays on the Internet. Not just a week in Spain, but amazing, once-in-a-lifetime trips. There are so many

251

things I want to do! Climb Machu Picchu in Peru; take the Trans-Siberian railways across Russia; go on safari in Tanzania; or a round-the-world cruise. Can you imagine it?'

'They all sound wonderful,' Estelle said truthfully. It certainly beat slaving over a hot oven in Bristol.

'I want to go on one,' Sue confessed, her eyes sparkling with excitement. 'With or without George. Life's too short – you have to seize the day, Estelle! This is the cruise I was looking at,' she explained, pulling a crumpled sheet of paper out of her bag. 'I printed it out. You start off in Los Angeles – Hollywood! I've only ever been to America once, and that was when we took the kids to Disneyworld. But that's just the beginning. From there, you sail across the Pacific to Tahiti, then on to Australia and the Far East . . .'

Her hands were flying, her face animated, as she breathlessly described the ship's route. Estelle listened happily, enjoying the sound of the exotic locations Sue conjured up. Then the door clanged, and an elderly couple came in, shuffling up to the counter.

'I'm sorry,' Estelle apologised. 'I'll have to go and serve.'

'No problem,' Sue said easily.

Estelle quickly prepared the couple's lunch order and came to sit down again, but no sooner had Sue begun speaking (she'd made it as far as Egypt in her proposed itinerary) than the bell clanged again. This time, a harassed-looking mother with three young children came through the door. It took Estelle longer to serve them, and by the time she'd finished, more people had joined the queue.

Sue idly glanced round then looked at her watch, shocked to find it was almost midday – they'd been chatting away for well over an hour! This must be the lunchtime rush, she realised, as she watched Estelle for a few moments. She was moving swiftly behind the counter, focused and organised, yet still taking the time to be pleasant to everyone. The queue was growing, and Estelle began to look increasingly stressed as she dashed out to deliver orders to those seated at tables.

Sue became aware of a commotion behind her, and heard Estelle apologising profusely. She'd clearly taken over the wrong order, and hurried back to get the correct one. A rotund gentleman waiting at the counter let out a heavy sigh, rolling his eyes at those in the queue behind him.

Outraged on Estelle's behalf, and feeling sorry for her friend, Sue snatched up her bag and walked behind the counter to where Estelle was heaping salad on the side of two plates of cheese toasties.

'Where are these going?' Sue asked, stashing her bag underneath the till and snatching up the plates.

Estelle looked startled, but smiled gratefully at Sue. 'Table twelve – that's the one over there, with the two gentlemen. And thank you.'

'No problem,' Sue grinned, carrying the plates across and clearing the empty mugs. 'Can I get you another drink?' she asked the customers politely.

'We'll take two more teas, please,' the younger of the two men smiled at her.

Sue walked smoothly back over to where Estelle was slicing into a baguette. 'Two more teas for table twelve,' she called. Estelle turned to her, a look of panic on her face. 'Don't worry, I can do them,' Sue assured her.

'Could you?' Estelle asked gratefully. 'The teabags are—'

'Just here,' Sue interrupted, taking clean mugs down from the shelf and picking two teabags out of the Tupperware container that held them. 'And the sugar's in this pot, and the milk's in the fridge down here. Don't worry, I've seen you do it enough times at the book group.'

Humming to herself as she moved through the cafe, Sue delivered the teas and returned to the counter. 'What's next?' she asked Estelle brightly.

'Oh, don't be silly, you go and sit down,' Estelle insisted, as she attempted to froth the milk for a cappuccino and butter a roll at the same time.

'Nonsense. I'm quite happy to give you a hand. Just let me know what needs to be done.'

Estelle hesitated, but when she saw the restless queue now stretching out of the door, she smiled in defeat. 'You'd better put this on,' she advised, passing an apron to Sue, who was wearing light grey trousers and a pale pink shirt.

'Would you mind wiping down any empty tables?' Estelle asked guiltily, as she passed Sue a J-cloth and a bottle of D10 spray. Sue didn't look like the sort of woman who was familiar with scrubbing tables, but seeing as she'd offered . . . 'And when that's done, these jacket potatoes will be ready to take out.'

'No problem,' Sue said brightly, picking up the cleaning spray as though it was a weapon and heading out to do battle.

For the next two hours, the women worked solidly. Estelle served customers and prepared the food, while Sue made the drinks and fetched and carried.

By mid-afternoon, Cafe Crumb was finally starting to quieten down, with only a handful of tables still occupied. Sue wiped down all the empty surfaces, while Estelle hurriedly tidied up behind the counter, getting everything in order for the late-afternoon rush. She knew that once the schools closed, the cafe would be flooded with mothers bringing primary-school children in for an afternoon treat, while high-school kids, who bought a can of Coke and made it last as long as possible, giggled and whispered and obsessed over their mobile phones.

'All done,' Sue smiled, returning to the counter and taking off her apron.

'Oh Sue, I can't thank you enough,' Estelle said genuinely. 'I'm ever so grateful. It's been getting so busy at lunchtimes recently.'

'That's good news for you,' Sue noted. 'And don't worry about me – I enjoyed it!'

'You don't have to go that far,' Estelle laughed.

'No, I mean it,' Sue insisted. 'It was nice to keep

busy for once, and I enjoyed chatting to all of the customers.'

'You've completely missed your lunch – you must be starving,' Estelle realised. 'Let me get you something to say thank you.'

'You don't have to do that,' Sue waved her away.

'No, I insist.'

'Well . . . a ham sandwich wouldn't go amiss. I am rather peckish,' Sue admitted.

'Good choice. I'll have the same. I don't know how I'd have managed without you today,' Estelle confessed, as she began preparing their food.

'Not a problem. Like I said, I enjoyed it.' Sue watched as Estelle filled two baguettes, then deftly sliced them across the middle. They each picked up a plate and sat down at an empty table, neither of them speaking as they savoured the delicious food.

'I think I've worked up an appetite,' Sue joked. 'I'd forgotten how hungry working for a living can make you.'

'I know,' Estelle agreed. 'It can be dangerous in here as there's so much temptation, but I'm usually so busy I rarely get time to eat. I just grab something when I can.'

'And there's just you working here, every day?'

'We're closed on Sundays,' Estelle explained, 'but other than that, yes, it's just me. I have a couple of people who help me out from time to time – if I need a few days off, or if I'm ill. But to be honest, I can't afford to pay an assistant at the moment.'

'Then let me help out!' Sue said suddenly.

Estelle looked at her in confusion. 'What do you mean?'

'Exactly what I said! I'd be more than happy to come in a few lunchtimes a week, if that's when you're busiest. It doesn't have to be every day,' she added quickly, as she saw Estelle's face fall. 'I might actually be able to persuade George to get out and about some days. But I'd be more than happy to do two or three days a week. If you want me, that is . . .' she finished doubtfully.

'It's very nice of you to offer,' Estelle began awkwardly, 'but as I said, I really can't afford to pay someone – not even for a few hours.'

'You wouldn't have to pay me,' Sue insisted. 'I'd be happy to do it.'

'I'm not a charity case,' Estelle said, rather stiffly.

'You might not be, but I am,' Sue joked. 'I've been going stir-crazy, stuck in that house every day. I can't tell you what a tonic it's been to get out today and see some new faces – I actually felt useful for the first time since I retired. And if you throw the odd bit of cake my way, I'd be more than happy.'

'You're serious, aren't you?' Estelle said, scrutinising Sue's face.

'Absolutely! Why not? As far as I can see, it's win-win for both of us. If you'd prefer, we could start on a trial basis and see how it goes.'

Estelle stared at her for a moment, hardly able to

believe that Sue meant what she was saying. For Estelle, it was the answer to her prayers. 'Alright then,' she said finally, breaking into a wide grin as she clinked her coffee cup against Sue's. 'It's a deal!'

23

Andy Smith lay spread-eagled on the bed. He was stark naked, face down on the duvet, while his wrists were encircled by pink, furry handcuffs and chained to the headboard. A blindfold over his eyes meant that he couldn't see a thing, and the lights in the room were dimmed, tealights flickering on the chest of drawers in the corner.

'Have you been a bad boy?' demanded Rebecca. She was prowling round the room in six-inch heels, fully trussed up in a black peephole bra with matching panties, and fishnet stockings held up by a lacy suspender belt.

Andy lifted his head with difficulty, and managed to call out, 'Yes!'

'Yes, what?'

'Yes, mistress!'

'Hmm . . .' Rebecca continued to stalk alongside the

bed, although the stripper shoes she was wearing were proving more difficult than she'd anticipated. The heels kept getting caught in the fluffy carpet, and the muscles in her calves were aching already. It was all she could do to stop herself falling over.

'Then you need to be punished,' she continued gamely, as she picked up a PVC paddle from the bedside table and slapped it down on her palm with a loud thwack. Andy jumped at the noise, his white bottom clenching in anticipation.

'Naughty!' Rebecca cried out, as she brought the paddle down on the underside of his cheeks.

Andy flinched, but didn't make a noise, so Rebecca tried again, harder this time. 'Bad! Boy!' she exclaimed, with each hit.

The final time, Andy let out a cry and Rebecca panicked.

'Are you okay?' she asked worriedly, breaking out of character and coming to sit beside him.

'Fine, thanks,' he replied cheerily.

'And you remember the safe word?'

'Monkey,' he confirmed.

'Monkey,' Rebecca repeated sternly. 'Okay, let's carry on.' She stood up, taking a moment to regain her balance, before circling the bedroom once more. 'What am I going to do with you?' she purred, her voice low and sexy. 'I've got a bad boy who needs to be punished, haven't I?'

'Yes, mistress!' Andy replied, and received a spank on the bottom in return.

'Yes,' Rebecca repeated, beginning to feel just the tiniest bit silly. 'What am I going to do with you?' she asked again, but this time the question was genuine, as she was starting to run out of ideas. 'Do you want it harder?'

'Um . . . okay then,' Andy replied uncertainly, as Rebecca took another swing with the spanking paddle and saw a red mark appear on the soft skin of his bottom.

'Does it hurt?' she asked in concern.

'Yes, mistress,' Andy told her, thinking this was all part of the game.

'No, Andy, I'm being serious. Is it hurting?'

'A bit,' he admitted. 'But I haven't said "monkey" yet.'

'Oh. Okay then. Do you want to carry on?'

'Up to you,' Andy replied, as easy-going as ever and eager to please his wife. It was Rebecca who had suggested trying out some light BDSM, inspired by all those erotic books she'd been reading.

'Are you getting turned on?' she asked anxiously. 'I feel a bit ridiculous to be honest.'

'It *is* kind of exciting,' Andy admitted. 'For a change. I wouldn't want to do this every day though. And if you're not comfortable then we can stop. All you have to do is say "monkey",' he grinned.

'Maybe I'm not cut out to be the dominant one,' Rebecca sighed. 'Maybe I'm more Christina Cox than Alexander Black.'

'Who?' Andy asked in confusion. 'They're not neighbours of ours are they?'

'No,' Rebecca smiled. 'They're characters. From *Ten Sweet Lessons*.'

'Of course,' Andy nodded, recognising the names that seemed to be everywhere at the moment. 'You had me worried for a second there. I thought you were suggesting swinging.'

'Are you interested in that?' Rebecca asked, her face creasing into a frown.

'No,' Andy replied firmly. 'I wouldn't want to share my beautiful wife with anyone.' Rebecca smiled, happy with his response.

'You know,' Andy began, 'I'd probably feel a lot more comfortable having this conversation if I could actually *see* what was going on.'

'Oh, yes of course,' Rebecca agreed, hastily pulling the blindfold up onto Andy's forehead. He squinted as his eyes adjusted to the dim light, blinking rapidly. Then he craned his neck and looked over his shoulder at Rebecca.

'You look amazing, by the way. Incredibly sexy. I can't wait to get my hands on you.'

'Would you like me to untie you?' Rebecca offered.

'Go on then,' Andy agreed, as Rebecca got the keys off the dressing table and unlocked the cuffs.

Andy sat up and turned over, wincing as his bottom hit the bed. 'I'm not going to be able to sit down properly for a week,' he joked. 'What am I going to tell the guys at work?'

'Just tell them you sustained an injury during a sex

game with your gorgeous wife,' Rebecca dead panned. 'See what they say to that.'

'They'll all be insanely jealous of me,' he insisted, running his eyes over her body. There was a subtle change in the atmosphere of the room. Rebecca saw the way he was looking at her, the desire flaming in his eyes the way it used to when they were first together.

He was standing to attention, clearly excited, and Rebecca felt a clutching sensation in her belly, warm waves spreading through her stomach and moving down to her groin.

'Come here,' Andy said gently, taking her by the hand and pulling her down onto the bed beside him where he began to kiss her – softly at first, but quickly becoming more passionate, their tongues exploring each other's mouths as though discovering one another for the first time. And it *was* a rediscovery, Rebecca realised. It had been so rare over the past year for Andy to kiss her like this – with real wanting and passion, rather than just perfunctorily.

Her whole body was tingling with excitement as Andy climbed on top of her, pinning her down with the weight of his body. Rebecca felt thoroughly out of control and she loved it, wondering what Andy was going to do next.

He began to kiss her neck, licking and sucking as he moved up to her earlobe. Then he put his lips to her ear and whispered, 'Would you like me to handcuff you?'

Rebecca looked at him, her eyes dancing. She felt nervous and excited, but trusted Andy completely. 'Yes,' she agreed softly as she lay back, raising her arms in a Y shape and feeling the cool metal and soft feathers clamp around her wrists before clicking into place.

She stared up at her husband, slowly taking in every inch of him. She saw all the things she'd loved about him when they'd first got together, and all the things that had changed too. Like her, he'd put on a few pounds and developed a cute little belly, while his arms had lost their muscle tone now that he no longer went to the gym. His thighs were still bulky and strong, and a tangle of blonde hair began at his belly button and led the way downwards . . .

Rebecca gazed into Andy's bright blue eyes, then her vision went blank as he gently slipped the blindfold over her head.

For a moment nothing happened and Rebecca giggled nervously. She could feel Andy beside her and hear his breathing, but he didn't move.

Then he spoke, his breath hot against her skin. 'Everything okay?'

'Mmm-hmm,' she murmured.

'You don't want to say "monkey"?'

'No,' she replied emphatically, still laughing.

'Good.'

She felt the mattress move as Andy shifted his body weight, moving down to the bottom of the bed where he unhooked her suspenders and slowly rolled them down her legs, his hands lightly brushing her skin.

Rebecca's breath caught in the back of her throat as

he softly kissed her feet, nibbling gently before taking the whole of her big toe in his mouth and sucking hard. Rebecca gasped. It felt exquisite, lying in the darkness with no idea what was coming next, a slave to the sensations running through her body.

It was as though losing her sight meant that all of Rebecca's other senses had become heightened. She could smell the musky, wanton scent of her own body, could hear her own breathing coming fast, as Andy's mouth moved over her body, covering the inside of her thighs with little butterfly kisses.

'Do you like that?' he questioned.

But Rebecca could only moan in reply. For Andy, it was all the answer he needed.

Gently, he rolled her over, so that her arms were crossed but her bottom was exposed as he delicately peeled down the skimpy knickers she was wearing. Picking up the paddle and slapping it against his hand, he heard Rebecca inhale sharply.

'What are you going to do?' she asked, breathless with delight.

Andy grinned. 'Oh darling, don't worry. I'm going to do things to you that are amazing, incredible, mind-blowing and—'

24

'Vile!'

'Depraved!'

'Pure filth!' finished Sue, looking suitably disgusted as she regarded her copy of *Justine* by the Marquis de Sade.

'So nobody liked my book choice then?' Reggie asked cheekily. He was sitting across the table from Gracie, and the two of them were studiously ignoring each other, having decided not to tell the rest of the group about their date. In fact, their behaviour made it all the more obvious that something was going on between them, and pointed looks had been flying between Estelle, Sue and Rebecca from the moment they arrived.

'Well I must say, I was shocked,' Estelle declared, sipping her tea. 'I always thought you were such a nice young man, Reggie.'

'Hey, I didn't write it,' he protested, holding his hands

up in defence. 'Besides, with the Marquis de Sade, you have a pretty good idea of what you're getting.'

'Violence, rape, sodomy, masochism . . .' Gracie listed airily.

'Do you know that's where the word "sadism" comes from?' Reggie interjected helpfully. 'From the Marquis de Sade.'

'How lovely,' Sue said primly. 'You learn something new every day.'

This time, Reggie looked suitably downcast. 'Sorry everyone,' he apologised. 'Maybe it wasn't the best book to choose.'

'No, don't apologise,' Estelle leapt to his defence. 'I can understand why you picked it. And let's face it, the whole point of a book group is supposed to be to discover new material and share your views with others – whether you liked it or not.'

'Well I couldn't finish it,' Sue said, folding her hands tightly in front of her. 'I'm sorry – I know it goes against the spirit of the club, but it honestly made me feel sick to my stomach. It was just . . . gruesome violence,' she finished, unable to think of any other words to describe how disgusting she'd found it. 'Over and over again, each situation more ghastly than the last. How anyone could find that erotic – well, they'd need locking up.'

'Is it *supposed* to be erotic, Reggie?' Rebecca asked doubtfully.

'I think it was written more to shock than to titillate,' Reggie said thoughtfully. 'Sade used his writing as a

267

vehicle for his opinions on religion, philosophy and polit-ics. If you can manage to overcome some of the really quite obscene scenarios, his work is fascinating. In many ways, he was a genius.'

'And in many ways, he was a nutter,' Gracie quipped which made everyone laugh. 'A sick, twisted, misogynist who had to be locked up for his perversions.'

Reggie turned to her, his eyes twinkling. 'Well, let's agree to disagree. I'm sure we'll be able to find something else that we both enjoy.'

Gracie let out a naughty giggle, then flushed bright red as she realised the others were watching them.

'Anything you want to tell us, guys?' Rebecca asked pleasantly, raising an eyebrow.

Reggie's face was the picture of innocence. 'No, nothing. What did *you* think of *Justine*, Estelle?' he asked sweetly, changing the subject.

Estelle hesitated, choosing her words carefully. 'Generally, I don't think anything should be banned or censored, but I did find *Justine* very, very disturbing. I think reading it was a worthwhile exercise, but I shan't be picking up anymore of Mr Sade's novels. That was quite enough for me, thank you.'

'Hear, hear,' Sue chimed in.

'Back to *Ten Sweet Lessons*, and the delectable Alexander Black, is it ladies?' Rebecca grinned.

'Yes please,' Sue nodded, which raised a chuckle amongst the others. 'I don't consider myself to be a prude, or uptight when it comes to sex, but this really was very distasteful. In fact, it worries me that the human mind can dream up such scenarios. Compared to *Justine*, *Ten Sweet Lessons* is ridiculously tame.'

'But *Ten Sweet Lessons* is a fantasy for bored house-wives – no offence,' Gracie added quickly, as she saw the expression on the other women's faces. 'But it's a safe way to escape the reality of everyday life. Even though you might think you're reading some shocking material, it's nothing when compared with what else is out there.'

'In a way, the two books use many of the same scenarios,' Reggie pointed out. 'There's bondage, the idea of punishment and pain, and you have the virginal young girl manipulated by a powerful older man. The difference is, that in *Justine*, these situations are taken to the extreme and portrayed very cruelly.'

'Well it made me feel grubby. And not in a good way,' Rebecca declared, which made the others smile.

The conversation seemed to be drawing to a close already, and Estelle sensed that none of them were keen to discuss *Justine* in any depth. It was certainly a far cry from the light-hearted, fun reads they were used to, and it just didn't generate the same excitement amongst the women as, say, the image of Oliver Mellors shirtless and chopping wood, or Rupert Campbell-Black photo-graphing a naked stable girl before having his wicked way with her against a tree.

'Going slightly off topic,' she began, trying to move the meeting on as the others looked at her with interest. 'How have you all been finding this kind of material? I know *Justine* is . . . somewhat out of the ordinary for us, but how about everything else? We did say that this genre might only be temporary, so are you happy to keep on with the erotica reads, or would you prefer something different?'

There was a moment of silence as everyone considered their replies. Finally, Rebecca spoke up. 'I'm really enjoying it, actually,' she admitted. 'I never dreamt that this was what we'd be reading when I first joined the club, but I'm so glad we are. I bet this has really messed up your research, hey Reggie?'

'Not at all,' he disagreed. 'It's been very . . . rewarding,' he finished, sneaking a glance in Gracie's direction.

Gracie smiled, and began speaking quickly to cover it up. 'As you all know, I was quite against it at first, but it's shown me that there are other opinions and other ways of thinking out there. I suppose you could say it's opened my mind.'

'I completely agree,' Rebecca jumped in. 'I'm definitely open to new ideas, and willing to experiment . . .' she trailed off, realising that she'd given away a little too much information.

'Chance would be a fine thing,' Sue said archly. 'Without going into too much detail – I know none of you want to hear that,' she chuckled. 'It's made me realise how unfulfilled I've been all these years. I'd basically given up on *that* side of my life, assuming that at my age it was all done and dusted. But I don't see why it should have to be.'

'Good for you, Sue,' Gracie spoke up. 'I'm all for women going out there and getting what they want,' she said passionately, unable to resist locking eyes with Reggie for a second.

'Amen to that,' he murmured under his breath.

'Sorry?' Estelle turned to him.

'Just clearing my throat,' he said with an innocent smile, as his foot found Gracie's under the table. She slipped off her shoe, sliding her toes beneath Reggie's trouser leg and stroking the bare skin of his ankle.

'I was going to say,' Estelle continued, 'that I know exactly what you mean, Sue. Rebecca, do you remember at one of the earlier sessions, you said that I shouldn't neglect the sexual side of my life?'

Rebecca nodded, looking at her with interest.

'Well let's just say that I understand what you meant by that, and I'm taking action to remedy the situation.'

'Really?' Rebecca looked impressed. 'Do you want to give us the gory details?'

'No, not yet,' Estelle demurred, feeling her cheeks turn pink.

'Go on,' Sue encouraged. 'It'll give hope to the rest of us.'

Estelle shook her head, keen to change the subject. 'So as we're happy – positively ecstatic in fact – with the erotica titles, we'll carry on with those. Who'd like to pick a book for the next session?'

'Neither Rebecca or Gracie have chosen yet,' Sue pointed out, 'so it should be one of them.'

'Good point. Ladies?' Estelle asked, looking at them expectantly.

'Well, I did have one idea,' Rebecca began. 'Although Gracie, if you'd rather—'

'No, go ahead,' Gracie insisted.

'How about *Lace*?' Rebecca suggested, as she sat forward in excitement, her eyes sparkling. 'By Shirley Conran. It was a massive eighties blockbuster – or bonk-buster,' she giggled. 'I read it when I was about thirteen or fourteen. It got passed round everyone, and all the girls at school went crazy for it.'

'I remember that,' Estelle nodded. 'I might have read it myself, back in the day,' she continued, her forehead creasing as she tried to recall.

'And it would definitely offer some light relief after the Marquis de Sade – sorry Reggie.'

'I guess I'll just go back to being quiet and sitting in the corner, if this is what happens when I try to contribute,' he pretended to sigh, as the women drowned him out in a chorus of disapproval.

'No, we like the new, talkative Reggie,' Estelle insisted.

'It's almost as though something's given you a confidence boost, but I can't think what,' Rebecca said airily, her gaze coming to land on Gracie, who turned bright red.

'So, *Lace*, yes? Great idea, Rebecca,' she gabbled.

'If we're all decided on that, I could put it up officially on the Cafe Crumb website,' Estelle announced, looking around proudly.

Rebecca gasped, as Sue turned to her in astonishment. 'You mean, you've finally got it done?'

Estelle smiled happily. 'Yes, all up and running. It went live last weekend. I meant to email you all to tell you.'

'I'll log on as soon as I get home,' Sue promised.

'We can have a look now if you want,' Reggie suggested, pulling his iPad out of his bag and switching it on. 'What's the address?'

Estelle told him, and Reggie quickly typed it in, the home page popping up seconds later.

'Ooh, Estelle, it's gorgeous,' Rebecca gushed, as they all gathered round to look.

'I love the design – it's so cute!'

'It's very *you*,' added Sue. 'Sophisticated and tasteful.'

'Thank you very much, everybody,' Estelle replied, turning pink with pleasure.

'You're so clever,' Rebecca told her. 'I'd never be able to set up anything like that.'

'Oh, I had help. Joe's football coach offered to give me a hand,' Estelle explained, trying to keep her voice even. 'Tony – you met him at the Fifties Night, I think.'

'*Him?*' Rebecca burst out. 'The hot guy you were dancing with?'

'Is he hot? I hadn't noticed,' Estelle giggled.

'So you've been spending lots of time with him, have you?' Rebecca interrogated her. 'No wonder you said you were rediscovering your sexual side, you lucky thing!'

'I've just remembered,' Gracie suddenly interrupted

273

them, much to Estelle's relief. 'I've been meaning to tell you about the Fifties Night.'

'Ooh, yes,' Estelle turned to her excitedly. 'When's the next one?'

'That's the thing,' Gracie replied, her face falling. 'They can't have them at the community centre anymore. I don't know the whole story, but the organisers have had a falling out with the committee, and they've really put the prices up. They just can't afford to hold it there any longer.'

'That's such a shame,' Sue said sadly.

'I know. They're hoping to get them back up and running soon, but they just need to find a new venue.'

'How about here?' Reggie suggested, turning off his iPad and sliding it back in his bag.

'Here?' Estelle repeated doubtfully, as Gracie turned to her, looking thrilled.

'That's a fantastic idea!'

'I don't know . . .' Estelle began uncertainly. 'What would it involve? Is it even big enough?'

'You've got a great space here,' Rebecca chimed in, staring round. 'If you pushed all the tables back and stacked them on top of each other, there'd be loads of room. You could even get some strapping men in to help you take the chairs upstairs or something. I'd supervise,' she offered with a grin.

'And it would be a great way to raise some additional income,' Sue added. 'I don't mean to speak out of turn, but extra money's never unwelcome is it?'

'Look,' Gracie cut in, as she could see Estelle wavering. 'How about I give you Jake's phone number? He's one of the organisers, and he's a really nice bloke. Just give him a call, have a chat and run the idea by him. If it doesn't work for either of you, then it's no big deal,' she shrugged. 'At least you'll have tried.'

'Take the risk, Estelle,' Rebecca encouraged. 'If there's one thing I've learned from reading all this erotica, it's that you have to go after what you want. And it usually turns out very pleasurably for all involved,' she winked.

'Okay, okay,' Estelle agreed, holding up her hands in defeat. Pulling her mobile out of her handbag, she typed in Jake's number as Gracie recited it and had just pressed 'save', when her phone began to ring, startling her so much that she almost dropped it. Staring at the name on the screen, Estelle's lips curled upwards in a slow smile, a pink blush stealing over her face.

'Does anyone mind if I take this?' she asked, her voice higher pitched than normal.

The others barely had chance to shake their heads before Estelle was running out to the back room, her heart racing.

'Do you think something's happened?' Sue asked in concern. 'Something bad?'

'She didn't look worried,' Gracie disagreed. 'She looked delighted, if anything.'

'I think it was a man,' Rebecca said firmly.

'He ex-husband maybe?' Sue suggested.

But Rebecca shook her head. 'Oh no. This is a man she's excited about. Didn't you see how red she went?'

'Perhaps it was the chap from the Fifties Night.'

'Tony!' Rebecca exclaimed. 'Sue, I think you're on to something.'

'*And* he helped her with the website,' added Gracie, as the speculation reached fever pitch.

'Lucky her, if it is him,' Rebecca said, sounding impressed. 'He was gorgeous.'

'I bet she—' Gracie began, but broke off as Estelle walked back into the room.

Everyone fell silent, looking at each other guiltily, but Estelle seemed oblivious. Her eyes were dancing, her face flushed and glowing. It was impossible to hide how happy she was.

'Everything okay?' Sue asked her casually.

'Yes. Yes, everything's great,' she smiled, although she seemed somewhat distracted.

'That was Tony, wasn't it?' Rebecca said bluntly.

Estelle stared at her in astonishment. 'How did you . . .? Yes, it was,' she confessed, looking as excited as a child on Christmas Day.

'And?' Sue prompted.

'He asked me out on a date. A proper date!' Estelle burst out, as Rebecca squealed.

'Where?'

'When?'

'What are you going to *wear*?'

The questions came flying in thick and fast. Estelle

could hardly get her head straight to answer them. '*La Luna* restaurant. This Saturday. And I have absolutely no idea!' she wailed.

She turned, startled, as Reggie stood up, scraping his chair back. 'I'm very sorry, ladies,' he began. 'Estelle, I hope your date goes well, but this discussion sounds like it's going to stray from my area of expertise,' he chuckled. 'So if we're done here, I might head off.'

'Of course, no problem, Reggie. Sorry for turning this into some kind of therapy session for my love life,' Estelle apologised.

'Don't worry about it. I'll see you all next time.' He began to walk off, but when he reached the door, he turned and looked back. 'Um . . . Gracie? Didn't you want to . . . tell me about that thing?' he began awkwardly.

'Thing?' she repeated.

'Yeah, you wanted to show me . . . on the way home . . . That *shop* you said I might like . . .'

'Oh yes!' Gracie caught on, going completely over the top. 'I'd forgotten about that! Sorry, Estelle, I think I need to go too. But if in doubt tight, black, sexy, but never forget that you're a lady. Works every time,' she winked.

'Thanks,' Estelle smiled, as Gracie packed up her things and hurried after Reggie.

'Honestly, those two,' Sue rolled her eyes, as the door closed, and the pair of them walked past the window giggling. 'Are they ever going to get together?'

'Maybe they already have,' Rebecca suggested, raising

an eyebrow. 'But enough about them. This is about *you*, Estelle. It's so exciting!'

'I know,' Estelle breathed. 'I can't believe he's asked me out. I mean, what are we going to talk about? I'm terrified!'

'Don't be,' Sue assured her. 'He obviously likes you for you, so just be yourself.'

'Absolutely,' Rebecca agreed. 'But don't forget to be confident, assertive, and flirtatious too . . . Not that you're not already,' she added hastily, as Sue glared at her. 'And most importantly . . . Wear incredible underwear.'

'Rebecca!' Estelle exclaimed. 'This is only a first date. He is certainly *not* going to be seeing my underwear.'

But Rebecca refused to be put off. 'We'll see,' she said, with a knowing smile. 'We will see.'

25

Estelle walked into the smart Italian restaurant in Quakers Friars and looked around nervously. It was a Saturday night so the place was busy, filled with glamorous-looking couples. After a desperate rummage through her closet, and a hasty late-night shopping spree when she realised she had nothing suitable, Estelle had taken Gracie's advice and was wearing a little black dress that fitted her slim figure perfectly. She was glad she'd made the effort. *La Luna* was clearly an elegant, stylish venue, all blonde wood and champagne-coloured decor, with light fittings in crystal and chrome.

The maitre d' approached, and Estelle tried to smile confidently. 'I'm meeting Tony Ellis,' she explained. 'I'm not sure if he's here yet . . .?'

The man inclined his head respectfully. 'Right this way, madam.'

Estelle followed him through the restaurant, taking care not to trip in her higher-than-usual heels. Tony stood up as he saw her, and Estelle's stomach flip-flopped. In the low light of the restaurant, he looked unbelievably handsome, with the classic good looks of a film star or a rugged male model. He appeared to have gone all out for the occasion, wearing a sharp grey suit with a sleek black shirt underneath. Much to Estelle's delight, he wasn't wearing a tie and his shirt was open at the neck, giving her a tantalising glimpse of bare flesh.

Tony kissed her on both cheeks and Estelle sat down quickly, worried that her legs wouldn't hold her any longer. Simply being around him was making her whole body turn to jelly.

'This is lovely,' she commented breathlessly, staring around the restaurant to distract herself. The tables were covered with cream linen, dressed with shining silver cutlery and lit by thick pillar candles. It was certainly a step up from Cafe Crumb, Estelle thought wryly.

'Do you like it?' Tony asked anxiously, clearly wanting her approval.

'It's perfect,' she told him honestly. 'Have you been here before?'

Tony shook his head. 'One of the guys at work told me about it,' he explained, causing Estelle to instantly visualise him in a fireman's helmet and very little else. 'He brought his wife here for their anniversary and said it was a really nice place,' Tony continued, not noticing the way Estelle was blushing.

The waiter brought over their menus, and Estelle was grateful for the interruption.

'Do you like Italian?' Tony enquired.

'Oh yes, I love it,' she gushed. 'Well, to be honest, I like anything as long as I'm not cooking it. It's nice to be waited on for a change.'

'How's everything going with the cafe?'

'It's going very well, actually,' she replied brightly. 'Business is really picking up. I think the website's helping – the hits are going up every day.'

'Glad to be of service,' Tony smiled.

'And I might be holding the Fifties Nights there,' Estelle continued. 'Apparently they can't use the community centre anymore – isn't it a shame? So Gracie – the girl who sang – gave me the number for the organisers and suggested I get in touch.' Estelle sat back in her chair, looking thrilled.

'That's a great idea! You're turning into quite the entrepreneur. You know,' Tony began thoughtfully, 'you could do a lot of things with that space. Maybe I could add a page to the website, so that people could book it for private events? It'd be perfect for parties and meetings and so on.'

Estelle's eyes widened. 'That would be amazing.'

'I should hold an event for the football team there. It's not long now until the end of the season, and it'd be a nice gesture, don't you think? A way to thank the lads for all their hard work this year.'

'I'd be more than happy to host it,' Estelle beamed.

'And I'm so grateful for all the help you've given me, I really am. I don't know how to thank you.'

'I'm sure you'll think of something,' Tony murmured, raising an eyebrow.

Estelle stared at him for a moment, wondering whether he'd meant to sound so suggestive. Tony's gaze was unflinching, and Estelle felt the heat rise in her cheeks once more and a delicious squirming low in her belly.

The waiter came over and Estelle quickly glanced down at the menu; she'd barely paid any attention to it, and ordered hastily. But it didn't matter – tonight, it definitely wasn't the food she was interested in.

'So how's Chris?' she asked, moving the conversation back on to safer territory. She wished she was more confident, that she could reply to Tony's flirting with some effortless, witty banter, but every time he said something complimentary, Estelle panicked and changed the subject. Sue and Rebecca would be so disappointed in her, she thought wryly.

'Yeah, he's good. He's away this weekend actually, with one of the lads from school. His parents have a cottage in Cornwall so they've gone there, and the boys are going to try surfing. I'm very jealous,' he added, with that broad smile Estelle loved.

'So you're on your own this weekend?' she noted, trying to keep her tone neutral.

'Yeah. I was going to throw a crazy party as I've got the house to myself but . . . I thought this would be more fun,' Tony grinned, as the waiter returned with a bottle of red and poured them each a glass. 'And how's Joe?'

'He's okay too. He's staying over at his dad's tonight.'

'Ted, right?'

'Yes, that's him. I'm hoping everything's back to normal where he and Joe are concerned. I think I mentioned to you that Ted's wife is pregnant, and it took Joe a while to adjust, but I think he's feeling much better about the whole thing. You'll see him at practice tomorrow. He's obsessed with his football,' Estelle smiled fondly. 'I think he really looks up to you.'

'Well, that's nice to know,' Tony said sincerely. 'He's a great kid. How about you – is it strange for you, seeing your ex have a baby with someone else?'

Estelle wrinkled her nose in thought. 'Not really. Ted and I get on much better now we're not married, and I'm genuinely happy for him. Leila seems nice so . . . I'm just glad everything's worked out well.'

Tony nodded, breaking a piece off his bread roll before asking, 'And there's never been anyone else in your life, not since your divorce?'

Estelle shook her head.

'I find that hard to believe.'

'What with Joe and Cafe Crumb, it just never seemed to be a priority,' she replied, giving out the standard answer that she always did when questioned about her love life.

'Then you should make it a priority,' Tony said firmly,

his dark eyes warm as he buttered the bread and took a hearty bite.

'How about you?' Estelle asked, feeling braver now that the alcohol had kicked in. 'I imagine you're always out on dates.'

He shook his head, a wry smile on his face. 'I'll let you into a secret. This is the first date I've been on since Carole passed away.'

Estelle was stunned. 'Really?'

'Really. It took me a very, very long time to get over her.'

'What happened to her?' Estelle asked, her voice dropping almost to a whisper.

There was a long pause, as Tony steeled himself for the reply. 'Cancer,' he said finally. 'She was only thirty-three. Chris was nine, and we were both just . . . devastated. You don't ever imagine . . . I mean, when you get married, you think it's going to be for life. That everything will stay the same way forever, and you'll grow old together, and everything will happen just as it's supposed to . . .'

'I'm so sorry,' Estelle told him, knowing how inadequate her words were.

Tony shrugged, implying that there was nothing more she *could* say. 'These things happen, I suppose. It's not fair, but life's not fair. I'm certainly not the only person in this situation, but I had to pick myself up and keep going for Chris's sake. Left to myself, I'd have fallen apart.' He gave a half smile, as though remembering something. 'I suppose I did the same as you in a way. I threw myself into work and found solace in that, by doing the best job I possibly could.'

'You seem to really enjoy it,' Estelle smiled.

'I love it,' Tony grinned. 'It's very physical work, so I have to keep fit, but there's no better way to blow off steam than a good session in the gym. Well, maybe one way . . .' he conceded, as Estelle took a sip of her wine, blushing as she realised exactly what he was referring to.

'And they're a great set of guys,' Tony continued, as the waiter brought over their starters. 'There's a real sense of camaraderie – there has to be, I suppose, if you're going to work as a team like that. You'd love them,' he added, with a grin. 'I'll have to introduce you. And, of course, there's the satisfaction of a job well done. It can be a real adrenaline rush.'

'Do you ever get scared?' Estelle wondered, as she squeezed fresh lemon over her deep-fried squid.

'Me? What? No, never!' Tony joked, brazening it out.

Estelle rolled her eyes, amused by his bluster. 'And have you ever saved someone's life?' she asked dreamily, visualising him as an all-conquering hero, pulling people from burning buildings, just like in the movies.

'Yeah, it's all part of the job,' Tony said easily. 'Putting out fires, rescuing people. There was this one silly woman recently who nearly burned down her own cafe,' he teased. 'But it's okay. I forgave her because she was so attractive.'

Estelle smiled, unable to help herself. 'And what happened to her after that?'

'Well, I lusted after her for a few weeks, and then I finally plucked up the courage to ask her out on a date,' Tony admitted. 'Thankfully, she said yes.'

'And after that?' Estelle couldn't resist asking.

Tony looked at her for a moment, desire flaming in his eyes. In the flickering light of the candle, he looked more handsome than ever, with his strong jawline and broad shoulders. Estelle felt a powerful wave of longing surge through her.

'I don't know,' Tony said finally. 'But I'm looking forward to finding out.'

They held each other's gaze for a long time, until the moment was finally broken by the waiter bringing their mains.

'So,' Tony began, and Estelle could tell from the mischievous expression on his face that he was about to say something he probably shouldn't. 'Have you been browsing anymore specialist websites – purely for research, of course?' he added, a wicked gleam in his eyes.

'I might have,' Estelle said casually, as though she did that kind of thing every day, before breaking down in embarrassed giggles. 'I can't believe that happened – it was mortifying!'

'I thought it was kind of hot actually,' Tony admitted, deftly slicing a piece of steak. 'Very assertive of you.'

Estelle looked up, surprised by his reaction. 'Well, I'm not exactly . . . I wouldn't want to give you the wrong impression,' she murmured demurely.

'You haven't,' Tony assured her. 'You've made a great impression on me, actually.'

Estelle felt her pulse rate quicken, her heart beating faster. In a smooth, easy movement, Tony poured the remaining wine into their glasses, before raising his in a toast. Estelle followed suit, looking at him questioningly.

'To us,' he said softly.

Estelle couldn't take her eyes off him. The air between them was electric. 'Is there an "us"?' she asked, hardly daring to hope.

'Do you want there to be?'

A wide smile spread across her face and she nodded shyly, hardly able to believe that this gorgeous, sexy man wanted to be with her. She saw the look of relief in Tony's eyes, along with something else. Something that she recognised from the night she'd been at his house. It was lust. He wanted her . . . and she wanted him too.

The thought was both terrifying and wildly exciting, and Estelle quickly dropped her gaze, worried that Tony could read her every thought. She couldn't let her face betray how much she wanted him, even though her body was making it all too clear to her. She could feel the delicious warmth spreading through her, the telltale tingling sensation between her thighs as her breathing quickened.

Estelle put down her knife and fork, unable to concentrate on her food any longer.

'Have you finished, madam?' The waiter appeared instantly, and she nodded in assent as he smoothly picked up the plates, balancing them expertly on top of one another. 'And would you like to see the dessert menu?'

Tony looked at Estelle, who shook her head. 'I'm fine, thank you.'

'A coffee, perhaps . . .?' The waiter pressed.

Once again, Estelle declined, as Tony said, 'I think we'll just get the bill, thank you.'

'As you wish.' The waiter nodded smartly and retreated, returning moments later with the bill, which Tony instantly took and paid for.

'Thank you,' Estelle told him gratefully, as she finished the last of her wine. 'I had such a nice time tonight.'

Tony stood up, pulling on his jacket. 'It doesn't have to end here,' he said lightly.

As they made their way through the crowded restaurant, he let his hand rest on the small of Estelle's back, guiding her between the busy tables. She was already feeling gloriously woozy from the wine, and the feel of his hand above the curve of her bottom was almost more than she could take. Her powers of restraint were abandoning her by the second.

It was only a short walk from *La Luna* to Tony's car, and as Tony slipped in beside her, she was acutely aware that they were now alone together. Her powers of speech seemed to have deserted her; her mouth felt dry, and she could think of nothing to say.

Tony started up the ignition and pulled out into the road. As they stopped at the traffic lights, he turned to Estelle. 'Would you like me to drop you back at your place?'

For a moment Estelle didn't speak, the question hanging in the air between them. The lights changed to green, and all she could focus on were Tony's powerful hands gripping the steering wheel beside her. He drove with the same sense of focus with which he seemed to do everything, and Estelle couldn't help but wonder what it would be like to have all of his attention lavished on *her* in that way.

Plucking up her courage, she finally asked, 'What's the alternative?'

The smallest hint of a smile appeared as Tony considered her question. 'Well, you can always come back to mine,' he suggested. 'No pressure, though.'

Estelle knew exactly what he was implying, and exactly what she wanted to do. But fear held her back. There was fear of the unknown, fear of being with a man again after all this time. And there was also fear of rejection – what if he didn't want anything to do with her afterwards? What if she'd misjudged him and he was only after her for one thing?

Blow all that, Estelle told herself finally. Even if it turned out to be nothing more than a one-night stand, she would make sure it was a night to remember.

'Okay,' she agreed finally, hardly daring to look at him. 'A nightcap would be good.'

They barely spoke on the short drive to Tony's house, but the tension between them was building like a pressure cooker. They pulled into the driveway, and Tony took her by the hand as he led her into the house. As soon as the door closed behind them, Estelle knew she was lost; she fell into his arms without even trying to resist. It was impossible to say who made the first move, but the next moment they were kissing wildly, Tony's powerful body crushing hers as he pinned her against the wall in the hallway.

Estelle's body was singing. It was as though all the years of pent-up frustration were finally finding an outlet; all the weeks she'd spent lusting after Tony, and being taunted by the incredible sex she'd read about in the erotic novels, were about to culminate in a blissful release.

For a second Tony pulled away from her, his breathing coming fast as he stared hungrily into her eyes. 'Are you sure you want to do this? I don't want to push you into anything.'

Estelle hesitated for a moment, the same old fears flooding back. But then she saw the way Tony was looking at her and everything else was forgotten. For once, Estelle didn't care what was right or what was expected of her – she was going to do exactly what *she* wanted. And she wanted Tony.

Estelle didn't even speak, simply pulling his head down to meet hers and kissing him once again. Tony responded eagerly and Estelle felt her stomach doing somersaults. She was unaware of everything except his lips on hers, the feel of his skin against her body as she unfastened his shirt so urgently that half the buttons popped off.

This was better than any fantasy she'd had, any book

she'd read. This was real – right here, right now. She felt Tony's strong arms around her and then he scooped her up as though she weighed nothing, carrying her upstairs as Estelle lay back and surrendered.

26

'Oh my word! Tell me everything,' Sue demanded, as soon as she walked into Cafe Crumb the following Monday.

She could tell immediately that something had happened. Estelle was positively glowing as she stood behind the counter, with a beaming grin that split her face from ear to ear. Her skin was radiant, her eyes were shining, and she looked as though making cups of coffee for the busy citizens of Bristol was the last thing on her mind.

For her part, Estelle was delighted to see Sue. She'd dealt with the commuter rush by herself as Sue didn't start work until eleven a.m., and her head had been all over the place. She'd been mixing up orders left, right and centre, not to mention almost pouring boiling water over herself because she'd forgotten she was holding the jug. The worst incident came when she accidentally tossed a freshly made breakfast roll into the bin, handing the customer the dirty dishcloth she'd been about to throw away, neatly wrapped in a brown paper bag.

'Oh, Sue, it was amazing,' Estelle sighed, a dreamy, faraway look in her eyes.

'Spill it, Ms Humphreys,' Sue instructed, as she stashed her bag in its usual spot beneath the counter and slipped her apron over her head. 'This is my chance to live vicariously through you, so you'd better make it good.' But at that moment the door opened and a young couple came in.

'Two minutes,' Estelle promised Sue, as she went to serve them.

In fact, it was nearer to half an hour before the two women were finally able to grab a few minutes to sit down and talk, and Estelle had almost exploded by then. She'd been replaying the weekend over again in her head; Saturday night had been so incredible that it was impossible to forget a single moment. She was beginning to think that the amount of orgasms in *Ten Sweet Lessons* wasn't so far-fetched after all – she'd certainly had more than her fair share that night.

They'd barely made it to Tony's bedroom, having frantic, urgent sex on the carpet as they fell in through the door. For both of them it was an intense, cathartic experience, after which they'd hardly slept for the whole night. Following the initial, rushed affair, they made love in Tony's bed, but this time it was a much slower,

293

gloriously drawn-out experience that ended in mind-blowing sweetness for Estelle. They took their time to savour each other's bodies, with Tony concentrating on her pleasure, exploring every inch of her with his mouth, his tongue, his fingers.

They stayed up talking, kissing, fumbling like teenagers, finally falling asleep just before dawn. Tony had woken her after what seemed to Estelle like only minutes later, with breakfast in bed. He looked exhausted but elated. There were dark circles underneath his eyes, and his hair was a mess, but he smiled as he kissed her awake.

'We have to get up,' he'd murmured, as Estelle stretched her aching body, the unfamiliar sheets warm against her bare skin. 'Football practice.'

'Joe!' Estelle burst out, her hand flying to her mouth as she sat bolt upright. The sheet slipped from her body and she hastily covered herself, shyness stealing over her as she remembered everything they'd done the night before. 'I said I'd meet him and Ted at practice.'

'It's fine,' Tony assured her. He'd wrapped a towel around his waist, but his chest was bare and Estelle could hardly take her eyes off him. His body was incredible – all toned muscles and abs, like an athlete. 'We've got plenty of time.'

'How much time?' Estelle asked, her eyes sparkling naughtily.

Tony caught her meaning immediately. 'Why?' he asked, bending down to kiss her forehead, her nose, her lips, with light butterfly kisses. 'What did you have in mind?'

Estelle didn't reply. She simply reached up to him, wrapping her arms around him so that the sheet slid down once again. This time, she didn't bother to pull it back up. His heavy body landed on top of hers, almost crushing the breath out of her, and she giggled as their limbs twined together, Tony gently pushing her knees apart before . . .

'Estelle? Earth to Estelle,' Sue repeated, as she waved her hand in front of Estelle's face.

Estelle realised she'd been drying the same cup for about five minutes now; it was a miracle that she hadn't dropped it.

'I'm so sorry, I was miles away.'

'It looked like a happy place,' Sue smiled indulgently. 'I was just saying, shall we take a quick break while we can? I want to hear *all* about it.'

'It was incredible,' Estelle sighed, as she floated over to a spare table. 'He's such a lovely guy, and we get on so well. We just talked and talked.'

'Is that *all* you did?' Sue asked, raising a suspicious eyebrow.

'No, not quite . . . I went back to his,' Estelle confessed, looking shamefaced and ecstatic all at the same time. 'I spent the whole night there. If it hadn't been for football practice on Sunday morning, I don't think we'd have got out of bed the entire weekend.'

'You lucky thing,' Sue said enviously.

'It was amazing,' Estelle gushed. 'Honestly, I think *I* could write an erotica novel with all the things we got up to.'

Sue clapped her hands delightedly. 'Good for you! I'm glad someone's getting some.'

'Do you really think so? I've been thinking about it ever since – not just *that*,' she giggled, as she saw Sue's face. 'But everything was sort of strange afterwards. Joe spent the weekend at Ted's, and I was supposed to meet them at football practice, but of course I couldn't very well turn up in Tony's car, still wearing last night's clothes!'

'Ooh, you dirty stop out!' Sue teased. 'So what happened?'

'Tony dropped me off here. We were running a little late because we . . . um . . . *again*,' Estelle admitted, biting her lip. 'So I had to get ready really quickly, drive up to practice, then stand beside my ex-husband pretending everything was normal, while I watched the man I'd just had the best sex of my life with jogging up and down on the pitch beside my son,' she finished.

'Well, when you put it like that . . .'

Estelle thought back to yesterday's training session. It had, without a doubt, been one of the more surreal mornings of her life. Ted had been chatting away as usual, enquiring after her health as he thought she looked 'a bit peaky', and worrying that perhaps she was coming down with the flu. Estelle waved away his concerns, knowing that her bright eyes, flushed complexion and tired expression were down to something – or someone – else entirely. Someone that was running past them right now, his strong muscular thighs on display for all the world to see, while all Estelle could think of was how incredible it felt to have been pressed beneath them only a matter of hours ago.

'And I haven't heard from him since,' she continued anxiously. 'He came over briefly at the end of training to say hello, but obviously we couldn't really talk as Joe and Ted were standing right there. I know he was going home to sleep afterwards, as he was due for a twelve-hour night shift.'

'Well there you are then. He'll still be working now,' Sue said, glancing at the clock. 'Or if he's finished his shift he'll be sleeping.'

'But what if he's not getting in touch because he regrets what happened? What if he thinks that I'm . . .' here Estelle dropped her voice, '*a slut*? I mean, what sort of woman am I, giving it up on the first date like that?'

'Don't be silly,' Sue waved away her concerns. 'You're both grown-ups and you can do what you like. I think it's fantastic.'

'Maybe I got carried away because of the books we've been reading,' Estelle wondered. 'You know, ever since I started the group, I've been viewing the world in a different way. I just seemed to be surrounded by sex, and it was as though everyone out there was getting some, apart from me.'

'And me,' Sue added glumly.

'Still no progress with George?' Estelle asked sympathetically, temporarily forgetting her own excitement.

Sue shook her head. 'He's becoming intolerable. And he's furious with me about working here. We had a big row about it yesterday, actually. I was going to call you, to find out how your date had gone, but then he went and spoilt everything as usual.'

'I don't understand – why doesn't he want you working here?'

Sue looked uncomfortable. 'He thinks I'm being an idiot, working for free. It doesn't bother me,' she added hastily. 'You know I don't mind.'

'Oh dear. I bet I'm not his favourite person.'

'I swear he thinks you've brainwashed me or something. He just doesn't understand why I need to be so active – why I can't spend all day in the house watching television like he can. Honestly, the only reason he even notices I'm gone is because his lunch doesn't appear on the table exactly when he wants it.'

'Oh, Sue,' Estelle said sadly. 'I don't know what to say.'

'There's nothing *to* say. The more I think about it, the more I think divorce is the only option. I feel like I'm in my prime, and I don't want to spend my precious retirement being miserable. If I live to be a hundred, that's almost forty more years to be stuck with that man, and the thought is unbearably depressing.'

'Well, do what you have to – you know I'll be here to support you.'

'Thanks, Estelle.'

'You never know, it might be a good thing. It could be a second chance for you to find happiness.'

'Like you have, you mean?' Sue smiled. 'Anyway, let's change the subject. I don't want to bring down your good mood by talking about that silly husband of mine. Let's talk about Tony instead.'

'Oh Sue, I like him so much,' Estelle gushed, unable to help herself. 'He's gorgeous, and funny, and he gets on well with Joe too.'

'He sounds perfect.'

'But what if he's too good to be true? Maybe he does this every weekend, and I'm just the latest in a long line of women to be duped by that hot body and those puppy-dog eyes. Oh God, what if I'm rubbish in bed and now I'm never going to hear from him again?'

'I wouldn't worry about that,' Sue smirked, as she looked past Estelle and out through the cafe window.

'Why not?'

Estelle turned around, following Sue's gaze. What she saw made her mouth fall open in astonishment.

Pulling up across the road was a fire engine, bright red and impossible to miss, with half a dozen firemen climbing out.

'Is that Tony?' Estelle asked in disbelief, rising from her chair and moving over to the window for a closer look.

'It's a pretty big coincidence if not,' Sue laughed.

'What on earth is he doing here?' Estelle wondered, as she spotted him at the front of the group, leading the rest of the men across the road and towards the door of Cafe Crumb. Panic swept over Estelle's face, as she ran a hand hastily through her hair. 'Sue, what am I going to do?'

But it was too late to do anything as the door opened with a clang and Tony marched in, followed by the rest of his crew. The sight of six firemen in full uniform striding through the cafe was causing a great deal of interest amongst the customers, and conversations dropped to a murmur as everyone turned to stare.

Estelle's heart was racing. She knew her face must be flushed, and she could hardly bring herself to look at Tony, suddenly overcome by a bout of crippling shyness.

Tony, however, was suffering no such qualms. He strode confidently up to the counter, a wide smile on his face. 'Hello, you,' he grinned.

'Hi,' Estelle replied hesitantly, feeling hugely self-conscious. Her panic increased even further when she realised she couldn't think of a single thing to say to him. Her head was completely empty, and all she could do was gaze helplessly into those deep brown eyes. She was abundantly grateful when Sue came to the rescue.

'Tony? I'm Sue, we met at the Fifties Night.'

'Yes, I remember. How are you, Sue?'

'Very well, thank you. Can I get you all anything while you're here?' she asked, unable to keep the flirtatious note out of her voice. The opportunity to make eyes at six strapping firemen was just too good to resist.

'We'll take six teas to go – all with milk and sugar

'– and an assortment of pastries. Half a dozen of anything you've got, please,' he requested.

Sue began preparing the order, as Estelle remained rooted to the spot.

'Are you . . .' she began, then trailed off. She tried again. 'I mean, how come you're here?'

'We're just on our way back from a call-out. This was the nearest cafe, so we thought we'd pop in.'

'Nearest cafe?' snorted one of Tony's colleagues, a younger looking man with dark skin and a physique like a boxer. 'We've practically driven halfway across Bristol for this.'

'Yeah, thanks Mo,' Tony retorted, but he didn't look the least bit ashamed of this revelation.

'You've just been out on a call?' Sue looked awestruck, as Estelle spotted an escape route and scurried over to help her with the order. 'Was it a real fire?'

'Nah,' Tony shook his head. 'Nothing so exciting. Cat stuck up a tree. The usual.'

Sue turned her attention back to Estelle, just in time to stop her spooning salt into the polystyrene cups. 'Wrong one,' she said brightly, swiping the tub from Estelle. 'I'll deal with the order – you go talk to Tony.'

'But I don't know what to say!' Estelle protested. She turned round nervously to see Tony watching her. His eyes were soft, and there was an amused smile on his face.

'So . . .' Estelle began hesitantly. 'How are you?'

'Never better. You?'

'Yeah, I'm good too,' she murmured, feeling that oh-so-familiar tug in her stomach.

Sue plonked the cakes and tea down on the counter, and the men eagerly snatched them up.

'We'd best be heading back,' Tony said reluctantly, as his colleagues made a move towards the door. 'I'll call you later, okay?'

'Okay,' Estelle nodded. 'I'll—'

But whatever she was about to say was cut off as Tony leaned across the counter and pulled her into his arms, planting an enormous kiss on her lips. His friends began whooping and wolf-whistling as the customers turned round to stare and Sue's eyes widened in shock, her face a picture of incredulity.

Estelle was oblivious to the commotion they were causing, aware of nothing except Tony's stubble against her chin, the feel of his lips on hers and the way her knees felt dangerously as though they might buckle at any moment.

Then Tony pulled away and Estelle was faced with the realisation of what had just happened – and in front of a cafe full of witnesses! Part of her was mortified, but at the same time she was utterly thrilled. Her inner sexpot was dancing a triumphant jig!

Tony threw her a final, cheeky grin that almost made her combust with happiness, before he and his colleagues strolled out of the door and climbed back into the fire engine.

He waved as they drove off, and Estelle turned to Sue, her face radiant.

'Are you still worried that you've given him the wrong impression?' she teased.

'Oh Sue, isn't he wonderful?'

'Do you think he's got a friend for me?' Sue replied, only half joking. Seeing Estelle so happy threw into stark relief the lack of passion in her own life. 'Seriously though, I'm thrilled for you. I mean, why bother daydreaming about Alexander Black when you've got Tony Ellis,' she added, looking after him admiringly. 'Now *that* is a real man!'

27

Reggie and Gracie were stretched out on Reggie's single bed, their bodies pressed together as they kissed passionately. They'd seen each other half a dozen times over the past couple of weeks, and things were hotting up between them. Tonight after their date at Mambos, a bar where Gracie had convinced Reggie to attend a jive beginner's class with her, she'd agreed to go back to his house for the first time.

Music was playing in the background – Reggie had selected a playlist of timeless classics, and Etta James was crooning *At Last* as Gracie slid her leg between his. She sensed that Reggie was nervous. She was too. They'd talked about their past experience, and neither of them had a great track record; Gracie had been through a string of short-term affairs with men who turned out to be either cheats, bastards or freaks – sometimes all three

– while Reggie had had a couple of insignificant relationships at university, both of which fizzled out not long after they'd begun. Each had their reasons to be hesitant and insecure, but the sheer excitement of this new relationship was causing them both to throw caution to the wind.

Gracie pulled him closer, her fingers scrabbling at the bottom of his t-shirt as Reggie took the hint, sitting up and pulling it masterfully over his head. His body was better than Gracie had expected; slim, but toned, with a smattering of dark hair in the centre of his chest. She brushed her hands lightly over the pale skin of his shoulders and down towards his belly button, her fingers weaving through the tangle of hair that disappeared into his waistband. Then her gaze landed on the bulge in his trousers and she let her hands continue to wander, stroking him through the fabric as Reggie groaned in delight.

In a sudden, unexpected movement, he grabbed her wrists, pinning her hands behind her as he used his free hand to unbutton her blouse. His eyes widened as he took in her full, heavy breasts in the delicate lace bra, and Gracie felt pleased that she'd chosen one of the prettiest sets she owned. She was even wearing matching knickers, as she'd had a sneaking suspicion that they might be on show tonight.

Come to think of it, she'd been spending a fair chunk of her salary on underwear recently, browsing lingerie websites and buying online, with new packages arriving for her on an almost daily basis. But she wanted to feel good, and she wanted to look nice for Reggie. While Gracie might once have scoffed at the idea of dressing to please a man, she realised that recently she'd become far more open-minded. She was gradually coming round to the idea that the things she'd read about in the erotic novels could be fun and consensual – they didn't have to be degrading or anti-feminist. And, of course, a big part of the reason for her change of heart was the fact that she'd met Reggie.

Right now he was nuzzling her neck, running his thumbs over her taut nipples. She'd never been with a man who really took his time before, someone who seemed to care about her pleasure as much as his own. Reggie might be an amateur, but he was learning quickly.

Slowly, he slipped her blouse off her shoulders, as Gracie sighed with pleasure. She felt completely comfortable with him, completely unselfconscious. Usually, she would have been sucking her belly in and worrying about how she looked, but for some reason, she didn't feel like that with Reggie. He brushed his fingertips over the rose tattoo on her collarbone, and kissed it gently.

'How old were you when you had this done?' he murmured.

'Seventeen. I was underage, so I lied and said I was eighteen. Typical teenage rebellion really. I was already different to the other kids at school, so I wanted to stand out even more, I suppose.'

'Why did you choose a rose?'

'No reason,' Gracie shrugged. 'It sounds naive, but I hadn't really thought it through, so I just picked the first thing I saw. I thought it was pretty,' she smiled.

Reggie let his fingers trail across her collarbone, dancing over her shoulder and along her arm. He came to a stop at the next tattoo, depicting a 1950s pin-up girl dressed in a red bathing costume. 'And this one?'

'I was twenty-one, and it was my birthday present to myself. I love it,' Gracie said fondly, angling her neck to admire it. 'I was going through a pretty bad time – my confidence had taken some knocks – and to me it represented absolute glamour and beauty. It was everything I wanted to be, and everything I wasn't – everything I'm still not.'

'But you are,' Reggie told her, absolutely genuine. 'You're stunning and sexy and confident and . . .'

'Keep talking,' Gracie grinned, leaning in for a kiss.

'And seductive,' Reggie murmured, as he sucked on her lower lip. 'And voluptuous,' he continued, as he moved down to her breasts and Gracie giggled delightedly.

'You know,' she told him, 'I do have another tattoo.'

Reggie looked up with interest. 'Where?'

'That's for me to know and you to find out,' she grinned naughtily. 'You'll have to keep exploring.'

They kissed again, more deeply this time, as Gracie felt a shiver of excitement and thought how incredible it felt to be discovering each other. There were new tastes, smells, textures, as their tongues pushed against each other, hands sliding over bare skin and exploring beneath clothes . . .

Suddenly, there was a sharp rap on the bedroom door and they jumped apart guiltily, Gracie snatching the duvet to her chest.

'Did you lock the door?' she whispered fiercely.

Reggie nodded. 'Let's pretend we're not in here. Maybe they'll go away.'

They both held their breath, hearts knocking so loudly that Gracie was convinced the noise alone would give them away.

After a few seconds, the knocking came again, louder and longer this time.

'Reggie?' A male voice called out.

'Oh, bloody hell,' Reggie muttered.

'Who is it?' Gracie asked, her eyes wide. Her mascara had smudged onto her cheeks, and her lipstick was non-existent from the amount of kissing they'd done.

'My housemate, Josh. He's an idiot,' Reggie explained in a low voice. 'One of those rugby types who thinks he's God's gift. He's always strutting around the place, talking at the top of his voice, or staggering around drunk.'

'Doesn't sound like you have much in common,' Gracie smiled.

'Reggie, mate, I know you're in there. I can hear the music!'

'I'm sleeping,' Reggie yelled back irritably.

'Then why have you got the light on? I can see it shining under the door.'

Reggie pulled a face. 'He's like bloody Columbo.'

'I don't think he's going to go away,' Gracie whispered astutely.

Reggie sighed and jumped off the bed, buttoning up his jeans as he walked across the room. He opened the door just a crack. 'What?'

'Oh, hey mate.' Josh was standing outside, swaying gently. His eyes were bloodshot and he looked wasted. He stared at Reggie for a moment, taking in his ruffled hair and lack of shirt. 'Sorry if I woke you. You weren't masturbating were you?'

Reggie didn't give him the satisfaction of a reply, settling instead for a withering glare.

Josh's gaze landed on Reggie's naked torso. 'Hey, if you want to tone up your abs, I know some great exercises. You should come down the gym with me – try and get a body like mine,' he suggested arrogantly, flexing his bicep muscles.

'What do you want, Josh?' Reggie asked wearily, trying to keep his temper.

'What? Oh yeah, can I borrow your iPhone charger? Mine's broken, and Pankesh has only got some crappy Samsung thing. What a dickhead, hey? I've got this bird on the go who's waiting for a call from me, and she'll probably be crying all night if I don't ring her.'

Reggie hesitated, his dislike for Josh growing by the second. He hated lending things to him – he invariably lost them or broke them, Reggie thought, remembering the *Star Trek* box set that never got returned, and the remote control helicopter he'd found in pieces behind the television unit. Tonight, however, he had Gracie to think about, and giving Josh what he wanted might be the quickest way to get rid of him.

'Okay. Hang on a minute.' Reggie pushed the door closed and ran across his room, quickly unplugging the charger. He blew a kiss towards Gracie, and she struck a naughty pose on the bed, one hand behind her head as she thrust out her chest in a typical pin-up style.

Waiting outside, Josh heard the creak of the bed, and saw the smile on Reggie's face as he reopened the door.

'Hey, Reg, have you got someone in there?' he asked incredulously, squinting as he tried to look over his shoulder into the room.

'No,' Reggie lied, turning the colour of a beetroot.

'You have, haven't you? You sly bastard! Got a bird in there, have you?'

'Leave it, Josh,' Reggie warned.

'Oh Jesus, it's not a guy is it? You're not gay are you, Reggie?'

'No, I'm not gay, Josh. Here's the charger,' he said, pressing it into his hands. 'Now get out and leave me alone.'

'Ooh, proper touchy, aren't you?' Josh grinned annoyingly, with no intention of going anywhere. 'Why are you being so secretive? I can't believe you've finally pulled! Let's see her then.'

'Don't be stupid,' Reggie said impatiently, eager to get back to Gracie. Arguing with Josh was really killing the mood. Deciding that rudeness was the only option, he went to shut the door, but his housemate quickly stuck out his foot, stopping it from closing. Reggie could smell the alcohol on his breath as Josh leaned in towards him, and when he spoke again, Josh's tone was aggressive.

'Bet she's a right munter, isn't she? Is that why you're ashamed of her?'

'Piss off, Josh.' It took a lot to make Reggie swear, but Josh was really testing his patience.

His anger was lost on Josh, who continued to grin inanely. 'Sorry mate, don't want to disturb you if you're about to lose your virginity.'

'You really are a dickhead, you know that?' snapped Reggie, sick of being the butt of Josh's jokes, and furious at being spoken to so disrespectfully when he knew that Gracie could hear every word.

'Steady on mate. What's your problem?'

'*You're* my problem. And I'm *not* your mate.'

Alone on the bed, Gracie was listening unhappily. She pulled on her blouse and padded over to the door, putting a hand on Reggie's arm. 'Leave it, Reggie. Come back to bed.'

'Ooh, there she is! Not bad at all. You've done alright for yourself mate.'

Gracie turned to him, her eyes like steel. 'Fuck off, you misogynistic twat.'

Josh erupted into peals of laughter. 'Proper little fire-cracker, isn't she? Never mind, I like that in a woman. Hey, if he doesn't know which end to put it in, my room's just across the corridor. I'll show you a good time,' he finished, winking lasciviously at Gracie.

The next moment Reggie's fist had shot out and connected with Josh's jaw. There was a loud crack as he fell to the floor, clutching his face and looking stunned.

Reggie and Gracie seemed equally shocked.

'Josh,' Reggie began. 'I'm . . . um . . .'

But Josh spoke up first. 'Shut up, Reggie, you fucking bell end. What the hell's wrong with you? Can't you take a joke?' He was sprawling on his back like a drunken beetle, backing away from Reggie as his feet scrabbled on the floor, trying to get purchase. His back hit the stair rail and he grabbed onto it like a drowning man, pulling himself upright.

'Look,' Reggie began. He stepped towards him, and Josh visibly flinched.

'Whatever, man. I wouldn't have shagged her anyway. Ugly little slag.' And with that parting shot, he scurried into his room and slammed the door. They heard the lock being turned, and then there was silence.

Reggie was still fuming; the vein in the side of his neck was throbbing and his breathing was coming fast. He turned to Gracie. 'Are you okay?'

'Yeah,' she nodded, as they walked back into his room and closed the door. 'Don't worry about me. I've come up against men like him before. Odious little shits. But Reggie,' she continued, gazing up at him in awe, 'I can't believe you punched him!'

Reggie hung his head guiltily. 'Me neither. I feel really bad.'

'Don't! He was asking for it.'

Reggie shrugged. 'Yeah, maybe. I can't believe I let him rile me like that.' He shook out his hand then inspected it carefully, his gaze running slowly over his knuckles.

'Is your hand okay?' Gracie asked, peering at it too.

'It will be.'

There was a pause, as Reggie flexed his fingers, blowing lightly over the back of them.

'It was pretty sexy actually,' Gracie admitted, unable to keep the smirk off her face.

'Was it?' Reggie asked in surprise.

'Yeah. My very own knight in shining armour.' Gracie slid her arms around his waist and pulled him closer, loving the feel of the tight muscles under his skin. She leaned up to kiss him, letting her breasts graze his chest through the thin shirt she was wearing, and murmured seductively, 'Now, where were we?'

But for Reggie, the moment was lost. Dutifully, he kissed her back, but he was too distracted by the thought of Josh across the hall.

'I'm sorry,' he apologised. 'I really don't feel like staying here now.'

'He's probably listening outside, the pervert,' Gracie

joked. 'Anyway, I bet he doesn't get half as much action as he reckons he does.'

Reggie smiled, but she could tell he was upset by what had just happened.

'We can go to my place if you want,' she suggested. 'Mum's out – she's meeting a friend, so she won't be back until later.'

'Are you sure?' Reggie asked, brightening at the thought.

'Yeah, positive.'

'Okay. Let's go.'

Gracie grabbed her bag, as Reggie pulled on a clean t-shirt, then they headed down the stairs and out into the street. It was slow progress getting to Gracie's house; they meandered along, their arms wrapped tightly around one another, and every few metres they stopped altogether for a long, lingering kiss.

They were so focused on each other that they didn't notice when Sue drove steadily past them, almost crashing into a lamp post as she realised what she was seeing. Her mouth fell open in amazement, and the driver behind beeped angrily at her erratic behaviour. Reggie and Gracie continued to kiss, joyously oblivious to everything and everyone around them.

Eventually, they arrived at Gracie's house and fell through the front door, kissing and giggling.

'My bedroom's this way,' Gracie murmured, taking Reggie's hand and leading him up the stairs. He watched the sway of her bottom, mesmerised, as he followed her, feeling the familiar stirring in his groin. There was always a lot of stirring in his groin whenever he was around Gracie.

Then they both froze as they heard a noise. A downstairs door creaked open, and a voice called, 'Gracie? Is that you?' as Maggie appeared in the hallway.

Gracie and Reggie turned guiltily, hardly daring to look at each other. It was blindingly obvious what they were about to do, and it was far from the ideal way for Reggie to meet Gracie's mother. Any stirrings that he'd been feeling instantly vanished.

'Oh, I didn't realise you had company,' Maggie apologised, looking equally flustered. 'You must be Reggie.'

'Yes, I am. Pleased to meet you,' he said politely, leaning over the banister to shake her hand.

'Mum, I thought you were going out!' Gracie exclaimed, unable to keep the frustration out of her voice.

'Obviously,' Maggie replied tartly, but her eyes were twinkling. 'Janice cancelled, so I ended up staying in. Sorry if I spoilt your night.'

'No, it's fine. Reggie was just . . . walking me home.'

'All the way to your room?' Maggie's mouth twitched in amusement.

'I like to be thorough,' Reggie confirmed, the comment popping out before he knew what he was saying. Fortunately, Maggie didn't seem to mind, smiling despite herself.

'Well don't let me disturb you. I'll go back in the living

315

room and turn the television up. It was good to meet you, Reggie. Hopefully I'll get to meet you properly sometime.'

And with that, she made a tactful retreat. As soon as the door was firmly closed, Gracie and Reggie burst into embarrassed laughter, which they desperately tried to stifle.

'I should go . . .' Reggie said reluctantly.

'No, stay, it's fine. Mum's cool with it, honestly.'

'I wouldn't feel comfortable, knowing she was just downstairs. Maybe we should call it a night. I'll go home, apologise to Josh.'

'I wouldn't bother,' Gracie muttered darkly, her good mood plummeting at the memory of what had happened earlier. She pulled Reggie towards her, leaning over to whisper in his ear. 'I'm getting so frustrated,' she murmured, gently nibbling on his earlobe.

'I know,' he sympathised, as he stroked her hair. 'Me too.'

'It's ridiculous,' she continued, beginning to get angry. 'We're both nearly thirty and we're still living like teenagers, sneaking around, with no privacy. I just want some time alone with you,' she pouted, stroking his chest with her fingertips.

Reggie knew exactly how she felt. It was like a very sweet form of torture, being alone with Gracie but constantly thwarted in their attempts to actually consummate the relationship. 'Look, I'll sort it out, I promise.'

'What are you going to do?' Gracie asked excitedly, sensing that he'd had an idea.

'It's a surprise,' Reggie smiled mysteriously. 'Leave everything to me. I'll be in touch.' He kissed her one final time, then disappeared into the night.

28

'You'll never guess what I've just seen!'

Sue burst through the door of her house, throwing her handbag down with wild abandon and rushing through to the living room where she knew she'd find George in his usual spot. He looked up at her disinterestedly, vaguely wondering what she'd got herself in such a tizzy about.

'A squirrel?' he guessed, saying the first thing that came into his head.

'A squirrel?' Sue repeated, sounding baffled. 'George, what on earth are you talking about? No, I've just seen Reggie and Gracie. *Together*,' she added meaningfully, in case he didn't quite grasp what she was saying.

But George merely stared at her in confusion, not sharing her excitement. 'Say it again?' he requested, thinking he must have misunderstood.

'Reggie and Gracie,' Sue repeated impatiently. 'You

know – from the book club. You met them at the Fifties Night – the singing one and the tall chap. We've had our suspicions about them for a while,' she chattered on, coming to sit in the chair beside him. 'But now I've got proof. I was driving back from Waitrose when suddenly – there they were! All over each other on the pavement, holding hands and kissing, without a care in the world who saw them.'

George grunted, looking distinctly unimpressed.

'They looked terribly sweet together,' Sue continued, thinking how lovely it must be to get so carried away with passion that you were oblivious to everything around you. Even when they'd first been married, George was rarely demonstrative in public; it was impossible to imagine him stopping in the middle of the street to sweep her up in his arms and kiss her as though his life depended on it.

'Pawing each other in front of everyone, were they?' George replied, an expression of distaste on his face. 'That's the thing with these young people – no shame. If you want to stick your tongue down someone's throat, do it in the privacy of your own home and don't subject the rest of us to it.'

'It wasn't quite like that,' Sue began. 'They were just happy, in love . . .'

'Love?' he snorted. 'The people from that book group of yours seem to be jumping in and out of bed with each other like it's the last days of Rome. Are you sure it's a book club and not a swingers club?'

Sue frowned. 'Don't be ridiculous. What's wrong with you?'

'I just don't know if I like the idea of you going there anymore. What about that Estelle woman? It sounds like she's got the morals of an alley cat.'

Sue's mouth fell open. 'How dare you! She's my friend.'

'Such a good friend that she's got you working for free,' George shot back.

'Oh, we're back to this again, are we?' Sue folded her arms and glared at him. 'I've told you before – *I volunteered* to help out. What part of that don't you understand?'

'She's playing you for a mug,' George retorted. 'Giving you some sob story about how she can't afford to pay you. She shouldn't be in business if she can't afford to pay her staff. And now she's gallivanting around with her son's football coach. I bet she's got enough money to buy new shoes and fancy dresses to go out on dates with him.'

Sue stared at George, hardly able to believe what she was hearing. Was this really the man she'd married? Tonight he seemed like a stranger to her; a miserable and bitter old man with whom she had nothing in common.

When she spoke again, her voice was icy cold. 'You can make your own dinner tonight. I'm not hungry. The shopping's still in the boot – you'll probably want to get the frozen food out before it melts.' And with that, she threw the car keys in George's direction and ran upstairs.

'Off to play computer games, are you?' she heard George shout after her.

Shaking with fury, she headed into the box room that served as their home office and slammed the door behind her. It shut with a loud bang, and Sue felt a brief moment of satisfaction, before the fury overtook her once more. She leaned against the wall, letting it support her weight as she took a few deep breaths, trying to calm her irate mind.

Almost on auto-pilot, she crossed the room and switched on her PC, feeling instantly soothed as she heard it whir into action. This was her link to the outside world, a reminder that there was more to life than her po-faced husband and his petty, small-minded taunts.

She sat down on the swivel chair and logged onto her email, pleased to see that Helen had sent her some new photos of Bella. They'd obviously been on a day trip to the coast recently and there were a dozen pictures of her granddaughter, each one cuter than the last: Bella on a donkey; Bella eating a cone with ice cream smeared around her mouth; Bella screaming with delight as she rode the kiddies' train at the funfair.

Sue smiled sadly, clicking reply to send an email back to Helen. She opened with the usual chit-chat and queries about how they all were, but almost before Sue realised what she was writing, the email turned into a long, cathartic rant, spilling out all of her feelings and frustrations about George. The more she wrote, the more she wondered why she hadn't left him months ago. She could hear him moving around downstairs; he'd turned the television up loud, but Sue could make out the clanking of plates and cutlery as he attempted to make himself some food.

Where had it all gone wrong between them? she wondered desperately. When had their lives and interests diverged so radically? Here she was, dreaming about travelling the world, whilst George's ambitions didn't extend beyond figuring out whodunit before Poirot did.

Suddenly, Sue sat bolt upright with excitement, the beginnings of an idea forming in her mind. Why did it *have* to be a fantasy? How many more years was she going to waste, dreaming of the life she could have, when it was all there for the taking? She just had to be brave enough to take the plunge.

Abandoning the email she was composing, she quickly clicked on the Internet icon, pulling up her favourite sites that she'd bookmarked. Each of them was more tempting than the last, offering one amazing destination after another – she could tour Alaska and watch the Northern Lights and the killer whales; she could fly to New Zealand to see the majestic snow-topped mountains; or relax on a deserted beach, miles away from anywhere, in the heart of the Indian Ocean.

With a tantalising sense of anticipation, Sue snatched up a notebook and pen from the desk beside her, scribbling ideas in her small, neat handwriting. For the next hour she worked solidly, absorbed in her task as she set about planning different itineraries, researching various locations and calculating the cost of the whole escapade.

Of course, her children would think she'd gone utterly mad – and perhaps she had. She'd miss her grandchildren, naturally, but it would only be for six months – nine at the most, depending on which option she chose. And it would mean taking a hiatus from the book group. She felt bad for leaving Estelle in the lurch with Cafe Crumb, but it had only ever been a temporary arrangement, and she felt sure Estelle would understand.

Sue was busy drooling over pictures of the Cook Islands when there was a knock on the office door. She didn't bother to respond, but a moment later George poked his head round, a conciliatory cup of tea in his hand. Sue knew it was his way of apologising, even if he wouldn't actually utter the words.

'How are you?' he asked stiffly.

'Fine,' she replied, her tone equally brusque.

'What are you up to?'

'Oh, just browsing,' Sue said lightly. 'You know me.' She felt a pang of guilt about the email she'd composed to Helen, and quickly hit the delete button before George could see it. Maybe she'd taken this whole thing too far, she thought ruefully, all her earlier exhilaration suddenly fading when faced with reality in the shape of her husband.

'Helen sent some photos through of Bella,' she told him cheerfully, trying to make an effort. 'Do you want to see them?'

George grunted in assent, placing the tea down on a coaster then leaning in towards her as he began to scroll through.

'Did you get yourself something to eat?'

'I made myself a sandwich,' George replied, trying to keep the resentment out of his tone and not quite managing it. 'You're making them all day long in that cafe, so you're probably sick of the sight of them.'

'Not at all. I enjoy what I do. That's why I'm doing it.'

'I'm not sure she's a good influence on you, that Estelle woman.'

'George,' Sue snapped. 'Don't start that again. She's my friend.'

'And I'm your husband.'

'That doesn't give you the right to decide who I can and can't see.'

'No, but it should give me some sort of input,' George retorted, as Sue shook her head in disbelief. He closed down the file with the photos of Bella, and a website showing the aquamarine waters and sweeping palm trees of some exotic, faraway land, with a gleaming white cruise ship in the foreground, popped up.

'Oh, looking at holidays again, are we?' he scoffed, his voice laced with sarcasm.

'Yes George, I am. Why, do you fancy going on one?'

'No, thank you.'

'Now why doesn't that surprise me?'

George stared at her through narrowed eyes, as though she was a strange new species he'd just discovered. 'Why on earth would you want to go on a cruise?' he demanded, glancing disparagingly at the website. 'Stuck on a boat with the same group of people, day in and day out;

getting sea sick; all herded on and off the boat like cattle; and probably catching the norovirus or something equally unpleasant. Why in God's name would you want to do that?'

'Actually, George, I think it sounds wonderful.'

'Do you now. Well how about you add it to the list of fanciful ideas you've been having recently. You're not living in the real world, Sue,' he chastised her. 'People like us don't go on fancy cruises or holidays to Tuscany. Have you been reading those celebrity magazines again?'

Sue rolled her eyes at his patronising attitude. 'We're not living in the 1920s, George. I'm not going to have to travel in steerage. It's perfectly possible for someone like me – or even you – to go out and do these things if they have the ambition. In fact,' she continued, her eyes blazing as she made her split-second decision, 'I *am* going to go.'

'Don't be ridiculous.'

'I'm not being ridiculous! You're the one who's dull and boring and unadventurous. I'm *miserable* George,' she yelled at him. 'You're not making me happy anymore – and I'm not making you happy. Why do you think I love going to Cafe Crumb? Because I get to talk to people, and laugh with them, and have a life. Even working for free is better than being stuck here with you!'

'I see,' George replied, with deadly calmness.

As she realised what she'd said, Sue felt a moment's guilt at being so brutally honest, but that was quickly tempered by the relief at finally getting her feelings off her chest. 'And you know what else?' she continued. *In for a penny, in for a pound.* 'I want to have a sex life! I may be sixty-two, but I'm not some dried-up, shrivelled old prune just yet.'

'Anything else?' George's voice dripped with sarcasm.

'Yes, actually.' Sue was shaking with anger, adrenaline coursing through her body. Now was the moment – it was do or die. 'I'm booking a cruise, George,' she told him gleefully. 'A round-the-world cruise. It leaves on the first of September, from Los Angeles, and takes six months. I'll arrive in Southampton the following March.'

George stared at her in horror. 'Have you taken leave of your senses, woman?'

'Maybe,' Sue shrugged. She was feeling utterly reckless.

'And you're going on your own, are you?'

'That's up to you. You're welcome to come if you want.'

'Don't play games, Sue,' George warned her.

'I'm not,' she replied, a sense of calmness stealing over her now that she'd finally made her decision. 'I tell you what, I'll book it a week today. That gives you seven days to decide whether you want to come. If not, I'll go alone.'

'Is this an ultimatum?'

'Yes, I think it might be,' Sue told him honestly. 'Now, I'm going to pour myself a nice glass of wine and go to bed with a good book.'

'Still reading those sex novels are you?' he snorted derisively.

'Yes, George, I am, and I'm thoroughly enjoying them. They're showing me exactly what I've missed out on all these years – and what I don't intend to miss out on any longer.'

George recoiled as though he'd been slapped. Sue stood up from the computer and practically skipped out of the room, feeling happier than she had for months.

29

Rebecca stretched lazily, rolling over in bed and snuggling down beneath the cosy duvet. It was late on Sunday morning, but Rebecca didn't care; today she was determined to relax and get up whenever she fancied. And speaking of things that she fancied . . . She stretched out her arm, expecting to feel the warm, familiar body of Andy beside her, but instead there was nothing. She opened her eyes, noticing that his side of the covers had been pulled back, and sat up, puzzled.

'Andy?' she called out sleepily.

At that moment, the bedroom door opened and Andy crept in, carrying a breakfast tray loaded with food. 'Perfect timing,' he grinned, bending over to kiss her before placing the tray in her lap.

'What's all this?' Rebecca marvelled, staring at the selection in front of her. There was pain au chocolat, fresh fruit salad, buttery toast, orange juice and a mug of coffee, with a single red rose lying beside her plate.

'Breakfast in bed,' Andy stated matter-of-factly.

'I can see that,' she laughed. 'But what have I done to deserve this?'

'Nothing in particular. I just wanted to treat my beautiful wife and tell you that I love you.'

'Aw, thank you, darling. That's so sweet of you,' said Rebecca, genuinely thrilled as she nibbled on her pain au chocolat. 'I love you too,' she told him, blowing him a kiss.

Andy took off his dressing gown and hung it on the back of the bedroom door. Rebecca couldn't help but check out his body as he strode across the room in just his underpants, climbing back into bed beside her.

'So, what do you fancy doing today?' he asked, as he leaned over and pinched a strawberry from the fruit bowl. 'Do you want to go out somewhere?'

Rebecca pulled a face. 'Not really. Let's have a lazy day at home, just the two of us.'

'I'm glad you said that,' Andy smiled, looking particularly pleased with himself.

'Why?' Rebecca asked suspiciously.

'I'll tell you in a minute.'

'Tell me now!' she protested, wondering what his mysterious secret could be.

'No, finish your breakfast first. You'll need your strength,' he winked.

Rebecca giggled, feeling self-conscious as Andy watched

her eat, making sure she finished every bite. Eventually, she drained the last of her coffee and turned to him excitedly. 'Why are you being so strange? What's happening?'

'I have a surprise for you.'

'A surprise?' Rebecca repeated in delight.

'Yeah.' Andy bit his lip nervously. 'I'm not sure what you'll think – I hope you like it.'

'I'm sure I will – but what is it?'

'Wait here.' Andy jumped out of bed once again, and headed through to the spare room. Rebecca could hear him rustling at the back of the wardrobe. Had he bought her some new clothes? she wondered. Underwear, perhaps?

He peeped his head round the door so that she couldn't see what he was carrying. 'I went shopping yesterday,' he explained, looking oddly guilty. 'I bought a few things for us . . .'

He handed over the bag he'd been concealing, and Rebecca tentatively peered inside.

'Oh my God, Andy!'

'Do you think I'm a pervert?'

He looked so worried that Rebecca burst out laughing. 'No, of course not. But I can't believe you bought all this.'

'It was one of the most humiliating experiences of my life, believe me. There was this extremely friendly female sales assistant—'

'How friendly?' Rebecca cut in, narrowing her eyes.

'No, nothing like that,' Andy added hastily. 'But she asked me all these questions, and went into so much detail. It was very embarrassing. All I could think about was getting out of the shop before I saw anyone I knew.'

Rebecca leaned over to kiss him, feeling touched that he'd gone to so much trouble for her.

'I just wanted to make you happy,' Andy shrugged. 'I know you're into this sort of thing at the moment.'

Rebecca tipped the contents of the bag out onto the duvet, astonished at everything that Andy had purchased. She felt as though she was opening a stocking at Christmas – albeit one with a very adult theme. There was a copy of the Kama Sutra, strawberry-flavoured lubricant, a set of love dice, chocolate body paint, and a terrifying implement that looked like something Estelle might use in her baking.

'What's this?' Rebecca asked, looking alarmed as she held it up. It had a long metal stem, with lots of tiny spikes at one end.

'That's a Wartenberg wheel – also known as a pinwheel,' Andy explained knowledgeably. 'You run it over your skin and it makes you tingle. See?' he added, taking it from her and gently running it down her collarbone and over the top of her breasts.

'Mmm, that does seem like good fun,' Rebecca purred.

'And *this* is the pièce de résistance,' Andy went on, picking up a small plastic box and opening it. 'It cost an absolute fortune.' Inside was a strange looking device, which looked like a thick pair of tweezers made out of

331

pink rubber. 'You play with this,' he said, handing it to her. 'And I get to control the strength of the vibrations with this remote control.'

'This is amazing,' Rebecca breathed. 'I'm not going to be able to leave the bed all day.'

'You don't have to. We've got plenty of food in the fridge, and we can always order a takeaway later if you want. It's been a while since we've had one, and believe me, we'll burn off the calories today.'

'You've really got this planned out, haven't you? I don't even know where to start!' Rebecca turned to him, her eyes sparkling, as she picked up the copy of the Kama Sutra and casually flicked through. 'Oh wow, how on earth do you get into *that* position!' she exclaimed, her eyes goggling.

'We can try it if you like,' Andy suggested. 'I think my arm goes here, and your leg goes *here*,' he chuckled, as he pulled Rebecca's ankle up behind his head, and she screeched in terror.

'No, that's not physically possible,' she cried, as the pair of them burst out laughing.

'Maybe we need some foreplay first, to get you warmed up,' Andy grinned, reaching for the love dice. There were two of them – one which had a different part of the body written on each side, and the other with an instruction, such as stroke, suck or massage.

'I'll go first,' Rebecca told him, leaning across and playfully stealing them from him. She rolled the dice in front of her, her face falling as she read how they'd landed. 'Apparently you have to rub my ears,' she said, sounding hugely disappointed. 'That's not very sexy. I want another go!'

'No,' Andy shook his head at her protests. 'That's what the dice say, so that's what we have to do. Mmm, do you like that? Is that turning you on?' he teased, as he put a hand on either side of her head and dutifully rubbed her ears.

'I'm not very impressed with your technique,' Rebecca told him. 'It's doing nothing for me.'

'Maybe you have frigid ears,' Andy suggested, as Rebecca hit him. 'My turn now then,' he grinned, snatching up the dice and blowing on them before he rolled. They both moved over to look.

'Lick genitals!' Rebecca exclaimed. 'Did you cheat?'

'The dice have spoken,' Andy said smugly. 'If I had to rub your ears, then you've got to take your turn.'

'Bloody dice,' Rebecca muttered, but she was smiling as she slid down the bed, tugging off Andy's underpants and carrying out the dice's instructions.

'I like this game,' Andy smirked, as Rebecca surfaced from beneath the sheets.

'Do you know what would make it even more fun – for me at least? Chocolate body paint.'

'I thought you might enjoy that,' Andy smiled, his eyes crinkling at the corners.

'We could put it on whichever body part the dice suggests.'

'Or whichever body part we'd like to be licked.'

'Well that's obvious,' Rebecca rolled her eyes good-naturedly.

'It doesn't have to be – we could start off well-behaved.'

'That doesn't sound like fun.'

'Well, not *too* well-behaved,' Andy clarified.

'Okay then,' Rebecca agreed, unscrewing the cap from the tube and squeezing out a small quantity onto her finger. 'Not bad,' she commented, as she sucked it off seductively.

'You're very good at that,' Andy commented cheekily, as he watched her.

'Why thank you.'

'I think you should take off your clothes,' Andy suggested, nodding towards the silky negligee she was wearing. 'You don't want them to get messy.'

'Aw, you're so considerate,' Rebecca teased, as she wriggled out of it. 'Always thinking of me.' She caught her breath as she saw the way Andy was looking at her, the tension in the room cranking up a notch.

'You go first,' he offered, his voice growing thick.

'Okay.' Rebecca took the paintbrush and squeezed the chocolate out onto her tummy, using the paintbrush to draw a circle around her belly button. When she'd finished, Andy moved in eagerly to lick it off and Rebecca giggled, his warm breath and wet tongue tickling her skin.

'Nice?' she asked, raising an eyebrow.

'Not bad,' he agreed. 'Although this game could get very sickly very quickly.'

'Your turn,' Rebecca said, handing him the paintbrush.

Andy smiled, as he painted an arrow along his thigh, pointing upwards towards his groin.

'Very funny,' Rebecca smiled, as she bent down to slowly lick it off.

The game carried on, with their requests getting ever filthier, until Andy finally broke down, saying, 'No more! I'm going to be sick.'

'Hmm, you're not a very good sex slave,' Rebecca chastised him. 'I thought today was all about pleasing me?'

'Let me make it up to you,' Andy begged. 'I think now might be the time to use this.' He picked up the vibrating toy, handing it to Rebecca. 'Now you just put it where you want to – and remember, I have complete control.'

He smiled, as Rebecca giggled nervously, but as soon as Andy turned it on, her expression changed to one of absolute pleasure. She moaned softly, as Andy picked up the pinwheel, running it along her arms and over her breasts, before turning up the vibrations with the remote.

Rebecca writhed on the bed sheets, hardly able to believe all the trouble Andy had gone to for her. His idea of staying in bed all day was exactly what she wanted – and she had a feeling it was going to be one of the best days of her life.

30

The Langdale was one of Bristol's most exclusive hotels, and Gracie felt a pang of nerves as she arrived at the imposing entrance. It was a grand, Georgian building, with elaborate columns in honey-coloured stone and a smart black awning over the main door. Gracie walked carefully up the low steps in her red patent heels, drawing on all her reserves of confidence as she tried to look like she belonged there.

Ordinarily, it was not the sort of place she would go to, but Reggie had insisted on meeting her in the hotel's plush piano bar. He'd told her to dress smartly, but that was all he would reveal, explaining to Gracie that the rest of the evening was a surprise.

She smiled graciously at the uniformed man on the door. 'Could you tell me where the piano bar is?'

'Certainly, madam. If you carry straight on, you'll see

the main reception on your left. Just past that is a staircase that takes you down to the bar.'

'Thank you.' Gracie felt his eyes flash over her appreciatively and, although it was going against all her principles to admit it, his admiration gave her a much-needed confidence boost. She'd dressed well – albeit demurely for her – and was channelling Dita von Teese in a tight black dress that hugged her curves like a second skin. It had a square cut neckline that showed off her ample cleavage, and neat cap sleeves, while the hemline fell to just below her knees. The tight skirt caused her to walk with a pronounced wiggle, as she made her way carefully across the tasteful lobby and down the stairs.

Music was playing softly in the background, and as Gracie glanced quickly around the largely empty bar, she realised Reggie hadn't yet arrived. She shimmied her way onto a zebra-print bar stool, feeling somewhat self-conscious as the young barman caught her eye and smiled flirtatiously. Gracie looked away, picking up the bar menu and scanning the cocktail list. It wasn't long before she became aware that someone was standing beside her, a little too close for comfort, and she turned angrily, only to see Reggie standing there. Her expression softened immediately, and she broke into a wide smile.

'Is this seat taken?' he asked. He looked amazing, in a smart black suit (definitely *not* the one he'd worn for the Fifties Night) with a crisp white shirt. He was wearing contact lenses instead of his old-fashioned glasses, and his dark hair had been cut and styled. He looked incredibly handsome – Gracie barely recognised him.

'Sorry, I'm waiting for my boyfriend,' she teased.

'He must be one lucky man,' Reggie quipped, playing along.

'Oh, he is.'

'Well, I hope he appreciates it.'

'So do I,' Gracie returned, enjoying the exchange.

'Perhaps I could buy you a drink while you wait for him?'

Gracie cocked her head to one side as she considered the offer. 'That would be acceptable,' she decided finally. 'Although you'll have to leave as soon as he arrives. He gets very jealous.'

Reggie raised his eyebrows. 'Does he?'

'Oh yes. He once punched a man.'

Reggie flushed, remembering the incident. 'He sounds terrifying,' he dead panned. 'I imagine he must be very masculine, very tough. Is he a boxer?'

Gracie bit her lip to stop herself from laughing. 'No, he's . . . an intellectual,' she finished, carefully selecting the word. 'He's very clever, and very well-read. Although between you and me,' she lowered her voice, 'he can be a little *worthy* at times.'

'Oh?' Reggie looked taken aback.

'Yes. I thought he was arrogant and a real know-it-all when I first met him.'

'And what do you think of him now?'

'Now? Now, I think he's incredibly sweet. And handsome.

And sexy. Just looking at him makes me want to tear his clothes off,' she confessed, her eyes flashing naughtily.

'Lucky him,' Reggie smiled delightedly. 'But you know, maybe he wasn't too fond of you when he first met you.'

'Do you think so?' Gracie asked, a challenging tone in her voice.

'Well, I can only guess. I don't know him personally of course.'

'Of course,' Gracie conceded, with a tilt of her head. 'But as you've only just met me, perhaps you could give me *your* first impressions.'

'Hmm . . .' Reggie pretended to think about it for a moment. 'On first impressions, you seem extremely confident – almost *too* confident in fact. Some would say bolshie, bordering on annoying,' he added, unable to stop himself laughing at the outrage on Gracie's face. 'But now I've been talking to you for a few minutes, I can see that a lot of that is a facade. That really, you're quite shy and uncertain. But at the same time, you're also funny and sexy and gorgeous, and from the second I walked into the room, I couldn't take my eyes off you.'

Gracie's smile lit up her face. She couldn't deny it – this role play was making her extremely horny. She loved flirting with Reggie like this, and it amused her to think that if the barman was listening in, he'd probably wonder what on earth was going on.

Noticing a break in the conversation, he made his way over to them. 'Can I get you anything, sir?' he asked, directing the question at Reggie.

'Yes, thank you, I'll have a Scotch on the rocks.' He turned to Gracie. 'Would you allow me to buy you a drink?'

'Thank you. I'll have a Slow. Comfortable. Screw,' Gracie requested, stretching out the words to make it sound as filthy as possible, and fighting to keep a straight face as she placed her order.

'Certainly,' Reggie replied, turning to the barman. 'And a Slow Comfortable Screw, please,' he repeated, a red flush stealing over his face.

The barman nodded, completely unfazed as he went off to prepare their drinks, while Reggie turned back to Gracie, shaking his head. 'Naughty,' he whispered under his breath, as Gracie giggled.

'So how did you meet this boyfriend of yours?' he continued, inching to the edge of his stool so that their bodies were almost touching.

'We met at a book club, specialising in erotica,' Gracie told him, letting the word linger on her bold, red lips.

'Wow, that sounds very open-minded. What sort of things have you been reading about?'

An impish grin spread across Gracie's face. Their drinks arrived, and she took a sip of her cocktail, before standing up and moving closer to Reggie. He was sitting with his legs apart and Gracie slid herself between them, bending over to whisper in his ear. 'All kinds of things,' she murmured, her breath hot against his neck. 'Bondage . . . spanking . . . fellatio . . .' She drew the words out slowly, making each one longer than the last.

Reggie could barely breathe, mesmerised by Gracie standing so close to him. He took a fortifying drink of Scotch, draining half the glass in one go. 'Your boyfriend must be very good in bed if he's read all of these things.'

But Gracie shook her head sadly, her eyes downcast. 'I've never had the chance to find out,' she whispered, running a scarlet-painted fingernail along his thigh, all the way from his knee to his groin.

Reggie swallowed. 'What a shame,' he managed. His throat felt thick, and when he spoke his voice sounded hoarse.

'Yeah. We've just never had the time or place,' she explained, still stroking his thigh.

'You know,' Reggie began, reaching round to rest a hand on her lower back, letting his fingers splay out over her bottom. 'I don't think this boyfriend of yours is going to turn up. Why don't you come upstairs with me?'

His fingers were stroking the top of her thighs, and Gracie was finding it difficult to concentrate. 'Upstairs?' she questioned.

'Yes. I've got a room here, and it's a very nice one. It seems a shame to be alone in there.'

Gracie couldn't keep the smile from her face as she realised what Reggie's surprise was. 'But I've only just met you,' she protested. 'What kind of girl does that make me?'

Reggie leaned in close, his lips brushing her ear as he spoke. 'I know exactly what kind of girl you are.'

Gracie's eyes were sparkling as Reggie took her hand

and led her out of the bar towards the lift. Neither of them spoke; Gracie was breathless with anticipation, but doing her best to appear normal as the other patrons of the hotel passed by, nodding to them with a polite 'Good evening'. Then the lift pinged open, and to her intense relief there was no one inside. As she stepped in, she saw that the walls were mirrored, reflecting their image back at them over and over so that the lift was filled with dozens of Reggies and Gracies. Reggie pressed the button for the fourth floor and the doors closed. The next moment, the mirrored Reggies and Gracies were all kissing passionately, just like the real pair.

'Well, that was fun,' Reggie murmured as they came up for air. 'I didn't know you were into role play.'

'Neither did I,' Gracie giggled. 'But I want us to be Reggie and Gracie again now. I want to be with you – not anyone else.'

Reggie nodded, kissing her gently on the nose. 'Hi, Gracie,' he smiled.

'Hi Reggie,' she grinned, a delicious shiver running through her. 'Thank you so much for doing this.'

'Well, I did promise. And I always keep my promises.'

The lift opened and they stepped out into an elegant hallway, all thick cream carpeting and low lights. Reggie led her along the corridor, stopping outside a nondescript wooden door and slipping in the key card.

'It's gorgeous,' Gracie breathed, as she entered the room and took in the rich colours, the smart furnishings and the king-sized four-poster bed that dominated the space. The marble bathroom boasted a giant tub and walk-in wet room, where Gracie could imagine getting up to all sorts of naughty things. 'I thought you were supposed to be a poor student?'

Reggie smiled. 'I have an emergency fund. This counted as an emergency.'

He caught her eye, and there was a split second of shyness between them, both of them suddenly overcome by nerves at the realisation of what they were about to do.

But then Gracie slowly turned around so that her back was to Reggie, and glanced coquettishly over her shoulder. 'Could you help me with my zip, please?'

Reggie moved forward, his hands trembling as he took hold of the zip and slid it down with excruciating slowness, revealing a tantalising glimpse of the black lace and bare flesh that lay beneath. Gracie gave a little shimmy and the dress slithered off her shoulders, landing in a heap on the floor.

Reggie gasped.

Gracie was wearing a black lace corset that pulled in her waist and pushed her breasts up enticingly. The suspender straps hanging off it were attached to sheer black stockings, and below that was a tiny wisp of fabric that passed for matching panties.

'Wow,' he gulped.

'Do you like it?' Gracie asked shyly.

'You look beautiful,' Reggie told her honestly. And she

343

did – there was no other word for it. Her legs seemed endless in the enormous heels she was wearing, and her body was insanely sexy. 'I found your other tattoo,' he grinned, his gaze falling on the intricate swallow design on her inner thigh.

Gracie smiled. 'You can take a closer look if you like.'

Reggie didn't need to be asked twice. Pulling Gracie to him, they fell backwards onto the bed, quickly lost in an exquisite tangle of limbs and hands and tongues, skin on skin, body to body, as mouths kissed and fingers explored, yielding moans and sighs of rapture.

This time there were no knocks at the door, no annoying flatmates or interrupting mothers. Just Reggie and Gracie together. And it was perfect.

31

It was 6.50 p.m., and Estelle and Sue were huddled in the doorway of Cafe Crumb, looking anxiously up and down the street as they beckoned hastily to Rebecca.

'What's happening?' she asked excitedly, loving the intrigue as Sue practically hauled her through the door, closing it firmly behind her.

'Gossip,' Estelle replied succinctly, as the three women quickly sat down, crowding around the table like a witches' coven.

Rebecca's eyes lit up. 'Ooh, tell me everything!'

'Reggie and Gracie – we have proof.'

'I saw them,' Sue confirmed. 'Kissing and cuddling in the street. *Really* kissing,' she emphasised, to make sure there was no misunderstanding.

Rebecca squealed, clapping her hands together

delightedly. 'I knew it!' she declared triumphantly. 'Ohhh, that's so lovely. So do we tell them that we know?'

'I suppose we should leave it and see if they want to tell us,' Sue said diplomatically. 'They might be keeping it a secret for some reason, and I don't want it to seem like I've been spying on them.'

'I don't think I'll be able to hold it in,' Rebecca wailed. 'As soon as I see them, I'll have to say something or else I might burst!'

'Let's play it by ear, then,' suggested Estelle. 'We don't want to embarrass them.'

'Okay,' Rebecca agreed, although from the ecstatic look on her face it was evident that keeping it quiet was going to prove exceptionally hard for her. Then her expression suddenly changed, and she stared hard at Estelle for a moment. 'Oh my gosh, I forgot about your date with Tony! How did it go?'

Estelle beamed, unable to hide her happiness. 'It went really well. I had such a lovely night.'

'That's an understatement,' Sue cut in. 'She's been floating around this cafe like Christina Cox after a night with Alexander Black. He even turned up to see her in his fire engine the other day.'

Rebecca looked between Sue and Estelle in astonishment. 'Really? How romantic! Sounds like he's smitten.'

'I think they both are,' Sue added, in a stage-whisper.

'So he got to see you in your underwear after all?' Rebecca said slyly.

Estelle's cheeks flamed, but she couldn't help but look thrilled at the memory. 'In my underwear, out of my underwear . . .'

Rebecca squealed once more, an ear-piercing cry, that startled Gracie who was coming in through the door.

'Hi ladies,' she called out cheerily.

Everyone fell silent, knowing expressions on their faces. Sue raised an eyebrow, as Rebecca began to giggle uncontrollably. 'Please can I tell her?' she begged. 'I can't hold it in much longer.'

'Tell me what?' Gracie asked suspiciously, as Reggie strolled casually through the door behind her. 'Oh, hi Reggie,' she continued, as nonchalantly as she could manage. 'You must have been right behind me. I didn't notice.'

'Yeah, I thought it was you up ahead but I wasn't sure. Anyway, it's nice to see you again,' Reggie replied, blissfully unaware that he and Gracie were fooling no one. 'How is everyone?' he asked, turning to the rest of the group.

They were all staring at him and Gracie, disbelief written across their faces.

'What?' Reggie exclaimed.

'Nothing,' Estelle smiled, as she turned and winked at the others. 'And we're all fine, thank you for asking.'

Rebecca quickly caught on to what Estelle was doing. 'Good to see you, Reggie. What a coincidence that you were just behind Gracie all this time, and you didn't notice her.'

'It's not *that* much of a coincidence,' Sue played along. 'After all, they were heading to the same place at the same time, so there's a high probability of them meeting outside.'

Throughout this exchange, Reggie and Gracie were swapping confused, nervous looks.

'Although,' Rebecca continued thoughtfully, 'it *must* have been purely accidental that you saw them together the other night, Sue. I suppose they bumped into each other again.'

'What? When?' Gracie burst out, panic written across her face.

'*When*?' Rebecca repeated with emphasis. 'You mean there's been more than one occasion?'

'Oh no, of course not,' Gracie laughed a little too loudly. 'It must have been . . . last Thursday?' she hazarded a guess, watching Sue's face carefully.

'Thursday?' Sue pretended to frown. 'No, it was last Tuesday.'

'Tuesday! Yes, that's what I meant to say,' Gracie cut in quickly. 'I'd just finished work, and Reggie was on his way back from the university. Isn't that right, Reggie?'

'What? Oh yes, absolutely . . .'

He trailed off and the cafe fell quiet; Estelle, Sue and Rebecca relishing the awkward silence.

'Well, I'm glad that's all been sorted out,' Estelle said eventually, leaving it just long enough for them to feel uncomfortable. 'Can I get anyone anything to eat or drink?'

Gracie got her order in quickly, grateful for the change of subject, and the group went through their usual preliminaries of getting out their copies of this session's chosen read and choosing a piece of cake. Sue helped prepare the drinks, so just minutes later they were all sitting down and ready to go.

'What did you all think of *Lace*?' Rebecca asked eagerly. She felt a sense of responsibility, as it was her pick, so she hoped everyone liked it.

'Great choice, Rebecca,' nodded Estelle. 'Much more my thing than the Marquis de Sade. Sorry, Reggie.'

'No problem,' he shrugged resignedly.

'I can see why it's become such a classic,' Estelle continued. 'It's epic. It spans decades, and covers so many issues, with all the interwoven plotlines . . . And the sex of course. Great sex scenes.'

'Like the goldfish scene!' Sue exclaimed.

'Oh my God, the goldfish scene!' Gracie spluttered.

'Is that really a thing?' Reggie asked uncertainly. 'I mean, do people do that?'

'I've never had a goldfish up my hoo-ha and I don't want one,' Rebecca declared, as everyone fell about laughing.

'I love the boarding school aspect of it too,' Estelle continued. 'The idea of female friendship – these girls bonding from a young age, and getting up to all sorts of things that they shouldn't while they're away from home.'

'Like a raunchy Enid Blyton,' Sue interjected.

'Yes, I think the female friendship aspect is very important,' Rebecca added. 'If you have good female friends, you should tell them *everything*,' she finished, with a pointed look at Gracie.

'I agree,' nodded Estelle, as Gracie squirmed uncomfortably. 'It's not really a proper friendship if someone's keeping secrets. What do you think, Gracie?'

'Well, of course, friendship is very important, although I wouldn't say it's the main thrust of the book,' she began, unsure as to why the others were placing so much emphasis on the subject. 'As you said, Estelle, there are so many plotlines, and when it comes to sex, I think it's great that there's so much focus on the woman's pleasure.'

'And what did we think of the male leads in *Lace*?' Estelle continued.

'It was definitely the women who were the strongest characters,' Sue spoke up. 'The men were a fairly useless lot, on the whole.'

'Were there any men for you to fancy this time, Rebecca?' Gracie teased.

'Not really,' Rebecca sighed. 'Prince Abdullah was in the running for a while, but I think he was just a bit too nasty. There was probably none for you either, Gracie – none that are your type.'

'My type?' Gracie repeated.

'Yes. You know – tall, dark, kind of handsome on a good day . . .'

'A little bit shy, but getting braver,' added Sue.

'Working towards his PhD and very dedicated to his

thesis,' Estelle couldn't resist adding, leaving them all in no doubt who she was referring to.

'What? What are you talking about? Don't be ridiculous!' Gracie spluttered.

'Gracie, we *know*! You can stop denying it!' Rebecca burst out in frustration.

'Know what?' she continued, trying to brazen it out.

'About you and Reggie. Together. So you don't have to keep pretending that you accidentally bumped into each other on the street. God, you're both rubbish actors!'

'B . . . but how?' Gracie stammered, looking utterly bewildered.

'Sue *saw* you. You haven't exactly been discreet, have you?'

'Sorry,' Sue apologised, looking terribly embarrassed. 'I drove past you, like I said, but you didn't see me. You were . . . otherwise engaged, shall we say.'

Reggie and Gracie were sneaking worried glances at each other, apparently realising that the game was up.

'Okay, we admit it,' Gracie said finally, grinning from ear to ear as she cuddled up against Reggie, while he wrapped his arms around her protectively.

There were exclamations of excitement and congratulatory noises from the other women, as Rebecca began applauding.

'But why didn't you tell us?' she asked, unable to hide her hurt.

'We were going to, honestly,' Gracie told her, gazing up at Reggie. 'We were just waiting for the right time.

351

And we didn't want to detract from the book club, or make things awkward for everyone.'

'Not at all,' Estelle insisted, feeling quite emotional at the sight of them together. 'We're very happy for you both.'

'Yes, absolutely delighted,' echoed Sue. 'But you know, I would never have imagined, back at the beginning of all this, that you two would get together.'

'Oh, I could tell,' Rebecca insisted. 'There was all of that tension between you, and it was obvious that the only reason Gracie was so argumentative was because she was sexually frustrated,' she winked, as Gracie pretended to be outraged. 'Incidentally, you're looking far more relaxed these days,' she teased.

'Maybe I should start a dating service on the side,' Estelle suggested.

'You get to read the erotica novels, then go home and practice what you've read!' Rebecca laughed.

'Well *you've* certainly been doing that,' Gracie smiled, knowing how happy Rebecca had been recently. 'Things going well with Andy, are they?'

'They might be,' she replied coyly, leaving them all in no doubt as to Andy's prowess in the bedroom. She was happier than ever with the way their relationship had been going, and they were making love on an almost daily basis, wherever and whenever the mood took them – just like when they first got together.

'Sue, are you okay?' Estelle asked suddenly, noticing that Sue looked close to tears.

'Yes, yes, I'm fine,' she insisted, as everyone turned to her in concern. 'I'm just being silly.'

'What is it? You can tell us,' Estelle assured her, placing a caring hand on her arm.

'It's just . . . Oh, I know it sounds ridiculous, but the rest of you have so many new and exciting things happening in your lives, it just makes me realise what's lacking in mine. All the things I've been missing out on, and how unhappy I am with George,' she finished sadly, as Estelle handed her a paper napkin from one of the tables and she dabbed at her eyes.

'Oh Sue,' she murmured sympathetically.

'Take *Lace* for instance,' Sue continued, holding up her copy of the novel. 'I know it's only fiction, but I found it so empowering. Those women went out into the world like trailblazers, starting their own businesses and travelling the globe. And it was back in the 60s and 70s, which is the era I was growing up. I should have been founding a multi-million dollar empire, not worrying about having George's dinner on the table.'

The others stared at her, taken aback by her response. They'd never seen her so vocal or so animated about any of their other reading material. Even *Ten Sweet Lessons* hadn't provoked a reaction like this.

'I have a confession to make, actually,' Sue began, finding that now she'd begun opening up, she couldn't seem to stop. 'I hope you don't mind me speaking to you all so frankly, but over the months, I've come to look upon you all as friends. And some of you have been very good friends,' she added, smiling at Estelle, who was still clutching her arm supportively. 'I've given George an ultimatum. I'm booking a holiday – a six-month world cruise in fact – in the next few days, and he has until then to decide whether he's going to come with me. If not, then I'm going alone.'

There were gasps around the table, and Estelle stared at her in alarm. She'd sensed that something had happened – Sue had been unusually distant all week in the cafe, but for once seemed unwilling to confide in Estelle.

'Surely he'll come with you,' Gracie insisted.

But Sue shook her head. 'I don't see why. He has no interest in doing it. We're just arguing all the time, and I think I might even prefer to go on my own.' She forced a laugh, but everyone could see that she was far from happy about the situation.

'When . . . When will you be leaving?' Estelle asked, feeling a tell-tale lump beginning to form in her throat.

'Soon,' Sue admitted. 'A few weeks – maybe less. I'm so sorry, Estelle. I meant to talk to you about it before, but I just wanted to pretend it wasn't happening. I still thought there was some way George and I might salvage . . .' She broke off, unable to continue.

'It's fine,' Estelle assured her. 'As I said before, I'll support you whatever you decide to do.'

The mood in the little cafe felt distinctly downbeat, a far cry from the giddy, giggly atmosphere earlier in the evening.

'Sorry everyone,' Sue apologised. 'I don't want to be a killjoy. Let's change the subject.'

'Well I did have one thing to ask you all,' Gracie began tentatively, hoping to lighten the mood and take the attention off an emotional Sue. 'Is anyone up for going to a burlesque night?' she finished excitedly.

'Burlesque?' Estelle repeated doubtfully. 'Women taking their clothes off?'

'Yes please!' Reggie held his hand up, which made everyone laugh.

'Actually,' Gracie told him, 'I was thinking women only – let's make this a girls' night,' she suggested, to Reggie's obvious disappointment.

'Ooh, burlesque's supposed to be really sexy, isn't it?' chimed in Rebecca.

'Yeah, it's fabulous, and I've heard really good things about this show.'

'Well count me in – although Andy's going to be furious he can't come!'

Estelle looked uncertainly at Sue. 'I'll go if you do . . .'

'Oh come on, Sue,' Gracie enthused. 'It could be just what you need – a night out with the girls, have some drinks, see a show. We'll have so much fun!'

'Why not,' Sue agreed, throwing her hands up in defeat. 'I could do with a night out.'

'Fantastic,' Gracie beamed. 'I'll book the tickets. Is this Saturday okay for everyone?'

The others nodded their agreement, although Reggie looked somewhat put out.

'Saturday? I thought we could do something together . . .'

'I'll make it up to you, I promise,' Gracie assured

him, her eyes sparkling naughtily as she cuddled up to him.

'So now all that's left on the agenda is to choose a book for next time,' said Estelle. 'And this time it's the turn of . . .' She made a drum roll on the table with her fingers. 'Gracie! The only one of us who hasn't picked yet.'

'Make sure it's a good one,' Rebecca warned her.

'Well, I have been thinking about it,' Gracie confessed, letting her hand rest on Reggie's thigh, 'and I decided I wanted something fairly modern – no Chaucer or Marquis de Sade,' she smiled. 'We haven't really explored the true-life, confessional style of erotica, so I thought why not choose that? And I've opted for *100 Strokes of the Brush Before Bed*,' she announced decisively.

'I haven't heard of that,' Estelle admitted. 'Can you give us a brief summary?'

'It's the diaries of an Italian schoolgirl, recounting her first sexual encounter and everything she gets up to after that. And from what I've heard, she gets up to a lot! She's keen to have as many different experiences as she can, and she records them all in her journal.'

'That doesn't sound very feminist,' Rebecca teased her.

'Maybe not,' Gracie acknowledged. 'Maybe my views have softened for some reason,' she added, smiling up at Reggie. 'I just thought it would be a different area to explore.'

'Well I think it sounds fascinating,' Estelle came to her defence. 'And on that note, I think we're done. I'll see all you ladies on Saturday for the burlesque show – Gracie, can you email us all the details?'

As the others began to make their way out of the cafe, Sue hung back to speak to Estelle.

'I'm so sorry,' she apologised again. 'I didn't want to announce everything like this, and I should have told you sooner, but I think I was embarrassed. It just feels as though I've made a huge mess of my marriage. Of my life, even.'

'Oh Sue,' Estelle said, enfolding the older woman in a comforting hug. 'I'm sure everything will turn out alright, and I'm so proud of you for making the leap. Of course I'll miss you so much, but do what you have to do. Just remember to send me a postcard or two, okay?'

'I promise,' Sue nodded. Then she quickly turned away and picked up her bag, hurrying out of the door before Estelle had a chance to see the tears that she was powerless to prevent.

32

'Oh my, look at this place!' Sue exclaimed, as she and Estelle descended a narrow stone staircase into the burlesque club. Known as The Underground, due to its cellar location, the room was dark and sumptuous, with burgundy painted walls and a bar area that ran the length of one wall. There were small circular tables set up to face the stage, where five shiny silver poles had been erected in a 'W' shape, leaving a performance area in the centre, while black velvet curtains provided a backdrop to the whole scene.

'There's Gracie and Rebecca,' Estelle pointed out, waving at them as they made their way over.

The small room was already beginning to fill up, the lively buzz of conversation creating a real atmosphere. The other tables were occupied by an eclectic mix of people, from a hen party at the back of the room, to a group of what looked like businessmen in smart suits, as well as a handful of couples dotted around.

'Hi!' Gracie squealed excitedly, standing up and kissing them in greeting. 'I'm so glad you're here.'

'It looks wonderful,' Sue assured her, glancing around her as she sat down.

'Let me pour you both a drink,' Rebecca said, removing a bottle of cava from the silver ice bucket in front of them.

'Ooh, bubbles,' Estelle smiled. 'I can tell this is going to be a fun night! You both look gorgeous, by the way.'

Rebecca was wearing a tight, one-shouldered fuchsia dress with royal blue stilettos. The bold colours and sexy style showed just how much her confidence had grown; even her hair was a lighter shade of blonde, in keeping with the summery weather.

Gracie, however, had gone all out on the burlesque theme, in black sequinned hotpants with fishnets underneath, and a sleek black corset. Her hair was styled in soft waves, and she'd drawn a beauty spot high on her cheek bone.

'So do you,' Gracie assured her. 'I bet Tony was mad that he missed out on tonight.'

'I swear he thinks I'm some kind of nymphomaniac,' Estelle giggled. 'I always seem to be reading erotica, or visiting burlesque shows, or looking up naughty things on the Internet.'

'I thought I was the only one who did that!' Sue exclaimed, as the others burst out laughing. 'Honestly, some of those websites out there are unbelievable. Not that I've been looking at *porn*,' she added quickly, lowering her voice. 'But I have been browsing websites like Lovehoney, looking at all the things you can buy. It's a whole other world.'

'Did I tell you Tony caught me looking?' Estelle confessed. 'He saw my Internet history when he was helping me with the website, before we got together. I was mortified – but it all turned out well in the end. In fact,' she began, her cheeks flushing pink at the thought of what she was about to say, 'sometimes we look at things on the Internet together . . . it can be a real turn-on, you know.'

'Estelle!' Rebecca squealed in shock, as Estelle tried to hide behind her hands.

'Quick, pour me another drink,' she demanded, giggling at their reaction.

But at that moment, the lights went down and a woman dressed like a Las Vegas showgirl in a red, glittery costume that left little to the imagination, stepped on stage. The crowd went wild, and the woman drank up their applause, relishing her moment in the spotlight.

'Ladies and gentlemen, my name is Miss Liberty Blue, and I am your *mistress* of ceremonies for tonight,' she introduced herself, as she prowled around the stage, looking out at the audience from beneath black-kohled eyes.

'I do hope you all behave this evening, or else you'll

have to see me to receive your punishment,' she purred, receiving another round of excited cheers in return. 'But without further ado, let me introduce to you your first act of the night. It's the wonderful, the gorgeous, the divinely sexy . . . Miss Trixie La Folle!'

The book group girls clapped heartily, along with the rest of the audience, as the MC left the stage to be replaced by a woman dressed in a top hat and tails, her only accessory a simple straight-backed chair. Her hair was styled in a sharp, black bob, her legs encased in sheer stockings tapering down to very high heels.

Mein Herr from *Cabaret* rang out over the speakers as Miss Trixie La Folle began to dance, gradually removing items of clothing in a slow, seductive manner. The women watched, unable to take their eyes off her. There was nothing sordid in this strip show; it was powerful, beautiful and sensual. Trixie was in absolute control, stripping down in deliberate, teasing movements as she straddled the chair, using it like a dance partner.

She slowly pulled off her black waistcoat and white shirt to reveal a black sequinned bra and, as the music grew faster, rising to a crescendo, she turned her back to the audience. Then, in one swift movement, as the audience cheered encouragingly, she whipped off the bra to reveal her naked back.

Estelle held her breath as Trixie span back around, wearing nothing but a pair of nipple tassels on her top half. As the song reached its climax, Trixie began to spin, the tassels whirling so fast they were a blur, before she dropped into a low bow and took her applause, shimmying off stage behind the black velvet curtain.

Sue was open-mouthed in shock and admiration, while Rebecca leaned over to Gracie and gushed, 'Wow, that was incredible! I didn't even know some of those moves were possible.'

'You'll have to practice,' Gracie told her, laughing at Estelle's wide-eyed expression across the table.

Liberty Blue returned to the stage and, after bantering with the table of businessmen, announced that they would be taking a short break.

'I'll go get us a bottle of wine,' Sue offered, rising from her seat and heading to the bar.

'So, would Tony be impressed if you could do that?' Gracie asked Estelle, referring to the performance they'd just seen.

'If I could do that, I'd be showing everyone – not just Tony,' Estelle chuckled.

'They sell nipple tassels here – you can buy them after the show,' Gracie informed them.

'Really?' Rebecca's eyes lit up. 'I might have to get a pair of those to add to the collection.'

Gracie almost choked on her drink. 'The collection?'

Rebecca giggled at her reaction. 'Andy came home with a whole carrier bag full of kinky stuff the other day,' she explained. 'Bless him, he's really making an effort.'

'What sort of stuff?' Gracie asked, intrigued.

'*Everything*. You name it, he'd bought it. Lube, love

dice, a copy of the Kama Sutra – even a remote control vibrator!'

'Bloody hell, I'm surprised you could walk the next morning!'

'Was it fun?' Estelle asked curiously.

'Oh, we had a great time. I've never had such intense orgasms in my life,' Rebecca confided. 'Of course, it's nothing like the smooth, slick experience you see in the movies, but we were just messing around, having a giggle with each other. And the sheets were totally ruined afterwards – that's chocolate body paint for you.'

'Maybe I need to experiment more,' Estelle said thoughtfully. 'I hope Tony doesn't think I'm boring – we haven't really used toys or anything like that.'

'Oh, you're alright – both of you,' Rebecca insisted, nodding towards Gracie. 'You're both in new relationships, so everything's exciting. When you're five years down the line like Andy and I, then you might need to think about spicing it up.'

'Speaking of long-term relationships, where's Sue got to?' Gracie turned round in her seat to see a long queue at the bar. Sue was staring off into space, an unhappy expression on her face.

'How is she?' Rebecca asked.

Estelle shrugged. 'Okay, I suppose. Just down about George, I think. She still doesn't know whether he's going to come with her on this cruise, but she's adamant that she's going regardless.'

'Good for her!' Rebecca exclaimed.

'Maybe tonight wasn't such a good idea after all,' Gracie said glumly.

'No, I think it was a great idea,' Estelle assured her. 'It's the best thing for her really. She needs to get out of the house and not dwell on everything that's happening. And speaking of getting out of the house, I totally forgot to tell you,' Estelle exclaimed. 'Gracie, I spoke to your friend Jake, and the bad news is that they've decided to put the Fifties Nights on hold for the time being – just for the summer at least. They're going to resurrect them in the autumn, so for now they're scoping out venues. He's going to come in for a chat and a look round, and we'll see what comes of it.'

'Brilliant,' Gracie smiled happily.

'*But*, when I first spoke to him, he said the committee were thinking of organising a street party in the road outside Cafe Crumb. They were waiting for council permission, which is why I didn't mention it at the time, but since then he's got back to me and they've been given the go-ahead to close the road so it's happening next Saturday. Isn't that great? Hopefully that'll be a fantastic boost for the cafe – and for all the shops along the row. Sue already knows about it – she's offered to work – so hopefully you'll both be able to make it.'

'I'll be there, and so will Andy!' Rebecca confirmed happily.

'I'll check with Reggie, but I'm sure it won't be a problem.'

'What's that?' asked Sue, finally returning with a chilled bottle of rosé.

'I was just telling them about the street party,' Estelle began, but she fell quiet as the lights over the audience dimmed and Liberty Blue took to the stage to introduce the second act, Peaches von Cream.

After the energy and glitz of the first performance, the second act was much more dreamy and romantic. The woman, who glided on to stage to *One Day I'll Fly Away* from *Moulin Rouge*, was dressed in a floor-length, ivory satin slip trimmed with marabou feathers. She'd paired it with matching long gloves and a faux-fur cream-coloured shrug around her shoulders, while her platinum hair was styled in ringlets. It was a real change of pace from the previous act; slow, seductive and sensual.

'She's gorgeous,' Gracie whispered to Rebecca, who nodded in reply.

Peaches von Cream was far from being the slimmest girl, but she was utterly confident up on stage, relishing in her glorious, milky-white curves. There was something almost wistful in the way she languorously removed her clothing, slowly stripping right down to nothing but a pair of silky knickers, completely at ease baring her near-naked body in front of the audience.

As the final notes of the song died away, the reception she received brought the house down, the audience whistling and stamping their approval.

'I found that really beautiful,' Sue told Estelle. 'I don't know how someone taking their clothes off can be moving, but that really was!'

Estelle opened her mouth to reply, but at that moment one of the bar staff appeared at their table.

'Can I get you ladies any more drinks?' she asked. 'Another bottle of wine, or some shots?'

'Ooh, let's do shots,' Gracie squealed excitedly. 'What should we get?'

'What's that one called?' Rebecca asked, as she saw one of the hen party walk past with a tray of cream-topped shooters.

'That's a Blow Job,' grinned the waitress. 'Baileys and Amaretto, topped with whipped cream.'

'Four of those,' Rebecca said instantly.

'No, not for me, thank you,' interjected Sue.

'Yes, for you,' Rebecca argued. 'Four shots, please.'

'And another bottle of rosé wine,' Gracie grinned at the waitress.

Their order came back quickly, and there was much giggling as they all downed their shots – even Sue.

'I've never done that before,' she confessed, as she slammed her glass back down on the table.

'What – a shot or a blow job?' Rebecca asked raucously, as they all burst out laughing. Estelle poured them all another glass of wine, as Rebecca turned to Gracie and said, 'Right, I'm drunk enough to ask the question that we're all dying to know the answer to – what's Reggie like in bed?'

There were squeals of protest from Gracie, and exclamations of horror from the other women.

'No one wants to know that, Gracie,' Estelle assured her. 'You don't have to answer.'

'*I* want to know,' Rebecca insisted. 'I want to know if there's a burning hunk of love underneath that geeky exterior.'

'Oi!' Gracie cried, not thrilled with Rebecca's description. 'Since you ask, he's great actually. No complaints from me.'

'Oh, I knew it!' Rebecca clapped her hands excitedly.

'You know,' Sue began, sounding somewhat tipsy. 'I'm so jealous of you young ones. For you, sex is all about fun. Spicing it up and keeping it fresh. But it was never like that for me – you just got on with it, and if it wasn't great then you had to accept that you'd got a dud.'

'It's not too late, Sue,' Rebecca assured her.

'Oh, I think it might be,' Sue replied sadly, taking a large slug of her wine. 'God, what if I never have sex again? What if this is it? Sixty-two years old and no more sex, ever. I might as well be dead.'

The table fell silent for a moment, as they all sipped their wine and contemplated the thought of no more sex.

'Well it won't happen,' Rebecca insisted, raising her voice to be heard above the rising noise levels. 'If the worst comes to the worst, we'll all club together and hire you a lovely young thing for the night. Do what you want with him and send him back in the morning.'

'I know what you mean though, Sue,' Estelle chimed

in through her laugher. 'Before Tony, I wondered if I'd ever meet anyone. But I've gone from worrying that I might never sleep with a man again, to having the best sex of my life.'

'That's probably because you're older,' Rebecca said thoughtfully. 'You can have better sex because you're not as self-conscious and you can just go for what you want. Plus, you know your own body better too.'

'Yes, after being single for five years I know it pretty thoroughly,' Estelle confessed, emboldened by the wine.

She was still blushing as the lights went down for the final time, and Liberty Blue came back on stage in an incredible gold-sequinned costume.

'Now, ladies and gentleman, we have something very special for the finale,' she purred. 'A little treat for you from two ladies who are some of the very best pole dancers in the world. Believe me, you ain't seen nothing like this. Well, *you* probably have, sir,' she laughed, singling out one of the suited businessmen. 'Please give it up for Ivana and Ivanka.'

The crowd went crazy as the two lithe, athletic and incredibly sexy-looking women slunk onto the stage. They were wearing flesh-coloured body stockings covered in diamante, giving the impression that they were naked apart from a few strategically placed diamonds, while waist-length extensions gave them both an impressive mane of blonde hair.

Circus by Britney Spears began to play, and at an invisible signal the two girls mounted the pole at the exact same moment. Their routine was incredible; acrobatic and skilful. It clearly required extraordinary strength, yet the women made it look effortless and graceful as they hung upside down, their legs parting in the splits, swinging round the pole and even hanging by just their feet.

The audience were mesmerised; it was hard to believe that the human body could contort itself into some of those positions.

'I bet they're amazing in bed,' Gracie murmured to Rebecca.

Rebecca nodded. 'I'm glad I didn't bring Andy,' she whispered. 'He'd be expecting me to do that next.'

There was a huge round of applause as the routine finished, the audience rising to their feet and giving Ivana and Ivanka a standing ovation. Everyone from the book club was stunned, their faces full of admiration for what they'd just seen.

The two women stayed on stage, as Liberty Blue came back to join then.

'So now we come to the final part of the evening, which is where I need your help. We're going to indulge in a little . . . audience participation,' she murmured suggestively. 'And I was wondering if there's anyone here tonight who'd like to learn how to pole dance.'

Before she had time to think about what she was doing, Rebecca's hand was instantly in the air. 'Me!' she yelled. 'And my friends!'

'Well-volunteered, come on up,' Liberty Blue smiled,

as Estelle and Sue tried desperately to refuse. But the rest of the audience were having none of it, insistent that they should go up. As they all arrived on the stage, there was wild cheering and applause.

Each of the women took hold of a pole, as Ivana took the centre one to show them how it was done, and Ivanka moved between the women, helping them to perfect their moves.

'Okay ladies,' instructed Ivana, in a strong, Eastern European accent, 'I want you to grasp the pole with both hands, firmly and confidently – imagine it's your boyfriend and you don't want to let him go,' she winked. 'Now sway your bottom from side to side, and slowly move down the pole – that's it, very good ladies,' she said encouragingly.

'Now turn around, so that the pole is resting against your bottom. Raise your hands above your head, grip the pole and slowly shimmy down. If you're wearing the right clothes – or if you want to give the audience an extra treat – you can open your legs on the descent. Very sexy, that's right!'

Gracie and Rebecca were loving their time on the pole, although Estelle was giving them a good run for their money. Sue was moving more slowly, clearly self-conscious at being in front of an audience, but she was beginning to relax.

'Grip the pole with your right leg, push gently off the ground, and you should be able to spin. Fantastic! And now, you can freestyle!'

Gracie was flying round the pole like she'd been born to do it, her hair streaming out as she tipped her head upside down and rippled her body. It made her feel strong, sexy and empowered, and she wished Reggie was here to see her perform.

Rebecca was equally confident, but her style was slightly wilder than Gracie's, flinging her body round with gay abandon despite being hindered by the short, tight dress she was wearing. One of the hen party members had thrown Sue a pink feather boa, and she was having more fun with that, waving it round her head and wiggling her hips, while Estelle was determined to master the pole, grateful that she was wearing black skinny jeans which allowed her to preserve her dignity.

'A huge round of applause for our amazing dancers,' cried Liberty Blue, as the women made their way down from the stage to raucous applause. As they sat back down at their table, still drinking in the frenzied cheers and whistles, the waitress swung by and deposited a bottle of champagne on their table.

'We didn't order this,' Sue told her worriedly.

'No, the gentlemen at that table sent it over,' she explained, pointing to the group of suited businessmen.

'Well, I could definitely get used to this,' Rebecca grinned, as she opened the bottle and the cork flew out with a loud pop.

'Christina Cox eat your heart out,' Estelle joked, as they each raised a glass of champagne, and toasted the solicitous men across the room.

33

'Reggie!' Gracie shrieked gleefully, as she staggered out of The Underground and into the taxi where Reggie was waiting for her. He'd been working late in the university library, and had offered to pick her up whenever she finished. By now it was almost midnight, and the book club girls were huddled on the pavement waiting for their various lifts and taxis.

'Look after her, Reggie,' Estelle called through the window. 'Make sure she gets home safely.'

'I will,' he smiled, as Gracie blew kisses at them all.

'Don't do anything I wouldn't do,' Rebecca winked.

'I think that leaves us with plenty of options,' Gracie shot back cheekily, waving at them as the taxi pulled away. On the back seat, she snuggled up against Reggie, tilting her head up to kiss him.

'Did you have a good time tonight?' he asked, gazing at her lovingly.

'Oh, I had a great night! I missed you though,' she told him, her fingers playing with the collar of his shirt.

'You look amazing,' Reggie told her, running his hands over her fishnet-clad thighs. 'I don't know if I should have let you go out looking like this.'

'Can we go back to yours?' Gracie whispered. 'I want to show you what you've been missing.'

Reggie groaned softly. 'I just feel so uncomfortable at mine after all that stuff with Josh. Saturday night's even worse – he'll probably be drunk and even more of a dickhead than usual. What about your place? Is your mum in?'

Gracie nodded. 'She went out earlier, but she'll be home by now. She doesn't mind, you know,' Gracie breathed, as she began to lick his ear. She felt more than a little drunk.

'I know, but I do,' Reggie protested. They'd been over to Gracie's a couple of times when Maggie was out, but Reggie never felt completely comfortable in Gracie's childhood room, squashed into her single bed and having to rush what they were doing before Maggie came home. It always left him feeling slightly seedy afterwards.

'But I need you,' Gracie murmured seductively. 'I'm horny, Reggie.' She let her hand slip down to his crotch, fondling him through his trousers in case he was in any doubt as to what she meant.

Reggie's eyes widened, and he looked nervously in the direction of the taxi driver, wondering how much he could see in the darkness of the cab. Gracie's jacket was on the seat beside her, and she swung it over their laps discreetly, unzipping Reggie's trousers and working her way inside.

Reggie gulped, trying his best to behave normally. 'S– so you had a good night, then?' he stuttered.

'Fantastic,' she replied brazenly, squeezing him tighter and finding her rhythm. 'I think the girls all really enjoyed it.'

'That's good,' Reggie panted.

'Yeah, the show was excellent. Lots of sexy girls taking their clothes off.'

'Remind me again why I wasn't allowed to go?'

Gracie grinned, continuing to stroke him. 'There's only one sexy girl who'll be taking her clothes off for you.'

'Believe me, that can't come soon enough . . .'

'And we all had a go at pole dancing,' Gracie told him tantalisingly, knowing that this was like torture for him and relishing every minute. 'Grinding up and down the bar, rubbing against it and wrapping our legs around it. Even Sue had a go.'

'That's a very off-putting image,' Reggie frowned. 'I'd prefer it if you didn't talk about Sue while you're . . .' he nodded towards his crotch, and Gracie giggled.

'Well you might not appreciate Sue's dancing, but there were some men in the audience who certainly did. They sent over a bottle of champagne when we'd finished.'

'Did they indeed?' Reggie raised an eyebrow. 'I'm not sure what I think about that.'

'Don't worry. We just drank the champagne and ignored them.'

'Good,' Reggie told her possessively. 'Because you're mine.'

'Mmm, I like it when you're dominant.'

'*All* mine,' Reggie added, pulling her towards him and kissing her deeply, not caring what the taxi driver thought. 'Every part of you belongs to me,' Reggie continued, his bravery building as he slyly slid his hand beneath the jacket on their laps, fumbling with the waistband of Gracie's hotpants and finding his way inside.

She gasped with excitement, pressing herself against his hand as his fingers began to explore. Neither of them spoke anymore; normal conversation was impossible as they tried to concentrate on not giving away what they were doing. Gracie's breathing was growing faster the more aroused she became, and she forced herself to look away from Reggie, gazing unseeingly out of the window. Houses, shops, pedestrians and streetlights all flashed past, but she didn't care about any of them.

It was only when she saw the familiar sight of the Clifton Suspension Bridge up ahead that something clicked in her brain. She sat up abruptly, letting go of Reggie.

'Could you stop here, please?' she called out to the driver.

Reggie looked at her in confusion.

'Trust me,' Gracie winked, when she saw his expression.

'Here?' the taxi driver asked doubtfully, peering out through the front window. The street was deserted, with nothing but a row of smart-looking houses on one side and a grassy area on the other.

'Yes, that's fine, thank you,' Gracie replied, straightening her clothes as the cab pulled up to the pavement. Reggie paid the bill and they jumped out, the welcoming light of the car disappearing into the darkness.

'Gracie, what are you doing?' Reggie asked, wondering if she'd taken leave of her senses.

'Now I can kiss you properly,' she told him, wrapping her arms around him and kissing him passionately. Reggie's mouth was warm, and she could feel herself getting turned on all over again.

'This is great, but how are we going to get home?' Reggie puzzled, still none the wiser as to what Gracie was planning. One thing he'd come to learn was that life with her was never dull.

'We'll worry about that later,' she told him, taking his hand and pulling him across the road. The night air was warm, and they walked along the grass verge for a while until Gracie stopped, turning around to look at the view. 'Isn't it beautiful?'

The bridge was just ahead, an incredible feat of engineering spanning the River Avon below. It was a dramatic sight, lit up against the dark night sky where a brilliant crescent moon sat amongst the silver stars.

'It's very nice, Gracie, but I've been living in Bristol for almost a decade now, and I've seen the bridge plenty of times. I hope you didn't stop the taxi just to show me that.'

Gracie shook her head. 'No. But while we're here, why don't we get a little bit closer?' She led him across the grass verge and through a gap in the bushes to where a rough path led a short way down the cliff.

'I'm not sure this is a good idea,' Reggie began, but Gracie cut him off.

'Come on, you only live once. I used to come down here all the time as a kid. It's perfectly safe.'

She disappeared, giggling, into the trees, and Reggie had no option but to follow her, as they made their way carefully down the uneven path. They hadn't gone far when the ground levelled out, and Gracie doubled back through a gap in the undergrowth. As Reggie caught up with her, he found that they were in a small clearing, hidden from view by sprawling ash trees. A huge slab of rock jutted out from the ground, and Gracie leant against it, her eyes sparkling in the moonlight.

'Now we can finish what we started,' she smiled.

'Here?' Reggie was incredulous.

'Why not? We don't have anywhere else to go.'

'Is it even legal?' he asked worriedly.

'It is if we don't get caught,' she grinned naughtily. 'Reggie, I want you,' she murmured, her voice growing soft. 'Right here, right now.'

Reggie recognised the challenge in her words, thinking

377

how sexy she looked in her corset and fishnets. As he watched, she began to dance, showing off the burlesque moves she'd learnt earlier. She raised her hands above her head, slowly rotating her hips, her breasts bouncing invitingly in the tight corset top.

Reggie swallowed, unable to take his eyes off her. One of the things he loved most about Gracie was her wild spirit, her sense of adventure. She was constantly pushing the boundaries, forcing him out of his comfort zone, and that was something he found a huge turn-on.

He stepped closer, powerless to resist and unable to tear his gaze away from her gyrating body. All he could think about was how much he wanted to be inside her right now. 'Okay,' he growled, his voice low and husky as his hands gripped her waist, pulling her sharply towards him. 'You're on. Right here, right now.'

34

The front door closed with a bang, and Sue winced, trying to be quiet as she tiptoed through the house. She knew she was a little tipsy – well, more than that, if she was being honest – but she'd had a great night, and the alcohol was flowing in her veins, making her giggly and upbeat. The bright pink feather boa still hung around her neck, and she smiled to herself as she remembered the pair of red sparkly nipple tassels she'd bought, now nestling at the bottom of her handbag. She couldn't imagine ever actually *wearing* them, but still, the very act of buying them had given her a mental boost. All the other women had purchased them too, and she'd felt like one of the girls, the whole gang of them laughing and excited as they handed over their money.

Sue crept down the corridor to the kitchen, switching on the light and pouring herself a glass of water. It was late – after midnight – and she imagined George would have gone to bed by now. Lost in her own world, she jumped so high she almost hit the ceiling when he walked into the room.

'George, you startled me,' she exclaimed, putting a hand to her chest. Something about the whole situation suddenly struck her as hilarious, and she began to giggle uncontrollably. From the expression on George's face, he didn't find it nearly as funny.

'Where have you been?' he demanded. His clothes and his face were creased, and Sue guessed he'd fallen asleep in the chair.

'Oh George, you know where I've been.' Her voice was louder than normal, her words slightly slurred. 'On a night out with the girls,' she clarified, giving a little shimmy.

'Until now?'

'Yes, until now. I wasn't aware I had a curfew.'

'I've been waiting up for you.'

'Well, no one asked you to.'

There was a tense silence, neither of them willing to back down. Sue felt the earlier exhilaration leach out of her, like water draining from a bath. She'd been on such a high tonight but, as ever, George could instantly bring her crashing back down to earth.

'What on earth are you wearing?' he asked sharply, as though noticing for the first time. 'You look ridiculous.'

'It's called a feather boa,' she informed him haughtily,

as she began to dance around the kitchen, humming a burlesque-style song and twirling the ends of the boa seductively. She wiggled over to George, shaking the feathers in his face, imagining she was back on the pole in front of a cheering audience. Okay, so she might not have been very good at it, but that hadn't seemed to matter at the time. It had been terribly exciting; a glimpse of what her life could have been if only she'd dared to dream a little bigger and run off to Paris to be a dancer in the Folies Bergère . . .

Sue was abruptly pulled from her reverie as she realised that George was quite literally spitting feathers, backing away from her as he pushed the boa out of his face.

'Stop it!' he snapped angrily. 'Are you drunk?'

'I may have partaken in an alcoholic beverage or two,' she told him flirtatiously, only to be met with a steely glare. 'Oh, lighten up, George.'

But George didn't have any intention of lightening up. 'I'm going to bed,' he told her shortly.

'Fine. I'm surprised you're not there already.'

'Like I said, I was waiting up for you.'

'Like *I* said, no one asked you to.'

George's eyes narrowed, his forehead creasing into a frown. 'And I had some thinking to do.'

'Oh yes?' Sue replied blithely, not really paying attention as she drained her glass of water and poured another.

'Yes. About whether or not to accompany you on this crazy trip you've proposed.'

Sue's hand froze in mid-air. George's gaze was fixed,

his eyes giving nothing away, but Sue's heart had begun to pound. She tried to keep her expression neutral, to not let him see how much of a big deal this was to her, but inside her emotions were running wild.

'And?' she asked coolly. 'Did you make any decisions?'

George paused. 'Yes. As a matter of fact, I did.'

Sue seemed to have sobered up remarkably quickly. Her pulse was racing as she realised how much she cared about what George's answer would be. 'And? Don't keep me in suspense,' she tried to joke, but her comment fell flat.

There was another long pause, before George sighed heavily. 'I'm not coming, Sue.'

Sue inhaled sharply, almost dropping the glass she was holding. 'Are you serious?' she demanded, scanning his face for signs that he might be joking.

'Of course,' George replied, trying to sound more confident than he felt. 'And I don't think you should go either.'

It was the comment Sue needed to propel her out of shock and into anger. 'I'm going,' she retorted furiously, 'And you can't stop me.' Her voice was shaking with emotion as she realised what this meant. As far as she was concerned, if George rejected her now, it was all over. How could they possibly carry on like normal after this?

George rubbed a hand wearily across his brow. He looked old and tired, exhausted by the constant fighting.

'But *why*, Sue?' he asked desperately, unable to

understand the way his wife seemed to have changed beyond all recognition in recent weeks. 'Why can't we just carry on as we are, without having to go off gallivanting around the world?'

'We've been over and over this!' Sue cried, unable to hide her frustration. 'I don't want this life, here, with you.' The alcohol made her cruel, and she blurted out the first thing that came into her head without attempting to censor it.

George stared at her for a long moment. 'Right,' he said finally, and his voice was quiet. 'I guess I'll be off to bed then.'

He turned around and headed for the door, but Sue called out to stop him.

'George,' she began. 'George, I *need* to go, to get away for a while. And if you don't come with me, I don't see how we can find a way back from this.'

George hesitated, letting the words sink in.

'If you walk out on me now, you walk out on this marriage,' Sue warned, desperation in her voice.

'Sue, I'm sorry,' George said, his voice cracking with emotion. 'I've tried, really I have, but I just can't do this anymore.' Then he walked out of the door, and Sue heard his heavy tread as he tramped up the stairs to bed.

As the door swung shut behind him, Sue crumpled as though she'd been punched in the stomach, sinking to her knees on the cold, tiled floor. The feather boa still hung jauntily round her neck, but now it just seemed garish and ridiculous, a pathetic attempt by a sad old woman to inject some fun back into her life.

Where had it all gone so wrong? Sue wondered desperately. At what point had George decided to give up on them – to give up on *her*. It felt like a complete rejection, as though he was saying that whatever they'd once had was no longer worth fighting for. It seemed unbelievable that he would rather stay here alone than come and see the world with her.

Did that mean it was over? Sue wondered, as the tears began to fall, streaking down her cheeks and ruining the mascara she'd applied so carefully at the beginning of the night. Did George want a divorce? To throw away four decades of marriage without even trying to salvage it? She felt like a complete failure, old and useless and good for nothing.

Feeling utterly hopeless, Sue collapsed on the kitchen floor, her body wracked with sobs as she wept for her lost marriage.

35

'You did *what*?' Rebecca screeched, causing people in the pub to turn round and stare. It was Wednesday evening, and she and Gracie had decided to meet for a catch-up in the New Inn, Rebecca's local. Although it was busy, Rebecca's voice still carried above the crowd, causing Gracie to turn bright red.

'Sssh! You heard me the first time. I'm not saying it again.'

'But outside? At night? With Reggie?' Rebecca looked aghast and impressed all at the same time.

'Of course with Reggie! Who else?'

'And was it good?'

'Yeah, it was pretty exciting,' Gracie confessed, adding with a giggle, 'I wouldn't recommend it in winter though.'

'Were you drunk?' Rebecca wondered.

'A bit,' Gracie replied honestly. 'You saw me when I

left The Underground. But honestly, Bex, it's so frustrating. We had a bit of an incident with one of Reggie's housemates, so we can't really go to his, and I'm still living with my mum, so it makes it hard to get any time alone.'

'Oh, I didn't think of that,' Rebecca sympathised.

'Sometimes you've just got to grab it where you can – if you'll pardon the pun,' Gracie grinned. 'The risk factor was a real turn-on, to be honest. It was hot and heavy and intense.'

'Couldn't you just book a hotel instead?' Rebecca teased.

'We did that before, actually. Our very first time – Reggie planned it all as a surprise.'

'Did he?' Rebecca's face lit up. 'That's so romantic.'

'Yeah, it was amazing,' Gracie remembered dreamily. 'Really special.'

'I can't imagine Reggie being like that. I mean, he's a nice guy and everything, but he always seems quite uptight. I'll never be able to look at him in the same way again, after the things you've told me!'

'He's actually really chilled out when you get to know him,' Gracie said, her eyes sparkling as she talked about her lover. 'He's funny, and sensitive, and caring . . .'

'You really like him, don't you?' Rebecca said softly, thinking what a different side she was seeing of Gracie. She'd been so abrasive and defensive back at that first book club meeting, never shy of voicing her opinion and always ready to argue with anyone who disagreed. Now, she still had her feisty side of course, but she seemed far more relaxed in her own skin.

'Yeah, I do,' Gracie admitted, taking a sip of her cider. 'I know he's not the best-looking guy out there, or the coolest person in the world, but neither am I. We just seem to suit each other,' she finished happily. 'Anyway, enough about me and my sexual exploits – how are you and Andy? It sounds like things are good.'

Rebecca nodded. 'He's really making an effort at the moment, and we're getting on so well. I think the sex is even better than when we were first dating, to be honest. He's so much more willing to experiment, and we're just having fun, going with the flow.'

'We really need to thank Estelle,' Gracie laughed. 'If it hadn't been for her and all those naughty books, I doubt we'd be as satisfied as we are now!'

'I think she's doing fairly well out of it too,' Rebecca replied wryly. 'Tony's gorgeous – lucky woman. She really seems to have blossomed recently.'

'You can definitely tell when someone's getting some,' Gracie nodded sagely. 'They just have this happy glow about them. You're definitely glowing.'

'Really?' Rebecca pulled a face. 'I feel rubbish.'

'Why, what's the matter? Are you coming down with a cold or something?'

'No, nothing like that. *Time of the month*,' she mouthed.

'Oh,' Gracie nodded sympathetically. 'Maybe you should have a Scotch to numb the pain.'

Rebecca shook her head. 'I feel really queasy actually. I haven't felt right since the burlesque night – it's like my hangover's never gone away.'

'Well they do say they last longer when you get older.'

'Not for four days! I was actually sick this morning, which is really unlike me – hence why I'm on the lemonade,' Rebecca explained, nodding at the glass in front of her. 'I'm trying to settle my stomach.'

'Weird. Shall we get something to eat?' Gracie asked, picking up the menu and scanning the choices. 'That might help.'

'I couldn't. I really don't feel like anything. Even the smell of food turns my stomach.'

'How about a dessert instead?' Gracie suggested. 'Ooh, they do hot chocolate fudge cake. We could share?'

'You get one if you want, but I don't think I could stomach it.'

'You're not like me,' Gracie continued cheerfully. 'I'm normally ravenous for chocolate when I've got my period. Can't get enough of the stuff.'

'Me too,' Rebecca realised. 'Well, usually. I don't know what's wrong with me today.'

'You're not pregnant are you?' Gracie joked. 'Oh, I suppose not. Not if you're on your period.'

'But I haven't . . .' Rebecca began, then trailed off.

'Haven't what?'

Rebecca swallowed hard, the colour draining out of her face. She'd attributed her sore, sensitive breasts, stomach cramps, and general feeling of not-being-quite-right to her impending period – something she thought was imminent due to the fact that she was now almost two weeks late.

The alternative hadn't even crossed her mind until Gracie had blithely suggested it just now, but the more Rebecca thought about it, the more it made sense. She was usually regular as clockwork, out by only a day or two at the most. And recently, she and Andy had been getting increasingly carried away, their usual precautions falling by the wayside when the mood swept them up.

Rebecca took a deep breath and realised she had to face it – there was a very real chance that she might be pregnant.

Gracie was watching her intently. 'Rebecca, you're not . . .?'

'I might be.'

'But I thought you were on your period.'

Rebecca shook her head. 'I'm due. I thought this was it.'

Gracie's eyes widened in alarm. 'Pharmacy. Now.'

'What?'

'You need to know, don't you? We can get a test.' Gracie was already on her feet, gathering up her bag. 'There's a late-night place down the road. Let's go.'

Which was why, half an hour later, Rebecca found herself locked in a toilet cubicle in the New Inn, with Gracie standing outside offering moral support.

'Have you done it yet?' Gracie called out.

'No, I haven't,' came Rebecca's muffled reply. 'Are you sure this is the best place? I'd much rather do it at home.'

'Don't you want to find out as soon as possible? I would.'

'I suppose so,' Rebecca admitted.

'Besides, you've got me here for moral support. Whatever the answer turns out to be . . .'

'Mmm-hmm . . .'

On the other side of the cubicle door, Rebecca closed the toilet lid and sat down on it, her mind racing so much she could barely concentrate enough to read the instructions on the enclosed leaflet. She thought she had a fairly good idea of what needed to be done – pee on stick, wait two minutes – just like in the hundreds of movies and TV dramas she'd seen over the years. But this was different. This affected *her*, and the outcome could change her whole life.

Of course she wanted children, and she knew Andy did too, but she'd always imagined that they'd wait until the timing was perfect and then have the discussion. Conception would be a planned, organised event – not some panic-inducing bombshell that Rebecca discovered in far from salubrious surroundings. She certainly hadn't imagined finding out in the grubby New Inn toilets, with their peeling paint and creaking plumbing.

Outside the door, she could hear Gracie pacing impatiently. She seemed almost as nervous as Rebecca was.

'Are you okay in there?' Gracie shouted once again. 'Do you need anything?'

'A shot of tequila,' she replied jokingly. Then realisation dawned and she added, 'Although depending on how this goes, I might not be drinking again for another nine months.'

'Or eating sushi,' added Gracie.

'Or raw eggs,' giggled Rebecca.

'Such a shame – they were your favourite too,' Gracie laughed, both of them becoming slightly hysterical.

Then they calmed down and the mood grew serious once again, as Rebecca pulled the stick out of its plastic packet and stared at it.

'I'm going to do it, Gracie,' she told her, trying to summon up her courage.

'Okay,' Gracie shouted back. 'Good luck!'

Taking a deep breath, Rebecca clambered unsteadily to her feet, pulling up her skirt and pulling down the beautiful silk knickers she was wearing. They were champagne-coloured, and part of a matching set. She'd planned to seduce Andy in them later, and the irony wasn't lost on her now.

Instead, she was crouched over a cracked toilet seat beneath a flickering strip light, her knickers round her knees as, in a most undignified manner, she weed on the absorbent tip.

And then it was done, and all she could do now was wait. She flushed the toilet, closed the lid and sat down as she prepared for the longest two minutes of her life.

'All done,' she called out to Gracie.

There was silence for a few moments, then Gracie called out. 'Bex?'

'Yeah?' she replied.

'What do you want the result to be?'

Rebecca swallowed hard, not even sure whether she knew the answer herself. 'I don't know,' she admitted.

It was no exaggeration to say that the test results of this test could change her life forever. If she *was* pregnant, then everything for the next eighteen years at least would revolve around the child. Her sleep pattern, job, holidays, sex life would all be affected by the new arrival. And there was part of her that felt as if she'd only just got Andy back – would this mean losing him all over again? Their identities swallowed up as they became Mummy and Daddy instead of Rebecca and Andy?

But on the other hand, what better time could there be for a baby? They were young, financially stable, and their days of going out clubbing were long behind them. Maybe they *were* ready for this.

Tentatively, Rebecca touched her stomach, wondering if there was already a new life in there – one which she and Andy had created. Her emotions were all over the place, swinging between pure, unadulterated joy and excitement, to sheer terror and back again. The wait was simply agonising.

Rebecca looked down at the stick in her hand but it remained frustratingly blank, apparently not appreciating the urgency of the situation. She estimated that there were about thirty seconds left to go before the result revealed itself, but until then there was nothing more she could do. She simply sat on the cold toilet seat and waited.

36

Estelle was gliding round her kitchen, moving dreamily from the oven to the scales to the work surfaces, where she rolled out the dough for another batch of chunky cheese scones. It was Friday night, and she was preparing an extra-large supply of goods for the weekend rush. Right now, there was nowhere she would rather be. She hummed delightedly to herself as she went through the familiar motions, everything perfectly under control, focusing on what she did best.

Business had really been booming in recent weeks, partly due to the warm weather that had arrived now they were moving into summer, and Estelle had set up a handful of tables and chairs on the pavement outside to take advantage. But even without that, footfall and profits were both up compared to this time last year, and she was hugely excited to see what the forthcoming street party would bring.

But there was something else adding to her good mood . . . Something that was making her emotions soar and plummet as though she was riding a rollercoaster; that made her stomach leap with nerves and anticipation; and that caused delicious tingles in other parts of her body too . . .

Her mobile beeped and Estelle snatched it up, as giddy as a teenager. Almost as if she'd conjured him up with her thoughts, there was a text message from Tony:

Are we still on for Saturday night? T xxx

Estelle broke into a wide smile, hugging the phone to her. Just knowing that Tony was thinking about her – that he was excited about seeing her too – sent her into a veritable tailspin.

She thought for a moment, then quickly typed back:

We sure are. Wear your fireman's helmet (and nothing else) ;) xxx

She was still beaming when Joe walked into the kitchen. 'Hi Mum,' he said, his eyes darting over the dough Estelle was rolling out, the cakes cooling on wire racks and the slabs of tiffin waiting to go into the fridge. He wandered aimlessly round the room for a few moments, taking everything in, before leaning against one of the units and letting out a heavy sigh.

'Hi Joe. Are you okay?' Estelle asked curiously. It was rare for him to linger.

'Yeah, fine,' he added, as he picked up a triple chocolate cookie and broke it in half. The dough was still warm, and the melted chocolate chunks dribbled luxuriantly onto the biscuit as he took a large bite. 'Do you want a hand?'

'No, I'm fine,' Estelle replied automatically. She knew he'd rather be playing computer games or texting his friends than stuck in the kitchen with her.

'Are you sure? I don't mind,' he insisted.

'Well . . . okay then,' Estelle agreed, deciding to play along. She knew he must have some reason for offering to help, so she would wait it out until he was ready to talk. 'You can do the flapjacks if you like. Now you know the rules – wash your hands thoroughly . . . That's it . . . Right, if you could weigh out five hundred grams of rolled oats to start with,' she instructed, passing him the bag.

He did as he was told, while Estelle melted the butter, sugar and honey together in a large pan and watched him fondly, remembering the way they used to bake together when he was a child. Back then, she was still with Ted, and they lived in a much larger three-bedroomed house with a beautiful kitchen-diner. Baking was still just a hobby, and she and Joe would often make fairy cakes or rice krispie buns, with mess splattering all over the worktops and Joe throwing a tantrum if he didn't get to lick out the bowl afterwards.

He'd grown up so much since then, Estelle thought with a pang – quite literally in fact, as he was now taller than she was. At almost fifteen years old, he was on the cusp of adulthood, stuck in the no-man's land of adolescence where he was neither boy nor man. Joe was currently at the awkward stage where he hadn't yet got used to his lanky frame and hunched his shoulders self-consciously. He was constantly eating, yet remained skinny as a rake, and dark, downy hair peppered his jawline and upper lip.

His face was currently scrunched in deep concentration, as he carefully poured the oats into the butter mixture and stirred the whole thing together with a wooden spoon. Estelle knew she could have done it herself in half the time, but it was sweet of him to offer to help.

'So how's everything going with you?' she asked, in a subtle attempt to broach whatever was on his mind. They very rarely had mother-son bonding time like this, so she was pleased that he'd come to her now.

'Yeah, it's all okay,' he shrugged, tipping the glacé cherries and desiccated coconut that Estelle handed him into the pan.

'And everything's alright at school?'

'I suppose so. I don't find it very interesting. I'd rather be playing football.'

'I know, sweetheart, but unless you're very lucky, you can't make a living out of playing football.'

'Tony does,' Joe said randomly.

Estelle paused, taken aback for a moment. 'Well, not quite,' she began, recovering herself. 'He works full-time as a fireman. He doesn't get paid for teaching you guys, you know – he does because he enjoys it.'

Joe fell silent, digesting what his mother had said. Eventually, he spoke. 'He's a nice guy, Tony, isn't he? I like him.'

'Yeah, he seems to be okay,' Estelle said casually, with huge understatement. She could feel the heat rising in her face, convinced her expression was giving her away, but fortunately Joe was concentrating on stirring the sticky mixture on the hob. 'You can tip that out now,' she told him. 'Spoon it onto this baking tray.'

'You get on well with him, don't you?' Joe continued, apparently oblivious to Estelle's attempts to change the subject.

'I suppose so. As I said, he seems like a nice man.'

Estelle had been meaning to have a chat with Joe about her relationship with Tony, but it never seemed to be the right time. Or, if she was being brutally honest, she'd been putting it off. She had no idea how Joe would take it, and while everything was so new there didn't seem any point in unsettling him. Now, however, it was looking as though it might develop into something more serious, and she knew she couldn't put it off any longer.

'You know, if you wanted to start dating again, I wouldn't mind,' Joe said presciently, as Estelle stared at him in shock. 'I'm just saying. I mean, Dad's got Leila, but it's been ages since you've been with anyone.'

'Joe!' she exclaimed, unable to do anything apart from splutter helplessly.

'I'm not going to be around forever,' Joe continued. 'I'll probably be going to university in a few years – if I get the grades, that is. It'd be good to know there's someone looking after you.'

He slid the baking tray into the oven, and Estelle felt close to tears. Her son was far more mature – and far more perceptive – than she'd realised.

'I know you haven't dated anyone since you and Dad got divorced . . .'

'Joe, I don't think this is an appropriate subject—' Estelle began, but he cut her off.

'It's no big deal, Mum. Me and Chris were talking about it, and—'

'Chris?' Estelle queried, alarm bells beginning to ring. Obviously she and Tony hadn't been quite as discreet as they'd thought.

'Yeah. Look, we don't mind if you and Tony want to get together.'

Estelle turned the colour of a glacé cherry. 'Well, I . . .'

'I'm not stupid, Mum. I'm not blind either.'

'Well, it's true that Tony and I have become . . . very good friends.'

Joe rolled his eyes. 'Yeah, yeah, I know what that means. I'm nearly fifteen, Mum, I know all about that stuff. We had the talk – remember?'

Estelle flushed even deeper.

'Okay, well, thanks for speaking to me about this,' she managed finally. 'It shows a lot of maturity.'

'S'okay,' Joe shrugged, as though he couldn't understand what all the fuss was about.

'Anything else you want to talk about while we're

399

chatting?' Estelle asked tentatively, keen to take the attention off her, and unsure when they'd next get the chance to talk so openly.

Joe shrugged again.

'How are you getting on with Leila?'

'Yeah, she's alright. She's getting pretty big now. We don't really have much to talk about, but I'm cool with her. I know Dad's getting on with his life – I just wanted to make sure you were getting on with yours.'

Impulsively, Estelle dropped the pastry cutter she was holding and flung her arms around Joe. 'I'm so proud of you! You're growing up into such a great young man.'

'Yeah, yeah . . .' Joe endured the hug until Estelle finally pulled away, planting a kiss on his forehead.

'But you'll always be my baby.'

'Stop getting mushy, Mum,' he protested, wiping his face where Estelle had left traces of lip balm.

Her phone suddenly beeped, indicating that she'd received a text message. She read it quickly, unable to stop a smile pulling at the corners of her mouth.

'Tony?' asked Joe.

Estelle looked up guiltily. 'Yeah, it was actually.'

'I could tell. You go all soppy around him.'

'No, I don't!'

'Whatever, Mum,' Joe grinned.

'He's a good guy, you know,' Estelle told him softly.

'Yeah, I know he is. I told *you* that.'

'So you wouldn't mind then? If we started seeing more of each other?'

'I guess not,' Joe said, with a dramatic sigh. 'As long as you don't start getting off with him at football practice or anything. That would be gross.'

'I won't. I promise.'

'Does Dad know?'

Not yet. I didn't think it was worth mentioning until I knew whether it was going to turn into something serious.'

'Well he can't have a problem with it. I mean, he's got Leila.'

They carried on working in silence for a few moments, as Joe began stirring the ingredients for a chocolate cake. He poured everything into the mixer and whizzed it round, before saying casually, 'There was one more thing I wanted to ask.'

'Mmm?' Estelle said distantly, her head full of Tony and Ted and red velvet cupcake recipes.

'Could I have some money? Twenty quid maybe . . . or thirty?'

'Oh, I see. Getting your mother all soppy and sentimental so you could tap her up for cash, were you? I know your game.'

'It wasn't like that,' Joe protested.

'You know money's always tight – although the cafe has been doing better recently,' she admitted. 'What do you want it for?'

Now it was Joe's turn to blush. 'I just do,' he said evasively.

Estelle narrowed her eyes, looking at him suspiciously.

'I'm not going to hand money over to you without knowing what it's for. Help me out here.'

'I'm going into town tomorrow. I just need some extra cash to spend.'

'Oh. Are you meeting up with Chris and Harry?'

'Not exactly.' Joe was squirming under his mother's questioning. 'There's this girl at school, called Lauren.'

'Yes . . .' Estelle said encouragingly, willing him to continue.

'We're meeting up at Cabot Circus, and I wanted some money so we could grab some food somewhere. Maybe take her to Nando's.'

'Like a date?' Estelle teased.

'*Mum*!' Joe looked mortified.

'Hey, I'm nearly forty-three, I know all about that stuff,' she parodied him gleefully, revelling in the fact that the tables were turned. 'So do you really like this Lauren?'

'I dunno,' he replied defensively. The last thing he wanted to do was discuss his love life with his mother. 'Yeah, she's nice. I just want to hang out with her a bit more.'

'I tell you what,' Estelle suggested, thinking on her feet. 'How about you help me out in the cafe for a bit tomorrow morning? Say, nine until twelve? Then you can have the cash and do whatever you want in the afternoon.'

'What?' Joe screwed up his face in disgust.

'It'll be like having a part-time job. You're old enough

to start working, and it'll be a good way to get you out of bed.'

'But that's child labour!' Joe complained. 'Isn't that illegal?'

Estelle gave him a look. 'That's the deal, Joe. Take it or leave it,' she threatened, holding out her hand.

He eyed it uncertainly for a moment. 'Okay, deal,' he agreed, reaching out to shake on it, but Estelle pulled him forward into another hug.

'Aw, my boy's growing up so fast,' she sniffed, feeling genuinely emotional.

'Stop it, Mum,' he protested, pulling away and going back to the cake mixture, tipping it into the tin that Estelle had greased and lined. She watched with a smile as he made a beeline for the empty bowl, plunging his hands in and scooping out the delicious gooey mixture before licking it off his fingers with a contented sigh.

Her son might be grown up enough to start dating girls and discussing her love life, Estelle reflected with amusement, but he would never be too old to lick out the cake bowl.

37

By mid-morning on the day of the street party, the road outside Cafe Crumb was teeming with people. Families with pushchairs strolled along, enjoying the warm, sunny weather, while young children begged for ice cream and excitable dogs on leads scurried underfoot, eager to get their noses into everything.

The street itself looked fantastic – bright and festive. The road had been closed off at all access points, and to the left of Cafe Crumb a red and blue bouncy castle had been erected. The lamp posts had been hung with strings of bunting that criss-crossed overhead, while helium-filled balloons were tied to street signs, and outside the gift shop a face-painter was doing a roaring trade, churning out dozens of miniature tigers and butterflies.

Most of the shops had stalls outside, and Cafe Crumb was no exception. Joe and Chris were currently manning it like professionals, the table laden with a selection of Estelle's most popular cakes and pastries, as well as cups of home-made lemonade and orange squash. They were doing shuttle runs inside to grab teas and coffees on request from Sue, who was helping Estelle inside the cafe.

Estelle couldn't help but worry about her friend. Although Sue insisted she was excited about her upcoming adventure, she had been distinctly subdued, and Estelle knew that however bad things were with George, Sue would rather he'd decided to come with her. His decision to stay behind was almost like a rejection, an admittance that something had gone badly wrong in their relationship that he had no desire to try and fix. Of course, Sue knew that she wasn't entirely blameless – it had been her decision, after all, to leave their cosy domesticity and book a round-the-world cruise – but George just seemed to be burying his head in the sand, making no attempt to compromise.

'How're you holding up?' Estelle asked sympathetically, as Sue smiled bravely.

'I'm surviving. I'm starting to get excited about my trip – I think I need to look to the future, rather than the past. But the best thing for me at the moment is to keep busy – it's great for me to be here.'

'Well, if you're sure,' Estelle told her.

'I am. Anyway, what are you still doing in here? Won't Tony be here at any moment?'

Estelle looked out of the window and saw that one of the barriers at the far end of the road was being removed. Seconds later, a large, red fire engine rolled slowly into view.

Estelle turned to Sue, excitement written across her face. 'Are you sure you're okay on your own for a few minutes? I'm just going to run out and say hi.'

'I'll be fine,' Sue nodded. 'Besides, I've got the boys to give me a hand if it gets too busy.'

'I'll tell them to keep checking on you,' Estelle promised, the door clanging as she headed outside. She was wearing a light cotton summer dress with a pair of ballet flats, and the beaming sun felt wonderful on her bare skin. 'How's it going boys?' she asked, as she passed the stall where Chris and Joe were throwing ice cubes at each other. They stopped as soon as they spotted her.

'Fine,' Joe replied, doing his very best to look innocent.

'Looks like your dad's arriving,' she said to Chris, as the fire truck reversed into position. 'Do you mind helping Sue out if she gets busy? I'm just going to pop over and say hello.'

'Mum, don't snog him in the street or anything,' Joe pleaded, looking mortified.

But Estelle merely smiled and skipped off, as Tony jumped down from the cab and strode over to her, throwing his arms around her before kissing her in front of everyone.

'Hi,' he grinned.

'Hi,' she replied, the same silly grin on her own face. 'You look great.' As it was a warm day, he'd left his jacket in the cab, wearing just his reflective trousers and a tight grey t-shirt that perfectly showed off his chiselled chest. Estelle found herself wishing he was topless, smeared in baby oil like one of those firefighter calendars you could buy.

'You're not so bad yourself,' he murmured into her ear, running his hand down her back and over her bottom. 'Uh-oh, here comes the craziness.'

Estelle looked up to see a group of young children, all descending eagerly on the fire engine.

'I'll see you later, okay?' he promised, striding off and swinging an excited little girl up into the cab so that she could look around.

Whilst it was technically Tony's day off, he and three of his colleagues had volunteered to bring one of the vehicles down to the street party, for the kids to explore and learn about fire safety. And judging by the amount of fathers hanging around examining the fire engine with more than a passing interest, Estelle guessed that quite a few of them had harboured dreams of becoming a heroic fireman at some stage in their lives as well.

Smiling as she watched the children cheer delightedly when Tony turned on the blue flashing lights, Estelle turned around and headed back towards Cafe Crumb, stopping in her tracks as she spotted Reggie and Gracie strolling down the street. She waved enthusiastically, thinking how good the pair of them looked together. Gracie looked incredible in high-waisted denim shorts, which she'd teamed with a plaid shirt, knotted at the waist, and a pair of chunky wedge shoes, while Reggie was looking distinctly laid-back in a casual t-shirt and a pair of knee-length khaki shorts.

'Nice legs, Reggie,' Estelle couldn't resist commenting as he drew closer.

Reggie rolled his eyes. 'Gracie made me wear them.'

'It's hot!' she protested. 'You have to wear shorts when it's hot, it's the law.'

'I just do what I'm told,' Reggie smiled resignedly to Estelle.

'You're learning fast,' she quipped. 'So how are you enjoying the street party?'

'It's great,' Gracie nodded enthusiastically. 'I can't believe how many stalls there are – everyone's made a real effort.'

It was true, thought Estelle, as she surveyed the street. Two doors down, the bric-a-brac shop had a whole host of furniture outside on the pavement, while the charity shop had a popular table crammed with books and DVDs. At the butcher's and greengrocer's, the queues were stretching out of the door, while the Greek restaurant had opened early and was selling generous tubs of feta and olive salad, fragrant dolmades and sticky pieces of baklava. There was even a stall selling glasses of Pimms.

'Oh, and there's Rebecca,' Estelle exclaimed, as she saw her and Andy making their way over to join the group. 'You look great,' she commented, giving her a hug. 'Honestly, what have you been doing? You're positively glowing!'

Rebecca flushed, seeming stuck for an answer, and Andy quickly stepped in. 'That's what happens when you're married to me,' he joked, as everyone laughed and said their hellos.

'Sue's inside by the way,' Estelle explained. 'So do pop in and say hi. I offered to swap with her, but she said she'd rather be indoors. I don't think she's up to socialising much at the moment.'

'Still no joy with George?' Rebecca asked worriedly.

Estelle shook her head. 'Honestly, I'd like to give that man a piece of my mind. I don't know what he's playing at, but he's making Sue's life a misery. It's—' she began, but stopped in her tracks as Tony appeared behind her, accompanied by a man and a woman that she didn't recognise.

'Estelle, this is Lesley Robertson, a reporter from *The Bristol Chronicle*,' he said, raising his eyebrows meaningfully. 'I've met her a few times as she's covered some of the incidents I've been called to, and she's writing a piece about the street party today. I suggested it might be a good idea if she interviewed you,' he continued, his eyes twinkling as he looked extremely pleased with himself. 'You know, get a bit of local colour in there, and spread the word about your business . . .'

'That sounds wonderful,' Estelle beamed, shaking hands as Lesley introduced herself.

'And this is Eddie, my photographer,' Lesley explained, indicating the scruffily dressed man who was hovering beside her. 'You own Cafe Crumb, is that correct?'

'Yes, it is,' Estelle said, suddenly feeling as though she was on trial.

'Great, well perhaps we could get some photos of you outside. Maybe serving on the stall? Tony, would you like to be a customer?' she suggested, jostling them both into position, as Eddie snapped away.

'I feel like a model,' Estelle joked, as she mimed selling Tony a piece of cake, while Joe and Chris looked on in hysterics.

'Perfect, that's exactly what I need,' Lesley smiled. 'Eddie, would you mind taking some general shots, just to get a feel for the day? Now, Estelle, do you have a few moments for me to interview you?'

'Absolutely,' she replied, trying to sound positive, although her stomach was dancing with nerves. What if she said something stupid and they wrote it down in the newspaper! As Lesley was busy flicking open her notepad, Estelle widened her eyes in alarm at Tony, but he merely gave her the thumbs up and jogged back over to the fire engine. The members of the book group were equally unhelpful.

'We'll pop in and see Sue,' Rebecca called to her. 'See you afterwards.'

'You'll be fine,' Gracie mouthed reassuringly, as they all disappeared, leaving Estelle with the slightly terrifying reporter.

'So,' Lesley began, turning to Estelle with her pen poised. 'Tony tells me you also run a book club. Could you tell me a little more about that . . .?'

* * *

It was more than fifteen minutes later when Lesley finally decided she had all the material she needed, and Estelle gratefully escaped, running back inside Cafe Crumb where she found the others sat round a table chatting to Sue.

'How was it?' Gracie asked.

'Okay, I think ...' Estelle said uncertainly. 'I don't think I said anything I shouldn't have done. We'll have to see when the article comes out.'

'Did you mention us?' Rebecca demanded, as Estelle laughed.

'Well, not by name, but I told her about the book group. Hopefully it'll be a nice piece, and bring a little extra publicity.'

'Who's she interviewing now?' Gracie asked, craning her neck through the window to try and see.

'You lot get back outside and enjoy the sunshine,' Sue chided them. 'Don't be stuck indoors for my sake.'

'Are you sure?' Rebecca pressed.

'Absolutely. I can handle the customers in here, and you should enjoy the weather while it's nice.'

They all looked at each other reluctantly, but in the end, the outdoors proved too tempting and it didn't take much persuasion before they all trooped back out. Tony ran over as he saw them, and the others discreetly walked off, giving him and Estelle some time alone.

'I can't believe you did that!' she exclaimed.

'What? I thought it was a great idea,' he grinned. 'Didn't I tell you I'm a one-man publicity machine?'

'Just one of the many things I'm learning about you,'

Estelle smiled, her eyes sparkling. 'I can't believe I'm going to be in the paper!'

'Congratulations, my little media star,' he chuckled. 'You wait, you'll be running a business empire to rival Donald Trump any day now.'

She stepped in closer to him and he wrapped his arms around her, leaning down to kiss her . . .

'Estelle?' A shocked voice called out.

She pulled away sharply, looking up to see Ted standing beside a very-pregnant Leila.

'Ted!' Estelle exclaimed, instantly feeling the awkwardness of the situation. 'I didn't realise you'd be here today.'

'Obviously,' he replied, with a pointed glance at Tony. 'Joe told me about the street party, so I thought I'd come along and check it out, see how you were getting on. But it looks like you're getting on fine.'

Estelle cleared her throat, wondering what to do for the best. 'Ted, you know Tony don't you?' she asked uncomfortably.

'Not as well as you do, it seems.'

Estelle flushed at the remark, and Tony stepped forward looking angrier than Estelle had ever seen him. 'Is there a problem here?' he asked coldly.

'You tell me – is there?'

'Ted,' Estelle interjected, looking worriedly between him and Tony, as Leila put a steadying hand on Ted's arm.

'Ted, leave it, it's none of your business,' she told him quietly.

'None of my business? I think I have a right to know if someone's going to be playing a significant role in my son's life, don't you?'

'I was going to tell you, but I haven't properly had a chance to speak to you,' Estelle explained, her words tumbling out in a hurry. 'We were waiting to see if it was serious.'

'And it is,' Tony confirmed, wrapping a protective arm around Estelle and pulling her closer.

She saw the surprise in Ted's eyes at the gesture, the readjustment as he realised his ex-wife was in her first serious relationship since they'd divorced. Not that he could really object – after all, he was standing there with his heavily-pregnant new wife. But knowing that Estelle had finally moved on, and that Joe had another male role model in his life, would take some getting used to.

'Tony, I think you're needed back at the fire engine,' Estelle told him, looking across to where the kids were running riot as his colleagues struggled to control them. One boy was hanging off the ladder, attempting to climb onto the roof of the truck.

'It's fine,' Tony said dismissively.

'No, go,' Estelle insisted, trying to communicate with her eyes that it would be better if he left then she could talk to Ted without him there.

'If you're sure,' he said reluctantly, finally getting the message.

Estelle nodded, and Tony leaned down to kiss her, before jogging off. She stared after him for a moment,

413

marvelling at how fit and strong he looked as he sprinted effortlessly across the street.

'Estelle?'

Ted's questioning tone brought her rudely back down to earth, and she turned to him defiantly. 'He's a good man, Ted. You can hardly begrudge me some happiness after all these years.'

'I suppose not,' he grunted. 'But it would have been nice to be told, that's all.'

'Well now you know. I didn't want you to find out like this, but it's happened,' Estelle replied through pursed lips, annoyed at Ted for ruining her day like this.

Ted was silent for a moment, staring off into the middle-distance. 'And what does Joe think?' he asked eventually.

'He . . . he seems happy for me,' Estelle admitted. 'He likes Tony, and he gets on well with his son, Chris. You remember him – he plays for the football team too.'

Ted nodded thoughtfully, as Leila nudged him. 'Speaking of Joe . . .' she smiled, as she slipped her arm through Ted's and nodded towards where Joe stood chatting self-consciously with a pretty blonde girl.

As he saw them staring, he walked over.

'Mum, Chris is going to man the stall for a bit. I'm going for a look round with Lauren,' he announced. 'Hi, Dad. Leila,' he added quickly, before heading back to Lauren. Shyly, he linked his hand through hers and they set off into the crowd.

'Well what can I say?' Ted remarked, a defeated look on his face. 'It seems as though everyone round here's

414

getting together and falling in love. What are you putting in that lemonade of yours?'

'So you're fine with me and Tony?' Estelle asked hopefully, sneaking a glance at Leila who smiled back, giving the tiniest of nods.

'It's serious, you say?' Ted remarked, running one hand over the stubble on his chin as he contemplated the situation.

'I think so,' Estelle confessed. 'It's certainly heading that way.'

'Then who am I to stand in your way?' Ted shrugged resignedly. 'He seems like a nice enough fella, I suppose, and he knows his football, I'll give him that. Now, I'm off to have a look at this fire engine, while you have a chat with Leila. Take her inside, and give her a huge piece of chocolate cake. She's had wicked cravings for it, so she has.'

Estelle looked on anxiously as Ted strode off in Tony's direction, but Leila smiled reassuringly.

'Don't worry, it'll all be fine. You know Ted – he'll feel like he has to bluster and make a bit of noise – give poor Tony a full on interrogation – but his bark's worse than his bite.'

Estelle smiled at her gratefully, as they headed into the cafe and placed their order with Sue. Estelle was a little nervous; she and Leila didn't know each other very well, and Ted was the only thing they had in common. Right now, her ex-husband was the last thing Estelle wanted to talk about.

She was busy staring out of the window, trying to check that Tony and Ted hadn't come to blows out there, when Leila leant across to speak to her.

'Ted says you've been reading *Ten Sweet Lessons*,' she murmured, a naughty gleam in her eye. 'I want to know exactly what you thought of it!'

And with that, Estelle knew that everything would be alright between them.

38

'Have you seen this week's paper?' Estelle squealed in delight, as she laid out her copy of *The Bristol Chronicle* on the table at the book club meeting. 'It just came out this morning.'

Everyone crowded round to look, ooh-ing and aah-ing over the double-page spread featuring the street party.

'Look, there's you and Tony!' Sue exclaimed, pointing at the photo on the top right. The caption underneath read: *Estelle Humphries, owner of Cafe Crumb, serves cake and lemonade to local firefighter Tony Ellis.*

'They've spelt my name wrong,' Estelle huffed in annoyance.

'Never mind,' Rebecca consoled her, a wicked gleam in her eye. 'You won't be Ms Humphreys for very much longer at this rate!'

'Look at this interview with you,' Gracie interrupted,

sparing Estelle's blushes. 'It's brilliant. There's a whole piece on the book group: *The Cafe Crumb book club covers a wide range of novels, from Thomas Hardy to Jilly Cooper,*' Gracie read out in her best speaking voice, as everyone stopped to listen.

'*They've even explored the controversial erotic best-seller,* Ten Sweet Lessons. "*We're a small, friendly group, and we like to think we're very open-minded in our choice of reading material", said cafe owner and book club chair, Estelle.*'

'Ha! You make it sound as though we actually read other things apart from erotica,' Rebecca teased.

'Well, I thought that while *Local Book Club Focuses on Erotica* might be a good headline, it didn't sound particularly family-oriented.'

'*Sordid Den of Vice in guise of Friendly Local Cafe?*' Reggie suggested as an alternative, as Gracie hit him on the arm.

'But whatever they've written seems to have worked. I've had over a dozen people contact me today, expressing an interest in joining the group.'

'Really? That's fantastic!' Rebecca exclaimed.

But Reggie didn't look so sure, knitting his eyebrows together. 'New people? I'm not sure I like the sound of that. We don't like strangers round here,' he finished, in a strong West Country accent, which earned him another smack on the arm from Gracie.

'I even had someone get in touch through the website to ask about hiring the space,' Estelle continued. 'They're looking to use it on Wednesday evenings, to set up a sort of open-mic arts night, where anyone can come along and read poetry, or extracts of novels, or even sing,' she finished, looking pointedly at Gracie.

'Yes, when are you going to do some more singing?' Sue asked. 'You've got such a wonderful talent, it'd be a shame not to use it.'

'Well, I am hoping to do some more,' Gracie admitted bashfully. 'The Fifties Night was such a great confidence boost for me, and I absolutely loved performing. But . . . well . . .' she began hesitantly, casting nervous glances at Reggie. 'It's a good job that you've got some new people interested in the group because Reggie and I have some news.'

'You're getting married!'

'You're pregnant!'

'No,' Gracie burst out laughing at their wildly inaccurate guesses. 'But we have decided to move in together,' she explained, moving closer to Reggie and wrapping her arms around his waist.

'Oh, that's wonderful news,' Estelle gushed.

'Yes, it is,' Gracie agreed. 'It was proving really tricky trying to find time together – Reggie's housemates aren't the nicest people, and I still live with my mother at the moment, so this seemed like the perfect solution. But it does mean that we might not be able to come to the meetings anymore.'

'We can get so much more for our money if we rent somewhere in St Pauls or St Philips,' Reggie explained, as Gracie bit her lip nervously. 'And obviously it's quite a trek across town to get here.'

'But won't that be really inconvenient for your work, Gracie?' asked Estelle.

'That's another thing I have to tell you,' she began, a proud smile creeping over her face. 'I applied for a new job, as assistant manager at the Central Library and . . . I got it!'

'That's fantastic,' Rebecca exclaimed, coming over to give her a hug as everyone congratulated her.

'Yeah, I'm really pleased. I was quite happy where I was, but sometimes you have to take a chance, don't you? So it's a promotion, of course, which will mean more money, and I'll be working in the city centre.'

'Well done you,' Sue smiled, looking thrilled. More than any of them, she knew what it was like to take a leap out of your comfort zone and prepare to try something new.

'And come September, I'm going to be teaching some evening classes at the university,' Reggie added, 'so my time will be limited.'

'How's your thesis going?' Rebecca asked him. 'Have we provided plenty of material for you to write about?'

'More than enough, believe me,' he joked, as Rebecca giggled. 'Actually, I have a bit of a surprise for you all myself. Not even Gracie knows about this,' he continued, as she looked up at him curiously, 'but I wanted to tell you when you were all together. My original subject was going to be *The Cohesive Power of Literature in*

Communities throughout the Bristol and Avon area from the Middle Ages to the Present Day.'

Sue swallowed nervously.

Rebecca's eyes bulged.

Estelle stared at him in disbelief. 'Say that again?'

Reggie laughed. 'It doesn't matter anymore, because I've decided not to use it. In fact, my new thesis title is going to be . . .' He cleared his throat, steeling himself to make the announcement, and looked slowly round the group of women, hardly able to believe what he was about to say.

'Oh, get on with it,' Rebecca heckled, making everyone laugh.

'Okay, alright, my new thesis title is . . . *The Evolution of Erotica: The Erotic Novel from the Marquis de Sade to CJ Jones.*'

Sue inhaled sharply, as Estelle began clapping and Rebecca squealed. Gracie threw her arms around him, covering his face in kisses.

'That's amazing,' she exclaimed.

'I can't believe how far we've all come,' Estelle said, her voice breaking as she began to get emotional. Despite the celebrations and the good news, it felt as though everything was changing beyond recognition. With new members joining and the original group breaking up, it seemed as though this might be the last session with just the five of them together.

'Well if you've got a surprise for me, then I've got a surprise for you,' Gracie announced, her eyes dancing as she looked at Reggie. Her buoyancy lightened the mood once again, as she swiftly unclasped her watch and threw it onto the table, holding up her forearm for everyone to see. 'I was going to leave it until later, but . . .' she shrugged, as everyone crowded round, looking at the intricate 'R' tattoo on her wrist. All in black, it looked like a beautiful illuminated letter, with swirling loops worked in to a butterfly decoration.

'R?' Reggie questioned, raising an eyebrow. 'For . . .?'

'Oh, I don't know,' Gracie shrugged airily. 'Rainbows. Rabbits. Raunch. Whatever you want really.'

Reggie had turned pink with embarrassment, but from the smile on his face, it was clear that he approved.

'Gracie Bird, you are without doubt the coolest girl I know,' Rebecca affirmed.

'And if we split up, I'll have it turned into *two* butterflies,' Gracie declared, somewhat undermining the romantic gesture.

'Thanks,' Reggie huffed, looking grumpy as Gracie kissed him.

'Sue, you're not going to be with us much longer either, are you? We're dropping like flies,' Estelle tried to joke, but it was impossible to hide the sadness in her voice.

'Still no luck persuading George?' Rebecca asked sympathetically.

'No, I think that bridge has been well and truly burned. It's actually becoming so unbearable that I'm moving out to live with my daughter for a few weeks, and then I'm flying to America a month early.' In spite of herself, Sue couldn't help but feel the old enthusiasm return when she talked about her plans. 'I'm going to take a month to travel coast to coast,' she explained excitedly. 'I fly to New York on the first of August, and the ship sails from LA on the first of September, so in between those dates . . . who knows? I've got four weeks to make my way there.'

'Sue, that's incredible,' Rebecca marvelled. 'Can I come in your suitcase?'

'By all means. It might get quite lonely out there.'

'It sounds like an amazing experience,' Reggie marvelled. 'Good for you, Sue. I'm really impressed.'

'I'm going to miss you so much,' Estelle sniffed, as it finally hit her that Sue would be leaving in a matter of days. She'd offered to work the following week in the cafe, as usual, and then she was moving to Helen's where she intended to stay until her flight from Heathrow. 'You've been such a great help to me here, and such a good friend,' she wailed, dabbing at her eyes.

'While we're all making announcements,' Rebecca spoke up, 'I've got one too – hopefully this will cheer you up a little, Estelle. I'm . . . well, I'm pregnant!'

They turned to her in shock – all except Gracie, who was smiling knowingly – as Rebecca giggled at the expressions on their faces.

Estelle was the first one to recover. 'Oh, congratulations! I'm so happy for you. When are you due?'

'I don't know exactly yet,' Rebecca admitted, as she unconsciously cradled her stomach. 'I've actually told you a little earlier than I should have, but I wanted to join in with the announcements! I have my scan in a couple of weeks, so they'll be able to date it then, but I would think early next year.'

'It'll be a *Ten Sweet Lessons* baby,' Gracie smiled, referring to the phenomenon of women reading the famous erotic novel, then falling pregnant months later. 'You see, *this* is what happens when you read erotica!'

'I'll put it in my report,' Reggie smiled.

'To be honest, I don't know how much erotica there'll be for me from now on. I'll be swapping the sexy under-wear and bondage gear for maternity bras and breast pumps,' Rebecca admitted. 'But I can't deny that the books really kick-started mine and Andy's relationship. I was actually feeling quite down before I joined the group, and it's genuinely given me a real boost. Thank you so much, Estelle,' she said, tearing up as she crossed the room to hug her. 'Sorry if I'm getting emotional, it's the hormones.'

'Oh, we're all emotional, and we can't all blame it on the hormones,' Estelle joked, grabbing a paper napkin from the table and wiping her eyes.

'Before we all have complete breakdowns,' Gracie interrupted, 'what about *100 Strokes*? I thought this was meant to be a book club, not some kind of counselling session!'

'I suppose Gracie's right,' Estelle acknowledged. 'And this might be the final time we're all together – as the book group at least.'

'Exactly,' Gracie said decisively, looking pleased. 'I'd love to order some coffee and cakes, and then we can get down to it.'

'Do you know, I was thinking as I read this book,' Estelle said, as she began preparing the orders, 'I can't believe what a difference these few months have made. I mean, this book covered losing virginity, group sex, gay sex, oral sex, transvestism and I really didn't bat an eyelid. In fact, I was disappointed at the lack of detail. I really didn't find it erotic.'

'Ah, that's the problem you see, Estelle,' Reggie joked, '*Ten Sweet Lessons* is like gateway erotica. It just gets you hooked on the harder stuff.'

'And we all like it hard,' Rebecca couldn't resist saying, as everyone burst into outraged laughter.

'Rebecca, you can't say things like that now you're pregnant!' Gracie insisted. 'The baby might hear.'

'Sorry everyone,' she apologised, grinning cheekily. 'Last inappropriate comment, I promise.'

'Oh, I do hope not,' Sue chuckled.

'You see, this is what I mean,' Estelle continued, bringing over their mugs and cakes. 'Six months ago, we had Reggie running away screaming whenever someone said the word "orgasm", Gracie couldn't read about a woman saying "okay, darling" to her partner without protesting that she was being oppressed by a raving misogynist, while Rebecca . . . well, Rebecca's just as filthy as she ever was, and look where it's got her!'

There were peals of laughter at Estelle's summary, and

425

the mood in the little cafe was upbeat and reflective. It was true that they'd all changed so much over the past few months, and were now a mutual support group that had had a huge effect on each other, whether they were aware of it or not. But now they were all moving on, each ready to embrace the next phase of their lives, whatever it might bring.

The conversation meandered comfortably and aimlessly, with all of them seeming reluctant to leave. It was as though they all knew and understood that this was an ending of sorts; that once they'd left this evening, things would never go back to how they'd been before.

It was only when Rebecca's phone buzzed that they broke out of their cosy little bubble, aware that the session was drawing to a close.

'That's Andy,' Rebecca explained, as she read the text message. 'He's on his way to pick me up, so he'll be here any minute. He's getting hugely protective, and hates me going anywhere by myself.'

'Good,' Sue said. 'You take the time and put your feet up. Let him run around after you for a change – you'll need all the rest you can when the baby arrives.'

'Thanks Sue,' Rebecca said, getting to her feet, as she moved across to give her a hug.

Reggie and Gracie stood up too, as everyone said their bittersweet goodbyes. Estelle watched, a lump in her throat, as Andy pulled up outside, helping Rebecca into the car and kissing her gently. Reggie and Gracie walked past the window hand in hand, their bodies pressed close together as Gracie giggled at something Reggie had said. Sue was the last to leave, and Estelle hugged her tightly.

'Let me know if you need anything – anything at all,' Estelle insisted, as Sue nodded, unable to bring herself to speak.

Estelle closed the door behind her, turning the key in the lock and sliding the bolts across. The noise seemed to echo in the empty cafe, a poignant wave of sadness and loss hitting her unexpectedly as she switched off the lights, sitting for a moment in the darkness of the cafe as she thought about the changes that had taken place since this disparate group of people entered her life.

Then her mobile phone began to ring, the back-lit screen lighting up the cafe, as the jaunty ringtone broke the melancholy. Estelle picked it up, smiling as she saw the caller name.

'Hi Tony,' she smiled.

'Hi gorgeous,' he replied, and she could tell from his voice that he was smiling too. 'Has the meeting finished?'

'Yeah, not long ago.'

'How did it go?'

'It was . . . strange,' Estelle told him honestly. 'Rebecca's pregnant, which is fantastic news. And Gracie and Reggie are moving to a different part of town, so I probably won't get to see them as often.'

'Are you okay?' he asked, hearing the melancholy in her tone. 'You don't sound like yourself.'

'I'm fine,' she assured him, forcing herself to sound brighter.

'That's good. I missed you today.'

'I missed you too,' Estelle admitted, feeling the first stirrings of something else start to take over her body. She could imagine the glint in his eyes as he spoke, the way he could look right at her and instantly render her powerless.

'I can't wait to see you tomorrow night,' Tony continued, his voice dropping to that sexy growl that she loved. 'I've spent the day thinking about all the things I'm going to do to you when we're alone.'

'Really?' Estelle smiled into the darkness, glad that no one could see the way she was blushing fiercely. 'Why don't you tell me about them?'

She heard a throaty chuckle of delight at the other end of the phone. 'You know something, Ms Humphreys?' he began, his breath coming harder as Estelle felt that unmistakeable longing deep in her body. '*You* are a very naughty girl . . .'

Epilogue

Sue was standing on the deck of the *Morning Star*, her hands resting on the railing as the enormous cruise ship pulled into the port of Alexandria. It was early morning, yet the sun was already hot as it rose over the Egyptian city, bleaching the buildings and sparkling off the water. The dock was a hive of activity, dark-skinned men shouting to one another in Arabic as goods were loaded and unloaded from huge, rusting container ships.

Ports were never the prettiest parts of town, Sue reflected – and she'd seen more than her fair share over the past few months. But in spite of the ubiquitous metal containers, soaring cranes and tatty fishing boats, sailing into a new city was always an incredible experience. Each new country filled Sue with a sense of wonder and excitement, leaving her eager to explore and discover what each place had to offer. And this morning was no exception.

Shielding her eyes as she looked out at the view, Sue's spirits lifted as they drew closer to Alexandria. The dark blue water lapped at the side of the ship, while along the shoreline she could see high rise buildings mingling with towering minarets.

The ironic thing was that today she would hardly even see the city they were docking in. Like so many of her fellow passengers, she had booked a day tour to Cairo, from where they would travel out to see the pyramids at Giza. She was hugely looking forward to it (they were one of the Wonders of the World after all), but it was at times like this that she missed George more than ever. She knew he'd have loved this – he'd watched endless documentaries about Ancient Egypt, and it was just such a shame that he hadn't had the gumption to get out of his armchair and actually come and see them with her . . .

Sue let out a sigh, watching a pair of seagulls whirl overhead. There were six weeks left of the cruise, and in a couple of days they'd be back in Europe, on the final leg of their journey to Southampton. There was no doubt about it, the trip had been incredible, but if Sue was being honest, she was glad that it was coming to an end. It had been an amazing experience, but she was looking forward to staying in one place for more than a day at a time, to seeing Helen and Bella again . . . and George.

At first, Sue had revelled in her new-found sense of freedom – travelling across America and boarding the ship, she could do whatever she liked and was answerable to no one. Everyone she'd encountered had been perfectly friendly, instantly making her feel at ease, but at the end of each evening she went back to her cabin alone and, as the cruise wore on, she'd begun to feel unexpectedly lonely and homesick. She'd visited some of the most beautiful, exotic and remote locations in the world, but at every place she had the nagging sensation that something wasn't right. She'd functioned as part of a unit for so long that she'd taken it for granted, and whilst the initial liberation felt good, before long it became obvious that something – or some*one* – was missing.

As they left Australia, bound for Jakarta in Indonesia, Sue had swallowed her pride and called George.

It had sounded as though he was missing her too. After some initial awkwardness, they wound up chatting for hours, communicating far more in that short time than they had done for months before Sue went away. Soon, visiting the computer room and Skyping George became a regular part of her day. She would even miss out on excursions, or evening entertainment, if the time difference meant that was the only chance she had to speak to him.

She didn't regret going on the cruise – it was something she needed to do, and had undoubtedly been one of the best experiences of her life. But it had made both she and George reassess their relationship – in a positive way. Speaking of which . . . Sue took her mobile out of her handbag and quickly switched it on, but there was no message from George. She supposed it would barely be dawn back in the UK, so there was no way he would be up yet. Perhaps she would take a picture of herself on a camel beside the Pyramids and send it to him, Sue thought with a smile. That would be a nice surprise.

As she glanced down, she could already see the queues forming on the lower deck, with people eager to be off the boat and heading out for their day's excursion. She made her way down the steps to join them, saying hello to the people she recognised, and as the boat finally docked she made her way out onto the harbour side to look for her driver for the day.

There were dozens of men lined up on the bank, and as Sue walked along she was immediately hit by the heat and the noise of this bustling city, young children crowding round her and asking for baksheesh. She was dressed sensibly, in long, loose, light-coloured clothing with a wide-brimmed hat, and she moved swiftly, staring out from behind her sunglasses.

Finally she saw her name – SHEPHERD had been crudely written on a torn piece of cardboard, and she smiled in recognition, making her way towards it. But then something stopped her in her tracks, her mouth falling open as she blinked in disbelief. The man holding the card, wearing khaki trousers, a loose white shirt, and what looked suspiciously like brand-new sandals was, she realised incredulously, her husband.

'George!' Sue exclaimed, breaking into a run. He held his arms open and Sue flew into them, hugging him tightly as the pair embraced. 'What are you doing here?' she marvelled, barely able to believe that he was actually there in her arms, solid flesh and blood.

'Well, I couldn't let you see the pyramids without me,' he chuckled. He was beaming as he leaned in to kiss his wife and she eagerly kissed him back.

'I've missed you, Sue,' he murmured. 'More than I can say.'

'I've missed you too, George,' she began, feeling close to tears, but George put a finger across her lips to quieten her.

'I need to say that I'm so sorry about the way I behaved. I should have listened to you, and made more of an effort.'

'I'm sorry too, and—'

But George cut her off once again. 'I've behaved so stupidly, and I only hope that you can forgive me. I've been mean and selfish . . .'

'Of course you're forgiven,' Sue insisted, flinging her arms around him once again and holding him tightly.

'I love you, Sue,' George told her, his voice serious as he disentangled her arms from around his neck and took hold of her hands, squeezing them tightly. 'For better or for worse – isn't that what we said? Well we've had the worst, and there are better times to come, I promise you.

This is just the beginning.'

Behind her sunglasses, tears were pricking at Sue's eyes. She didn't think George had ever been quite so open with his feelings, declaring his love for her on the crowded quayside. He'd never been one for grand, romantic gestures, but here he was, having flown across a whole continent in order to surprise her.

'I love you too, George,' Sue insisted. 'But how come you're here? I mean, how on earth..?'

'It took a lot of organising, and Helen really helped me out. I think I've been driving her mad since you went away,' George chuckled.

Sue smiled, staring at her husband's familiar face as she tried to take it all in. 'There's so much to talk about, and I'm supposed to be going on this excursion today . . .'

'You could always give it a miss,' George suggested. 'We could sneak back to your cabin and catch up. You could even give those nipple tassels a whirl if you want,' he winked.

Sue raised an eyebrow in surprise, instantly realising what was on his mind. 'But what about the pyramids?' she asked, her body already tingling with anticipation.

George shrugged, wrapping his arm around Sue and steering her back towards the boat, pushing through the crowds of people surging in the opposite direction. 'They've been around for over four thousand years. They'll wait a bit longer.'

He bent down to gently plant a kiss on her shoulder

and Sue smiled. For once, her husband was right. She'd waited long enough for this moment, and right now, George was the only thing that mattered.

Estelle was wiping down the tables in Cafe Crumb, humming to herself as she cleared away the empty crockery. Her new assistant, Kara, a recent graduate of Bristol Old Vic theatre school, was stood behind the counter reading a script, completely unaware that there was work to be done.

Estelle sighed, heading into the store room to fetch a fresh supply of paper napkins. She knew she should be harder on the girl, but really, it was just quicker to do everything herself.

She'd employed Kara not long after Sue's departure, realising firstly that she needed an assistant to take the pressure off herself, and secondly, that she could now afford one as the cafe was doing much better. The extra help meant that Estelle could now take more regular days off, and she planned her free time around Tony's hours, meaning that if he was on a late shift she could take the morning off too. Once the boys had gone to school, they were free to spend the morning cuddled up in bed together. It was utter bliss – in more ways than one . . .

Estelle had her arms full of serviettes when she heard Kara say, 'Yeah, she's just out the back. I'll call her for you. Estelle!'

Estelle hurried out, almost dropping her bundle when she saw who it was.

435

'Rebecca!' she exclaimed, dumping everything on the counter as she hurried over to give her a hug. 'How wonderful to see you. Oh, and this must be Chloe,' she murmured in wonder, peeking inside the pram Rebecca was wheeling to see a beautiful, blue-eyed, gurgling baby girl.

'I'll get her out,' Rebecca smiled, folding back the pram cover and reaching inside. 'She's awake anyway.'

'Look at you,' Estelle smiled, cooing at her. 'Aren't you gorgeous! How old is she now?'

'Ten weeks,' Rebecca replied. She looked exhausted, but absolutely in love with the little bundle in her arms. 'This is the furthest I've been out since I had her. There's so much to think about – even popping to the shops takes so much planning. I honestly can't believe how easy my life was before, and I never appreciated it.'

'Oh, but I'm sure it's all worth it,' Estelle smiled, as Chloe balled her hands into fists then stretched out her arms.

'Do you want a cuddle?' Rebecca asked.

'I thought you'd never ask! Kara, can you bring over two teas and a couple of custard slices?' she called out, as she took the baby from Rebecca, and the two of them sat down at a table.

'So how have you been?' Estelle asked, as she gently rocked Chloe, making cooing noises as she stroked her back.

'Delirious from lack of sleep mostly,' Rebecca smiled.

'And I have absolutely no gossip, because I've been nowhere and done nothing, so I'm relying on you to give me my fix.'

'I'll do my best. How's Andy?'

'He's good. A ridiculously proud father – he absolutely dotes on her. He went back to work a few weeks ago, but he rushes home every night and can't wait to see her as soon as he gets in the door. It's a bit different to this time last year, when he was rushing home to see me.'

'And that's how you get one of these,' joked Estelle, gazing down at Chloe.

'I can't believe that was only what – a few months back? It's about a year since the first book club meeting, isn't it? It seems like a lifetime ago.'

'It does,' Estelle agreed ruefully. 'There've been a lot of changes since then.'

'How's the new book club going?'

'It's . . . different,' Estelle said after a pause. 'There're ten of us this time, and they're a very different group. We read a real range of things, and the whole tone is more serious. I sometimes miss the fun and the giggling that we used to have.'

'Ah, we were the original and the best,' Rebecca grinned.

Kara brought over their order, and Rebecca let out a groan of delight as she bit into her custard slice. 'God, I've missed these. I'd forgotten how amazing your baking is, Estelle.'

'Thank you,' she laughed, as she watched Rebecca tuck in with gusto. 'That's Kara, by the way,' she said, pointing out her pretty young assistant who was walking back to the counter. 'She's the new Sue.'

'Wow, Sue's looking good!' Rebecca chuckled, through a mouthful of pastry and cream. 'Speaking of which, have you heard anything from her?'

'Yes, I hear from her quite a lot actually – emails and postcards. She should be back any day now, come to think of it. Did you know she got back together with George?'

'No!' Rebecca exclaimed, her eyes widening. 'What happened?'

'Well, I think she was enjoying herself at first – from the sound of her emails, she was having a whale of a time. But then it almost became too much of a good thing, and I think she got lonely. Anyway, it turned out George was really missing her too, and to cut a long story short, he flew out to join her when the ship docked in Egypt, and they're travelling back together. Sue said they're having an amazing time – it sounds like a second honeymoon.'

'Aw, that's lovely,' Rebecca sighed. 'I'm so pleased they worked it all out.'

'Me too,' Estelle agreed. 'I can't wait to catch up when she's back. You should come too – we could have a mini reunion!'

'I'd love that,' Rebecca agreed. 'I could leave Andy on babysitting duty. Do you know, I can't remember the last time I had a night out.'

'Get used to it,' Estelle warned. 'It'll be a long time before your life is anything approaching normal again.' She looked down at Chloe, who was falling asleep in her arms. She was the spitting image of Andy, with fine, blonde hair and the cutest snub nose. 'Are you still in touch with Gracie?'

'Yeah, she came over not long after Chloe was born and we had a really good catch up. She and Reggie are still going strong, and she seems really happy in her new job. She's even joined a band, so she's singing again, and they're starting to do some gigs around Bristol. In fact . . .' Rebecca trailed off, glancing up at the clock on the wall. 'Right on cue,' she smiled, as Gracie burst through the door.

She looked exactly as Estelle remembered her, wrapped up warmly against the chilly weather in a leopard-print faux-fur jacket, her dark hair scooped up at the back and tied with a bandana.

'Gracie, what are you doing here? Did you plan this?'

'Kind of,' Rebecca admitted.

'I'm working in my old library today,' Gracie explained, dumping her bag on the table and sitting down eagerly beside Estelle. 'My old boss is off sick so I'm covering for him, which feels really weird, but Rebecca and I thought it would be a great opportunity to meet up.'

'Well I'm so pleased you did,' Estelle told her genuinely. 'It's lovely to see you. Rebecca said it's all going well with Reggie?'

'Yeah, he's great,' Gracie gushed, her face softening as she spoke about him. She looked across at Chloe, sleeping in Estelle's arms. 'I'm really sorry Estelle, but do you mind if I take her? I'm dying for a squeeze. She's got so big, hasn't she?' she said to Rebecca, as Estelle passed her across.

'Yeah, she's almost twelve pounds now. The health visitor said—' Rebecca broke off as she stared at Estelle's hand, emerging from the pile of baby blankets. 'What's that?' she demanded.

'What's what? Oh, *this*?'

'Yes, *that*!' Rebecca shot back. 'Is it . . .?'

With a beaming smile, Estelle held up her left hand, wiggling her third finger where a small, neat diamond nestled on a gold band.

Gracie realised she was holding her breath. 'Tony proposed!' she breathed.

Estelle nodded, her face radiant with happiness. 'On Christmas Day. We're planning to get married in the summer. It'll just be something very low key – probably a registry office. Both of us have been through the whole hoopla before, and aren't in any rush to do it again, but we just want to make it official. You'll all be invited though, of course,' she finished excitedly.

'I'm so happy for you Estelle,' Rebecca said, leaning across to hug her. 'You really deserve it. And Tony is *hot*, you lucky thing,' she added, lowering her voice.

Estelle couldn't help laughing. 'Same old Rebecca,' she joked.

'So what will you do about this place once you're married?' Gracie asked.

'I'll keep it on,' Estelle nodded, 'Although I'm thinking of hiring someone to manage it full-time, then I can take life a bit easier. Joe and I are going to move into Tony's house, which means I can rent out the flat above here and that'll bring in the extra money to cover a manager's salary.'

'Sounds like it's all worked out perfectly,' Gracie smiled, as she gently rocked a sleeping Chloe.

'And all thanks to some naughty books,' Rebecca added with a grin.

It was true in a way, thought Estelle. This time last year, she'd never have believed that she could be in this position – blissfully happy, engaged to a gorgeous man who just happened to be a strapping fire fighter, with business at the cafe booming and her finances back on an even keel.

'Thanks so much ladies,' Estelle smiled, feeling a pang of nostalgia as they sat around the table with their tea and cakes, just like the old book club meetings. 'I really miss having you all around.'

'But there'll be many more good things to come,' Rebecca said brightly, as she raised her teacup in a toast. 'To the future.'

'And to the Naughty Girls,' added Estelle.

'The Naughty Girls,' echoed Rebecca and Gracie, as they all dissolved into uncontrollable laughter.

Reading Group

Reading Group Questions for *The Naughty Girls Book Club*

1. Which character did you most identify with, and why?

2. Are Gracie's feminist views compatible with ideas of dressing up to please your man?

3. Sue struggles to adjust to her retirement – how much does having a career contribute to a woman's sense of self?

4. All of the members of the Book Club grow in confidence over the course of the novel. How does this manifest itself?

5. Reggie longs to be like the male characters in the novels they're reading. What qualities does he want to possess, and why are these considered so important for men?

6. Does Estelle put Joe and Cafe Crumb before her own happiness? Is this something many women are guilty of doing and, if so, why?

7. Many of the Book Club members find *Justine* by the Marquis de Sade distasteful. Should certain types of erotica be censored, or is freedom of speech more important?

8. Rebecca says that submission is powerful, because it's the woman's choice to give power to the man and she's ultimately the one in control. Do you agree?

9. Was Sue's decision to go on the cruise brave or selfish?

10. What would be *your* choice of novel for the Cafe Crumb Book Club?

Recommended Erotic Reads

The Cafe Crumb Book Club read a number of classic erotica novels. If this has inspired you, and you're looking for more suggestions, here are some recommendations:

Delta of Venus – Anaïs Nin

Delta of Venus is a collection of short stories, covering a wide range of topics from incest to necrophilia – so not for the faint-hearted!

Nin was asked by a wealthy collector to write erotic stories for him, and was paid $1 for every page she produced. He asked her to focus purely on the sex, and to omit any emotions or poetry in her writing, but Nin found herself unable to do this.

The result is beautifully written erotica with a female focus, which was first published after her death in 1978.

Chances – Jackie Collins

To be honest, I could have chosen any Jackie Collins novel; without fail, they're all racy, fast-paced and glitzy, packed with powerful, ruthless men and strong, sensual women.

I've opted for *Chances* as it's the first in the celebrated *Santangelo* series, introducing us to Italian-American gangster, Gino Santangelo, and his beautiful, headstrong daughter, Lucky.

This is the book that really cemented Jackie's position as a world-famous novelist, and it has everything – ambition, rivalry, intrigue, murder and, of course, lashings of sex.

Fanny Hill (Memoirs of a Woman of Pleasure) – John Cleland

This is one of the most famous and notorious English language works of erotica, having been banned many times since its publication in 1749.

It tells the story of Fanny Hill, an orphaned teenager who becomes a prostitute in order to survive after the death of her parents. Her fortunes rise and fall, as she falls in love, loses her love, works in a series of brothels, becomes mistress to various men and inherits a fortune, not to mention having numerous lesbian encounters along the way.

The book is also well known for its fascination with a certain part of the male anatomy (yes, *that* part), and uses a wide variety of descriptions for it, including the pretty hilarious 'red-headed champion'.

The Intimate Adventures of a London Call Girl – Belle de Jour

Many of us are familiar with the TV adaptation starring Billie Piper, but *The Intimate Adventures of a London Call Girl* was one of the first of the wave of 'confessional' sex novels published last decade (in the appropriately named 'Noughties').

The novel – which is somewhat racier than the TV series – began life as an award-winning blog, following the trials and tribulations of an escort working in London. It was published in 2005 under the pseudonym Belle de Jour – later revealed to be American research scientist Dr Brooke Magnanti, who'd turned to prostitution to help finance her doctoral studies.

The novel spawned various sequels and spin-offs, including *The Further Adventures of a London Call Girl* and *Belle de Jour's Guide to Men*.

The Story of O – Pauline Réage

Pauline Réage is the pseudonym of French author Anne Desclos; *The Story of O* was written for her lover, who admired the work of the Marquis de Sade. It has been claimed that she wanted to prove to him that a woman could write a novel as explicit and shocking as a man.

The heroine, O, is a beautiful Parisian fashion photographer who becomes a complete submissive to her lover, René, learning to be constantly available for his pleasure. She's blindfolded, chained and whipped, before being taken to the château de Roissy, where she is trained to serve a group of men and handed over to a new master, Sir Stephen.

The Story of O is cruel, disturbing and sadistic – it could be seen as the missing link between The Marquis de Sade and *Fifty Shades of Grey*.

Fifty Shades of Grey – E L James

This *had* to be included! Let's face it, if it wasn't for *Fifty Shades of Grey*, there probably wouldn't even be a *Naughty Girls Book Club*. It's the novel that really kick-started the recent erotica phenomenon, breaking all records and causing sales of sex toys to soar.

Fifty Shades of Grey is the story of virginal young student Anastasia Steele, who's seduced by sexy entrepreneur Christian Grey – a BDSM enthusiast who quickly introduces her to his own kinky world, leaving her panting for more.

We've all heard the criticisms, but there's no denying that E L James has massively connected with readers all over the world. It seems there are thousands of women out there fantasising about being spanked by their own smouldering multi-millionaire in his Red Room of Pain . . .

General Book Club questions for any erotic novel

1. Are the portrayals of men and women realistic?

2. How would you categorise this novel – erotica, porn, romance or something else?

3. Who was your favourite character and why?

4. Does this novel negatively portray women?

5. What scenarios from the book would you like to try out for yourself?

6. Who would you like to see play these characters in a film version, and why?

7. How and why do men and women view sex differently?

8. How do the characters develop over the course of the book? Do their experiences change them?

9. Did you find the language used in the novel shocking or realistic?

10. Which character would you most like to be, and why?